JUST THE TV

Georgie Capron

About *Just the Two of Us*

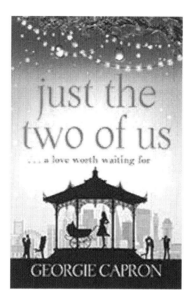

Lucy is the wrong side of thirty and tormented daily by the idyllic family pictures cluttering up her Facebook newsfeed. All of her friends seem to be getting married and having babies, and yet here she is, resolutely single, and no prospect of creating the perfect family she's always dreamt of.

How she longs for it to be her turn.

But finding love is complicated, and as time passes she wonders if there might just be another way to make her dreams come true. Is she brave enough to go it alone, or is the fantasy of 'baby makes three' just too precious to give up on?

Funny, warm, and a story for our time, Just the Two of Us will make you laugh and cry, and remind you never to give up on love.

To my husband Tom

Prologue

October 2016

'Aaargh!' groaned Lucy as another tidal wave of contractions careered through her, taking her breath away with the full and brutal force of its impact. She gripped Claudia's hand as the taxi hurtled through the streets of London at breakneck pace. Mid-grimace Lucy caught a glimpse of her unlikely knight in shining armour in the rear-view mirror. He appeared to be muttering frantic yet muted prayers under his breath, no doubt pleading that his Good Samaritan act of kindness would not result in the permanent tarnishing of his immaculate leather upholstery, or worse, the need for him to perform a heroic delivery on the side of Oxford Street.

Claudia's brown hair was plastered to the side of her face with nervous sweat as she tried to remain calm and in control of her own nerves. 'Don't worry Luce,' she said, reassuring her best friend that they were nearly there, that all would be well. Claudia's hatred of hospitals and all things medical was one of the reasons why she had never wished to put herself through the pain that was currently sending her best friend into anguished spasms beside her.

'This is not supposed to be happening!' groaned Lucy through gritted teeth as they careered around a sharp right-hand turn. Her knuckles whitened as she gripped the door handle in an attempt to steady herself.

'Plenty of babies come early, it's nothing to worry about!' reassured Claudia, her fingers firmly crossed behind her back as she leant across to rub Lucy's shoulders.

'You're hardly an expert,' said Lucy. 'How are we meant to know? Oh God, grab my phone will you and pass it over. I'm going to call the hospital again.'

This was not what Lucy had had planned for today. She and Claudia were meant to be enjoying a blow-out lunch to celebrate the start of Lucy's maternity leave. A last meal of indulgence before Lucy found herself struck off the social scene with sleepless nights and nappies taking over her life. The plan was to have lunch and then to do some gentle pottering around the shops in search of the somewhat curious combination of stretchmark cream and lingerie. No prizes for guessing which item on the list was for her, Lucy thought with a wry smile.

She had struggled to the restaurant in quite a bit of pain. In fact, she had been feeling niggling pains for the past few hours that had come and gone like a particularly bad bout of period pain. Erring on the side of caution, she had spoken to her midwife on her way to meet Claudia. The midwife had reassured Lucy that these 'twinges' were probably false alarms, harmless Braxton Hicks contractions that were to be expected at this late stage of her pregnancy.

The pains had grown more intense throughout lunch but Lucy hadn't said anything, not wishing to alarm her most un-maternal of friends, who, let's face it, was finding pregnancy by proxy a challenging enough experience as it was! Surreptitiously, Lucy tapped the *Contraction Monitor* app that she had downloaded on her iPhone, logging another twinge of pain as she tried to time their frequency. Her suspicion that she was, in fact, in labour was growing stronger by the minute, though she was determined not to make a fuss until she was sure. Lucy had long ago sworn to herself that she wouldn't fall into the category of hysterical first-time mother when millions upon millions of women had gone through the process of childbirth before her with nothing even as advanced as pain relief to ease the process. However, by the end of lunch she was feeling faintly terrified; if what she was currently experiencing were merely Braxton Hicks, how unutterably dreadful would the real thing be? It was hard to contemplate.

Her waters had broken, or more accurately, ruptured, in as explosive and humiliating a way as possible, all over the floor of Selfridges lingerie department just as she had tried to negotiate her enormous bump past a rail of silk briefs that would have been hard-pushed to cover a mere inch of her disproportionately large and swollen derriere. Shoppers had looked aghast as she shrieked in horror, puce with embarrassment, having realized what must have happened. Claudia had come hurtling out of the fitting room at the sound of Lucy's desperate yelp and, having rapidly assessed the situation, dragged Lucy towards the lift amidst mumbled apologies to the startled shop assistant who stared gaping at the floor, dumbfounded.

By the time they had made their way out of Selfridges and onto the heaving streets thronging with tourists and Saturday shoppers, Lucy had started to panic. With one hand on her lower back to support herself and the other shielding her protruding stomach, she began to sob. Claudia, in full protective tigress mode, sharpened her elbows as she pushed and shoved, yelling 'Get out of our way! She's in LABOUR for Christ's sake!' at the top of her lungs, clearing a pathway for Lucy to follow along behind.

Eventually they lurched over to a taxi rank and pounded on the window of the first unsuspecting driver in the queue – the man who was currently doing a good imitation of Lewis Hamilton in his desperate bid to deposit his unexpected cargo safely at the hospital doors.

Reassured by the midwife that all was well, Lucy dropped her phone in Claudia's lap as another agonizing surge of pain twisted through her. A garbled, inaudible screech escaped her lips.

'What was that, Luce?' asked Claudia, trying to ignore the bone-crunching grip of Lucy's fist as she reached for her hand once again.

Taking a deep breath in, Lucy looked at Claudia, her eyes pleading. 'Call him!' she begged. 'Please, Clauds, I need him…' she tailed off as she closed her eyes and began to concentrate on her breathing.

Claudia reached for Lucy's phone with her free hand. 'Okay, Luce, I'll call him now. Don't worry. It's going to be okay,' she muttered as she found his name and pressed the green button, sending a silent prayer that whatever he was doing and wherever he was, he would answer his phone.

Chapter One

June 2014

'You have *got* to be joking!' A wave of nausea rushed up the back of Lucy's throat. *Seriously?* she thought, *What is wrong with people? Is there no shame?* She peered again at her laptop screen and re-read the post from her long-lost school friend Eliza Longchamps-Delauney. Even the name made her stomach squirm. A far cry from her previous surname, Pratt, she noted with a wry smile.

Facebook Status Update:

Eliza Longchamps-Delauney: feeling blessed (1 hr: London)

Eliza is the luckiest girl in the world, thanks schmoopy for the best anniversary surprise – ten red roses. One for each year. You are my soulmate and I am so glad I found you!

'Oh, pleeease,' Lucy muttered to herself, 'spare me!'

She scrolled down her newsfeed and scanned the updates from her various friends and acquaintances. Lucy winced and swept her fringe away from her eyes, leaning closer in disbelief as she caught sight of yet another portrayal of blissful family life.

Michelle Murphy (2 hrs: London)

Thanking my lucky stars for my perfect family.

The caption accompanied a carefully posed photograph of Michelle and her ridiculously handsome husband with their three blonde children, all in neatly pressed matching sailor suits, sitting on the steps to their mansion. They looked like a Ralph Lauren advert.

Gorging on these cringeworthy posts had become Lucy's preferred pastime. Why did people insist on sharing their private thoughts and moments with the world on social media? Her favourite of all time was from an American ex-colleague called Brett Davies. His post from across the world in Chicago had made her want to share it on worststatusupdatesever.com to publicly shame him.

Had a proud fiancé moment today. My speakers crashed off the wall at 3 a.m. and I leapt on top of Danni to cover her body with mine in case she got hurt. So pleased my natural instincts were to protect her first.

Lucy didn't want to look at these displays of sickly-sweet marital bliss but she couldn't quite resist the urge. She found them bizarrely intriguing. They were a bit like the traffic jams caused by cars slowing down as they passed the site of a gruesome accident.

'I will *never* share sentimental crap like that on social media' Lucy vowed solemnly to herself, attempting to shove aside the familiar sneer that popped into her mind that she may never get the chance. She wondered briefly if there was something wrong with her, if she was missing some kind of 'romance' gene that would turn her into a simpering fool like Eliza or Brett. Perhaps all the romance-free years that fate's hand had dealt her had tarnished her tolerance. Or maybe, the cynical voice of reason suggested, she was just jealous. For, in truth, the one thing Lucy longed for more than anything else was her own other half, someone to stroke her hair and fall asleep with, someone to share her life with and, most specifically and heart-wrenchingly of all, someone with whom she could start a family of her own.

Before she could stop herself, she had tapped the letters 'JACK' into her Facebook search bar, clicking on the first name to appear in the scroll down list of her acquaintances, Jack Hawkins. Even the tiny icon of his profile picture was enough to get her heart racing. She knew it was pointless and would only serve to torture herself further but she couldn't help it. She scrolled down his wall looking for any new posts. There was nothing new, which wasn't particularly surprising considering that she had last looked at his page immediately before going to bed the night before. Unable to resist, she clicked on his cover photo, a picture-perfect family snap of his beautiful wife, Penelope, and their two children, Max and Arabella. She had never actually met them yet she felt like she knew them all pretty well thanks to her Facebook-stalking habit. She imagined snipping Penny's perfect face out of the picture and inserting her own instead. She scolded herself… this had to stop! How could she even consider breaking up such a happy family? She knew it was partly Jack's fault, despite being one of her superiors at work he flirted outrageously with her at any given opportunity. Over the past few months the flirting and flattery had escalated to such a point that she was starting to entertain the prospect that he might actually have feelings for her. She fantasized about a deeply unhappy marriage behind closed doors and dreamt of the day he would leave his wife and declare his undying love for her instead. Forcing herself to get a reality check, she clicked on the cross to close the page.

She rolled her eyes and sighed, rubbing her face with the palms of her hands to try and wake herself up. She had to stop procrastinating on these hateful social media sites and get to the task in hand. Her best friend was getting married. She still couldn't quite believe it. Today was finally the day when little Claudia, the scruffiest, scrawniest girl in school was to be wed. And Lucy was maid of honour. Claudia was, as her namesake might suggest, the Winkleman to Lucy's Tess. Though unfortunately for Lucy, the blonde hair was about as far as her own comparison went. Claudia, meanwhile, with her dark looks and waif-like figure, was a real dead ringer for the *Strictly* host.

Despite Claudia's obstinate refusal to pander to the opposite sex in any way, shape or form, she had well and truly pipped Lucy to the matrimonial post. Though, to her credit, Claudia was doing her best to soften the blow by promising Lucy the wedding's most eligible bachelor as her dinner companion. The prospect of this, and Lucy's determination to prove that she was not giving up on life or love just yet, trebled her resolve to transform herself from cygnet into swan for the occasion.

She slammed her laptop shut and chucked it on to her battered, floral sofa, rootling around amongst the biscuit crumbs in search of the remote. She found it, aimed for the TV and flicked through the music channels to find some suitably upbeat tunes. Satisfied with her choice, she looked at the clock: 9 a.m., one hour to get ready and out the door in time to catch the train from Paddington to Little Bedford. The service was not until 3.30 p.m. but Lucy was under strict instructions to be there by lunchtime to help with last-minute preparations and to steady Claudia's nerves. Though what there was to be nervous about when you were marrying someone as awesome as Dan, Lucy couldn't imagine.

At her bedroom mirror, swaying her hips in time to Beyoncé, Lucy took a long, hard look at herself. She patted her squidgy love handles and round belly, trying to repress the familiar critical thoughts that vied for her attention. She was relieved that Claudia had chosen a sculpted, shape-enhancing dress with boning that would squeeze her curves into all the right places. Today of all days she didn't need to worry whether any unsightly lumps or bulges would disrupt the contours of her bottom half. She released her blonde hair from its ponytail, checking her fringe, which she decided was in dire need of a wash and straighten, and examined her face. She moved a little closer to the mirror, scrutinizing the sprinkling of freckles, the slightly open pores, the smattering of broken veins on her cheeks and her cornflower blue, black-ringed irises. Thank god for make-up. Without its wonders, she looked like a puffy-eyed mole taking its first glimpse of daylight. A university boyfriend had once joked that make-up took her from a paltry five to a more impressive eight out of ten in the looks department. Of course, she had laughed it off at the time, but she hadn't forgotten the barbed compliment in the fourteen years that had since passed.

Brushing these thoughts aside, she jumped into the shower and turned the taps to full blast. A happy sigh escaped her lips as the invigorating, warm water sliced over her. She scrubbed herself with some mint shower gel, washed her hair and scraped a rusty old Bic over her armpits and legs to eliminate a couple of weeks' worth of unsightly stubble.

Lucy stemmed the flow of water and opened the shower door, watching the tiny droplets of spray swirl in the steamy condensation as they made their bid for freedom in the small bathroom. She hadn't done much to the flat since she had bought it six years ago. There hadn't been a penny left over from the money that Granny Annie had given her. She adored her little home more than anything and had done a wonderful job of making it cosy. She had invested all the love and attention that most people showered on their other half into her home instead. It was filled with bits and pieces from her extensive travels and she had scattered her beloved plants about the place in brightly coloured pots.

With one eye firmly on the clock, Lucy scanned the living area; the table in the kitchen was strewn with newspapers and magazines as well as the remnants of her breakfast. Not wanting to come back to a messy house, she quickly cleared the table, shaking the toast crumbs into the bin and stacking her plate and coffee cup into the dishwasher. In her bedroom, she gave her body a final, vigorous rub-down with the towel, made the bed and raked her hairbrush through her damp hair.

Lucy had always loved getting dressed up for any occasion. She prided herself on her ability to transform from the most disastrous of early-morning appearances in a surprisingly short amount of time. She had a well-established routine that had been perfected over the past decade of pre-first-date preparations. She luxuriated in the smell of cocoa butter as she smoothed moisturizer all over her skin. This was followed by several pumps of bronzing gel, which she rubbed into her chest, face, arms and legs to give herself a sun-kissed glow. After that she tousled her shoulder-length hair with the hairdryer before running her straightening irons over it, paying special attention to her fringe. She chose a new set of blue silk lingerie from her underwear drawer, the same striking cornflower blue as her eyes. There was nothing so confidence-boosting as the knowledge that a killer set of matching underwear lay hidden beneath your clothes, even if they were covered by a thick layer of Spanx. She wiggled into them to the beat of Madonna's 'Like a Virgin', wondering what tunes she might be dancing to that evening… and more importantly with whom?

She conjured images of the mysterious eligible bachelor that Claudia had mentioned holding her in his arms as they danced. A new man was just what she needed to knock all thoughts of Jack out of her mind for good. She tried to quash any hope that swelled within her at the thought. The truth was she was desperate to meet someone to settle down with and she knew only too well that men could detect desperation on a woman like a bad smell.

Lucy approached her mirror and her make-up bag with determination. She smoothed her foundation over her face, watching any red marks and uneven patches of skin tone disappear as though being airbrushed away. A dusting of bronzer, a touch of pink blusher and a thick line of smudged black kohl around her eyes and she was nearly there. A final double coat of black mascara made the striking dark rings around her irises stand out in contrast to the blue of her eyes. She fluttered her eyelashes seductively at herself in the mirror, practising, just in case.

Lucy looked at the clock, 10.05 a.m., perfect timing. She dashed to the loo one last time, grabbed her canvas overnight bag, already packed, and her beautiful satin dress in its protective plastic sheath, and closed her green front door behind her, clattering down the three flights of stairs and blinking in the early morning sunlight as she emerged onto

Mayfield Road. A feeling of huge excitement rippled through her, she was on her way! She whipped out her phone and sent Claudia a text.

All on schedule and so excited! Should be there by 12, can't wait to see the beautiful BRIDE! L x

With that, Lucy made her way to Baron's Court tube with a skip in her step. Not even the realization that the back of her skirt had been tucked into her knickers most of the way there, thanks to some rather overzealous honking of car horns, could dampen her spirits.

Chapter Two

A couple of hours later, as the train pulled slowly into the station, Lucy spotted Claudia's sister-in-law Tara waiting on the platform. She looked radiant in a coral maxi dress and white jacket, one hand resting on her bump. Lucy suppressed a familiar twinge of jealousy.

Lucy descended from the train and made her way over to Tara, enveloping her in a hug.

'It's so good to see you! Look at your bump... how exciting!' said Lucy. 'It's been far too long.'

'I know, isn't it ridiculous how time flies?' Tara agreed as she guided Lucy away from the station. 'I have to warn you, Luce, it's complete chaos chez Reynolds, as you no doubt expected! I'm *so* glad you are here. You can help Claudia do the final touches while Rob and I keep the rest of the family out of the way. You look amazing by the way, I love your dress!' Tara kept up a constant stream of chatter as she led the way out into the car park, telling Lucy amusing anecdotes from the pre-wedding build-up over the last couple of days. She always enjoyed Tara's company, she had a dry sense of humour which made Lucy laugh. 'How was the journey?' Tara asked as they clambered into her little red Nissan and began to make their way along the winding roads towards Claudia's childhood home.

'Oh, not bad at all, couldn't have been easier in fact,' Lucy replied. 'How's pregnancy suiting you? You look positively glowing!'

'Ah, you're too kind. I'm fine now, but bloody hell the morning sickness in the first few months nearly finished me off!' said Tara, shaking her head at the memory.

'And Rob? Is he excited?' asked Lucy.

'Oh, you know what Rob's like,' laughed Tara. 'He's been ready for this for the last ten years. He's over the moon!'

Lucy was so chuffed for her dear friend Rob, a brotherly figure to her just like her own brother, Ollie, though definitely more settled. The thought of Ollie, the eternal backpacker, being anywhere near ready for fatherhood made Lucy chuckle. Knowing him, he was probably reclining on a beach somewhere in Australia with a beer in one hand and a surfboard in the other. Claudia's brother Rob was the complete opposite.

Like Ollie, Claudia had always been one hundred per cent sure that she never wanted children. Dan was luckily of the same mindset; another reason why Lucy was convinced they were a match made in heaven. Claudia insisted she had been born without a single maternal bone in her body and was perfectly happy that way, a phenomenon that Lucy had never really understood. Though given that Claudia was verging on phobic when it came to all things medical, Lucy supposed it wasn't that surprising. In contrast, having children was an idea that Lucy was never more than a thought away from, her biological clock was ticking louder and louder with every passing year. This desire to procreate was a deep, primal urge that was impossible to describe but deeply rooted within her. During the hours when Lucy lay sleepless and awake in the middle of a restless night, the fear of never having children would sweep over her. It was her darkest worry. In those moments, Lucy reassured herself that should fate let her down she would always be able to take matters into her own hands, after all, you didn't need a man to have a child these days. But she prayed fervently that destiny would intervene and that she, too, would meet her perfect match, before it was too late for her to conceive. The trouble was, at thirty-five, her time was running out.

Lucy and Tara parked in front of the ramshackle cottage. Several of the latticed windows were thrown open to let the warm air into the house and the scent of freshly baked pastry came floating out to greet them.

Claudia's mother, Sue, opened the front door to welcome them.

'Welcome to the madhouse!' she said, wiping the flour from her hands onto her floral apron as she did so.

Graham, her husband, was following close behind her.

'Juicy Lucy!' he chortled, reverting to her childhood nickname and enveloping her in a hearty hug. 'Great to see you! How's the big smoke?' he asked.

'Oh, you know, hectic, busy, exhausting!' replied Lucy. 'Nothing changes! How's the bride?'

'Oh, you know, hectic, busy, exhausting. Nothing changes!' repeated Graham with a wink. It felt good to be back in Claudia's family home after so long. She suddenly felt nostalgic for her own beloved parents and made a promise to herself that she would sort out a visit home sooner rather than later.

Having brought Lucy's bag inside, Sue ushered Lucy straight upstairs. She found Claudia sitting serenely at the chintz dressing table amidst the clutter of her childhood bedroom, curling her eyelashes.

'Luce!' Claudia cried, putting down her tongs. 'You made it!'

'Oh my god, Clauds! I can't *believe* this is happening,' Lucy said, feeling her eyes well up at the sight of her dearest friend.

Claudia came over, skirting around the piles of discarded clothes, shoes and accessories that carpeted the floor, and gave her an enormous hug.

'Don't you start or you'll set me off too!' warned Claudia, patting the rollers that were secured haphazardly to her head, checking that they were still in place.

Lucy cleared a space for herself to perch on the corner of the bed as Claudia proceeded to give her a full report on the morning so far. The main drama had been caused by the seating plan. Each member of the family had refused point blank to sit next to drunken Uncle Alan, resulting in three entire tables having to be re-planned last minute. Claudia was laughing about it now, but she had clearly been at her wit's end. Luckily, despite the late alterations, Claudia insisted that Lucy's strategic placement next to the most eligible man at the wedding was non- negotiable. Apparently, he was a friend of Dan's who had just moved back to the UK from America. Despite Claudia's encouraging words, Lucy could picture him now: he was probably balding, had a paunch, and was nearly forty. She was only too used to the ever-shrinking pool of talent that remained available to a thirty-five-year-old woman. All the good-looking ones were already taken, like Jack. She did not have high hopes.

Having temporarily exhausted their chatter, they went into the spare room to admire the dress that they had chosen together back on a rainy February day in London. It hung like a work of art, glistening in its swathe of protective plastic. The art-deco silver beading that fringed the plunging back suited Claudia's bohemian style perfectly.

Suddenly feeling overwhelmed, Claudia reached out and grabbed Lucy's hand. 'Oh my god, this is really happening, isn't it, Luce?' She turned to face her, her big brown eyes shining with excitement, tinged with nervous anticipation and a hint of sadness in acknowledgement of the era that was drawing to a close. 'I'm not leaving you, you know. We're still going to be exactly the same; this isn't going to change us, right?' Claudia said. She was only too aware of how tricky this day must be for Lucy, and was filled with regret that her friend didn't have a plus-one of her own to accompany her.

Lucy said, 'Of course not,' and gave Claudia a friendly push. 'Don't be daft!' But they both knew that things would be different from now on, they already were. Gone were the days when Claudia and Lucy had shared a flat during their first years in London. Friends since their days at Fairview primary school, they had spent secondary school apart when the Reynolds had moved away from Cornwall, and then reunited once again at Exeter University, falling back into stride as the best of friends, wingwomen to each other and the centre pair of an ever-growing crowd of friends, always laughing and getting up to no good.

Claudia had been on the single scene with Lucy for the majority of their twenties following serious relationships at university. Lucy had broken up with her boyfriend of two and a half years after realizing they had become more like friends than anything that would last the distance. Since then both girls had had the odd fling, dalliance and holiday romance, but nothing too serious. Then Claudia had met Dan at a work party just before her twenty-ninth birthday and that had been it! They had moved in together the next year and had never looked back. Dan was an extremely laid-back guy, the perfect counterbalance to Claudia's chaotic lifestyle and personality. They complemented each other perfectly. Lucy was delighted that Claudia had found him and she was happy that she had gained a new friend in Dan, but she knew in her heart of hearts that the days of Claudia and Lucy, just the two of them, were over. She just wished she could find someone like Dan for herself.

At one o'clock, Sue called everyone down to the kitchen for a light lunch. She had made a quiche Lorraine with buttery, crumbly pastry that melted in Lucy's mouth, a mixed salad and some warm French bread straight out of the oven. As they devoured their food, Graham, Sue and Rob swapped stories about Claudia's childhood. Tara and Lucy wept with laughter as they heard about Claudia dressing up in her mother's white petticoat aged six and insisting on going to the church to demand a groom.

After lunch Lucy got changed and helped Claudia to apply her make-up, put the finishing touches to her hair and get into her dress. Everything seemed to be going smoothly until a last-minute panic erupted when Claudia couldn't find the glamorous beaded hairpiece that would complete her twenties-inspired look. Lucy searched high and low, frantically sorting through piles of mess whilst placating Claudia, who was sitting on the bed on the verge of tears, getting steadily closer to full-blown hysteria with every passing minute. Lucy breathed a sigh of relief when she spotted the culprit wedged firmly behind the bed, and with a quick wipe to remove the coating of dust and fluff it had acquired along the way, fixed it in place with some spare kirby grips from the emergency stash she had brought in her clutch. There was just time for Lucy to pin the delicate veil to the back of Claudia's head before she had to set off with Tara to drive the couple of miles down winding country lanes to the church.

Lucy was dropped off at the gate, where she spotted Rob on grandfather-sitting duty accompanying Graham's father Bill in his wheelchair. They were perched under a large beech tree, sheltering from the bright sun in the leafy shade.

She looked up as a white dove flew over her head and settled on the lopsided cross at the top of the old stone spire. A good omen, Lucy thought, as she walked down the curving path through the gravestones towards the church.

Chapter Three

The sweet smell of newly polished oak mingled with the fresh scent of lilies and the abundant swathes of honeysuckle that arched over the entrance to the church. Lucy stepped over the cool stone threshold and tottered down the aisle, taking care not to catch her stilettos in the air vents or slip on the floor, worn smooth by the constant footfall of the faithful. The thrum of chatter and the excited anticipation of Claudia and Dan's nearest and dearest filled the church. A riot of jewel-like colours and feathered fascinators tilted towards one another in hushed conversation. She found her allocated seat at the front, as instructed, in case she needed to get up and perform any emergency adjustments to the bride's train. She was relieved that Claudia had asked her to go straight into the church rather than accompanying her as part of the bridal party. Claudia hadn't wanted a gaggle of bridesmaids and Lucy had been grateful that she didn't have to walk solo down the aisle.

She caught Dan's eye and grinned at him as he stood nervously by the altar, waiting with Mark, his best man. He gave her a wave and a small thumbs up, straightening his tie and shifting uncomfortably under the weight of his tails.

Lucy scanned the people surrounding her, searching for familiar faces and smiling at everyone she knew. Just behind Dan, a handsome, dark-haired man with a strong jawline caught her attention. Probably gay or taken, Lucy thought to herself. She knew better than to assume that any remotely fanciable man might possibly be available. Just at that moment, the vicar came in and made the usual garbled announcements, asking people to silence their mobile phones and join in with the required responses. After he finished, there was a hushed air of anticipation until at last the organ broke the silence, cranking and groaning into life, emitting the first bars of 'Canon in D' by Pachelbel. The congregation, as one, turned to face the door.

A universal intake of breath announced the arrival of the bride. Lucy craned her neck to catch a glimpse of her best friend but she was unable to see her. She quickly turned to take one last look at Dan. She was moved by the look of sheer pride that was plastered across his face. Claudia and Graham had turned the corner and started to walk down the aisle, coming into Lucy's line of sight. Hot tears sprung into her eyes and she blinked her curly lashes several times to stop them from rolling down her cheeks and spoiling her mascara. As she had announced to Claudia earlier, she looked the most breathtakingly beautiful that Lucy had ever seen her. Her olive skin glowed with radiant happiness, her brown hair shone deeply and curled softly just as it reached her shoulders. The soft lace of the veil swept up and over the crown of her head, hanging gently down her back. As she walked slowly towards the altar, arm in arm with her dear old father, the material of her dress flowed over her body like liquid silk. When she arrived at the front, Claudia caught Lucy's eye and winked before taking her place next to Dan at the altar, beaming.

Lucy choked back tears as she listened to them make their vows. As they sung the hymns and listened to the sermon, she dreamt of a time when she might get the chance to be the bride. She allowed her thoughts to wander until she could see herself walking arm in arm with her father, Gus, down the aisle of her village church in Cornwall. She imagined the fragrant smell of sweet peas, the little bridesmaids in their taffeta dresses leading the way while the soft music of a cello filled the church to the rafters. In her mind's eye she could see Jack standing at the altar. He was smiling at her with the same tender and adoring expression that she had seen on Dan's face a few minutes earlier. Her heart felt like it would burst with happiness. All of a sudden the deafening strains of 'Widor's Toccata' wrenched Lucy back to the present with a jerk and she turned to face the aisle once again, slightly shaken from her vivid daydream, as the newly-wed couple made their way out of the church.

The wedding reception took place at a local hotel in a sumptuously decorated room. Round tables groaned under the weight of glittering glass and silver, each place-setting denoted with an ornately folded napkin. The tables were heavy with white linen.

Lucy accepted a glass of champagne from a passing waiter and sipped it gratefully; the cold bubbles quenched her thirst. She watched Claudia flitting happily around the room, greeting all her guests, never far from her new husband. Lucy chatted to a group of university friends and caught up on their news of work, babies and marriage; expertly deflecting any attention away from her barren love life with the practised hand of a long-term single. She saw the chiselled man from the church once again. This time he was talking to a tall blonde with a glossy ponytail that flicked from side to side coquettishly every time she laughed. 'Taken,' Lucy muttered to herself. 'Just as I thought.'

At that moment she felt a light tap on her shoulder and spun around to find her old friend Zoe standing before her. She was cradling the tiniest bundle that Lucy had ever seen in her arms.

'Oh my god, Zoe! How good to see you! Is this baby Lola?' squealed Lucy, kissing Zoe on the cheek and telling her how wonderful she looked. It amazed Lucy how some women could snap back into shape what seemed like mere moments after giving birth. Zoe looked radiant, if exhausted, and delighted in telling Lucy all about the arrival of Lola into the world a few weeks ago.

'Do you mind if I hold her?' Lucy asked, trying to keep the longing out of her voice.

'Be my guest!' said Zoe, draping a muslin cloth over Lucy's shoulder just in case Lola decided to ruin her dress with regurgitated milk.

Lucy caught her breath as she scrutinized the tiny features of her friend's newborn. She leant her cheek next to the impossibly soft, downy hair on Lola's head and breathed in deeply that sweet baby smell. Holding Lola's feather-light body as she nestled into the nook of her shoulder caused such pangs of longing in Lucy it was like physical pain. She rocked the baby gently from side to side, trying to keep her attention on Zoe as they swapped stories about mutual friends. They were all too quickly joined by Zoe's husband, Nathan, who whisked Lola off for a nappy change, the ultimate modern dad doing his bit. As she watched Nathan carry Lola away, noticing the look of adoration plastered across his face, she strengthened her resolve that she would have a baby of her own before it was too late.

Before long a gong sounded and the MC's voice echoed over the microphone, encouraging everyone to move over to the dining area for the wedding breakfast. Lucy would far rather have spent the evening cuddling Lola than anything else.

Lucy took her seat on one of the round tables in front of Claudia and Dan who were sitting with their close family members on a trestle table overlooking the rest of the room. She surveyed the names on either side of her place setting, the mysterious Alexander (the supposedly eligible bachelor) to her right and Claudia's Auntie Mabel to her left. Looking up, she spotted Mabel making surprisingly speedy progress towards the table for a ninety-year-old, still looking as youthful as the last time Lucy had seen her but with a slight stoop to her back and hunch to her shoulders.

'Little Lucy Johnston, I don't believe it!' said Mabel, clasping her face with wrinkled hands and kissing her cheeks.

'Auntie Mabel!' smiled Lucy. 'It's been far too long! How are you?' Lucy asked. She got up to help her into her seat and saw a plump, bald man making a beeline for her table. *This will be the eligible bachelor*, thought Lucy wryly, making a mental note to thank Claudia later.

Having ensured Mabel was safely seated, Lucy turned to her right to confront the bride's disastrous match-making skills face to face. With a deep breath, Lucy stuck out her hand to introduce herself. 'I'm Lucy,' she said. 'Pleased to meet you!'

'Alexander,' said the hairless wonder as he took his seat with a grunt, doing his best to tuck his sizeable belly underneath the table. The broken red veins that smattered his cheeks and the yellowish tinge to his teeth reminded Lucy of a walrus.

Gratefully, Lucy turned back to face Mabel who had begun reminiscing about Claudia and Lucy's joint tenth birthday party. She did her best to focus on Auntie Mabel, leaning ever so slightly closer to hear her fragile voice across the din of the party, happy to put even a sliver of extra distance between herself and the gentleman to her right. Lucy was nearly too distracted to notice another man approaching the table, causing a bit of a kerfuffle as he apologetically suggested that perhaps Mr Walrus was in the wrong seat.

Daring to believe her luck, she glanced up to see the handsome man that she had noticed earlier taking his seat to her right instead. Apparently both men were called Alexander, resulting in a case of mistaken identity on the seating plan. Much to Lucy's relief Mr Walrus was currently beating a hasty retreat to his rightful place on the other side of the room. His replacement introduced himself briefly as Alex, leaning across to shake hands with both Mabel and Lucy.

Taken aback by his good looks, she stammered, 'I'm Lucy, nice to meet you.'

Just as Alex looked ready to respond, Lucy received a pointed jab in the ribs from Auntie Mabel, obviously keen to pursue her journey down memory lane. Reluctantly, Lucy turned to face her, noticing disappointedly that Alex immediately struck up conversation with the vivacious Brazilian lady to his right. She found herself acutely aware of this handsome newcomer's presence and she struggled to focus on Auntie Mabel telling her about her latest WI project, punctuating her speech with the odd 'yes' or 'oh really?' but straining with half an ear to tune into the conversation to her right.

For their starter, they ate mozzarella wrapped in Parma ham, resting artfully on top of bundles of asparagus and washed down with sips of cold, velvety Chablis. Even the arrival of their food did nothing to stop Auntie Mabel's nostalgic reminiscing. By the time the starters were taken away and having somewhat run out of small talk, Lucy was relieved when Auntie Mabel excused herself to nip outside to smoke a Silk Cut, muttering something about 'old habits dying hard' as she went. Lucy immediately turned to her right just, as luck would have it, as Alexander offered her a top-up of wine.

'So, you must be the famous Lucy I've heard so much about!' said Alex, his umber eyes twinkling mischievously under his perfectly groomed brow. She noticed a flicker of irritation from the Brazilian who reluctantly turned to strike up conversation with the less attractive man seated on her right.

'Have you?' asked Lucy, praying that Claudia had bigged her up hugely whilst playing down some of the more embarrassing anecdotes from her enormous thirty-year collection. 'And what exactly have you heard?'

'Oh, all good things, don't worry,' Alex replied, oozing self-confidence and charm. 'Interesting, in fact. You work in advertising, don't you?'

'Yes, for my sins. Though the unadulterated joy of selling Listerine mouthwash to the faceless masses has somewhat lost its appeal over the years! I'm thinking of sacking it all in to work for some far more worthy cause.'

'And what might that be?' Alex enquired, his voice rich and smooth, like treacle, deep and resonant.

'Gosh, I don't know, perhaps I'll go and work for a charity one day... or travel the world and teach?' said Lucy.

'I love travelling,' Alex said. 'In fact, I once fancied myself as a sort of Robinson Crusoe type and drove around south-west France with a tent and a clapped out old car. But after about two weeks trying to cook my own food on a campfire, I rather lost the will to live and checked into the nearest hotel for a hot shower and a juicy steak!'

Lucy laughed, he was proving to be rather an irresistible combination of good-looking, funny and modest. 'I know the feeling. I did a lot of travelling in my twenties, but I'm not sure that I could face doing it on such a shoestring budget now. Some of the places we used to stay in don't even bear thinking about!'

'Whereabouts did you go?' asked Alex.

'South East Asia mostly. I backpacked for a year after I left uni with a friend who went on to teach. We were such good travelling companions that every summer I would save up my holidays and join her wherever she was travelling during her summer break... God how envious I am of teachers and their bloody holidays! Twelve weeks! Ridiculous, isn't it?' said Lucy.

'Quite unbelievable!' Alex replied. 'Perhaps we should all retrain?'

'Mmmm... not a bad idea. What do you do for a living?' she asked.

'I'm a lawyer, I'm afraid. Terribly unexciting,' he said as he broke into a crusty brown roll and helped himself to butter.

'What kind of lawyer?' Lucy asked, watching him take a bite and feeling strangely envious of the crumbs that fell onto his blue shirt, nestling there.

'Corporate stuff mainly. Though recently earning a living has taken me across the pond for a couple of years, so I can't complain. It's been amazing, but it's good to be back, I must admit. I've missed it here more than I had realized,' he said, looking at Lucy with such intensity that she felt herself blush. 'Yes, I am glad to be back,' he leant closer to Lucy and muttered, 'very glad indeed!'

Lucy was pleased to see that Mabel was now chatting merrily away to Claudia's cousin who was sitting on her left, yet another relation of hers. She was clearly having a lovely time so there was no need for her to tear herself away from Alex quite yet. During the course of dinner, the conversation between them flowed easily. They found that they had lots in common – they both loved travelling, food and literature, as well as a shared hatred of pretentious foreign films. Lucy felt herself glow like the embers of a fire under the warmth of his attention. A tide of nerve-jingling anticipation rose up from the pit of her stomach and she found a joyous grin spreading across her face as she laughed along with him. She was entranced by his dashing good looks, the knowing twinkle in his eye as he looked at her. She admired his strong, determined jawline, resisting a crazy urge to trace her finger along the angular lines of his face. He ran his fingers through his wavy brown hair, brushing it off his forehead as he laughed raucously at the tales she told from her travels around Laos. Lucy felt the fluttering of a thousand fireflies stirring deep within her. For once, she couldn't believe her luck… this man, this incredibly gorgeous man was flirting with her!

She took another sip of rich Chablis, savouring the sharp tang of liquid on her tongue and leant closer to Alex, squeezing her arms together to emphasize her ample cleavage. His eyes flickered towards the seductive shadow of her breasts and, for a moment, their eyes locked. Lucy felt an electric current pass between them and she was sure that he could feel it too. A thrill of excitement and hope rushed through her as a tiny voice asked, *Could it* finally *be my turn?*

A tinkle of glass caught their attention. Lucy wrenched her gaze away from Alex and turned to face the Master of Ceremonies, Claudia's best friend from work Louis. He announced the speeches and Lucy leant back in her seat, giddy with happiness for Claudia and Dan, filled with excitement from this new, unshakeable feeling that something momentous was happening to her.

Her leg was pressed firmly against Alex's thigh. She was acutely aware of his presence next to her. Neither moved away as they laughed at the speeches, raising their glasses to the bride and groom, cheering and clapping as each speech ended.

Taking the microphone for one last time, Louis announced Mr and Mrs Brightman's first dance and the wedding guests all raced over to the dance floor to watch. Lucy pushed her way to the very front of the crowd, determined to get a good view.

Lucy was so thrilled for her best friend, watching as Dan spun her around like a white bird of paradise. Claudia's feet barely touched the floor and her face beamed with happiness. It was definitely true love, Lucy thought. As the newly-weds beckoned for their guests to join them, Lucy looked around. Unfortunately her dinner companion was nowhere to be seen but even this realisation couldn't bring her down from the buzz of happiness she was currently experiencing,. She grabbed Auntie Mabel instead and they danced the fox trot, Mabel's favourite from when she used to frequent the dance halls during the war. Lucy found herself twirling into a group of university friends and they jived to 'Let's Twist Again', giddy with laughter as they snaked their hips up and down.

Suddenly, the hairs on the back of her neck stood on end as she realized someone was standing directly behind her. A male voice bent down and muttered in her ear, 'May I have this dance?'

Lucy found herself spinning around and pressing into Alex's chest. As they moved in time to the music she was only too aware of his hard torso just millimetres away from her body, the peppery smell of his aftershave made her feel dizzy with longing.

The rest of the evening passed in a blur of dancing, drinking and laughter. Lucy and Alex were inseparable and at one point the ethereal bride grabbed her and said, 'So, do you like him?!'

'Are you kidding?' replied Lucy, grinning. 'He's divine!'

Claudia smirked, 'I told you so! If only he hadn't been bloody working in Chicago, I would have introduced you years ago!' she said as she twirled around to find Dan. True, Lucy thought, but she didn't even care, because there was Alex, down on his knees, strumming an imaginary air guitar, the life and soul of the party, with a crowd surrounding him, cheering him on.

Seeing her looking at him, he stumbled over to her, threw his arms around her and flung her backwards in a dramatic Hollywood-style embrace. He looked into her eyes, 'You're beautiful, Lucy,' he whispered. 'I am so glad I met you.' Then, putting on a good show for their audience, he kissed her. The dance floor erupted into hysterical cheers and claps. Lucy's head spun with joy and her body fizzed and tingled as he kissed her, her knees going weak beneath her.

Chapter Four

'Beep, Beep, BEEP,' shrieked the alarm rudely. The shrill tone pierced Lucy's skull and reverberated a thousand times around her head like a hammer to the brain. She reached over to the bedside table to silence it, cursing herself for being so efficient yesterday in setting it. She had planned to get up in time for a hangover-destroying fry-up, but there was no way given her current head spin that she would be making it down to breakfast. She looked at her phone to check the time, ten o'clock; she had an hour to be out of her room. Lucy groaned. She tried to swallow but her tongue felt alien, swollen and heavy, stuck to the roof of her mouth. She brushed her fringe from her eyes and groped for a glass of water, gratefully gulping it down as she pieced together the reason for her hangover. With a few too many years of practice, she began at the church service, searching through her memories, reordering them and joining them together like a jigsaw puzzle.

'Oh my god! Alex! Alexander Hayes!' Her heart leapt sky-high and an enormous grin spread across her face as the memories of last night came flooding back. A bubble of laughter rose through her, erupting in a manic giggle. She grabbed her phone to check for messages, nothing yet.

Lucy and Alex had spent the whole night dancing, flirting and swapping stories, revelling in their mutual attraction. She had been dizzy from the delicious smell of him, combined with vast quantities of champagne and wine. She remembered Alex's taxi coming to pick him up, to take him to his friend's house nearby where he was staying for the weekend. They had parted exchanging numbers and lingering kisses with promises of dinner soon.

Lucy wished and hoped that he would text her, sending up fervent prayers to whoever might be listening that this wouldn't be yet another first encounter that never developed. But this time Lucy just knew he would get in touch. It had been different, she couldn't explain why but she knew that it had.

She phoned Claudia but predictably got her voicemail, the first morning of newly wedded bliss was not to be interrupted. So she left her a rambling voicemail telling her how she was dying of a hangover, how it had been the best wedding ever, how she had been the most stunning bride and Dan the most handsome groom and how she wished them the best honeymoon ever and could she text her the minute she arrived?

Heaving herself out of bed, Lucy showered and packed before calling a taxi to take her back to the train station.

She bought a bacon bap and a cup of tea at the station kiosk, found an empty seat and collapsed heavily into it. The journey passed in a blur of sleepy daydreams, mostly about Alex. Unable to resist, Lucy let her imagination run riot. She raced through a string of indescribably perfect dates, a whirlwind romance followed by heartfelt declarations of love. She imagined their first home together, allowing herself to relive her daydream from the church but this time it was Alex standing there waiting for her, exchanging their vows in front of all their family and friends, including Jack. She even saw them strolling through the park on a summer's day, pushing a pram with their first child giggling up at them from inside. As the train rolled into London Paddington, she drifted out of her reverie, opened her eyes and glanced at her phone. A message! Her heart leapt into her mouth. She frantically clicked on the open button and her heart plummeted back to its resting place as she saw Claudia's name appear on the screen. She opened the message:

Darling Luce, best MoH ever. D + I on cloud 9. On way to Maldives! OMG! Will call when I land xx P.S. Alex??! He was def keen. You were all over each other! Keep me posted! C x

Lucy chuckled as she gathered her stuff before heading for the tube. She swiped her Oyster card and braced herself as she was sucked into the momentum of the underground network, eventually being propelled back into the daylight at Baron's Court. She walked slowly home, looking forward to the rest of the day. She was going to spend it under her feather duvet on the sofa, watching reruns of *Friends* and *Sex and the City*. She decided to treat herself to a curry from the local Indian and felt her tummy begin to rumble at the thought. She remembered her mother Ginny's much-used expression 'a watched pot never boils', but she knew that she would be checking her phone every five minutes for a text from Alex nonetheless.

Chapter Five

'Rough weekend?' asked Caitlin, the pierced and punky secretary at J&L Communications, as Lucy pushed through the revolving door on Monday morning, sunglasses firmly in place despite the grey clouds outside.

'Wedding,' Lucy grimaced, pushing her glasses on top of her head.

'Ouch!' Caitlin grinned sympathetically.

Lucy walked up the stairs and pushed open the door to her office, approaching her pod unenthusiastically as she surveyed the pile of work she had left in her 'To Do' tray on Friday. She felt sure that today was going to be more than a little bit painful, marvelling at how much longer a hangover took to disappear in your thirties than it had in the previous decade. Her spirits were flagging; she still hadn't heard from Alex and was mentally preparing to add him to her long list of failed first encounters and disappointments. She had spent the whole weekend constantly checking her messages to no avail. It almost felt worse this time because she had had such high hopes for him. To add insult to injury, Jack walked past at that very moment. Her stomach lurched at the sight of him.

'Lucy,' he said as he strode past her desk. 'Good weekend?'

'Lovely thanks,' she said, simpering like a nervous schoolgirl.

'Get up to much?' he asked with a flirtatious smile.

'It was my best friend's wedding actually. I was her maid of honour.'

Jack moved slightly closer so as not to be overheard and muttered 'Any fumbles with the best man?'

'None of your business!' she laughed. She found his sheer arrogance alarmingly attractive, the way he raised an eyebrow and smiled knowingly when she spoke to him as though mentally undressing her. She was sure that he never listened to a word she said. He gave her a wink and made his way across the room to his office.

Trying to steady her beating heart, Lucy was grateful for the arrival of her pod mates, Lettie and Simon. She pushed all thoughts of Jack to one side and spent the first hour or so chatting to them both about their weekends whilst simultaneously scanning the right-hand column of the *Daily Mail* website, updating her already impressive knowledge of inane celebrity gossip. She knew that this was about all the intellectual capacity she was currently capable of.

A beep from her mobile interrupted her while she was deep into a depressing article about how many women were now childless at forty. She reached for her phone. 'Alex' was displayed on the screen. She felt like she had been punched in the gut with adrenalin and let out a yelp of excitement, prompting a flurry of questions from both Lettie and Simon, asking her what, exactly, she had neglected to tell them about her weekend. She ignored them and frantically read the message:

Dear Lucy. Sorry I didn't get in touch yest – no charger. Just got to office – Sat night was amazing. Drinks/dinner soon? Alex

Lucy's mood rocketed from somewhere near the bottom of her boots towards the ceiling. She felt as though she had been given a shot of Red Bull to the heart. She punched the air, shouting 'YES!' before leaning back in her chair, a grin splitting her face from ear to ear.

Simon and Lettie were fighting over themselves to grab her phone and read the text, bombarding her with a thousand questions and demanding to know the surname of this mysterious Alex so they could Google him immediately. Alexander Hayes of Westbury's law firm was one of the top results, as Lucy knew only too well having done the exact same thing many times over the last couple of days. Simon and Lettie both swooned over his photograph, declaring him too handsome to be true. Lucy was inclined to agree and had to use every ounce of self-restraint to resist texting him back immediately to say yes. She knew how important it was to play it cool despite feeling ready to burst with excitement at the thought of him.

It was, as predicted, a long, arduous day at work, despite the added bonus of Alex's text to distract her. At the best of times, Lucy found her job painfully dull. The initial thrills of office life – gossiping with friends at the water fountain, the coffee machines, the hum of chatter and clacking of busy fingers on keyboards – had seemed an exciting new world to a wide-eyed twenty-three year old fresh out of university. She had even enjoyed the commute, the buzz of Londoners going about their busy lives and the surge of bodies thronging the pavements from five o'clock onwards, either making their way home or, most often in Lucy's case, to the nearest wine bar. But as the years had passed the novelty had worn off, and she longed for something more meaningful, a sense of doing something worthwhile, something which would have a positive impact on the world. She was envious of those around her who could find that sense of purpose through their work, and she struggled with the feeling that all the efforts she put in on a daily basis were meaningless. It felt like nothing more than a waste of time and energy.

Today was no exception and she sat through her final meeting brainstorming ideas to market the latest super food, daydreaming of Alex and planning a reply to his text, one eye on the clock as the minutes ticked slowly by. Lettie and Simon had agreed that she had to wait until nine p.m. to reply.

As the clock reached six, Lucy shut down her computer. After a short battle with the lazy part of her mind which wanted nothing more than to slump on the tube, she forced herself to go to the bathroom and change into her running kit. These days she tried to run home a couple of times a week in an effort to keep her weight under control. She had always loved her food but the older she got the harder it was to eat what she liked and keep the pounds from piling on. She also relished the opportunity to straighten out her thoughts, unclutter her mind and appreciate the effects that the changing seasons had on her route home. Sometimes she would stop off to see her granny on the way; she adored her grandmother Annie more than anyone and tried to see her at least once a week. Annie had been down in Cornwall for the last couple of weeks staying with Lucy's parents and Lucy missed her. She would love to tell her all about Alex, but it would have to wait until she was no longer in her mother's earshot!

As her feet pounded the pavements the music from her iPod danced in her ears. Spring was Lucy's favourite time of the year. She saw the buds blooming to bursting point in the hedges and flower beds as she ran around the Serpentine Lake in Hyde Park. The setting sun cast a soft pink glow on the still waters, a flutter of birds skimmed along the surface of the lake.

Lucy quickened her pace and felt her breath coming in faster gulps, gritting her teeth as she felt the burn in her legs, still stiff from the dance floor and her stilettos.

Her energy levels depleted rapidly as she left the park and headed for home. She decided to walk the remainder of her route, taking the opportunity to phone her mother, Ginny, to tell her all about the wedding. She skimmed over the encounter with Alex for fear of raising her mother's hopes. She was only too well aware of her desire for grandchildren and had lost count of the number of times Ginny had 'subtly' hinted that Lucy might like to get a move on and settle down. She was convinced that Lucy was too picky, that she needed to lower her standards and expectations. If she had any idea that Lucy's fantasy of late involved a married man with children she might change her opinion of her daughter in this respect. Gus, Lucy's beloved dad, was constantly telling his wife to butt out and leave her alone, for which she was eternally grateful. He knew that she would settle down when the time was right for her. Ginny passed her onto Annie and Gus for a quick word; she had to bite her tongue not to spill the beans to her granny knowing full well that Ginny would be eavesdropping close by. She rounded the corner onto Mayfield Road just as she said her goodbyes.

Lucy slid her key into the lock and pushed open the front door with a click. She unstrapped her backpack as she climbed the three flights of stairs to her flat, unlocking the door of her little haven and flinging her bag and keys onto the kitchen table.

Once showered she settled into the familiar routine of making spaghetti bolognese, opening a bottle of red to go in the sauce and pouring herself a glass at the same time. She looked at the clock, eight thirty p.m., half an hour until her self-imposed deadline.

She watched an episode of *Masterchef* while eating her dinner, savouring the rich, hearty flavour of the meat sauce, scattered with large flakes of salty parmesan. She took a slug of Malbec, enjoying the slightly light-headed feeling that increased with each sip as the stress of her day ebbed away.

At nine o'clock, she allowed herself to send her reply:

Alex, great to meet you on Saturday. My feet are still aching from my dancing shoes! Drinks/dinner sounds good. Let me know when, L x

With a pang of excitement, she pressed send. She hoped her reply would show him that she was keen, but not desperate. She wanted him to think she had plenty of other offers, not that he was the first man to have piqued her interest this much in years.

As Lucy poured herself another glass of wine, she reflected on her single status. She had always assumed that, at thirty-five, she would have been married for years and have at least two children by now. She wasn't entirely sure how her life had turned out so differently. She had started off in the same boat as all of her girlfriends; endlessly analysing every little detail about all their crushes, lovers and flings. Slowly working out who or what they were looking for, shared experiences and failed romances offering new wisdom. One by one, they had met their matches and paired off, a slow and steady process, each new coupling filling Lucy with excitement and anticipation, as well as a touch of jealousy. As she watched the final years of her twenties disappear, she and Claudia would toast each other every New Year's Eve and vow that this, *this* would be their year. Finally, their turn would come. And, for Claudia, at twenty-eight, it did. So the probability grew higher that Lucy would be next. Surely.

As she turned thirty, she became less convinced. She began to feel bitter and resentful whenever she thought about how unfair life was. As the years continued to roll by, Lucy was stricken with moments of doubt. Sheer panic would set in. *What if there was something wrong with her? What if she* never *met someone? What if* she *was the exception to the rule?* No one could guarantee that there was someone out there, perfectly suited, just for her. And even if there was, what actually were the chances of that person crossing paths with her? There were seven billion people on this planet... And what if the man she was meant to be with was already married, to the wrong woman? What if he already had children?

As hard as she tried to push these negative thoughts out of her mind, she struggled to keep them at bay, settling on keeping them to herself instead, and developing a dry and sardonic approach to her single status when asked, using humour as a method of defence as she regaled couples with hilarious tales of her forays into the dating scene. Her go-to story guaranteed to have everyone in stitches was the time when a so-called friend had set her up on a blind date with a guy called Henry. They had met in a pub in central London after work. Henry had appeared perfectly normal at first; they had enjoyed some small talk over several glasses of wine before ordering some dinner. Just as Lucy had begun to think maybe this blind dating malarkey wasn't such a bad idea after all, Henry had leant seductively across the table to give her a kiss. Alarm bells should have rung: rather than a gentle graze of lip across lip Lucy was left with a curious wet patch on her chin. Not to be deterred, she finished her meal. Henry had insisted on settling their bill which was always a good sign as far as Lucy was concerned. After fetching their coats they had made their way to the tube. As they said goodbye, Henry leant in for another kiss. Lucy angled her face bravely towards him and closed her eyes. Nothing could have prepared her for the horror that followed. Henry's mouth was somewhere between a washing machine on full spin and a Hoover on full suction – the lower part of her face was incomprehensibly engulfed in wet slobber. Lucy squirmed in protest and tried to wrench herself free from Henry's grip, wiping her mouth with the back of her sleeve in disgust as she did so. An awkward barrage of excuses followed from Lucy as she beat a hasty retreat into the underground system, desperate to get away from Henry before he mounted a repeat attack. As she sat on the tube, she grappled in her handbag for her mirror, pulling it out and inspecting the damage. To her absolute horror she found the red bruising of a love bite smattered across her mouth and chin. She had had no choice but to pull a sicky the next day and she refused to leave the house until the marks had disappeared. Needless to say she had not seen Henry again. She had given the friend who had set her up strict warnings against allowing some other unsuspecting soul to fall victim to the same fate. As she entertained the masses with her stories she would see a look of quiet relief in their eyes that they were not standing in her shoes; a look of thanks aimed at their partner.

Lucy's phone beeped, shaking her from her reverie. She opened the message:

Dancing shoes currently hanging in cupboard, recovering. Mondays always hard but doubt my clients got much out of me today! Something to look forward to? Friday, Piccadilly Circus, 8pm? A x

Lucy's heart danced the tango and she did a victory jig around her coffee table. A date! Hooray! She immediately texted Simon, Lettie and Claudia.

How refreshing, Lucy thought, *to receive a text from a man who has taken control, suggested a time and a place, and got on with it.* Unlike so many men before him who were just all talk and no action.

She finished her wine and her episode of *Masterchef*, a contented smile playing at the corners of her mouth, before getting ready for bed. As she pulled the warm duvet around her, feeling the reassuring weight of it settle over her body, she reached for her phone and texted back:

Great idea. See you on Friday, looking forward to it. L x

She lay back and closed her eyes, falling asleep within minutes, her mind full of possibility.

Chapter Six

The week passed in a frenzy of activity at J&L Communications, the whole team were working around the clock to create the perfect pitch for a new home-furnishing brand. The office was full of employees working well into the night on Wednesday, surviving on numerous cups of coffee and regular deliveries of takeaway as they put the finishing touches to the campaign. Lucy was grateful for the distraction. It meant that she had less time to fret about Friday night.

She had hoped that the prospect of a date with Alex would stop her from thinking about Jack, but sadly this was not the case. She couldn't stop herself from tracking his movement around the office with the diligence of a deranged stalker. It was as though she was fitted with a homing device fixed permanently on his whereabouts. She had perfected using only her peripheral vision to keep tabs on him, managing to fix her eyes on her computer whilst simultaneously tuning into his presence wherever he was in the large, open-plan room. She adored him even more when he was under pressure. He was what her dear mother Ginny would call a 'silver fox'. She had to stop herself from staring at him in meetings. The last thing she wanted was for anyone to find out about her illicit crush; if Simon and Lettie knew, she would never hear the end of it. Lucy found the way he ran his fingers through his short, greying hair and rubbed his temples absurdly attractive. She longed to run over to him and take him in her arms. What was it about him? She strongly suspected that the fact that he was so clearly and completely taken was part of the appeal. It was ludicrous to even entertain the idea that she had feelings for him. He was married. And worse, he had two gorgeous children, whose gap-toothed grins in the photograph on his desk should have been enough to quell any amorous thoughts in an instant. She surmised that there must be something seriously wrong with her. Thank god she now had a legitimate prospect on the cards for once, to put an end to this madness.

On Friday morning she got dressed carefully, choosing a floaty emerald dress with a tie around the waist, some low heels and a pair of gold hoop earrings. A good night's sleep had restored her flagging energy levels and reduced the size of the bags under her eyes. As she walked to the tube for her final commute of the week, she was filled with anticipation. Would he be just as she remembered? Where would they go? What would they do? She had received a lovely text from Alex the day before:

Hi Lucy. Looking forward to tomorrow evening. See you at 8pm by the statue of Eros. A x

Lucy hoped that his choice of the notorious statue of love was a promising sign of things to come.

The team was in a celebratory mood on Friday after a huge victory winning the pitch and the MD had filled the offices with cupcakes and wine to say thank you for everyone's hard work. Lucy and Lettie passed the day munching on cake and gossiping, doing very little work having given themselves a day off 'actual' work. Simon gave Lucy his usual spiel about appropriate first date behaviour, though given that his love life was in a worse state than hers she largely ignored him. He did, however, tell her not to follow in his usual footsteps of trying to bed the man on the first date, suggesting that Alex may not respect her in the morning if she did so. Lucy reassured him that she had absolutely no intention of doing anything untoward, a chaste kiss would be the furthest she would go. In her experience anything more resulted in an immediate lack of interest. She was a firm believer in the old adage 'treat them mean, keep them keen,' acknowledging that treating them mean merely meant keeping them waiting! Men were simple creatures, after all!

At six o'clock she went to the wine bar next door where most of the office could be found on a Friday evening kick-starting the weekend with a pint or two, or in Lucy's case, a huge glass of cold Sauvignon Blanc. As soon as she walked in she spotted Jack in the corner. Lucy resisted the urge to make a beeline for him; instead she talked to Mark, one of the directors, about his two daughters and cooed over photographs of their recent holiday to Greece. She could feel Jack's eyes on her and tried hard to focus on the conversation she was having, knowing she would rather be talking to him. She got chatted up by bald Brian from HR, and tried to keep her eyes from roaming down to his distractingly large paunch lest he should take it as a sign of encouragement. After getting trapped with Marjorie from the sales team talking about her latest yoga retreat, she managed to excuse herself and make her way to the bathroom, realizing that she would need to leave soon to get to Piccadilly Circus in time. As she got to the top of the stairs, she bumped into Jack coming back up from the Gents.

'Lucy,' he said, 'you're here! Can I get you a drink?'

'I'm about to head off actually,' she said, resisting the urge to ditch her plans and spend the rest of the evening gazing into his steel blue eyes.

'Off? What do you mean, off? You can't leave!' he said in mock horror. 'We're celebrating!' He raised one perfectly groomed eyebrow suggestively.

'Well I'm sorry but it can't be helped! I've got plans.' Feeling a bit mean, she added, 'Congratulations on winning the pitch though, I thought it was amazing.'

'It's thanks to all of the team's hard work that we won.'

'And your winning powers of persuasion!' laughed Lucy.

'They don't seem to be working very well on you. Where is it that you are running off to exactly?' he asked.

'I'm meeting someone for a drink.'

'Aaah, a date?'

'Maybe.'

'Some guys have all the luck...'

'You shouldn't say things like that,' Lucy said, secretly loving the flattery.

'You're right!' he replied with a knowing twinkle in his eye. She could tell that he'd had a few drinks already.

'Right, well I'd better go.'

'Don't!' said Jack. 'Stay...'

'I really don't think that would be a good idea!' said Lucy. 'Anyway, as I said, I've got plans. Have a good night!' she said, pushing past him down the stairs, forcing herself to walk away. As she brushed past him, he grabbed her fingers and held on. She turned to look at him. She felt a shot of electricity pulse through her, the attraction she felt for him was real, there was no doubt about that. She let his hand drop and carried on down the stairs, determined not to look back.

Peering into the dimly lit mirror in the Ladies, Lucy gave herself a stern talking-to. Pushing all thoughts of Jack out of her mind, she focused on the evening ahead of her. She decided to refresh her make-up, hoping the dull light would not leave her resembling a cast member of *TOWIE*. She sprayed Chanel no.5 on her wrists and behind her ears then reached into each cup of her lacy bra to hoist up her boobs and give her more cleavage. She admired the effect of her readjustments. She felt confident, sexy and a little tipsy. The encounter with Jack on the stairs had bolstered her self-esteem. Dangerous though this flirtation was, she had to admit it felt good to be wanted. She was in the perfect mood for a first date.

With a final goodbye and good luck wishes from Lettie and Simon she headed for the door, dodging Brian on the way out.

The sense of calm she had felt at the bar disappeared as she sat on the tube, her Dutch courage was wearing off. All thoughts of Jack had disappeared as she relived each moment she had spent with Alex the previous Saturday. Her nerves jangled with every step she took as she climbed the stairs to exit the tube station. She wondered whether he would be there already, deciding that would be preferable to waiting around gormlessly for him to arrive. She navigated her way through the crowds surrounding the fountain, momentarily distracted by an incredible beat-boxing act busking in front of the famous neon signs. She looked around, trying to distinguish Alex from the masses, wishing he had chosen somewhere less hectic to meet. Suddenly she spotted him opposite the fountain. She stared at him for a few seconds, marvelling at his chiselled good looks and gearing herself up to approach him. She was glad she had come. Taking a deep breath, she walked towards him and called out his name.

Alex spun around, searching her out and crying 'Lucy!' with a huge smile as he came towards her. He kissed her on both cheeks, causing her stomach to flip over like a pancake as the memories of last Saturday night came flooding back.

'You look stunning!' he said as he ushered her away from the crowds towards Haymarket.

'Thank you,' Lucy replied. 'You don't look too bad yourself!' she said. *A huge understatement*, she thought to herself.

'I thought we could have a drink at this little wine bar I know,' said Alex. 'It's got a fantastic roof terrace with an amazing view of the city.'

'Sounds great!' said Lucy, falling into step with him as they made their way down the busy road. Alex chivalrously ensured that he was on the side of the pavement facing the oncoming traffic. Lucy appreciated his good manners, one of the most attractive qualities in a man as far as she was concerned. They turned down a narrow, cobbled side street and came to the entrance of the bar.

A porter at the door tilted his hat and said, 'Good evening, Mr Hayes, good evening madam.' Lucy was impressed by the personal greeting.

'I come here a lot with work,' Alex said by way of explanation as they entered the lift, pressing the button for the top floor. 'It's a great place to try and impress clients… I'm hoping it's going to have the same effect on you!'

As the doors slid open, they stepped into the room. A huge glass bar lay in a 'U' shape in front of them, surrounded by tables; a jazz pianist tinkled the keys of a grand piano over to the right. The opposite wall of the room was made entirely from glass, revealing an open-air terrace with spectacular, panoramic views of London. Lucy exclaimed in delight and headed straight through the open door to the railing to peer out over the city. The emerging stars twinkled above her, little pulses of light, and the street lights illuminated the surrounding buildings with a rosy glow.

She spun around to face Alex, saying 'What a stunning view! I'm definitely suitably impressed.' She saw a fleeting glance of relief flash over his face. *He's nervous too*, thought Lucy, thrilled that she was capable of having that effect on him.

He asked her what she would like to drink and they made their way back inside to the bar. She ordered a gin and tonic and they took their drinks to a table near enough to hear the relaxing music from the piano, but still close enough to the window to admire the view. They toasted the end of the working week and laughed at stories from the wedding. Alex informed her that Claudia's Uncle Alan had been found wandering through the town in the early hours of the morning singing 'Lady in Red' whilst dancing with an imaginary partner. Lucy burst out laughing at the thought.

'I've been dying of jealousy all week at the thought of Claudia and Dan in the Maldives,' moaned Lucy. 'If she would stop sending me photos of her painted toenails with nothing but white sand and turquoise sea stretching beyond I would be extremely grateful! I mean, what is it with honeymooners, and in fact holidaymakers in general, about rubbing salt into the wounds of those of us stuck at work?!'

Alex laughed and asked her to show him the photos she had received. Lucy happily obliged, relishing the opportunity to lean closer to him, allowing his delectable smell to work its hypnotic magic on her. He snorted with mirth as he found a picture of Dan looking as red as a freshly cooked lobster and proceeded to tell Lucy about their post-finals trip to Malaga. One night, in the early hours of the morning, Dan had infamously passed out drunk on a pool-side lounger wearing nothing but his underwear, failing to rouse himself until midday. Unfortunately by this point he had managed to acquire third-degree burns all over his body and had been unable to wear clothes for the rest of the week. Lucy chuckled as Alex asked the waitress for another round of drinks. They regaled each other with stories about Claudia and Dan's misspent youth, a surprisingly easy source of entertainment, it turned out. Lucy was sure that, given the cause, Claudia would forgive her for any indiscretions.

As they finished their G and Ts, Alex glanced at his watch. 'I have booked a table at a great little place around the corner, but if you'd rather stay here, or if you have other dinner plans...?' he trailed off, leaving the ball firmly in her court. Lucy was touched at his lack of assumption and appreciated his foresight in planning their evening so thoughtfully.

'I'm starving,' she said, 'that sounds like a great idea!'

Alex paid for their drinks and escorted her down the stairs and across the road, guiding her through the backstreets of the West End to a small red-brick building. As she crossed the threshold of the restaurant, Lucy was immediately struck by the enticing smell of garlic. She loved the red and white chequered table cloths, the buzzing atmosphere of happy diners, the fairy lights strung haphazardly across the walls. They followed the waiter to their table and sat down as he gave them their menus and explained the day's specials, catching each other's eyes and sniggering at his absurdly fake French accent.

'Poor thing,' Lucy said. 'You obviously have to be "French" to work here!'

Alex burst into a stream of stereotypical Frenglish, in an extremely over-the-top accent, culminating in 'Would-a you like-a ze ketch-up wiz-a your steak and cheeps? What do you think?' he asked. 'Would I get the job?'

'Definitely,' Lucy chuckled, 'I'd give you a job any day!' The two gin and tonics had had a wonderful effect on her, she felt full of sparkling conversation and bags of energy. Actually, perhaps it was Alex's impact, not the G and Ts, she thought.

A few minutes later, Gaspard, their waiter, came over and took their order. Alex chose a bottle of Côtes du Rhône, and they both ordered Coquilles St. Jacques followed by the steak and chips. As Gaspard poured their wine, Alex told her about his father, a wine expert who had taught him everything there was to know on the subject. Alex showed her how to swirl it properly in her glass to release the vapour, and told her to look out for the smell of spice. She inhaled and instantly identified it, surprised at herself.

'Wow, you're very good at this!' she complimented him, relaxing into her chair. They chinked glasses and she took a sip, savouring the deep, peppery flavour as she rolled the wine around her mouth. She was really starting to enjoy herself.

A short while later, their starter arrived. The impeccably cooked scallops melted in her mouth, perfectly accompanied by the smooth and salty Gruyère cheese. She soaked up the remaining sauce from the shells with a piece of bread.

'God, I love food,' sighed Alex. 'Especially French food.'

'Mmm,' agreed Lucy, 'this is unbelievable. It's been years since I have eaten scallops. Imagine life without food… it wouldn't bear living!'

'It's so refreshing to meet a girl who enjoys eating proper food. I can't tell you the number of dates that I've been on where the girl has just ordered a mixed salad with the dressing on the side. There is nothing more unattractive,' Alex said firmly.

'Well you certainly don't have to worry about that with me… clearly!' grinned Lucy, gesturing towards her empty plate.

'Good!' said Alex. 'Is there anything about you that I'm not going to love?'

Lucy blushed at his compliment and shrugged, 'I hope not!' as Gaspard approached the table, asking 'Ow were zee starters? You like?' which prompted another set of conspiratorial winks and barely suppressed giggles.

As their juicy steaks arrived with baskets of stick-thin French fries, Alex asked Lucy to tell him about her family.

'Siblings wise it's just me and my younger brother Ollie, then there's my mum Ginny and my dad Gus!' Lucy told him. 'They live down in Cornwall in a little village on the north coast, where I grew up.'

'It's so beautiful in that part of the world,' Alex said. 'We used to go on holidays to Devon when I was young, which I imagine is quite similar.'

'Yes it is, very.' Lucy nodded in agreement. 'The rugged coastline full of wonderful little paths that almost propel you into the sea on a windy day!'

'Pasties, clotted cream, fudge…' said Alex.

'Clotted cream ice-cream!' said Lucy, dreamily.

'Surfing on flimsy bits of polystyrene, salt water up your nose…' said Alex, laughing. 'Oh, the memories!'

'Oh yes! Especially squeezing yourself into wetsuits you've long since outgrown…. in fact, when Ollie and I were really small, mum and dad refused to buy us new ones for years, so we had to slip carrier bags over our feet to reduce the friction and wrench ourselves in!' Lucy remembered. 'Such a palaver!'

'What does Ollie do?' Alex asked.

'Oh, he's sort of an eternal backpacker, really. He's in Australia at the moment. He was doing some work on a cattle ranch last I heard, but really he just wants any excuse to avoid coming home and joining the "real" world. He's still surfing mad; though I'm sure he doesn't need a wetsuit over there! What about your family?' enquired Lucy.

'Well, there's my father, Michael, the self-titled sommelier, and my mother, Lillian… she gave up banking to become a housewife, I've got two older sisters, Sarah and Isabel,' explained Alex. 'Sarah is the oldest at forty-two, she's married to Nat and they have two children, a boy and a girl. Isabel is the middle child and she's thirty-nine, she's got a daughter too and is married to a guy called Nick. And I'm the youngest, clearly letting *everyone* down by not being married *or* having procreated yet!' screeched Alex mischievously, clearly mimicking his mother.

'Tell me about it! An unmarried daughter and a son living on the other side of the world… I'm sure my parents think we've got some kind of conspiracy theory against them having grandkids at all!' Lucy rolled her eyes.

'I propose a toast. To the reprobate offspring who have thus far failed to reproduce!' announced Alex.

'Hear, hear!' concurred Lucy as their glasses met, chiming. Lucy hoped that Alex was in the same category as her, wanting to have children but waiting for the right person to come along before starting a family. She stopped herself short of asking him directly, for fear of sounding deranged.

For dessert they shared a lavender crème brûlée with two glasses of golden, syrupy pudding wine and Alex told her about his nephew and two nieces, whom he clearly adored. Lucy took this as a positive sign. He said that he loved buying them presents and always chose the most annoying ones with the special effects and noises, toys that were strictly banned when Uncle Alex was not around as they drove his sisters to distraction but definitely gave him huge brownie points from the kids.

Much later, realizing that they were the last table there and that the waiting staff were setting up for the next day's lunch shift, Alex asked for the bill. He batted away Lucy's hand as she offered to pay half, insisting that it should be his treat.

Wrapping their jackets around them, they stepped out into the coolness of the night, a swollen moon hovering above them as they made their way to the nearest tube station. Alex took hold of her hand and she enjoyed the reassuring presence of his palm against hers, smooth and warm.

As they approached the tube, Lucy said, 'I've had such a great time tonight. Thank you so much.'

'It's been fun, hasn't it?' agreed Alex, stopping on the side of the dimly lit street and turning to face her.

Lucy was aware of the traffic whizzing past on the main road up ahead and was grateful that they were on a quiet street with no one to disturb them. She nodded in agreement, suddenly aware of how much taller he was than her. He stood in front of her, strong and steady, his brown eyes looking intently at her under thick black lashes.

Still holding her hands, he said, 'I would very much like to see you again. Would that be okay with you?'

Lucy muttered, 'I'd love to,' sure beyond certainty that he must be able to hear her heart, which by now was hammering on her ribcage like a bird trying to escape from captivity.

He held her gaze and said, 'Good,' brushing her fringe away from her eyes, then he slowly lowered his face to hers. He grazed his lips gently against her mouth, cupping her chin in one hand as he did so. At the touch of his lips, Lucy's stomach did a back flip; she felt as though she had been plugged into the mains as electricity shot through her. Noticing her reaction from the wide-eyed expression on her face, Alex smiled, and, holding her firmly with his free arm, he kissed her again, softly at first and then more passionately. Each tantalizing kiss dissolved into the next one; the spicy smell of his aftershave made her dizzy as he kissed her on and on. She thought she might collapse with longing. Eventually, she pulled away. Finding inner strength from god knows where, she steadied herself against his chest. Breathless, they grinned at each other and, without a word, walked hand in hand to the tube.

Chapter Seven

The next morning Lucy flung open her bedroom curtains, allowing the daylight to come streaming in, creating a patchwork of sunbeams all over her bed. She smiled to herself, stretching like a cat arousing from a deep sleep. She felt on top of the world as she relived her evening. It was a wonderful feeling to fancy someone who was actually available. The fact that it was the start of the weekend was the icing on the cake.

She wrapped her fluffy white dressing gown around her, luxuriating in the softness. Pulling on her slipper socks, she padded into the kitchen to put the kettle on, reaching for her cafetière and spooning in some real coffee. Opening the freezer, she took a cinnamon bagel out of the packet and popped it into the toaster. This was her standard routine to start the weekend: coffee, bagels and a lie-in.

She decided to text Alex to say thank you for the date, resulting in an instant flashback to the night before, her insides dissolving once again at the very thought of his irresistible kisses. She couldn't wait to see him again… she hoped that she wouldn't have to wait too long! She sent him a text:

Morning! Thanks for a wonderful evening. I'm still full from all that yummy food! Hope you're having a fun day at the zoo with Sarah + fam. L x

Lucy thought of him playing the role of naughty Uncle Alex with Sarah's little ones. She imagined that he was extremely good at it. Sarah and Nat were in London for the weekend, staying with Nat's brother and sister-in-law, and Alex had offered to take them all to London Zoo. She chuckled to herself as she imagined the children dragging him around all the different animal zones before no doubt holding him hostage in the gift shop! The fact that as an experienced uncle he was no doubt amazing with children added to her excitement about him as a prospective partner.

After showering, Lucy called Tor, her best friend from secondary school, and checked their plans to meet for lunch. Tor confirmed they were meeting at half past one at their usual cafe in Holland Park, next to the Orangery. Lucy dressed in jeans and a navy and white stripy T-shirt, put on her sunglasses, and left the house, slinging her handbag over her shoulder. She strolled leisurely up Edith Road, revelling in the feeling of the sun beating down on her, soaking up the badly needed Vitamin D, before turning right to make her way towards her favourite park in London. She loved all the different parts that made up Holland Park – the Dutch gardens that were full of tulips at this time of year, the zen Japanese garden with its peaceful water features, the peacocks parading their bejewelled beauty, trying to impress a mate. Lucy and Tor had fallen into the habit of meeting there during the warmer months for lunch and a catch-up, walking around the park afterwards with steaming cups of coffee, putting the world to rights.

As she arrived at the café, she could see Tor sitting at one of the metal tables outside, basking in the early summer sunshine. Her curly blonde hair was tied back into a ponytail, her Ray-Ban aviators keeping the hair off her face to allow for maximum sun exposure. *She really is a girl after my own heart*, smiled Lucy as she approached the table. Both girls had spent much of their time at school 'revising' in the garden of either of their family homes, far more interested in the depth of their tan than anything else.

'Hi Tor,' Lucy said as she bent down to kiss her friend on both cheeks. 'I love your top – very boho chic!'

'And look at you – very nautical! Aren't we bang on trend?' chuckled Tor, placing her sunglasses onto the bridge of her nose to stop her from squinting. 'I'm dying to hear everything about Claudia's wedding. How was it?' she asked.

'Oh, it was just wonderful!' Lucy said. 'She looked amazing, they were the sweetest couple ever and, you'll never guess what… I met a guy… a *real* guy!'

'*Whaaaat!!*' screeched Tor. '*How* have you kept that quiet for a whole week?!'she demanded.

Lucy laughed and began to fill her in as they went inside to order their lunch, telling her all the details of the wedding, and, much more importantly in Tor's eyes, of last night's date.

As they sat back down at their table, Tor demanded a snoop at his Facebook page. Lucy hadn't befriended him yet, but she knew that they would be able to look at his profile picture if nothing else. A notification popped up on her homepage, Lucy clicked on it and saw to both of their delight that it was a friend request from Alex. Lucy wondered when he had sent it, was it before last night or since? She responded, befriending him, and they spent the next few minutes munching on their sandwiches and poring over his photos, analysing any that included females, all declared 'dog-ugly' by Tor immediately, despite looking as though they had just stepped off the nearest catwalk. Tor certainly couldn't be criticized for being disloyal!

As Lucy talked about their date, she couldn't help the massive grin that spread across her face.

Tor spotted it, 'Oh dear, you've got *that* look!'

'What look?' Lucy asked, still beaming.

'You know, that goofy grin that means you've met someone special, when you can't stop smiling like some kind of loon!' explained Tor.

Lucy knew exactly what she was talking about, she felt so happy and, what was even better, she had none of those nasty feelings of doubt she sometimes got when she was trying to talk herself into fancying someone, knowing they weren't quite right. This was definitely different. So far, Alex was faultless. Charming, funny, polite, fascinating to talk to, interested in her and the world in general. Kind, sexy… the list could go on!

'God, you *are* lucky!' Tor said. 'After my first date with Will I wasn't so sure. He was ill and I was exhausted and we ended up going home after a couple of drinks. The only reason I gave him a second chance was because I was desperate and you told me I might as well!'

'Whatever, Tor! You might have had a bad first date but look at you now!' chided Lucy.

'I know,' Tor shrugged. 'Ten years! Oh my god! How did that happen?'

They went and ordered coffees in takeaway cups and began to stroll through the fragrant, flower-filled gardens. Lucy checked her phone surreptitiously to see if Alex had replied… nothing yet, she noticed with a pang of disappointment.

As they walked, Tor filled Lucy in on the latest trials and tribulations of her battle with IVF. She and her husband Will had been told they couldn't conceive naturally due to a blockage in her fallopian tubes. Tor had been utterly heartbroken when she had discovered that their only hope lay with IVF. She was at the final stages now and would soon be going in for the last procedure where her fertilized eggs would be implanted back inside her. She was clearly very nervous about this, having already had one failed attempt, not least because of the cost of each round of treatment. Lucy reassured her that what was meant to be would be and that she would be okay no matter what, not wishing to raise her expectations with empty reassurances that it would definitely work. Tor and Will were rock-solid; their relationship had grown much closer during their struggle to conceive. It must be hard, thought Lucy as they talked, to hear of so many school friends falling pregnant during their first month of trying. She had been standing next to Tor at a wedding recently when a friend had asked, 'So, you've been married quite a long time now, any children yet?' and Tor's eyes had filled up with tears.

'No, not yet,' she had replied, smiling with false cheerfulness. Lucy had wanted to kick the man for his insensitivity. She had been the sounding board for Tor as she waded her way through the many possibilities before finally settling on IVF. Lucy found it comforting to know that science could always lend a helping hand, should she fail to conceive naturally – either through lack of a suitable partner or fertility problems of her own. Lucy had everything crossed that this round of IVF would work out for Tor and Will. She knew that Tor wanted a baby just as much as she did.

They ended up walking to the cinema on Kensington High Street, Tor wanted to watch a chick flick that Will had put his foot down about seeing. He was playing golf all day, so Lucy had Tor to herself for the whole afternoon. As Lucy settled into the comfortable chair, swapping her sunglasses for her actual glasses to help her see the screen, she reached for her mobile to turn it onto silent. She saw a message from Alex and elbowed Tor, who yelped and was swiftly hushed by the surrounding cinema-goers. Lucy loaded the message onto the screen and saw a photo of him with his nephew and niece, arms full of candy floss and stuffed animals, laughing and looking up at their uncle adoringly. Knowing exactly how they felt, Lucy read the message underneath:

Glad you enjoyed it. I loved it too. Having a great time, too much candy floss = hyperactive children = bad idea – note to self. What are you up to? Ax

Lucy hugged herself with glee at the encouraging text and settled back into her seat, popping popcorn into her mouth and slurping her Diet Coke contentedly as the opening credits rolled.

Chapter Eight

A series of text messages had pinged back and forth between Lucy and Alex all weekend and well into the following week. Alex had suggested going to watch some comedy at the famous 99 club in Leicester Square the following Wednesday night. He had booked tickets and suggested that they meet before the show started to have dinner. Lucy was thrilled at the prospect of a second date and was buzzing all week on a tremendous high. Lettie and Simon stared at her enviously, shaking their heads from time to time and quipping that they wanted the old grumpy Lucy back, she was far less nauseating. Lucy told them both to shut up and continued humming happily to herself, suddenly finding her job much less painful, walking from meeting to meeting with a spring in her step.

'So, how was it?' Jack asked, sidling over to her at the coffee machine. Lucy felt the usual rush of excitement in his presence.

'It was great, thank you,' smiled Lucy. 'Not that it's got anything to do with you!'

'Who is the lucky man?'

'His name is Alex.'

'Alex?'

'Yes.'

'And what does he do? This Alex?' asked Jack in a slightly mocking tone.

'He's a lawyer,' said Lucy.

'A lawyer indeed? Very nice! And… will you be seeing him again?'

'I certainly hope so. He's lovely,' she said, adding 'and, what's more, he's single!' Lucy looked at him pointedly, determined not to show him how much she wished that he was single too.

'Yes, yes. That certainly helps,' he acknowledged with a rueful smile. She noticed that he had dark bags underneath his eyes. Her heart went out to him as she allowed herself to imagine once more that he truly was unhappy in his relationship. So what if he was unhappy, a voice popped into her head. It was absolutely not her concern.

As Wednesday evening approached, her excitement levels almost reached bursting point. She found herself daydreaming about Alex's handsome face, his curly eyelashes, that angular jaw, his strong, big hands touching her here, there and... she had to constantly wrench her attention back to the task in hand. Sometimes her daydreams morphed from Alex into Jack, and back again. She marvelled at the powers of physical attraction, at how she could be so drawn to such different men at the same time. But there was no doubting she couldn't wait to see Alex again and was slightly worried that she might pounce on him uncontrollably and rip his clothes off the minute she did. It had been a long time since she had been physically intimate with a man, and she had missed it. She would have to exercise some serious self-restraint.

At five thirty on Wednesday she met Claudia for a pre-date drink outside her office. Claudia was an even darker shade of olive with her Maldivian tan and looked radiant despite the come-down she was apparently experiencing: a combination of post-wedding anticlimax and post-honeymoon blues. She grilled Lucy for every detail of their date, read every single text message between Alex and Lucy and then declared that she was satisfied, this was definitely love, saying how *exciting* it was that her best friend was going to marry Dan's friend and live happily ever after and have lots of babies. Lucy told her to stop getting carried away with herself, allowing a very secret, deep part of herself to scream *'I know!'* silently whilst the rest of her tried its best to remain calm, with realistic second date expectations.

'How is the forbidden work crush?' asked Claudia. She was the only person that Lucy had dared tell about Jack. 'Hopefully meeting Alex has put paid to that?'

'If only… I know it's ridiculous and I am disgusted with myself, really I am, but I still can't help it. There's just something about Jack. He's so confident and so good at what he does and he flirts with me *all* the time which doesn't help.'

'Do you flirt back?'

'I am trying really hard not to. I keep bringing up his wife and I've even told him about Alex.'

'Good. I'm glad to hear it. He shouldn't be flirting with you at all. It's so unfair. His poor wife!' said Claudia.

'Don't!' said Lucy. 'I feel guilty enough already. I should never have encouraged him,' she said.

'Why did you then?' she asked with a slightly accusatory undertone. Lucy supposed she was sticking up for married women now that she had joined their ranks.

'It started as harmless banter, or so I thought. And he's way more senior than me, so I hardly thought he meant it…'

'How has his seniority got anything to do with it?!' asked Claudia. 'He'd hardly be the first man to have an affair with a junior at work… it's the old cliché of a man and his secretary!'

'Look, Clauds, nothing's going to happen, I promise. Hopefully if things work out with Alex, then he'll get the message loud and clear that I'm taken and give up!'

'Yes, thank god for Alex,' agreed Claudia. 'The whole thing sounds like an absolute recipe for disaster.'

Feeling slightly exhausted by this mini-interrogation, Lucy expertly deflected the attention away from herself and back onto the honeymoon, listening with envy about the five-star treatment that newly-weds receive in the Maldives. Rose petals scattered on the bed and in the bathtub, your own private sunbeds overlooking the sea, sun downers on little glass-bottom boats to look at the tropical fish swimming below. All in all, it sounded like paradise.

They chatted happily over their white wine spritzers until, before she knew it, it was time for her to go. She checked her make-up in her hand-held mirror, applied some bright pink lipstick to 'make her eyes look naughty', as Granny Annie always said, and set off for Leicester Square, kissing Claudia goodbye.

Lucy loved that feeling of London as the summer began. Now they were in the month of July, the weather was starting to get warmer. She walked through the streets watching the tourists admire the beautiful majesty of the buildings and parks and feeling extremely fond of her city. At Leicester Square she wove her way through the masses towards the comedy club and saw Alex leaning against the wall, holding two tickets in his hand. He looked up as she approached him, smiling warmly at her, and enveloped her in a massive hug. The peppery smell of his aftershave combined with the touch of his skin made her stomach lurch like a car being jumpstarted; he briefly kissed her on the lips and said, 'Good to see you, Luce.'

'Hi Alex. Good to see you too. I've just been having a drink with Claudia,' said Lucy. 'She sends her love.'

'Ah, Clauds, how is she? Sickeningly loved up and on a honeymoon high?' asked Alex.

'Actually feeling a bit sorry for herself now that it's all over. You know, not being the centre of attention anymore – it's hard for a woman!' said Lucy, shrugging her shoulders with a grin.

Alex chuckled and they fell into an easy rapport, catching up on the last few days as the guy on the door checked their tickets and they made their way downstairs to the underground comedy club. They sat down at a little round table a few rows back from the stage, not wanting to be in the comedians' direct line of vision in case they became the target for some improvisation. There was nothing more cringeworthy than being used as cannon fodder when on a date. Lucy was sure that comedians could spot a couple in the early stages of a new relationship from a mile away; perhaps like a bloodhound they could smell their fear.

Happy with their choice of seat, they perused the menu, deciding on different variations of burgers and fries: cheddar cheese for Lucy and blue cheese and bacon for Alex. Lucy ordered their food and a couple of bottles of Budweiser at the bar and returned to the table, where she filled Alex in on the rest of Claudia and Dan's news as they sipped their beers.

When their burgers had arrived, Lucy suddenly had an idea, a way of tempting Alex to agree to a third date. Everyone knew what could happen on the third date, after all, and that tantalizing thought was never very far from Lucy's mind. 'Have you tried the burgers in Borough Market?' asked Lucy. 'They have this burger shack which has all sorts of different toppings like blue cheese or caramelized onions… you can choose whatever you like and the meat is so tender it is unbelievable. I have never eaten anything so delicious!'

'Sounds amazing!' said Alex, enjoying Lucy's enthusiasm for food.

'I should take you there,' suggested Lucy. 'Are you free this weekend?'

'I'm free on Saturday. It's a date!' said Alex, chinking his beer bottle against hers. 'I shall leave myself entirely in your hands.' The way he looked at her when he said that made Lucy flush a deep red, she knew he wasn't talking entirely figuratively, and the prospect of what might happen on Saturday night was too much for her to handle. Distracting herself by dunking her last remaining chips into the little pot of mayonnaise, Lucy was relieved when Alex went to buy them another round of beers. Just as he was sitting back down, the lights began to dim and a spotlight shone brightly onto the small stage. A sweaty, northern MC came on to warm up the crowd and announce the first act, Dermot O'Donnell, and Lucy and Alex settled in to be entertained.

At the end of the evening, on their way out of the club, they agreed that they had been given a particularly amazing line-up. Apart from the one act who had absolutely failed to get a laugh, a standard feature of any comedy night it seemed, they had all been hilariously funny. Lucy and Alex had cried with laughter at an ancient old New Yorker's sardonic take on London. They had collapsed with mirth at some wry social observational comedy in the vein of Michael McIntyre, and finally, they had been treated to a preview from a well-known Iranian female comic who was testing her set on the 99 Club before taking it to *Live at the Apollo* the following week. Lucy and Alex both felt in perfect sync with each other in the way that only shared laughter can achieve, it was a relief to find out that they shared the same sense of humour. They had noticed a couple next to them who were also clearly on a first or second date. The girl was having a fantastic time, hooting with laughter at every joke, while the guy sat there looking disparagingly at her, shaking his head in despair, clearly wishing he was elsewhere.

The evening air felt warm as they walked to the tube side by side. Lucy was desperate to reach out and grab his hand in hers, the distance between them felt torturous. Just as she thought she couldn't wait another second, Alex stopped and turned to face her, indulging in another set of lingering, stomach-churning kisses.

As soon as Lucy left him she started to count down the days, minutes and seconds until she would see him again. Her body tingled with the possibility of what was to come. She wanted to make sure that their third date, the date she was in charge of organizing, was amazing. And she also wanted to ensure that she could have her wicked way with him at the end of it. She texted Tor and Claudia on the way home.

Just had second date, he took me to the comedy. Such fun. He is SO amazing. I'm taking him to Borough Market on Sat! Call me tomorrow for full debrief! L xx

Chapter Nine

Lucy opened her eyes with a start on Saturday morning, looking at the clock on her bedside table in panic. 9.55 a.m. *Yikes!* she thought, that gave her one hour and ten minutes till she had to go. She jumped out of bed and went through the motions of preparing her breakfast: bagel in the toaster, kettle on for the coffee, while simultaneously running around the flat, tidying up frantically in preparation for a potential visitor later that night. She gathered old newspapers, magazines and junk mail into a huge pile and shoved it into the recycling bin. She put shoes away, coats on the correct pegs, and wiped down all the surfaces. She ran her duster around the TV and over the mantelpiece, plumping up the cushions with one hand as she munched her bagel in the other. Satisfied with the house makeover, she turned her attention to herself. Stripping off her cotton nightie and throwing it into the laundry basket, she selected a sexy negligee from her underwear drawer in a blue-green teal colour and laid it on her bed, ready for later.

Lucy stepped over to the long mirror in preparation for Step One: The Body, and examined her naked form. She was an hourglass shape with a substantial bust and shapely bum. She tried her best to embrace her curves but it wasn't always easy, especially with a best friend like Claudia who was naturally skinny and had always looked amazing in a bikini. Lucy battled with herself on a daily basis to try and stop any negative thoughts from raising their ugly heads. She tried to reassure herself that a little bit of extra padding was nice for a guy, after all she couldn't think of much worse than someone's hip bones jutting into you at an inopportune moment. The smattering of cellulite on the back of her legs was a genetic curse inherited from her mother on which no amount of running, treatments, creams or dry-brushing seemed to have the slightest impact. Lucy tried her best not to think about the more unsightly parts of her body, choosing to focus on the good bits instead, like the seductive line that ran over her hip bone and into her waist like an ancient marble sculpture.

Focussing on the task in hand, Lucy realized that she needed to start the depilatory procedure a.s.a.p. As she got older the process seemed to get lengthier with the increasing amount of hair that seemed to sprout from ever more unexpected parts of her body. She plucked her eyebrows and then jumped in the shower, shaving any remaining hairs, including her bikini line. She was fed up with spending thirty quid every month on an excruciating Brazilian wax and hadn't had time, frankly, to get around to it recently, so shaving would have to do.

She washed and conditioned her hair, lathered her whole body in foam burst shower gel and finally stepped out of the shower to rub her body down with a towel, spraying a mist of moisturizer over herself.

Having dried her hair and run her straighteners through the ends and especially through her fringe, she embarked on stage two: The Face. She primed, bronzed and buffed her skin before paying careful attention to her eyes, ringing them with smoky eyeliner and coating her lashes with mascara. Working her way methodically through her usual routine was extremely satisfying.

She dressed in black jeans and a bright blue silky top, carefully selected in Topshop on her lunch break yesterday to match the exact colour of her eyes. She flung her leather jacket around her shoulders, admiring the total effect of the makeover. She felt pleased with her reflection and smiled to herself as she sprayed her perfume generously in a cloud in front of her, stepping through it to ensure an even coating.

Checking the time, she saw the clock had just gone past eleven so she grabbed her handbag, stuffing in some emergency make-up along with her mobile. As she gave the flat a final once-over, she noticed a magazine lying open on the sofa at an article entitled 'How to win your man.' Squealing with embarrassment at the thought of Alex seeing that later, she quickly shoved it on the shelf before closing the front door behind her, clattering down the stairs in her heeled boots out on to Mayfield Road.

Lucy took the District line all the way to Tower Hill, one of the best sightseeing spots in the city, with the mystic old Tower of London to the right and the famous Tower Bridge rearing majestically out over the Thames to the left. She walked under the pathway linking the Tower to St Katherine's Docks behind her, sidestepping bundles of tourists and their cameras as she made her way to Tower Bridge. As she reached the south side of the river and headed to Borough Market, she phoned Alex to find out where he was. He tried to explain his whereabouts but the hordes of people made it virtually impossible to pin him down. They played a game of hide-and-seek trying to locate each other amidst the crowds. Eventually catching sight of him by a little cafe selling macaroons and hot chocolate, she headed towards him.

'Hi!' she said.

'Hello there!' said Alex, kissing her on the lips, sending a thrill of shivers down her spine, and handing her a raspberry macaroon the size of a small Frisbee.

'Trust me,' he said, 'they are amazing! You have to try one.'

'Pudding before lunch... I see!' laughed Lucy. Obliging, she bit into the crumbly sweetness, the gooey middle dissolving on her tongue, sharp with the flavour of raspberries.

'Mmmm, you're right. That is heavenly!' Lucy said, offering him a bite. 'It's not the best weather today, sadly,' she complained, looking up at the dull sky.

'I know, but apparently it's going to brighten up later,' said Alex optimistically.

'Let's hope it doesn't rain, there isn't much cover around here,' said Lucy, steering him into the market. 'Have you been here before?' she asked.

'A few times,' said Alex. 'I don't know why I don't come here more often to be honest.'

'It's a real treasure,' said Lucy. 'Though it's slightly ruined by the tourists nowadays. And the prices are not exactly cheap!' she laughed as she picked up a stick of dried salami that cost £13.99.

'Wow!' said Alex. 'That better be some seriously good sausage!'

There were hundreds of stalls bustling with activity, selling freshly made produce and huge vats of hot food, from chorizo and prawn paella to hoi sin duck noodles. They marvelled at all the mouth-watering dishes, their senses inundated by the tantalizing aromas pervading the air.

'Where is this burger stall?' asked Alex.

'It's somewhere around here,' replied Lucy, trying to remember which of the many twists and turns would lead them to the correct place.

'Aha!' said Alex, catching sight of the burger van.

'Here we are!' said Lucy, pleased they had managed to find it after a momentary panic that it was no longer there.

'I'm never going to be able to choose!' moaned Alex as he surveyed the options chalked up on the blackboard next to the van.

After several minutes of indecision, they ordered their lunch and then found an old stone wall to perch on while they devoured it, licking their fingers and laughing at their unsightly table manners.

'God, you are right… this is hands down the best burger I have ever had!' laughed Alex, wiping his chin with the back of his hand.

'I told you!' said Lucy mid mouthful. 'Best burgers in London.'

When they had finished their lunch they pottered around the market. Lucy bought a bag of fudge in all different flavours, from cinnamon to chilli peppers, and they aimed for the Thames Path, heading back over the bridge to the Tower of London, taking it in turns to choose a piece of fudge and guess at the flavour as they walked.

'I think the Tower of London has to be one of my favourite buildings,' said Alex. 'I love the history.'

'I still remember going to visit the crown jewels with my granny when I was little,' said Lucy. 'I loved all the Beefeaters in their traditional dress.'

'It's a seriously random nickname, "Beefeater",' mused Alex.

'True. I wonder where it came from,' added Lucy as they neared the ancient landmark.

When they reached the side of the Tower overlooking the dry moat, Lucy and Alex gasped in unison. A sweeping display of red poppies ebbed from one of the castle windows like blood seeping thickly from a wound. Artists were hard at work installing what appeared to be a war memorial.

'What is going on?' asked Alex.

'I've got no idea…' said Lucy. 'It's beautiful!' She whipped out her iPhone and googled it to find out what was happening. 'Oh my goodness… how amazing. This is in memory of the First World War, they are going to fill the moat with ceramic poppies. Each poppy represents a soldier whose life was lost.'

'How incredible,' said Alex.

'There are going to be nearly 900,000 poppies altogether.'

'Unbelievable,' said Alex. 'There must be several thousand already… it will be breathtaking when it is finished.'

It was a sobering sight; each life represented by one hand-crafted, lovingly made poppy, standing in the grass and nestling against the golden bricks. Lucy was moved to tears at the thought of the sacrifice they symbolized. Alex stood behind her and she allowed herself to lean back into him, feeling the comfort of his presence. They stayed there in quiet contemplation as they watched the artists work, before moving further along the moat. They shared stories about their grandparents and what they had done in the war. Lucy's paternal grandmother had worked at Bletchley Park on the Enigma machines, something she was extremely proud of. Alex's grandfather had flown in the air force and had sadly lost his life at the age of twenty-eight when his plane was shot down, making the memorial even more poignant for him.

Afterwards Lucy took Alex to a nearby church. 'This is called All Hallows,' she said. 'It's the oldest church in the City of London.'

'It's lovely,' said Alex, wondering around the church and admiring the stained glass windows, the paintings and statues that lined the walls.

'Alex, come over her,' said Lucy, beckoning him to a little staircase at the back of the church.

'What's down here?' he asked.

'There's a secret underground chapel in the crypt,' said Lucy as they climbed down the staircase to find a little museum crammed full of ancient artefacts. Alex was fascinated as he explored the church, imagining all the beheaded bodies from the Tower that were brought here awaiting burial to be cared for by the clergy.

Blinking as they made their way back into daylight, the sun pushing through the clouds, Lucy asked, 'What would you like to do now?'

'How about the South Bank?' suggested Alex, so they looped back over Southwark Bridge and walked along the pathway overlooking the river. It was buzzing with both Londoners and tourists enjoying the buskers and book stalls, the open-air bars and the many street entertainers. They pottered around the various stalls, stopping to laugh at the performers. They sat for a while on a bench overlooking the river, just as the sun made an appearance through a gap in the clouds. The city sparkled under the rays of light and Lucy felt her spirits soar.

'I don't know about you,' said Alex, 'but all this walking has made me extremely thirsty.'

'I could murder a glass of wine!' agreed Lucy.

'Follow me,' said Alex. 'I've got just the place in mind.'

They crossed the river at Embankment and settled in the underground vaults of a famous wine bar. A long-established watering hole for the city, each little table was nestled in a small candlelit cavern; it was a very romantic spot. Alex ordered them a bottle of red of a particularly good vintage and they sat there chatting, slowly getting drunk whilst nibbling on a platter of cheese.

After the second bottle, they found themselves leaning close together as they talked, their heads almost touching. With no inhibitions left, Alex's hand had found a resting place on Lucy's thigh. Normally at this point she would have started to worry about whether he thought her thighs were fat, but not tonight. She felt so comfortable in his presence that she just didn't care. He moved his hand ever so slightly further up her leg, igniting a flame of desire so powerful in Lucy that it left her breathless. He bent to kiss her and whispered in her ear, 'I think we had better get out of here, don't you?'

Lucy nodded, unable to speak.

Alex paid the bill and they made their way out onto Villiers Street, heading up to the main road to flag a taxi.

In the back of the black cab, they sat pressed up close to each other; Alex's hand remained firmly on her thigh. As the taxi pulled up outside her house, she fumbled in her bag for her keys, her hands unsteady. Alex paid the taxi driver and followed her up the steps, admiring her house from the outside as he did so. She led him up the three flights of stairs and groped at the lock, scrabbling with her keys to open it, his body pressing closely behind her as she did so. As the door sprang open, she stepped in, feeling suddenly nervous, as though she had forgotten what to do next. She mumbled something about 'Home, sweet, home,' and laughed nervously.

'Would you like another glass of wine?' she asked.

Alex shut the door behind him, slowly taking off his coat. He said, 'No, I don't want a glass of wine, thank you.'

He was so handsome standing there, such a huge presence in her small flat, she felt quite overwhelmed at the sight of him. She took off her jacket and her bag as he stood there, watching her, his eyes dark and gleaming.

Just as she thought she would burst with longing, he crossed the room and took her in his arms, kissing her passionately, no longer holding back, showing her exactly how much he wanted her. She lay on the sofa feeling the heavy weight of him on top of her, her body fizzing and tingling with longing. He took off her silk shirt and kissed her neck, trailing kisses along her collarbone, making her squirm underneath him. He stroked her cheeks and ran his fingers through her hair. She groaned with pleasure as he moved his attention to the top of her jeans, unbuttoning them and sliding them over her hips, continuing with his slow, exquisite torture. They lost themselves in each other, moving in perfect synchronicity, before collapsing in an exhausted, sweaty heap, their limbs tangled.

'That was amazing,' Alex said afterwards, kissing her tenderly on the lips.

Lucy grinned, stretching luxuriously, 'Yes, it most definitely was!'

Alex said, 'I hope you haven't got any plans tomorrow, because I am not letting you leave until we have done that again, and again… and again… and again…'

Lucy laughed and said nonchalantly, 'Oh well, if we must…' receiving a playful nudge from Alex, before taking his hand and leading him into her bedroom.

Chapter Ten

As the summer passed by, Alex and Lucy moved from a couple in the early stages of dating to boyfriend and girlfriend; a real couple in a real relationship. Lucy had to stop and pinch herself at times. She couldn't believe this was actually happening to her, and what was more, that she had bagged herself a gorgeous, eligible lawyer, not someone like Jack with the myriad of complications and baggage that would have come with him. And Alex was a proper catch! Even more surprising to Lucy, and to Lettie and Simon, whose eyebrows seemed permanently wedged up somewhere near their hairline these days, Alex was totally smitten with Lucy. He was the one who had done the majority of the pursuing, he was the one who had asked her out, chased her and brought up the conversation of their exclusivity. He had fallen hook, line and sinker for Lucy and she just couldn't believe her luck. In fact, she had almost been wary at first, thinking that his keenness was a bit strange, but eventually she had accepted it. As unbelievable as it might seem to her, this insanely attractive, available man had chosen her, of all the girls that he could have picked, and she accepted that, relaxing into their relationship as though she had never been apart from him. They formed new routines and traditions, found new places together, and built up a steady stream of memories and shared experiences, the building blocks of a long-lasting partnership. Lucy felt so lucky to be in a relationship that she never questioned it if things felt as though they were running less than smoothly. She put up with any vices: the snoring, the rather short temper, Alex's tendency to see the world as a glass half empty rather than her glass half full approach to life. She was determined to focus only on the positives and to embrace the relationship in full. She knew that hard work was the key to success and she was prepared to do anything to make this new relationship work, to make it last the distance.

Even better, now that she was taken, Jack had begun to accept the fact that she was in a relationship and had toned down his behaviour towards her accordingly. He still flirted with her, and he made it perfectly clear that the offer of dinner or a drink was there if she wanted it, but that was all. She had made it clear that she was not interested and as her feelings for Alex had developed, her interest in Jack had finally begun to wane. She was relieved. Being attracted to a married man was the last thing she needed. She refused to be the kind of woman who broke up a family.

In August Lucy introduced Alex to her grandmother, Annie. Ginny's mother had been brought up in Monmouthshire, near Wales, but she had adopted the mantle of a Londoner in her twenties, having moved to the capital with her husband. Nowadays, she wouldn't live anywhere outside Chelsea, the erstwhile bohemian centre of the city. She lived in a tiny artist's studio, flowers blooming everywhere and paintings lining the walls from top to bottom. Alex and Lucy picked her up from the studio; they were going to the Chelsea Physic Garden and had decided to collect Annie en route. Lucy was glad that she had managed to persuade Alex to come. At the last minute he had said that he wasn't sure he felt up to it, that he quite fancied a quiet night in by himself. Lucy had known how much Annie was looking forward to meeting him and had used all her powers of persuasion to get him to change his mind.

'Granny, I'd like to introduce you to Alex,' said Lucy.

'Very pleased to meet you, my dear,' said Annie, offering him her hand as she eyed him up and down. She had very high standards when it came to potential suitors for her granddaughter and Lucy could see she was sizing him up.

'It's lovely to meet you,' said Alex as they waited for Annie to lock the house before setting off towards the river.

'Have you ever been to the Physic Garden before?' asked Annie. 'I'm a member there and I've been going for years. It's quite charming!'

'I'm afraid not,' said Alex. 'But I'm very much looking forward to seeing it this evening.' Lucy was grateful that now that he had decided to come he was on his best behaviour. He wasn't withdrawn or sullen and this was a huge relief to Lucy. She knew her grandmother would have picked up on it instantly.

'Do you go there often?' asked Lucy. 'It's been a while since I heard you mention it.'

'Well I used to go with my friend Delilah, but since she moved into the nursing home I haven't been going nearly so often. I'm so glad you are coming with me today.'

They walked slowly, arm in arm, through the streets of Chelsea. Annie made polite conversation with Alex, enquiring after his family and asking him about work. Inside the Physic Garden, a little walled garden tucked behind the Thames, Annie took great pleasure in sharing her expertise with Lucy and Alex as they wandered around the flower beds.

'Do you know this garden was founded in the seventeenth century?' asked Annie. 'It was used by apothecaries to study the medicinal qualities of plants, hence the name.'

'How fascinating!' said Alex as they looked at the plants, carefully labelled with the ailments that they were used to treat.

Despite his earlier reluctance to join them, he seemed to be genuinely enjoying himself. She hoped that he was glad that he had made the effort to come and she wondered where his earlier reluctance may have stemmed from. Could it have been nerves? Or worse, disinterest? She hoped he was just genuinely tired and had fancied a night in.

After walking through the gardens, they sipped glasses of gin and tonic at a table outside the restaurant. If Lucy wasn't mistaken, she felt a slight chill emanating from her grandmother towards Alex. She wished she would be a tiny bit less suspicious of the male sex. Despite the bouts of moodiness, the odd impatient reaction or bad-tempered moment, Alex was mostly faultless. Her grandmother should be thrilled that he had taken a shine to Lucy and welcome him with open arms. Lucy felt sure that he would win her over by the end of the evening and was relieved to detect a gentle thawing in Annie's manner by the time they deposited her safely back at home.

A couple of weeks later, Tor telephoned Lucy with the happiest news in the world; she and Will were expecting a baby. The IVF had finally worked, and although they were going to wait until three months had passed to share their news, she couldn't help but tell Lucy. Tor was over the moon with excitement and Lucy was thrilled for her friend. She compared her reaction to the news now that she had Alex (and her own hope of a happy ending) to how she would have felt a few months ago, in the depths of being single. She knew that whilst being happy for her friend she would have felt deeply envious of her pregnancy. She would have despaired about her chances of a similar turn of events, knowing that before she could even think about getting pregnant, she had to find a man. Now that she was safely happy with Alex she felt much more content. She knew that if things were to carry on developing at this fast pace, she would probably find herself in a similar position sooner rather than later. They had talked about the future and Alex, though not exactly jumping at the bit to settle down, had seemed to want similar things to her.

The weekend after receiving Tor's happy news, they spent a long weekend down in Cornwall with her family. Lucy took Alex to all her favourite places from her childhood, grateful for the blissfully hot weather to really show her home county off at its best. Ginny, Lucy's scatter-brained but charming mother, had been a massive fan of Alex. Always an incredibly generous hostess, she had pulled out all the stops, cooking yummy roasts, baking freshly made scones for cream teas and huge fry ups every morning for breakfast. Alex got on well with Lucy's father, Gus, an academic who had spent many years working at the local University. They discussed the nearby Roman ruins that Gus was researching with interest.

There were several occasions during the course of the weekend when Lucy found Alex to be somewhat withdrawn, where he seemed to retreat inside himself and get lost in his thoughts. She tried her best to lift him out of these reclusive spells, suggesting all sorts of activities to raise his spirits. She felt as if it were her duty to make him happy, to use her sunny personality to bring him out of his shell when he felt low. Lucy relished the opportunity to act as a ray of sunshine in his life, knowing how lucky she was that she never really felt down, as so many others did, and enjoying being able to help him through the days when he didn't feel quite as bright as usual. She loved the idea of being there for him, of serving a purpose within the relationship. Together Alex and Lucy paddled in the icy sea, walked along the treacherous coastal paths with her parent's excitable spaniel Tiggy, surfed in the sunset and munched on vinegary fish and chips wrapped in newspaper with the sand between their toes. Despite Alex's bouts of the blues it was one of the happiest weekends of Lucy's life. Every time she looked at Alex, her heart burst with pride at his dazzling good looks. He looked like he belonged in a Levi's advert with his chiselled torso and perfect hair. She noticed other women's reaction to him and could sense their envy as they watched him with her, but he only had eyes for Lucy.

After Cornwall they plunged back into their daily office life, spending as much time together as possible, evenings and weekends devoted to the hedonistic pleasures of fine wine, gourmet food and adventures exploring London.

The last weekend of August was the bank holiday and Alex had asked Lucy to stay with him at his parents' house in Gloucestershire. He warned her that Sarah, Nat, Isabel and Nick were going to be there with their children so it was going to be quite full on. Lucy couldn't wait to see how the Hayes family interacted en masse. She had met both Sarah and Nat and Isabel and Nick before separately at various dinners in London, but she hadn't met Lillian and Michael yet. She was intrigued to see from whom Alex had inherited his looks, as well as certain elements of his personality.

As soon as they arrived they were swept into a cacophony of screaming children, toys, dogs and general chaos; a happy tide that set the scene for the rest of the bank holiday weekend. Lillian was an extremely beautiful older woman, very elegant and refined, the opposite to Ginny's homely, happy-go-lucky appearance. It was clear to Lucy that Alex had inherited his brains from his ex-financier mother. His father Michael, slightly volatile, slightly full of himself with a naughty twinkle in his eye, had clearly passed on his 'smooth' character to his son. Lucy surmised that Alex's sensitive side and his tendency towards occasional bouts of withdrawn behaviour were also from his father. It was a trait that, if she was honest with herself, she would rather he didn't have, that sort of gloomy edge which gave her the feeling that, no matter how many goals he achieved or how much he got out of life, he would always be left feeling unsatisfied. Instead of focusing on the negative though, she acknowledged that no one was perfect and counted her blessings, listing all the wonderful things about him until the less than perfect parts faded into insignificance.

Lucy was incredibly popular with Phoebe, Archie and Nathalie, Alex's nephew and nieces. They adored her and spent the whole weekend bouncing on her lap, hanging off her sleeves and dragging her along wherever they wanted to go. They went on some lovely blustery walks, wrapped up warm because of the late summer chill. Michael gave them some exquisite wines to sample from his collection; Lucy was impressed to find out how he had turned a hobby into a career by setting up his own local wine merchants. Lillian cooked them some pretty tasty meals, though they would fail miserably in comparison to Ginny's culinary talents. Lucy felt perfectly at ease with his family, she slotted in comfortably as though she had been around for years. It seemed that Alex and Lucy had crossed all the hurdles they needed to cross to ensure their compatibility with each other. Lucy couldn't stop thinking about what the future might have in store for them. She hoped beyond hope that they would settle down together, get married and have a family.

As the summer drew to a close and the September evenings started drawing in, they fell back into their by-now familiar routines of London life. One Thursday evening, they decided to go up the road to Alex's local pub, 'The King's Head,' for supper. Alex scooped up a pile of unopened letters that had been gathering by the front door on his way out. As they ordered their food, a chicken pie and mash for Lucy and sticky ribs for Alex, he opened his post. He took a sip of his pint of ale and frowned. 'Oh, bugger.' he said. 'I knew I should have sorted through all of this weeks ago, I just don't seem to have had time for any personal admin lately...'

'What's up?' asked Lucy.

'It's a letter from the estate agents. The flat's lease is coming to an end in December, and I am not being given the option to renew,' Alex said.

'Oh no!' Lucy said. 'That's annoying.'

Alex sighed and rubbed his eyes with his hand, pushing his thick brown hair away from his face. 'Things are building up at work with this big case I've been roped in on, it's going to be pretty bad timing to start looking for somewhere else to live.' He hadn't been in the best frame of mind recently. This was the last thing he needed.

'Yeah, it's not a great time, is it?' Lucy said, an idea slowly forming in her mind. Part of her wasn't sure they were ready for the next step in their relationship, but another part of her thought why the hell not? They weren't exactly spring chickens anymore and she had a house that she owned. 'Why don't you just move into mine?' she asked casually, taking a sip of her glass of Chardonnay.

Alex's face paled slightly, he seemed lost in his thoughts for a moment or two. Then he said, 'Well, it does make sense, I suppose.'

Not exactly the ecstatic response she had been hoping for but not an outright refusal either, she thought, hopefully.

'Well, it's totally up to you. I think it would be fun to live together! I have a place... you need somewhere... why not?'

'Okay, let me think about it for a couple of days and I'll let you know. I'm fairly sure the answer will be yes, but there are a few logistics that I need to work out before I fully commit.'

Lucy felt slightly uncomfortable about the whole conversation but, a few days later, when Alex confirmed that yes, he would love to move in with her, she brushed her concerns about his initial lack of enthusiasm to one side and began to get excited about the prospect of taking this huge step together. She immediately phoned Claudia and Tor to tell them that Alex was moving in.

'No way!' said Tor. 'This is absolutely massive news!'

'I know!' said Lucy. 'I can't believe it really. After all these years, I'm finally being a grown-up and living with a man.'

'You're definitely going to get married if it carries on at this rate… you'll be up the duff in no time!' laughed Tor. 'Bloody brilliant!'

Claudia shrieked down the telephone, 'I'm coming over immediately. I'll bring some champers!' Within fifty minutes they were having a full debrief on the sofa, brimming glasses of bubbles in their hands.

'How did it happen? Who asked who?' asked Claudia, desperate to hear every tiny detail.

'I asked him,' said Lucy as she explained about the situation with his flat.

'But he was super keen, right?' asked Claudia.

'Well, yes… though I think it might have come as a bit of a surprise,' said Lucy. She couldn't quite bring herself to tell Claudia just how unenthusiastic his initial reaction had been.

'He better be thanking his lucky stars that he gets to live with you!' said Claudia before toasting, 'To Lucy and Alex… cohabiters!' and chinking her glass against Lucy's.

With the arrangements put in place, Lucy began the countdown to Alex's moving day, the twentieth of December. October and November flew by, Alex was working hard on his big case and Lucy was inundated with Christmas advertising campaigns from all the big brands. They saw each other late at night and in snatched visits rather than enjoying leisurely lunches and dinners as they had done in the earlier stages of their relationship. Alex's work meant that he was even working weekends, so Lucy used the time to spring-clean her flat, creating space for Alex's things and taking endless bags of old clothes and possessions down to the charity shops. With Alex busy working she began to hang out with her work colleagues more frequently, going for drinks in their local bar as she had done so regularly before Alex came along. She realized that she had missed it.

One Friday after work, after one too many glasses of wine, Lucy found herself alone at the bar with Jack. She hadn't seen much of him lately. He had been running a huge new campaign that had kept him squirreled away in boardrooms and flying off on business trips. Everyone else had drifted off with various weekend plans. Alex was working late and so Lucy had nowhere to rush off to.

'Can I buy you a drink?' asked Jack. She contemplated this for an instant, deciding that she should be perfectly capable of having a harmless drink with Jack now that she was in a stable relationship.

'Sure,' said Lucy. 'A glass of Chablis please.'

'That'll be a large Chablis and a whisky and soda for me please,' Jack instructed the barman.

'Thank you,' said Lucy a few moments later as she took her drink. 'So, how are things with you?'

'Not too bad, thanks,' replied Jack, taking a sip of his drink. 'It's been a hectic few weeks.'

'Tell me about it! Hopefully things will settle down for a while and we can all take it a bit easier.' They chatted about work for a while, catching up on various bits of news.

'So how's it going with the new man… what was his name again?' asked Jack, swivelling on his bar stool to face her, his knees grazing hers. She could tell that he was drunk. He swayed slightly on his stool, using his hand to steady himself on the bar.

'Alex. It's going really well,' said Lucy. Jack nodded and there was an awkward pause. 'In fact,' she hesitated, 'he's moving in soon.' She didn't know why she was telling him this; they didn't usually discuss anything too personal. Maybe she just wanted him to know how committed they were.

'Really?' Jack raised an eyebrow. 'Must be getting serious then.'

'Well it's about time,' laughed Lucy. 'I'm getting past it!'

'No you're not. I'd say you are anything but past it,' he said, slurring slightly. He had definitely had too many whiskeys.

She looked down at her drink, unable to meet his gaze. 'Thanks.' Desperate to end the awkward silence that followed, Lucy babbled on, 'It's about time I settled down though. I spent most of my thirties single and I'm thirty-five now… forty is not too far away.'

'I suppose your biological clock is ticking?'

'You could say that!' said Lucy, laughing nervously. She was embarrassed at the tangent their conversation had taken.

'I admire you, you know. It takes guts to wait for the right person to come along, not to settle. How my wife puts up with me… I'll never know,' Jack shook his head. 'We were so young when we met. No better than children really. I often wonder who I would have ended up with if I had just waited a bit longer. Maybe I'd be happier now if I had held out…'

Lucy was surprised that he was speaking so candidly to her about his marriage. It must have been the drink talking. She wondered whether he was just saying it to make her feel sorry for him, or whether it was true. Whatever his reason, it was working. She did feel rather sorry for him. In that moment she was grateful for all the single years, for all the frogs she had had to kiss in order to meet her Prince Charming. Alex was worth waiting for.

Jack leant closer towards her, clearly enjoying offloading his marital woes onto Lucy. 'I guess I wouldn't have my kids if I hadn't married Penny though, and they are fantastic. But it's not always that easy. I mean, I love Penny, I do, but it becomes more like a sort of brotherly affection after a while, not quite how a man should feel about his wife. Do you know what I mean?' he asked, looking at her intently.

Despite herself she felt her insides begin to fizz at the possibility of him feeling something more than brotherly affection towards her. This took her by surprise, she had thought that her feelings for Alex would have stopped her reacting to another man in such a way. She was now close enough to see the graze of stubble against his chin, the specks of grey in his eyes. He was still looking at her. She felt pulled towards him as though by an invisible magnetic force. He reached out slowly and ran his thumb across her cheek with the lightest touch. She could feel an electric current running through her at the exact point of contact. Her spine tingled. She felt frozen to the spot as though paralysed. This was getting dangerous. He was just drunk, she should know better, and, anyway, she had Alex. Using all her powers of self-restraint, she took a deep breath and said, 'I think I had better go.'

Jack nodded and took another sip of his whisky.

'Thanks for the drink,' she said as she reached down for her bag. As she left the bar, she picked up her phone and dialled Alex's number. It went straight to voicemail. She listened to the familiar sound of his voice asking her to leave a message then she hung up before the beep. She knew that she had been wrong. She shouldn't have put herself in a position where she was alone with Jack. She wasn't as strong as she thought. And clearly, she was still susceptible to his considerable charms.

Chapter Eleven

Although Lucy missed having Alex around during her days off, she was glad that she had more free time to spend with her beloved Granny Annie. She regretted the fact that her weekly visits pre-Alex had dwindled significantly during the course of their relationship, for at ninety years old, she didn't know how much longer her granny would be with her.

Lucy arrived at the studio but her granny was nowhere to be seen. Without a moment's hesitation, she crossed the street and headed for the local church gardens, knowing full well that her grandmother would be sitting on the bench, getting her daily dose of fresh air as she watched the children totter about. This, combined with sunbathing in the summer months, was her main source of entertainment, as well as her daily scrutiny of each page of the newspaper, which gave her an impressive general knowledge of current affairs; her in-depth understanding of the premier league football teams particularly amused Lucy.

Scanning the benches in the park, she spotted her sitting under a tree. With a smile she remembered one afternoon last summer. Once again she had come to the park to look for Annie but had failed to find her. A sense of panic had risen within her as she worried that her darling granny might have had another awful fall. She had fallen over in church while taking communion at the beginning of the year and been rushed to hospital with a huge gash on her forehead. Suddenly, she had caught sight of a tiny figure lying on the grass behind the bench, clearly right as rain and enjoying a spot of sunbathing. Laughing, she had walked over to the spot, calling out, 'Granny Annie, what on earth are you doing down there?!' Annie had peered up, trying to focus on Lucy's face despite the bright sunshine, 'Oh, hello darling! What a nice surprise! I'm trying to get the back of my legs brown!' she had explained, as though it were perfectly normal for an eighty-nine-year-old to be lying on the ground.

She chuckled to herself as she marvelled once again at the lengths Annie would go to achieve a tan! Her grandmother had a tanning addiction that would rival Magda's in *There's Something About Mary*. She found winter quite depressing without her daily dose of Vitamin D, however she had taken to using what she described as 'brown make-up' on her face to keep up her healthy perma-tan glow.

Granny Annie certainly was a character, she had bright blue eyes that still retained their sparkle and she wouldn't be seen dead without her bright red lipstick. She had recently purchased a pair of gold strappy sandals to wear around the house and had proceeded to paint her nails purple, all by herself. Lucy found this unbelievably adorable, and loved her granny even more because of her eccentricity.

'Granny Annie!' called Lucy as she neared the bench.

'Lucy, darling! How did you know where to find me?' asked Annie.

'Oh, lucky guess, I suppose!' laughed Lucy as she bent to kiss her granny's wrinkled cheek, her skin felt cold from the chilly winter air.

'How long have you been here?' Lucy asked. 'It's freezing!'

'Oh not long, darling, you know how I like to come and get some fresh air. I can't bear being stuck inside all day. But it is jolly cold, feel my fingers! They are numb!'

After a few more minutes spent watching a particularly sweet little boy in dungarees unsuccessfully chase a pigeon down the path next to them, Lucy and Annie set off to the shop around the corner to buy some lunch, arm in arm. They went back to the lovely, warm studio where Annie lived and Lucy heated up some soup. As they ate their lunch they talked about life. Her grandmother had met Alex several times now and, while they had got on well, it was clear to Lucy that Annie hadn't been as bowled over by his charm as others. However, she seemed happy to hear about them moving in together and Lucy hoped that this demonstration of commitment on Alex's part would encourage Annie to warm to him a little more. Perhaps she was just being wary of his intentions towards her beloved granddaughter. It was a shame, though, because it was very important to Lucy that her grandmother approved of her other half.

Later, Lucy set off for home. Annie bid her farewell, chanting her customary departing line, 'Don't talk to strange people!' and blowing her kisses, waving from the pavement outside her house until Lucy had walked all the way down the street and turned the corner. Lucy's heart melted as she turned every few steps to wave back at her, Granny Annie was only four foot ten, and the sight of her so small and alone broke her heart. She renewed her promise to keep up the visits and to phone her more frequently, knowing that her family was all she had left now that so many of her friends had passed away.

The big move was scheduled for December twentieth, giving them a couple of days to settle into the flat before they both went to their respective family homes for Christmas. The twentieth was a Saturday, so they had the whole weekend to move Alex out of the flat in Pimlico and into Lucy's. Dan was coming over in the Nissan to lend a hand with the removals,

Claudia having kindly opted to stay at home so as not to be a 'nuisance!' Lugging bags up and down stairs was not Claudia's idea of fun. Lucy helped Alex pack, sorting his belongings into those he wanted to keep and those he would have to throw away. They had both had to downsize their wardrobes dramatically so that two flats' worth of possessions would fit into one. Luckily, Alex had been renting a fully furnished flat, so he didn't have any furniture to deal with. Alex was ruthless with his clothes and shoes; anything that he hadn't worn in the last six months was bagged up for charity. Dan and Lucy did a run down to the local Oxfam, who gratefully received the bags of expensive labels, before helping Alex load the car up with the remaining suitcases. She was grateful for the two men's insistence on carrying the bags up the three flights of stairs to her flat, busying herself with pouring them both stiff drinks as a reward for their efforts.

Dan left a short while later, leaving them to settle in to their first night of cohabitation. Unenthusiastically they surveyed the scene of destruction that surrounded them.

'Arrrghhh…' groaned Alex as he did a mammoth stretch, 'I'm *so* stiff!'

'Me too,' agreed Lucy. 'It's exhausting work, moving!'

'Thanks so much for all this, Luce.' Alex said. 'I really mean it, you've been amazing. I couldn't have done it without you!'

'And Dan, he was great! We definitely owe him one, maybe we can get Dan and Clauds over for our first joint dinner party at 13 Mayfield Road?' Lucy suggested.

'That sounds like a fantastic idea,' Alex said as he made his way over to her, enveloping her in his arms. She felt so happy. For once Alex had remained in amazingly high spirits all day, despite the hassle of moving house. She couldn't help but see this as a good omen, a sign that he was ready to embrace the next stage of their life together. 'Do you know what else sounds like a good idea to me, right now?' he said, as he bent to kiss her.

'I think I can guess,' laughed Lucy, as he picked her up and carried her into the bedroom.

'I'm afraid those boxes will just have to wait!' announced Alex, kicking the door shut behind him and throwing her onto the bed.

Chapter Twelve

Christmas Day dawned bright and clear, a crunchy frost coating each leaf and blade of grass, sparkling like the glitter from Santa's grotto. Ollie had flown back to Rose Cottage from Oz for the festive period, his flights being a rather over-the-top Christmas present from his parents, who realized that shelling out the money was the only way they would get to see their son and heir. Lucy and Alex had parted company the day before Christmas Eve, each travelling back separately to their family homes. They had exchanged gifts before they left. Alex had bought Lucy a new wallet while she had given him a soft cashmere jumper. Lucy was missing him terribly and hoped fervently that this would be the last Christmas they would ever have to spend apart.

Lucy walked arm in arm with Ollie and Annie, Ginny and Gus following closely behind. They made their way along the winding road that cut through the village and led out to St Minver, the local parish church. Their breath was like puffs of smoke in the frozen air, their cheeks red from the pinching chill.

Exhausted, Lucy struggled to keep her eyes open during the sermon, having stayed up half the night with Ollie, catching up face to face for the first time in a year. He was spending the thirtieth and the thirty-first of December with Lucy and Alex in London and was eager to give her new man the once-over. Claudia and Dan were hosting New Year's Eve at their house, which promised to be huge fun. Claudia was renowned for throwing epic parties, the effects of which were guaranteed to stay with you for at least the following week. Lucy couldn't wait to spend her first New Year's Eve with Alex. It would make a pleasant change having someone to kiss at midnight at long last! She was also looking forward to meeting Sebastian, Tara and Rob's baby. Claudia had told her all about his arrival several weeks before and she couldn't wait for a cuddle. Even Claudia, the most unmaternal of people, seemed quite besotted with her adorable new nephew- she kept sending Lucy pictures of him.

The vicar, Maura, was a serious-looking woman who managed to do the whole service without breaking into a smile once, hardly a joyous celebration of the birth of Christ, Lucy and Ollie agreed. The choir was always the highlight of the Johnstons' annual trip to church. They were a mismatched brigade of old dears, all in various stages of toothlessness, squinting at music through glasses perched precariously on the edge of their noses. They all seemed to be singing an entirely different song to the person next to them, whilst the organist accompanied a different piece of music altogether. This always prompted fits of giggles from the parishioners, and today's masterpiece was no exception.

At lunchtime Ginny excelled herself, as always, with a roast turkey as tender and moist as could be, Brussel sprouts served with chestnuts and pancetta, crispy bacon, caramelized roast potatoes and thick white bread sauce. Tiggy sat patiently underneath Gus and the carving board, her eyes fixed on the golden bird with razor-sharp attention, waiting in case a piece of the succulent meat should fall to the floor. They devoured their meals, helping themselves to seconds and even thirds, savouring that unbeatable combination of flavours unique to Christmas Day. They drank champagne by the roaring fire as they unwrapped their presents, Annie taking care to fold all the wrapping paper neatly so as not to waste it. Finally they collapsed, slumbering on the sofas in a food- and alcohol-induced coma, the Christmas *Bond* movie flickering on TV in the background.

Bizarrely Lucy hadn't heard from Alex all day, which she thought was extremely peculiar. She wondered if he didn't have any signal, particularly given that she had sent him a sweet text message wishing him a happy Christmas at seven o'clock that morning, the moment she had opened her eyes. Maybe he was in one of his moods again, she thought. She was beginning to lose patience with him slightly in this respect. He really had nothing to complain about: he was a young, healthy, employed, financially stable man in a relationship, who should be counting his blessings in life, not wallowing in bouts of self-pity. She was finding it increasingly hard to be sympathetic towards him but she hoped that, now they were living together, he might turn over a new leaf.

Gus was in charge of dessert. His speciality was making the Christmas pudding, which they always left until the evening to eat, no one having a single ounce of space left in their tummies at lunchtime. He brought his pièce de resistance in to the sitting room, flickering with ghostly blue flames, and they ate the warm gooey cake, drizzled in melting brandy butter.

As Lucy went to bed she checked her phone, still nothing. She opened her WhatsApp and scrolled to her message chain with Alex. *That's weird*, she thought, *he was last active at 14.55 p.m. So he does have signal.* Feeling slightly unsettled, she sent him another text:

Hope you had a good day? Am so full, we have had an amazing day, love having Ollie home and Granny Annie too, so good to see them. Love you, L x

She didn't usually sign off with 'love you.' They had said it to each other a couple of times before and she had typed it without really thinking about it. She scrolled to her sent items and reread the message. Those two words suddenly made her feel like crying, a sense of vulnerability rose up inside her. She hoped he would hurry up and reply, and tell her that he loved her too. She couldn't shake the feeling that something was wrong. She closed her eyes, leaving her phone on loud in case she got a reply.

The next morning, Lucy opened her eyes and immediately clicked on her phone, still nothing. She scrolled through her Facebook feed, clicking on Alex's profile to see if there were any new posts or photographs, any clues as to why he might be ignoring her, but there was nothing new. She felt slightly pissed off and worried that something was up. Next she clicked on Jack's profile, unable to help herself. She looked at a photograph that Penny had tagged him in, posing with his kids underneath a huge Christmas tree. He looked so handsome. She knew she shouldn't be doing this to herself and that it was only because she felt upset with Alex. There was no point. She knew that she would never act on her feelings for Jack, no matter what happened.

She pulled on her tracksuit and trainers and took herself off for a run. The fresh air would do her the power of good and help her shed some of the frustration she was feeling at his lack of contact. She ran down to the beach and up along the coastal path that led to the next bay around. Her heart pounded and sweat began to trickle down the back of her neck. The familiar views, the salty breeze on her face and the effect of the sun as it bounced off the waves lifted her spirits. After half an hour or so she veered left through the sand dunes and took the shortcut back across the golf course towards Rose Cottage. The whitewashed walls and rambling rose that sprawled across the front welcomed her as she walked the last bit of the track, feeling her heart rate begin to slow down.

Pouring herself a glass of water from the tap when she got inside, she went up to her room to strip off her sweaty clothes. The rest of the family hadn't surfaced yet. It was still early and they were no doubt still sleeping off the excesses of the night before. Her phone was beeping as she walked in,

Hi! Glad you had a good day. Must be nice having O back. Home exhausting as ever. Looking forward to escaping back to London! Love you too, A x

Seeing that he had said 'Love you too' made her heart swell with happiness. Sighing with relief, she told herself off for being so silly. There was no rule saying that he had to be in touch on Christmas Day, after all. She pushed any feelings of unease to one side and made her way to the bathroom at the end of the corridor, ready to face the haphazard plumbing in the hope of procuring at least some hot water for a shower.

Before she knew it Lucy was making her way back to London, her bag laden with presents and her waistband straining ever so slightly after a week of Ginny's cooking. She was due back at work between Boxing Day and New Year, as was Alex. She felt as if they had been apart for weeks. She cooked him delicious meals and they snuggled up on the sofa together in the evenings catching up on the Christmas specials that they had recorded. Ollie came to stay at Alex and Lucy's for the night before New Year's Eve. The three of them had lunch together at the local pub, knowing that Ollie would be out all night catching up with his mates, before returning at god knows what time to pass out on the sofa. He often didn't return home at all. His sun-bleached shaggy mop of hair, boyish good looks and sun kissed tan were an unfailing hit with the ladies, and he was never short of a place to stay the night! This was the standard routine for Ollie's fleeting visits to London.

Alex and Ollie got on well, taking the mickey out of Lucy for her ability to say the wrong thing at the wrong time, swapping stories and killing themselves with laughter at her expense. Lucy chuckled along gamely, enjoying watching two of the most important men in her life get on so well. She had forgiven him for his lack of contact on Christmas Day, determined to start the New Year focusing only on the positive.

New Year's Eve at Claudia's was, as expected, a riot. Rob, Tara and their gorgeous son Sebastian made an early, fleeting appearance, appearing in a flurry of baby paraphernalia.

'Oh my god I can't believe I finally get to meet him!' cried Lucy, rushing over to kiss them hello. Sebastian was in his car seat gurgling merrily as his enormous eyes absorbed his new surroundings. 'He is just divine! Please can I hold him?'

'Of course you can,' said Rob, unclipping his son and passing him over to Lucy for a cuddle.

'How are you finding fatherhood? You look like such a natural!'

'I was absolutely terrified to begin with,' admitted Rob. 'I thought I was going to break him every time I held him!'

'But they're actually pretty robust little things, babies…'added Tara, deftly wiping some dribble from Sebastian's chin with a muslin cloth.

'You look amazing, Tara,' said Lucy, noticing her stylish black jumpsuit and smoky eyes.

'Oh thanks! I must say it's a miracle that I've managed to leave the house with clean hair and no baby sick on my clothing… trust me, it doesn't happen often!' laughed Tara.

Alex was hovering near the nibbles, so Lucy took Sebastian over to him. He cooed appreciatively and nuzzled his chubby red cheeks. Lucy was glad that he seemed to like babies. It was a good sign… surely? She was determined to have a chat with him to reassure herself that they were both after the same thing when it came to having kids. She had had many conversations about children and family with him before, scoping out how he reacted, and he had always seemed to be keen on the idea… but she was conscious that she had never actually asked him out right.

A couple of hours later, emboldened by a few of stiff drinks, Lucy broached the subject. 'Sebastian is such a sweetheart, isn't he?' she said.

'He is cute,' agreed Alex.

'I was wondering…' Lucy took a deep breath. 'Do you think you would like children one day?'

'Steady on, Luce!' laughed Alex, swiftly concealing the flash of panic that had darted across his features. 'It's only been six months!'

'I know, I know…' said Lucy, giving him a playful shove. 'I'm not asking if you want them now. I'm just asking whether you want them some day.'

'To be honest I haven't really given it much thought,' Alex shrugged. 'I'm not really sure yet.'

Lucy felt something inside her plummet. This was not the reaction she had been hoping for. How could he have not even thought about the one thing that Lucy couldn't stop thinking about? Perhaps that was the difference between men and women… men didn't have a biological clock ticking away inside them, there was absolutely no time pressure for them to procreate.

To mask her disappointment, Lucy marched over to the kitchen table that was currently acting as the bar. Claudia had pulled out all the stops as usual, including a never-ending supply of punch, which had become more and more heavily spiked as the night wore on. Tinsel and flashing lights were strewn all over the place and a fantastic playlist of cheesy Christmas tunes kept everyone dancing. The party went on well into the early hours of the morning ensuring a hung-over and rather depressing start to the New Year.

As always on January first, Lucy swore that next year she would definitely *not* drink, promising herself that there would soon come a time when she would welcome in the year in a zen and peaceful state of wellbeing, instead of dying a slow and painful death on the sofa surrounded by takeaway cartons. At least this year she was lying in Alex's arms, she reasoned to herself, a serious improvement on three hundred and sixty five days ago, when she was dealing with the depression of her hangover all alone.

After a few days, when her hangover still hadn't worn off, Lucy began to suspect that she was, in fact, ill... a sure side effect of drunkenly sharing drinks with a bunch of fellow party-goers. Her glands began to swell, her throat began to ache and she was overcome by a chronic sense of fatigue. She just wanted to stay in a cosy hole underneath her duvet and sleep. She phoned work to tell them that she was sick, not very impressive having only managed two days back in the office so far this year, but Lucy was beyond caring. She tried to sleep but the pain in her throat had become truly excruciating. She stumbled over to the mirror in her bedroom, finding a torch deep in one of her drawers and shining it into her open throat.

She located her tonsils, swollen and raw, with the telltale little white spots of tonsillitis. Reaching for the telephone, she made an emergency appointment with the doctor, knowing from experience that she was in for a rough few days, and that penicillin was the only solution.

As the illness passed, Lucy began to feel like herself once more, finally plucking up the strength to go back to work, feeling thoroughly uninspired at the prospect of another year at J&L Communications. She didn't want any more awkward encounters with Jack and she made a vow to herself that she would stay well away from him this year.

Chapter Thirteen

The sun made a welcome appearance in March after a dreary, drizzly winter. Lucy opened the curtains one Saturday morning and jumped for joy at the clear blue sky. She busied herself toasting bagels for her and Alex and made a cafetière of fresh coffee. Alex lounged in bed, unwilling to rouse himself, only emerging from under the layers of bedding when Lucy brought his breakfast to him in bed.

'Thanks babe,' he said, stretching like a bear emerging from hibernation. 'You're the best,' he mumbled sleepily.

Lucy bent down and kissed his stubbly cheek, admiring how completely sexy he could look having just woken up. She had good days and bad days, sometimes perfecting the tousled, just- got-out-of-bed look surprisingly well. She had realized that keeping her mascara and eyeliner on normally made her look much better, provided that she remembered to wipe the smudges away from under her eyes to stop her looking like a panda. Perhaps, this was because Alex had told her that he preferred her with make-up on – something Claudia had been furious about when Lucy had told her. The last couple of months had flown by. Alex had settled in well. His moods had been mixed as usual but Lucy had decided to accept him as he was. There was no use trying to change him, and the more she let his bouts of the blues stress her out the more it would have a negative impact on their relationship. He had really impressed her with the effort he had made on Valentine's Day the month before. Alex had booked a table at a local restaurant for a six course tasting menu with a matching flight of wine.

Lucy had been immensely touched by his thoughtfulness and had relished the chance to be one of those couples that she had always envied, staring lovingly into each other's eyes, on the night of the year when she had always felt at her lowest.

She left him happily munching his bagel as she curled up on her window seat next door to phone Tor. They were meeting for their regular lunch at Tor's insistence, despite her being in her ninth month of pregnancy. As soon as Tor answered she said, 'Holland Park?'

'That's exactly what I was calling about! It's such a beautiful day... but can you manage to get yourself there okay or will it be... too much?' asked Lucy tentatively.

'Lucy, I'm the size of a whale, I agree, but I can still walk, and I'll be damned if I'm going to let the elephant-child that has taken up residence in my womb stop me from enjoying myself,' Tor said. 'Besides, you're supposed to keep moving if you want the damn thing to come out!'

'Okay, fine. But don't go breaking your waters on me or anything like that!' warned Lucy.

'I'll try my best! Eugh, it's all so disgusting!' whined Tor. 'I'll see you at the usual time.' she said, hanging up the phone.

The usual time was one o'clock. Alex had made a last-minute plan to meet a friend on Ken High Street at midday so he dropped Lucy off early en route. She ordered a coffee at their usual cafe and sat inside at the table in the corner, thinking about Tor and how lucky she was to be having a baby so soon. The very thought of it stirred the maternal longings within her; she was so desperate to experience it for herself. Lost in thought, she stared blankly out of the window, stirring her coffee.

Suddenly an enormous copper dog, almost a metre high, came bounding over to Lucy, crashing into the table and causing her latte to spill all over the place. Jolted from her daydreams, Lucy looked up in shock at the huge animal, noticing its glossy chestnut-red fur and brown almond-shaped eyes. The dog was rooting around under the table, trying to gobble up the crumbs that were lurking in the corner, wagging its tail happily. Seconds later, the door to the cafe flung open and a tall, well-built man came striding through it, bringing a blast of fresh spring air in with him.

'Rufus!' he boomed in a deep, throaty voice; the 'r' rolling softly with the gentle lilt of an Irish accent.

At the commanding tone of his master's voice, Rufus, who Lucy presumed was the dog responsible for the disruption, sprang to attention: body frozen, ears pricked.

'Rufus!' bellowed the voice again, resonating with a note of warning.

At this, the dog began to retreat sheepishly from Lucy's table. Turning his long head to look expectantly at his owner, he paused.

Lucy followed Rufus's gaze, taking in the heavy boots, the worn jeans and the thick, knitted jumper; the dishevelled black hair lay in a riotous mess at the top of a ruggedly handsome face. The man's startling blue eyes were staring beneath dark lashes with a look of forbiddance at the dog; his mouth set in a stern frown.

'Rufus, *here!*' he shouted, pointing at the floor beside him. Rufus darted over to him in a flash, proffering his neck apologetically so that his owner could attach the lead to his collar.

Lucy grabbed a few napkins from the dispenser on the table and started to mop up the mess of her spilt drink.

The man, aware that his dog had wreaked havoc at her table, approached Lucy, clearing his throat awkwardly. 'Ahem,' he said; his voice was gravelly and gruff. 'Apologies for the behaviour of my ill-mannered mutt,' he muttered huskily.

Lucy looked at this huge hulk of a man and felt something kick-start deep within her. She had never seen someone so striking; his features looked like they had been carved out of stone, weathered by the outdoors. A dark layer of stubble covered his chin, his thick brow was crumpled with the effort of his apology; he was clearly uncomfortable with the situation.

Lucy laughed, trying to put him out of his misery. 'Honestly, it couldn't matter less!' she said. 'It might have looked like a big spillage, but it was only a couple of drops really.'

'Could I not buy you a new coffee, at least?' he asked, concern like a shadow cast over his face.

'No, not at all. Really, it was nothing!' she chimed, flicking her blonde hair over her shoulder in an effort to look relaxed in front of this strangely attractive man. His presence was having a peculiar effect on her. She felt like she was thirteen years old once again, when she and Claudia would try (and fail) to impress Rob's older rugby mates, massively out of their comfort zone.

'Well, if you're sure? I'm terribly sorry to have disturbed you,' he said, before turning on his heel, dragging poor Rufus along behind him and out the door, back into the park.

Lucy watched out of the window as he set off along the path, Rufus scurrying along with his tail between his legs, aware that he was not in his master's good books. Feeling bizarrely flustered, she took another sip of her coffee. She wondered what that salt-of-the-earth-looking Irish man had been doing in Holland Park; he looked like he belonged on some windswept island in the Atlantic.

As she stared out of the window, she noticed Tor's car crawling up the road towards the small car park that was located just south of the Orangery. Lucy was pleased to see that she had driven, that she was cutting herself at least a little slack given her current state. She watched Tor park the car and went over to help her haul herself and her tummy out from its resting place underneath the steering wheel. They made their way to the cafe, ordered their lunch and sat down, sunglasses firmly in place as they caught up on the recent gossip. Tor laughed at the story of Rufus the dog causing havoc a few minutes earlier and was jealous that she had missed the episode, particularly given Lucy's flattering description of his owner.

Later, as they were strolling at snail's pace around the Dutch gardens, Tor proceeded to tell Lucy about all the side effects to pregnancy at the later stages that everyone failed to mention; some of them very unpleasant indeed.

Lucy balked at the thought, squealing, 'Enough! There's a reason why people don't tell you, you know! It's enough to put anyone off!'

Tor laughed, 'I couldn't put *you* off, could I? You've always wanted kids more than anyone I know. Have you and Alex talked about it yet?'

Lucy said, 'Kind of. He said he hadn't really thought about it much when we first talked about it at New Year's Eve. But then the other day, after we had Claudia and Dan around, we had this conversation about why they are so dead set against having kids. I told him to imagine what life would be like for Granny Annie if she hadn't had any children. All her friends have died; the only people she sees are her children and her grandchildren. I can't think of anything worse than being all alone when you are old, with no family and... he kind of agreed. So I think he's definitely coming around to the idea.'

'Excellent... so when are you going to start trying? Hopefully soon and then our kids can be friends!' said Tor excitedly.

'I was just having the same thought this morning. The thing is, I think we would both want to be married first, and I'm hoping that Alex won't take too long to ask me. I mean, we are getting on a bit! I know it hasn't even been a year yet but I think when you know, you just know! Though I'm not sure Alex is quite as ready as I am....men take so much longer to get their heads around change.'

'True. Well, you're birthday is next month! Thirty six, you'll finally join the club! It'll be here before you know it...' teased Tor.

'Don't remind me!' groaned Lucy, clasping her hands over her eyes and shaking her head. 'How did we get so old, exactly?' she asked in disbelief.

'Hey, I'm six months older than you!' Tor said. 'You can't complain!'

'At least you will have a baby by next month, apparently your chances of conceiving rapidly decrease if you haven't had your first child by the time you're thirty-five. So I'm screwed,' moaned Lucy.

'No you're not, don't be daft!' Tor shoved her playfully. 'You've met the man of your dreams, a smoking hot one at that, he's moved in, and in no time at all you'll be engaged!'

'Maybe I'll come off the pill as soon as I get a ring on my finger!' chuckled Lucy.

'Why not?' said Tor. 'A quickie wedding and then nine months later, you can be on maternity leave with me and we can do this every day!'

'Bliss!' sighed Lucy, hoping fervently that Alex would get a move on, forcing any creeping doubts that he may not be quite as ready as she was to the back of her mind.

As Tor had predicted, Lucy's thirty-sixth birthday was upon her in a flash. She couldn't believe how the time was flying; it seemed only recently that she had entered this decade. On her birthday morning Alex woke her up with breakfast in bed: chocolate croissants, freshly squeezed orange juice and Columbian coffee. He said that she would have to wait until dinner for her present and told her to meet him at six thirty at Leicester Square tube. She wondered what mysterious plans he had in store for her as she set off for work, her mind coming up with all sorts of exciting scenarios of what their evening might entail. Every time the tiny voice inside her head peeped up with the suggestion 'maybe he'll propose!' she immediately drowned it out, wary of raising her expectations, but sadly unable to stop the thought from appearing in the first place.

At work, Lettie and Simon had organized a huge birthday cake for her. Jack sent her an email wishing her a happy birthday; there was no innuendo, she was pleased to see. He had reigned in the flirting since she had left him that evening in the bar. Every now and again she still caught him looking at her, his eyes lingering slightly too long, but mostly he retained a respectful distance and restricted his conversation to work-related topics. She missed their flirtatious banter but she knew that it was for the best.

Later that morning the whole department gathered in the boardroom and sang 'Happy Birthday', making a fuss over her and causing her eyes to well up with emotion. She may hate her job, but she really did love her work colleagues, they were such a well-meaning bunch.

She told Lettie and Simon off for going to so much trouble, but they insisted that they all go out to lunch together as a birthday treat. They asked many a leading question about what Alex would be getting her for the big day and she fobbed them off by saying probably something for the house.

For once, her clients seemed to be kind to her today, no complaining emails, whining voicemails or last-minute deadlines. Besides, she had far more important things to be doing with her time, such as reading all her birthday text messages, WhatsApps and Facebook posts, and listening to screeching voicemails from her friends, enjoying the one day of the year when she felt truly popular. Before she knew it, the clock ticked six o'clock and it was time to go and meet Alex.

At the tube station Alex gave her a hug and a birthday kiss before leading her into the French restaurant opposite. Not the most exciting place in the world, Lucy thought, but they did love steak and chips, she reasoned, thinking perhaps Alex had wanted to choose an old favourite to remind her of their first date. He ordered the usual minute steaks and frites in record timing, appearing rather uncharacteristically rushed. He then announced that he was going to give her his present now, if that was okay?

Slowly, he reached inside his suit jacket, retrieving something from the inner pocket. Lucy didn't even blink or catch her breath, she sat frozen, on tenterhooks, her eyes fixed on his hands as he pulled out... an envelope.

Oh! thought Lucy! *Okay, an envelope... plane tickets, a romantic holiday, a mini-break to Paris?* her mind whirled through the possibilities.

Alex passed her the envelope, grinning sheepishly. Without a second to lose, she ripped open the envelope and read the card.

Dear Lucy,

I know how much you have wanted to see this. Hope you like it!

Happy 36th Birthday!

All my love,

Alex

Two black and white tickets had fallen out. She read the printed script: **Shakespeare in Love, Stalls Row B3, Tuesday April 12th, 7:30 p.m.**

'Oh WOW!' cried Lucy, disguising her slight disappointment with an over-the-top, enthusiastic reaction. This was an art form that she had perfected over many years of receiving unwanted Christmas presents from her rather strange Aunty Gwynn. 'That is *so* kind of you! I have been dying to see this show. I can't believe we are actually going!' She got up and leant across the table, kissing him on the lips. Alex visibly relaxed, he was clearly worried that she would be disappointed with her present, and she chided herself for being so greedy. Not to mention for being so desperate for a ring on her finger. She told herself off. She needed to get a grip; it would happen when Alex was ready and not a minute sooner. She blamed the desperate ticking of her biological clock for her impatience.

'I'm so glad! I remember you saying that you couldn't wait for it to come out months ago.' said Alex. 'That's why I wanted to order so quickly so that we will finish in time for the start of the show!'

'Ha ha,' laughed Lucy. 'It all makes sense now! The devious goings-on in the mind of Alexander Hayes!'

They finished their meal with plenty of time to spare; walking hand in hand to the theatre, stopping off to buy some peanut M&M's en route to keep them going until the interval.

It was a wonderful performance, definitely more Lucy's cup of tea than Alex's, but he managed to stay awake throughout, bolstered by a stiff gin and tonic in the interval. After the show they got the tube back to Baron's Court where Lucy opened all the birthday cards that the postman had delivered for her.

As they got into bed, Alex said, 'Now it's time for your *real* birthday present!'

As he began to kiss her, she thought that as birthdays went, this one hadn't been bad at all.

Chapter Fourteen

Thoroughly fed up with the wintery chill that had been dragging on throughout spring, Lucy had suggested to Alex that they should book a holiday somewhere in the sunshine. She was slightly worried that the long working hours and stress of their day jobs was taking a toll on their relationship. They weren't spending as much time together as they had when they had first started going out, and the time that they did spend together felt rather snatched. She longed for the days when they had been more intimate with each other, spending hours and hours lying in bed and talking, snuggled in each other's arms. It was hard for Lucy to know whether there was actually something wrong between *them*, as a couple, or whether this was just natural for a relationship as the honeymoon period wore off and they became used to each other's company. Maybe this was what Jack had meant? She really didn't want to lose that initial spark, but noticed that whenever she tried to get closer to Alex he seemed to recoil slightly. So she tried not to force it, coming to the conclusion that some time spent together, just the two of them, might be all that was needed to bring them closer together again.

Alex seemed reluctant at first to take time off work but he eventually agreed. They decided to book a trip to Sicily, hoping to catch some early Italian sunshine before the summer kicked in. Lucy had spent a whole weekend while Alex was stuck in the office trawling through travel web sites and TripAdvisor, comparing the costs of flights and all the alternative options available. She finally settled on a sweet little farmhouse bed and breakfast just near the town of Cefalu on the north coast. With their flights and accommodation sorted, it occurred to Lucy that she would need to embark on a shopping spree at some point to find some new bikinis and beachwear for the trip.

Her Saturdays had become rather more empty since Tor had had baby Otto several weeks before, a beautiful bouncing baby boy. When Lucy had gone over to visit him she had marvelled at the radiant glow of motherhood emanating from her friend. She looked so unbelievably happy with this miniature bundle in her arms. It was a miracle of Mother Nature that one could look so amazing despite getting less than two hours sleep a night. Tor had thrust Otto straight into her arms, telling Lucy that she had better get used to him if she was going to be his godmother. Lucy was over the moon and said yes immediately, showering Tor and Otto in kisses while holding his tiny body against her, gazing in awe at every miniscule feature, every perfectly formed little part of him. By this stage her body clock was ticking so firmly that she could almost hear it. Her breasts ached when she was near a baby and she realized that she was going to have to do something about it soon before her body had some kind of phantom pregnancy.

A couple of weeks later, with Alex away on a business trip, she hit the shops with a vengeance. She hated the harsh reality of standing in the cold light of day, pulling bikini after bikini over her swollen thighs and squinting at herself in the unforgiving mirrors as she decided which ones were the most flattering, or rather the least unflattering! Every year she noticed that bikinis started to look less and less attractive on her; she was almost tempted to start wearing a swimming costume, but not quite. She couldn't wait for her skin to get a suntan, being slightly plump it was wondrous what effect the sun had on her general appearance. Lucy had come to the conclusion that you could get away with many more extra pounds on the scales if they were of a sexy, golden brown variety, rather than being white and flabby like raw pastry.

She arrived home grateful that that particular chore was over and done with for another year then set about unpacking her shopping bags into the ever-growing mountain of stuff that they seemed to have amassed.

The next day she decided to have a bit of a sort-out, taking clothes out of cupboards and drawers, folding them and reorganizing them. There was a corner of the walk-in wardrobe that Alex had taken over with his sports kit. Lucy hauled his golf clubs out from the cupboard, causing a cascade of bags and boxes that had been carefully wedged in to fall with a clatter, scattering onto the floor. Lucy sighed and began picking them up, sorting them out and stacking them into some kind of order. She couldn't imagine why men needed to have so much sports equipment, Alex rarely even played golf! A stray golf ball rolled across the floor and under the bed. Groaning, Lucy chased after it, flinging her arm as far as it could reach under the bed and stretching out her fingertips as she just managed to clasp hold of it. She knew that Alex kept his golf balls in one of the side pockets of his club bag, so she unzipped the pocket closest to her, reaching inside gingerly to see if there were any balls there, half expecting to lay her fingers on a smelly pair of socks or something far worse. Her hand closed around a small, velvet box. Without even thinking, she pulled it out.

'OH MY GOD!' she squealed, her vision suddenly becoming blurred as her head began to spin. She sat down with a thud on the floorboards, still clutching the box. She knew exactly what it was: a jewellery box. She sat there frozen to the spot like a statue for several minutes, staring at the blue velvet. Her mind was completely blank. She knew she should put it straight back where she had found it, but her fingers, as if acting completely of their own accord, flicked to the clasp and undid it. The box sprang open.

'AAAAAAAAGHHHHH!' she screamed out loud, as her gaze fell on the most beautiful ring she had ever seen. A huge diamond sparkled as though it was filled with its own light source, reflecting miniature rainbows off every facet, with two hexagonal aquamarines nestling on either side of it.

Grinning like a Cheshire cat, she slammed the lid shut, unable to believe her luck that not only had Alex decided to propose but that he had chosen such an exquisite ring, and furious with herself at the same time for having ruined the surprise before it had happened. This could explain why he had seemed a bit distant and remote with her of late. Tor had felt exactly the same way before Will had proposed, that he had been slightly awkward around her; she had even rung Lucy and complained that something was seriously wrong, but then he had proposed and when she had talked to him about it he had explained that he had been so nervous he couldn't act normally around her!

Lucy opened the box once more, staring in disbelief at the ring that she had been waiting for her whole life. She couldn't believe that it was finally going to be her turn! She was going to get engaged and be a bride and… it was too much for her to cope with. A tear trickled down her cheek and she lay back on the floor, a smile splitting her face from ear to ear.

Hands trembling, she silently packed away the ring in exactly the place where she had found it. She stuffed the golf clubs into the cupboard, followed by all the bags and boxes, trying to replicate the same random order that they had been in before she had begun tidying up.

She knew there was only one person she could tell. Claudia. She tripped over to her bed and flung herself onto it, grabbing her iPhone and pressing the speed dial for Claudia's mobile.

'Hello Juicy Lucy, how are you?' Claudia answered on the second ring.

'Is Dan there?' Lucy asked, trying to get her voice to sound normal.

'No,' said Claudia, 'why? What's up?' she asked.

'Nothing really, only I JUST FOUND AN ENGAGEMENT RING IN ALEX'S GOLF BAG!!!!!!' Lucy screeched ecstatically.

'WHAAAAAAAAAT!!!!' Claudia screeched back. 'Are you JOKING?!' she shouted.

'No!' replied Lucy. 'I'm totally serious!'

'Oh my god this is too exciting! You have to tell me everything. And I mean *everything*!' instructed Claudia. So Lucy recounted every detail, giving her an exact description of the ring and swearing her to total and absolute, eternal secrecy, invoking best friend rights over the marital vows that Claudia had made with Dan. Claudia agreed, swearing to secrecy, unable to stop shouting with excitement.

'So do you think he is planning on doing it in Sicily then?' asked Claudia.

'Oh my god, I hadn't thought of that. I wonder if that's his plan!' said Lucy.

'I bet it is, oh this is just too exciting, if only I could come in your suitcase!' cried Claudia.

'Don't get too carried away, Clauds,' Lucy warned. 'I mean, imagine if he doesn't do it then, how will I feel?'

'Oh shut up Lucy, of course he will do it then! You're thirty six, he's nearly thirty seven. It's bound to happen sooner or later!' said Claudia. 'It was always just a matter of time!'

When Lucy finally hung up the phone, she sat on her bed, quietly awestruck by the momentous events of the day. Her earlier worries about looking good in a bikini had disappeared completely. Now she knew once and for all that Alex truly loved her exactly as she was. She found that the most incredibly reassuring thought. Lucy vowed that whatever happened, she would never tell Alex that she had found the ring. She didn't want to ruin the surprise, after all. She would react as though she had never seen it before, and she knew that it would be such a genuinely emotional time that he would never suspect her accidental discovery.

Lucy was in such a state of shock and excitement that she didn't know what to do with herself. She looked at the clock; it was only lunchtime. She knew she needed to do something to fill her day or she would just spend it staring at the ring which she had forbidden herself from looking at again. Making the decision that she had to get out of the flat, Lucy pulled her running kit on, grabbed her keys and a fiver to zip into the disguised pocket at the back of her leggings as she did so. She skipped happily down the stairs and out into the spring sunlight. As her feet hit the pavement, it was as if they had a mind of their own, falling into a steady rhythm as they pounded along the roads. She had no specific destination in mind but soon found herself jogging the familiar route to Holland Park.

She felt as though she was radiating joy through every cell of her body, her feet barely touching the ground. A soundtrack of 'I'm engaged, I'm getting married!' played on repeat over and over in her mind. She just couldn't believe how her luck had changed.

She made a loop of the park, enjoying the sight of families picnicking, couples relaxing and children playing as she ran. Finally, she slowed her pace and began walking, making a beeline for the cafe as she cooled down. She was suddenly gasping for a drink. She entered through the back of the cafe, popped to the bathroom and then queued up at the counter for a cold bottle of water.

Breaking the seal as she twisted the cap off, she pushed open the door and sat at the nearest table, glugging the refreshing liquid gratefully down her parched throat. As she did so she noticed that the man with the huge dog who had spilt her coffee several weeks before was sitting at the very next table. The dog was lying peacefully at his feet. The man was smiling at her, his crow's feet creasing deeply as he squinted at her in the sunshine.

'You're the lady that my awful dog pounced on, aren't you?'

'Hi!' Lucy blushed, embarrassed that she must be as puce as a tomato and shining with sweat. 'It's Rufus, isn't it?'

'Err, Rory, actually. Rufus is down there, behaving himself for once!' said Rory, nudging his dog with his foot.

'Oh yes, I remember, Rufus is the dog. Sorry!' laughed Lucy. 'I'm Lucy, Lucy Johnston.' She stuck out her hand, having wiped it hastily on the side of her leg.

He took hold of it rather awkwardly and shook it, saying, 'Rory McCullan, pleased to meet you,' in that extraordinarily gruff voice.

'Am I right in thinking he's an Irish setter?' Lucy asked.

'You are indeed!' replied Rory.

'He reminds me so much of my little spaniel, Tiggy,' said Lucy. 'He looks just like a supersized version of her!'

'You have a spaniel?' asked Rory, looking around as if expecting to see one hidden underneath her table.

'Well, she's actually my parents' dog. So she lives in Cornwall, not exactly close by!' said Lucy. 'I wish she did though, I miss her terribly.'

'Spaniels are a great breed,' agreed Rory. 'They're such friendly, excitable dogs.'

'I know… I remember when she was a puppy, her whole body would just tremble with excitement whenever we came into the room. It was like she was plugged into the mains electricity, poor little thing. They are so eager to please!' said Lucy.

'Unlike this one,' Rory said. 'He has a mind of his own, I'm afraid.' At this, one of Rufus's long conker brown ears cocked, he lifted his head slightly as though he was listening to their conversation. 'Don't you, boy?' laughed Rory, bending down to stroke his glossy coat. Rufus emitted a contented sigh and rested his handsome head back on to his paws.

'He's a really gorgeous dog,' said Lucy, bending down to stroke him. 'How does he cope with city life?' she asked.

'He's pretty good, really. I take him for a nice long walk every day to make sure he can have a proper run around. I do feel guilty at times that he doesn't live in the countryside.'

Rory and Lucy chatted for a few more minutes about the pros and cons of dog ownership in the city, before parting ways as Lucy decided to return to the flat. Her head was buzzing with possibilities about her new life with Alex. Maybe they could get a dog of their own? Perhaps they would move out of London so they could bring their children up in the countryside, with plenty of space to run around and explore.

They would probably sell Mayfield Road and buy a house together… a cottage perhaps? But where? Maybe she could find a new job somewhere nearby. Her mind spun as she daydreamed her way home. She was determined to act normally when Alex arrived back later that afternoon. There was no way he could find out what she had discovered.

Chapter Fifteen

Gatwick airport was crammed full of passengers all trying to beat the system by getting cheap flights despite the extremely antisocial hour of the morning. Lucy was beginning to regret her decision not to fly with British Airways and pay the extra few hundred pounds that would have given them another couple of hours in bed. She watched Alex as they edged their way forward in the check-in line, looking for any clues or unusual behaviour that might betray his nerves. She wondered where he had hidden the ring, in his check-in bag or somewhere on his person? Would he have bought insurance, she thought to herself, in case something happened to it or to his bag. She couldn't bear the thought. She tried to stop herself from acting weirdly around him, telling herself that it was vital that she behaved completely as normal. Her nerves were on edge and she knew that they would be until the moment he asked her. But, she told herself, there will be a time and a place for the proposal, and the check-in queue at Gatwick airport was certainly not that.

As the plane took off, she gave Alex her blow-up pillow, noticing that the bags under his eyes were really pronounced. He must be exhausted, she thought. He had been working increasingly later and later into the evenings recently, seeming very stressed whenever he got home. He was being very quiet too, which was unlike him. If she hadn't have found the ring she might have been quite concerned as to whether or not everything was okay between them. She was thankful that they would have a whole week in Sicily with nothing to do but sleep and relax, thinking that would be exactly what the doctor ordered to restore Alex to his former self.

Settling back into her seat with a new book, she looked out of the window as the plane took off. She watched as the city disappeared beneath her, the familiar patchwork of mustard brown and green fields stretching out like a quilt as far as the eye could see. After only a couple of hours she looked out of the window once again to see crystal blue water shimmering beneath them and the majestic Mount Etna towering ahead as they began their descent.

The Sicilian farmhouse they stayed in was a dream. The owners Anna and Fede were as charming as could be, they didn't speak much English but, between the four of them and with lots of sign language, they managed to communicate quite well. They gave them bikes to use during their stay and Alex and Lucy explored the local area both on foot and on bicycle. They drove to different local beaches every day in their little hire car, each one glistening with golden sand, the sea sparkling turquoise. They ate mouth-watering pizzas with fresh basil, tomatoes and mozzarella, tasty concoctions of pasta and gnocchi, gelati of every different flavour under the sun. They went for walks along the coastal paths and lay in the sun, relishing the heat as it beat down on their bodies. Alex slept endlessly, on the beach, in the hammock and in bed. He would fall asleep the minute his head touched the pillow and Lucy would watch him as she lay awake, so handsome and so peaceful in his slumber, grateful that he had the chance to catch up on some sleep and hoping that he would recover some of his usual energy soon.

Her heart had jumped into her mouth on several occasions at the start of the week: as their drinks had been served in a little trattoria on their first evening, as they had reached the top of a hill on a bike ride with a panoramic view stretching out beneath them. But nothing had happened. It became obvious to Lucy that he was planning on proposing at the end of the week, on the last night perhaps. She had been pleased with his thoughtfulness, knowing that she would want to celebrate immediately with her nearest and dearest and that that would be possible the very next day as soon as they landed back home. Her nerves were still a quivering wreck, but she now had them at least slightly under control. A slow countdown to the end of the week ticked in her head as though emblazoned in neon lights around her.

On the last day of their holiday they sat on the beach watching the evening sun make its lazy descent onto the rolling waves, turning them into molten, liquid gold. The sand felt warm from the heat of the day as it nestled between her toes. She could taste salt and sun cream on her lips, her skin radiated with heat. As the sun began to set she knew that this would be the moment. She snatched a glance at Alex, he looked lost in thought. She had heard enough engagement stories from her friends to know to expect odd behaviour from their other half in the run up to popping the question. She had thought that Alex would be able to handle it better than this! He must be crippled with nerves, she decided. She took his hand and gave it a gentle squeeze, mentally willing him on. She couldn't take it any longer.

He turned to face her and said, 'It's such a beautiful sunset, isn't it?'

Lucy smiled at him, trying to stop herself from welling up with emotion. 'It really is.'

'It's been wonderful to get away from London for a week,' Alex continued. 'I really needed a break.'

'I know you did, you've been working so hard,' Lucy agreed, wondering what tack Alex was taking here.

He turned back to watch the last few minutes of the sun setting as it dipped behind the golden waters, disappearing to shine its light on the other side of the world.

She had to remind herself to breathe, realizing that she had been holding her breath.

He turned to face her again, 'Shall we go?' he asked, getting up as he did so and beginning to pack his towel, book and general beach paraphernalia into his red rucksack.

'Oh okay,' said Lucy, slightly nonplussed, but remembering that she wasn't meant to know anything, and forcing herself to be cheerful despite the sense of anticlimax that engulfed her.

They made their way up the beach and back to the hire car that was awaiting them, full of sand, in the car park.

'I quite fancy going back for a shower before we go out to eat,' Alex said. 'Is that okay with you?'

'Sure,' said Lucy. 'I feel like I've got sand in every part of my body, I'm dying to be rid of it.' She was disappointed that he hadn't taken advantage of the romantic setting of a sunset, especially knowing how much she loved them, but she decided that he had probably planned something special for later that evening. A restaurant proposal would be better anyway; she could get all dressed up and make sure she was looking her best.

They drove back to the farmhouse where they were warmly greeted by Anna, who was watering her plants in the garden, and then showered and changed for dinner.

Lucy made sure that her phone was fully charged in case she needed it to take some photos of this special event as a keepsake. She chose her outfit with care, wearing an olive green strappy dress that showed off her deep golden tan. Her hair had been bleached even further by the salt water and the sun, and her freckles had deepened, giving her a real sun-kissed look. She knew that she looked her best when she was on holiday, and added to her appearance with just a dusting of bronzer, a touch of blush and her usual eye make-up, making her eyes smoulder.

Alex was already ready and waiting for her downstairs as she came down the rickety wooden staircase.

'Shall we go to that Trattoria again from the first night?' he asked. 'It was nice food and quite cheap...' Alex tailed off, waiting for her confirmation.

Again slightly shocked but suspecting some kind of double bluff or attempt to throw her off scent, Lucy said, 'Sure,' and followed him out the door and along the path leading back towards the town.

They ate in the sleepy trattoria overlooking the bay, the moon shimmering on the moving waters. As she plunged her spoon into her pudding, she half expected it to hit something hard and find the ring buried within, like in the movies, but no, nothing happened. She tried to steady her trembling hand and calm her nerves. The anticipation was getting too much for her to bear.

They finished their carafe of wine and were given little glasses of sweet limoncello by the waiters as they paid the bill. She couldn't believe that he still hadn't asked her. What was he planning? She just couldn't figure it out. Alex led her back to the cottage, using a flashlight to light the way, without stopping or pausing, talking about this and that but nothing in particular. Lucy, more confused than ever, followed along behind him, mumbling the odd word in agreement but focussing her attention on making sure that she didn't stumble in her wedge heels. The proposal, or lack of proposal, was at the front of her mind.

Back at the room, Alex started packing, so Lucy followed suit; she was so full of nervous anticipation she couldn't even pack her bag properly, clumsily stuffing her clothes in at random, her mind racing and her body tingling with nerves, a sick feeling rose in her stomach. She went into the bathroom, taking deep, calming breaths and reassuring herself that if this was how nervous she was feeling, could she even begin to imagine how nervous poor Alex was right now? He obviously kept wimping out at the last moment; after all, it was a momentous step in any man's life.

With a final, long breath to steady her nerves, she opened the door, half expecting to see Alex down on one knee in front of her. Her eyes fell on the bed. Alex lay there, fast asleep. Lucy didn't know what to do with herself; she went back into the bathroom, closing the door behind her, a shuddering breath escaped loudly from her lungs. She didn't understand why he hadn't done it. Suddenly, an enormous feeling of exhaustion fell over her as though a pin had pierced the bubble of tension that had been holding her together. She opened the bathroom door and walked wearily into their room, folded back the sheets and got into her side of the bed. Alex was facing away from her, sprawled across the bed, mouth open, releasing soft snores into the room. She turned away to switch off the small lamp on her bedside table, plunging the room into darkness. She lay back onto her pillow and willed the familiar blanket of sleep to cover her, her cheeks burning with silent tears.

Chapter Sixteen

The journey back home passed in awkward silence, Lucy didn't feel in a particularly talkative mood and found herself being quite short with Alex. Her head was spinning in confusion and she rued the day that she had found the ring, wishing for the bliss of ignorance.

They got back to the flat and set about unpacking their bags, an almost palpable atmosphere of tension brewing in the room. It was as if they were trying to avoid making eye contact with each other, making only brief conversation about menial things such as where the cleaner might have hidden the remote, or what they might eat for dinner. Lucy couldn't shake the feeling that something was wrong. She couldn't marry this concern with her knowledge about the engagement ring: it was as if something didn't quite add up. She tried to tell herself not to worry, but deep within her bones an unshakeable feeling of foreboding brewed. Trying to put on a brave face, she offered to cook for him. She decided she would make his favourite, bangers and mash with onion gravy.

On the way to the local shop, she rang Claudia.

'Any news?!' Claudia answered on the first ring. 'I've been waiting by the phone!'

'Nothing,' said Lucy. 'I wish I'd never found that bloody ring.'

'How strange! I was sure he would do it on holiday. Maybe he thinks that's too obvious? That it wouldn't be a big enough surprise?' suggested Claudia.

'Mmmm, maybe,' said Lucy. 'I just don't know what to think.'

'Everyone gets engaged on holiday, I'm sure he is planning something much more romantic,' said Claudia. 'I've got a friend who came home from work to find the flat filled with roses and her boyfriend down on one knee! That could be you!'

'You never know!' said Lucy, hoping that Claudia might be right.

'Ah damn, I've got to go… Dan's calling me and I'm late – we're having dinner with his parents. And I haven't even heard about the holiday yet…' said Claudia.

'I'm seeing you on Wednesday, don't worry. I'll fill you in on everything then,' said Lucy.

'Oh yes. Okay, bye! See you Wednesday!' said Claudia as she hung up the phone.

The next day Alex and Lucy both returned to work, plunging straight back into the deep end. Lucy managed to find the time to share her holiday photos with Lettie and Simon, glossing over the low points and painting a fabulous picture of holiday bliss for them both. She didn't want to disappoint their romantic notions of Lucy and Alex as the ideal couple and was hugely relieved that she hadn't told them anything about finding the ring.

She had dinner with Claudia on Wednesday, having seen very little of Alex on Monday and Tuesday night; he had been working late again. She decided to voice her concerns to her oldest friend as they sat eating noodles out of cartons, Claudia's speciality. She was unable to put her finger on exactly why she was feeling uneasy but she was desperate to talk through the situation to try and work out what was going on inside her head. She also hoped that Claudia might be able to shed some light on Alex's increasingly withdrawn behaviour, his usual mood swings seemed to have got even worse. She thought perhaps Dan might have shared some insights that could explain his behaviour, but Claudia was unable to help. She shrugged it off, saying that all relationships went through good patches and bad patches, and that he was probably just really busy at work and unable to separate his work stress from his home life.

'Anyway', Claudia said, 'things can't be that bad between you two or he wouldn't have bought you a bloody diamond ring! Would he?'

Lucy agreed, smiling at her friend and changing the subject to talk about work, laughing at Claudia's hilarious stories. Lucy loved nothing more than listening to her chatter on and on, a perfect distraction from her thoughts, which she was finding it increasingly hard to escape from.

That weekend, Alex and Lucy were supposed to be going to stay with her cousin, Jo, and her husband Matt. Alex hadn't met them yet, and they had tried so often to get a date in the diary to meet that Lucy had begun to feel embarrassed at the amount of times they had had to say no. At long last they had finally managed to pin down a date, and Jo had been emailing excitedly all week with plans about what they were going to do that weekend. Matt was a farm manager and they had been given a lovely cottage on the estate. Jo worked as a teaching assistant in a local school and had fully embraced life in the country, even owning her own pigs and chickens. She was dying to show them around and to get to know Alex at long last.

On Friday morning Lucy received a phone call from Alex. She assumed that he was calling to make a plan about what time train they were going to aim for, and pressed the green button saying, 'Hi!'

'Hi Luce, how are things?' he asked.

'Fine thanks, you? Good day?' she replied.

'Busy. Look, Lucy, I hate to say this but this weekend is not looking good for me. I think I'm going to have to pull out of going to your cousin's.'

Lucy's heart dropped to the floor. 'What?' she said. 'We've had this in the diary for such a long time, you can't pull out now. God, poor Jo…'

'Lucy, it's not exactly as if I am doing this on purpose,' Alex said frostily. 'I have a tough job, and sometimes I have to prioritize work over pleasure. You probably wouldn't understand.'

'Don't patronize me, Alex, of course I understand. It's just that I hate letting people down. Jo has been so excited about meeting you; we've had to put them off so many times before. She's going to think something is wrong with us if we carry on like this.'

'If you carry on like this then there might well be something wrong,' Alex said acerbically.

'I'm not trying to have a go, Alex. I'm just disappointed. I'm the one who is going to have to phone her and explain after all,' complained Lucy. 'And I was looking forward to spending the weekend with you too.'

'We've just spent a whole week together, so there's no need for you to use that as a reason.'

'Look, arguing is not getting us anywhere. It's fine. You stay in London and work, I'll phone Jo and apologize that you won't be able to make it.'

'Fine,' Alex said, then after a pause he added, 'I'm sorry it's worked out this way, but that's life, I'm afraid.'

'Thanks for the apology,' Lucy said, sarcasm dripping from her voice as she hung up the phone. She wasn't sure if he had even heard her. She wanted to scream with annoyance. Salty tears sprang unwelcome into her eyes. God he was so infuriating when he was like this. She had a sneaking suspicion that he didn't *have* to stay and work, he just couldn't be bothered to go and spend the weekend with Jo and Matt. He would probably just do some emailing on his BlackBerry whilst sitting on the sofa watching *Game of Thrones*. But she couldn't exactly prove her suspicions, unless she cut short her weekend and came back to surprise him. She doubted that would go down well with Jo, either.

Gritting her teeth in frustration, she scrolled through her contacts until she found Jo's number. Pressing the dial button, she made the call, apologizing profusely on behalf of Alex, exaggerating about this enormous case that he had on at the moment and lying about how upset he had been to have to cancel. Jo, as always, was so sweet and understanding but Lucy could hear the disappointment in her voice.

Hanging up the phone, Lucy spent the rest of the morning ploughing through her work with flagging spirits, her emotions on a roller coaster from anger to sadness as she thought about their argument. To make matters worse she had been invited to go to a working lunch with Jack and another colleague, Sharon, to discuss ideas for a new social enterprise project that was in the early days of development. Lucy had been asked along because of her previous experience in the field and she had been looking forward to being involved in something more meaningful than her usual commercial projects but Alex's phone call had put a dampener on everything.

Despite her initial lack of enthusiasm the meeting turned out to be a very productive session. The three of them soon found that they were bouncing ideas off each other at the rate of knots. The creative energy lifted her spirits and gave her a much-needed boost. After lunch Sharon had to dash off, leaving Lucy and Jack to finish their coffees and settle up.

'That was really good,' said Jack. 'You have some great ideas.'

'So do you! It sounds like quite an exciting project,' agreed Lucy.

'So how are things with you?' he asked, leaning back in his seat and fiddling with his napkin. He turned to look at her and she was struck with that familiar feeling deep in the pit of her stomach. It was always the same; when he gave her his complete attention, she felt a nervous energy pulse through her, it almost made her feel uncomfortable.

Realizing she hadn't answered him, she cleared her throat. She suddenly felt like crying, the emotional roller coaster of the last few weeks had left her reeling. She felt like a boat that had become detached from its mooring. The clear path she had seen herself on had disappeared. She didn't know what to think or how to feel. She just felt lost. 'I'm okay,' she said but before she could stop herself, her eyes had welled up with tears.

'Lucy, what's wrong?' asked Jack. He moved slightly closer to her.

She shook her head, cross with herself for not being able to control her emotions better.

'It's nothing,' said Lucy. 'I'm just overtired.' He reached out and put his arm around her shoulders. It felt so natural, she did nothing to stop him. In fact, it felt nice to have someone paying her attention, to feel the warmth of physical contact. It had been a while since Alex had bothered.

'Is there something upsetting you at work?' he asked.

Lucy shook her head. 'No, it's not that. It's nothing to do with work… I'm sorry, it's nothing really. And I definitely don't want to bore you with it.'

'You're not boring me, I promise. If you want to talk, tell me.'

'I'm just having a few… personal problems,' she said quietly, dabbing at her eyes with the corner of a napkin. She didn't want to go into any details but felt she had to offer some explanation for her inappropriately timed tears.

'Relationships can be tough,' he said. He had rightly assumed that she was talking about Alex.

'I know… they really can be.' When she looked at him, she could see that he was talking from his own experience.

'To tell you the truth… and please, don't go spreading this around the office… my wife and I have decided to take a break from each other for a while. She's got the kids and I'm staying at my brother's while we try and figure things out.'

'I'm so sorry to hear that,' said Lucy, genuinely moved for him.

'We've talked a lot and we both feel like maybe the time has come for a change,' he explained. 'She thinks that we're stuck in a rut and we need some time apart to re-evaluate.'

'My goodness, you poor thing.'

They sat in quiet contemplation for a few moments, lost in their thoughts. Lucy was slightly taken aback by this sudden revelation. After a while she said, 'Do you think any relationships actually last the distance?' It seemed to her that most were doomed to failure. She clung to the thought of her parents' long and happy marriage as evidence that it was, in fact, possible. Thank god for them.

'I'm afraid I'm the wrong person to ask,' he said with a deep sigh. 'Look, I'm sure things will get better soon,' said Jack. 'But if you ever need someone to talk to, I'm here. Just remember that.' He tucked a curl of hair behind her ear and ran his thumb down the side of her cheek, just as he had done that night in the bar. A shiver ran down her spine.

'Thanks Jack,' she said. She reached over and hugged him, squeezing him tightly. He was so warm and comforting. She didn't want to let go. Neither of them broke contact with the other. They sat like that for a few minutes. Jack rubbed her back softly and she could hear him breathe in deeply. As they parted he leant closer and kissed her gently just on the corner of her mouth. Her heart looped the loop and she had to use all her willpower not to turn her lips up to his and kiss him properly, partly to spite Alex and partly because Jack was so irresistibly handsome. But she knew it was pointless. He was a great guy, despite his dubious loyalty to his wife, and she had to admit it felt wonderful to know the effect that she had on him, but she could never go there. It wouldn't be right. She gave his hand a gentle squeeze and smiled at him, then reached for her bag.

'I'd better get back to work, I've got a few things left to do before the weekend finally arrives,' she said.

'I'll settle up here and see you back at the office,' said Jack. 'I've got a couple of calls to make. Have a good weekend. Remember, if you ever need to talk…'

'Thanks Jack,' she said.

As she walked back to the office, her hand traced the corner of her mouth where he had kissed her.

Later on that evening as she sat around the fire sipping red wine with Matt and Jo in their cosy, ramshackle cottage in Hampshire, she envied their easy, happy relationship. She wondered if she and Alex would ever reach that comfortable stage acquired by so many years together, and hoped and prayed that things would get better between them. She kept her phone on vibrate in her pocket, half expecting it to buzz with an apologetic text from Alex like he would have done in the past after they had had an argument. But there were no texts, no calls.

On Saturday the three of them went for a long walk in the New Forest, the tall trees towering over their heads, whispering in the wind. Lucy was mesmerized by the wild ponies that roamed across the downs; the whole place had a mystical feel to it. In the evening they went to the local pub, The Frog and Forget-me-not, to sample their famous steak and ale pies. Afterwards, a local band began to play, and they stayed to listen to the live music, chatting with some of Jo and Matt's friends from the village. Lucy found she was really enjoying herself, forgetting all about Alex and getting quite tipsy on pints of the local cider.

The next day she got the train back to London after a scrumptious roast chicken prepared by Matt, her tummy full of good food and feeling as though the country air had blasted the cobwebs of London right out of her lungs.

As she let herself into the flat, she found Alex on the sofa, as predicted, watching an episode of *Game of Thrones*. He pressed pause as she came in, asking her a few cursory questions about her weekend, but she found herself unwilling to go into detail about what he had missed out on. She kept her answers short, went into the bedroom and unpacked; she didn't ask him about work or what he had been up to.

The next week passed in a blur of meetings, another pitch for a big campaign was on the horizon for Lucy, this time for a new brand of kitchen roll that was being launched. At the same time she was working on the new social enterprise project that Jack and Sharon were leading, so any spare time she might have had had disappeared. Alex and Lucy passed like ships in the night; she was working later and later as the pitch drew nearer, pulling the usual all-nighters as the deadline approached. Her feelings of unease grew but she slammed them to the side of her mind, focusing on work and ignoring the unspoken truth that was dawning on her, that something was really, very wrong. As soon as the pitch was over she decided that she would confront him that weekend, knowing that she couldn't put it off any longer. They needed to talk.

That Saturday morning Alex volunteered to go to the shops to buy some supplies for the weekend. While he was gone Lucy sat on the sofa trying to summon up the courage to confront him, suddenly feeling sick. Her stomach was literally churning with unease. She was so fed up with this deep, innate sense of disquiet that had been lurking within her for weeks and before she knew it tears had begun to roll slowly down her cheeks. She didn't even wipe them away. She knew she should busy herself with some task that might help snap her out of this mood but she couldn't summon the energy. She just sat there and let the tears fall, swollen with a sense of foreboding.

She was still sitting there when Alex got back an hour or so later, plonking the shopping bags on the kitchen table and asking her what time she wanted to eat. When he realized that she hadn't answered he turned to face her. Noticing her tears, Alex visibly paled. He came over to her and sat next to her on the sofa, saying, 'Luce, what is it?' and putting his arm around her.

Taking a deep breath and turning to face him, she whispered, 'Something's wrong, isn't it Alex? Something is wrong between us…' Alex didn't move, he just sat there, holding her hand quietly. 'Talk to me, Alex, *please*. I can't bear this silence any longer. You are always pussyfooting around me, avoiding any meaningful conversation, working all the bloody time. What is going on?' she said, feeling her voice tremble as she spoke.

Alex sat still for a long time, looking at his hand holding hers. He took a deep breath and slowly began to nod his head, 'I think you might be right, Luce.'

The second she heard those words she knew that the fears she had barely allowed herself to contemplate, were somehow, unthinkably true. A sense of total and utter panic rose up her throat; she felt the sense of security and happiness that had wrapped around her like a safety blanket for the last year slip through her fingers.

'I didn't know how to bring it up, what with the holiday and everything. It seemed so cruel.' He looked at her with eyes pleading for forgiveness. 'I don't know what to say,' he said. 'Things have been really hard recently, you must admit. I feel like we've been growing apart.'

She couldn't believe her ears. Suddenly furious, she shouted, 'NO!' her voice hoarse with bitter despair. 'You *cannot* do this to me, Alex. No, no, *no*… you can't.' Her body felt completely numb with shock, panic rose up her throat, choking her. 'What the hell do you mean, growing apart?' Lucy shouted, hating him for lying to her, misleading her when he was feeling like this. She felt as though he had given up without even the slightest fight. Surely their relationship meant more to him than that?

'I can't really explain it, Luce. Maybe it's me. I've been doing a lot of thinking, trying so hard to make it work between us, trying so hard to see a future. And I did, I swear. I really did, for the first six months of our relationship I couldn't get enough of you. I loved you so much... I was sure that it was forever.'

'You *loved* me so much? You're telling me that you don't even love me anymore?! Well thanks a lot for being *so kind* as to let me know,' Lucy shouted bitterly. 'What a pathetic fool you must think I am.'

'No, Lucy, you don't understand. I do love you. I do. Of course I do. Look at me,' Alex said, his eyes full of tears, his brow creased in deep, anguished furrows. 'Do I look like this is easy for me? Can't you see how upset I am to hurt you?'

'If you really do love me Alex then why are you telling me you don't see a future for us?' she said, hot tears dampening her cheeks.

'I just don't know if it's enough,' he said quietly. 'I don't love you enough.'

Those words were the final nails that hammered into her heart; she broke down into hysterical sobs, her whole body shaking. He tried to put his arms around her but she shrugged him off. He tried again and she hit him, shoving and pushing him away from her with all her strength.

'Just get off me!' she wailed.

He kept on apologizing over and over again but there was nothing he could do to comfort her. She kept repeating 'No!' She felt totally unable to accept what he had said. The happy future she had dreamt of, the children they would have had together, everything she had waited her whole life for; it was all dissolving before her eyes.

Suddenly remembering the ring, she lifted her head, still staring directly at the wall in front of her; she wiped her tears from her cheeks and whispered, 'The ring.'

'What?' Alex said.

'I found the ring… I was clearing out the cupboard, the golf bag… I thought you were going to propose. The whole time we were in Sicily I kept thinking, any minute now.' Shaking her head in disbelief, she slowly turned to face him, she felt nauseous to see the look of guilt and pity on his face. 'How could you? Look at what you've done to me!' she cried, her eyes were so swollen she could barely see out of them.

'I did buy a ring, Luce,' Alex admitted. ' I bought it a couple of months ago. It's been sitting there, burning a massive hole in my conscience, ever since. I thought that I was just freaking out, that I was nervous of making the final commitment, of actually getting married. I knew how much you wanted it, how much our families wanted it, our friends. I thought I was just too chicken to go through with it and that I needed to man up. I tried to do it, Luce, I promise, but when it came down to it, I just knew it wouldn't be fair on you. You deserve someone who has no doubts; you deserve someone who can make you totally happy.'

'But you *do* make me happy. That's the problem,' Lucy said, her throat burning with emotion, her heart breaking into tiny pieces. 'I chose *you*. I love *you*. I want to marry *you*…'

'I know you do. I'm so sorry, Luce, it's just not right. I can't do it. I just can't…' he trailed off, unable to say anything more. There was nothing left to say, just pain. Pain like Lucy had never known, never even imagined possible. It was as if someone had ripped out her heart. Stabbing pains were ripping through her, that feeling of dread, of your worst nightmare coming true in front of your very eyes. She was utterly powerless.

'What will I do?' she whispered, her voice barely audible, her body trembling.

He stood up, pulling her to her feet as she sobbed, muttering, 'Oh Lucy, please don't cry. I'm sorry, I'm so, so sorry,' as he wrapped his arms around her.

Too weak to protest, Lucy rested her cheek on his chest, so familiar to her, so dear and precious. The thought of not being able to do this anymore was unthinkable. She could smell that delicious smell of him and wanted to hang on to this moment forever, the feeling of protection he gave her when she was in his arms, it was bittersweet. They stayed like that for a long time, she didn't know how long.

Eventually, Alex said that he would go, that he would spend the night at Dan and Claudia's. Lucy couldn't even bring herself to speak; she just nodded her head, numb. She couldn't imagine Claudia's reaction when he turned up; the thought of telling her friends was too much. She just wanted the ground to open and swallow her. There was no way she could get through this.

She watched him gather a bag of his stuff; he took his phone from the kitchen counter and his house keys, leaving the untouched bags of shopping on the table.

He came over to her and kissed her one last time, on the lips, saying 'I'm sorry.'

Suddenly overcome with a rising tide of blind panic she cried, 'Don't do it, Alex. Change your mind. We love each other, we can get through this, I know we can!' She was desperate to stop this from happening, to stop him from leaving her. She had to stop him from going out that door. If he went, there would be no going back.

Shaking his head, he said, 'I can't, Lucy. I can't do it.'

'Please!' she cried. 'Please don't go. We can get through this, I'll change. We can work it out, I promise.'

'I'm sorry.' he said. 'I know it's terrible, I know how much you must hate me. I just hope that one day you will be able to forgive me. I'm sorry I couldn't make this work.' His eyes were so full of emotion, so honest, that she knew that he was finding this just as hard as she was, that the last thing on earth he would ever want to do was hurt her. But that somehow made it worse. If only he had done something bad, cheated on her, anything, then maybe she could hate him, but she didn't.

Slowly unfurling her fingers as they grasped his hand, he let her hand drop from his, his cheeks wet with tears. Turning and picking up his bag, he left, closing the front door behind him. Lucy stood there for a long time, staring at the door in utter disbelief at what had just happened. Without making a sound, she turned off her phone, shut all the curtains and got into bed. She didn't even have the energy to take off her clothes. Completely overcome with raw grief, she cried and cried, moaning and wailing like an animal in pain. Every part of her body ached with sorrow. Finally, in the early hours of the morning; she fell into a fitful sleep.

Chapter Seventeen

Lucy didn't move from her bed for the whole of the next day. She threw the covers over her head, burying herself under the duvet, unable to accept the new reality that faced her. The thought of people finding out, the pity and the disbelief that her friends would feel for her made her stomach churn. How could this have happened to her? She just didn't understand how life could be so unfair. Her eyes stung from the tears that she had shed; her pillow was damp with them.

She switched on her mobile, seeing a myriad of messages from Claudia, including several voicemails, but nothing from Alex. Her heart fell. Turning over, she closed her eyes and tried to slip back to sleep.

At midday she woke, forgetting for a moment where she was and what had happened. She sat up and looked in confusion at the drawn curtains, the clock showing 12.00. She turned to look for Alex before suddenly remembering what had happened, the reality slamming into her like a ton of bricks. There was nothing but an empty void where he should be. Unable to bear it, she grabbed her phone and typed him a frantic message, begging him to come back, telling him how much she loved him; that he was wrong, they *were* meant for each other, she knew it. She told him that she couldn't imagine her life without him. Pressing send, she prayed and prayed that he was sitting somewhere, at this moment, thinking exactly the same thoughts: that he had realized he had made a massive mistake; that this message would finally break his resolve and he would come running back to her, begging for forgiveness.

She allowed her imagination to run with this idea, pictured opening the door, letting him into her arms and holding him. She simply couldn't face the alternative: that she would never hold him again; that he would never make love to her, kiss her, tell her how much he loved her; that there would be no more lie-ins, breakfasts in bed, adventures; that it was all over, as though it had never even begun.

Her phone beeped in her hand and she hurried to open the message.

I'm sorry. I can't. A x

She let out a cry of grief and threw her phone against the wall, tears once again rolling down her cheeks. She didn't know where they were coming from, it seemed like she had an endless supply of them. She retreated once more into her bed, closing her eyes tight, wishing that all she had to do was shut her eyes to disappear from sight, like a small child playing hide-and-seek. She just wanted to fade away.

That evening as she sat on the sofa wrapped in her cashmere throw, still wearing her pyjamas, Lucy heard a gentle knocking on the door.

'Luce?' called Claudia softly. 'Are you there? Please let me in, I'm so worried about you.'

Knowing that she wouldn't go away until she saw her, Lucy stumbled over to the door and opened it to let her friend in.

Claudia took one look at her and said, 'Oh Luce, you poor thing,' before wrapping her in her arms for an enormous hug, prompting a new flurry of tears and sobs. She led her back over to the sofa, opened the curtains and the window to let some fresh air into the flat, turned on the lamps and took a bottle of red wine out of her bag. 'First, you need a drink,' said Claudia, getting two glasses out of the cupboard and pouring them one each. 'Right, now tell me everything,' she demanded.

Before Lucy could start she had to ask, 'How is he?'

'Pretty devastated, to tell you the truth. The bastard,' said Claudia through gritted teeth. She was clearly furious on behalf of her oldest friend.

Lucy proceeded to tell her what had happened, taking her time, pausing to catch her breath between juddering sobs. She explained about the holiday, the ring, his doubts, the whole sorry story.

They drank the bottle of wine and opened another one. Claudia cooked Lucy some pasta using some of the ingredients that Alex had bought the day before. She forced Lucy to eat at least a few mouthfuls, having not eaten anything all day, telling her that she needed to keep her strength up. Before she left she said, 'Look, Luce. We both know that this is going to be a totally shit time. You are going to have to grieve for this relationship, go through all the stages as if you are in mourning. But you *will* be okay. I promise you that. You will get through this; I'll be there every step of the way. Leave work to me, I'll call Lettie and Simon, I'll talk to your boss. You need to get the hell away from here. Go to Cornwall, Ginny will look after you. Alex can get his stuff while you're gone. When you feel stronger, you'll come back and you'll start over.'

Lucy nodded blankly, she knew that Claudia was right, but she couldn't imagine how it was going to happen. She would go back to Cornwall though. She knew that was the best place for her to be right now. One thing was for sure, she couldn't stay here, in their house.

Chapter Eighteen

The next day, despite Claudia's insistence that she would sort it out, Lucy phoned her boss to explain her change of circumstances. Luckily for Lucy she was very understanding. She told her to take a few days off work to look after herself. Lucy still had plenty of annual leave to tap into if she felt she wasn't ready to return to London for a while.

She made the telephone call to her mum that she had been dreading and was surprised at her reaction. No judgement, no comment, just 'Come home. We'll sort you out, darling, don't worry.'

Suddenly longing to retreat into the safety of Ginny and Gus's familiar domestic routines, she packed a suitcase of clothes and essentials, trying hard to ignore Alex's things, which were scattered all over the flat. She couldn't remember what the flat had looked like before he had moved in. No doubt he would be coming round soon to move his stuff out; she blanked the thought from her mind, knowing that she didn't have the strength for it.

Too tired to face public transport, she called a taxi to take her to Paddington Station. She found her seat on the First Great Western to Penzance, stowed her suitcase in the luggage rack and hoped that her neighbour would not try to initiate conversation. As the train pulled out of London she began to relax, feeling a little stronger and a little more detached from her sad situation with every mile that she put between them. She stared out of the window, watching the English countryside whizzing by, and marvelled at the surety that no matter what happens to you, life will and does go on. Nothing had changed for anyone else but everything had changed for her. Just like that, the perfect future she had envisaged had disappeared.

Ginny was waiting at Bodmin Parkway with open arms, her glasses swinging from her neck on their beaded string. She gave Lucy a huge hug and took her bag from her, carrying it to her trusty Land Rover, opening the boot and heaving it in to sit amongst the dog hairs and wellington boots. They set off for Rose Cottage at Ginny's usual breakneck speed, careering around corners and past oncoming traffic with scant regard for the paint surface of the car as it scraped against brambles and bushes. They slowed down as they came up the bumpy track leading to the house. All the while Ginny managed to keep up a stream of chatter about Tiggy's escapades, Gus's latest findings in his research project and the local parish council.

When they arrived, Lucy stepped through the thatched porch and inhaled deeply, the comforting smell of home washing over her, and she knew that she had been right to come here. This is where she would be able to start putting herself back together again, no matter how hard it was going to be.

Gus was standing by the Aga, pouring hot water into a cracked, old green teapot. He turned around as they came in, peering at his daughter over his reading glasses. 'Lucy,' he said, and came over to give her a hug, enveloping her in his soft cashmere jumper. 'There, there!' he said as she started to cry. 'It'll all be okay. You'll see.'

Lucy sat at the old pine table where a few months before she had sat with Alex and gratefully accepted a cup of tea. The warm, sweet drink calmed her nerves as she told her parents exactly what had happened. They shook their heads in disbelief. Lucy knew that they were as surprised as she was. They had really liked Alex and she was fairly sure they too had been expecting wedding bells at long last. She almost felt like apologizing for letting them down, but stopped herself short of that. It wasn't her fault. The relationship just wasn't quite right and it was better that Alex had told her now, rather than marrying her with doubts, and bitterly regretting it later. Maybe she had been right all along, maybe there wasn't going to be a perfect match for her. The sooner she accepted that reality, the better. No more daydreams, no more chasing fairy-tale happy endings. She had tried that already and look where she had ended up. She was back in her childhood home, sipping tea with her parents, single once again.

For the rest of the week she slept a lot in the familiar comfort of her little floral bedroom up in the attic, the wooden beams stretching over her head and the small window with views down to the beach. She phoned her boss and arranged to take a couple of weeks of her annual leave to give herself more time. Word of her break-up was clearly spreading around the office, as shortly after hanging up the phone she received an email from Jack saying that he was sorry to hear the news of her and Alex. She was touched that he had made the effort to write.

That afternoon she phoned Tor, who had been texting and calling non-stop since hearing the news from Claudia.

'Lucy my love, how are you?' said Tor as she answered the phone. 'I've been so worried about you.'

'Sorry it's taken me so long to call,' apologized Lucy. 'I've been hibernating.'

'I'm not surprised. How are you feeling?'

'Not too great to be honest.'

'What a massive shit! How the hell could he do this to you?' asked Tor, her frustration on Lucy's behalf clearly evident down the phone line.

'Do you know, I'm not even that angry now. Just incredibly sad,' said Lucy, rubbing her temples as a wave of exhaustion swept over her. She stifled a yawn.

'He is such an idiot. Does he not realize what he is letting go?' asked Tor.

'I don't think it's as simple as that,' said Lucy. 'He just can't see a future with me and he doesn't want to settle for less than perfect.'

'But you are perfect, Luce,' said Tor. 'That's what I don't understand.'

'Well I'm not perfect for him,' said Lucy, her eyes welling up with tears.

'You will be perfect for someone better though, Lucy, I promise you that. Sooner or later we will be looking back on this very conversation, remembering how we didn't know what was going to happen and thinking if only we had known then what we do now,' Tor reassured her. 'It could be just around the corner.'

Lucy tried to believe it could be true but her gut was telling her the opposite. She promised Tor that she would call whenever she needed to talk and thanked her for being there for her. She knew that she was supported one hundred per cent by her friends, and for that she was extremely thankful.

Often, in the middle of the night she would wake up, drenched in tears, aching for Alex, hugging her pillow in his absence and praying for him to come back. Her gut would twist with pain and she would scream into her pillow with grief. She spent hours thinking obsessively about what had gone wrong, wondering if she could have done things differently, what it was about her that had caused the relationship to fail. Why couldn't he love her enough? She felt so sure that if she could just see him again he would change his mind. She would daydream about scenarios where this might happen, playing hundreds of different happy endings in her mind. At times she thought about whether he might be with another woman, perhaps there had been someone else involved? She sent him messages begging him to come back to her. He would reply to each one with the same, steady apologies, the same certainty that this was the right decision, that he wouldn't change his mind. This did help her to begin to fully realize the unacceptable truth that he had gone. He didn't want her. He did love her, she was sure of that, but he didn't love her enough. That kind of love wasn't built to last a lifetime. It wasn't strong enough to raise a family, which would eventually end up suffering from the broken relationship at its core. She knew that if he wasn't happy, if he wasn't sure, then something was deeply and fundamentally wrong. Maybe she was too blinkered by love to see their relationship clearly. She had to believe that he was right and try to be thankful. It was the only way she knew how to move on.

As she slowly got used to her new circumstances she went for increasingly long walks, sometimes for hours at a time, finding a good spot to stop and sit, lost in her thoughts. Ginny fed her up with nourishing home cooking, making all of her favourite meals. Her appetite gradually began to pick up because of all the fresh air she was getting. Lucy spent her afternoons searching for cowry shells on a little sun-drenched beach just a bit further along the coast from her house. A twisting, treacherous-looking path cut through a hedgerow of wild flowers and led to a hidden cove where the tide washed them on to the seashore. In the olden days they had used cowry shells as currency in certain parts of the world. Lucy adored these shells; they were tiny and pale pink like the inside of a conch. Each shell looked as though it had been hand-sculpted in porcelain, curling delicately in on itself with crease marks like miniature wrinkles etched across. If you walked to the end of the beach you could find them nestling amongst the mussel shells and seaweed that the tide had washed in. Lucy and Ginny had spent hours there during her childhood, sifting through the pebbles on the beach, searching for these precious trophies. It was incredibly cathartic, a sort of mind-numbing therapy, and she spent hours on the beach lost in the rhythmic process.

When Lucy finally broke the news to her, Granny Annie was full of words of wisdom and encouragement. 'He was not good enough for you, darling,' her voice crackled slightly down the telephone line. 'I knew it all along.'

'I could tell you weren't quite convinced by him,' said Lucy. 'In fact, I find it quite reassuring in a strange way. Perhaps you had some kind of hidden intuition.'

'When you meet the right man, darling, I will know,' Annie said. 'There was something about him that I didn't warm to. He was a nice enough young chap, don't get me wrong, but not quite right for my little Lucy.'

'I just hope he wasn't all I was going to get!' laughed Lucy wryly. 'My time seems to be running out, I think I might be a hopeless case.'

'Nonsense!' said Annie. 'Everything will work out just as it is meant to. You'll see.'

As she passed the telephone onto Ginny for her nightly catch-up with her mother, Lucy remembered an article she had read that said it takes half of the amount of time that you are in a relationship to get over someone. Lucy surmised that she had a little under six months until she would truly be feeling fine. It was June now, so that gave her until November. She took out her phone and put a reminder alert in her calendar for the 13th November: **By today you will feel normal.** Giving herself a deadline made her feel strangely better, as though she had something to work towards. It was helpful to believe that these feelings of utter despair would not stay with her forever. She clung to the old Persian saying that 'this too shall pass' and repeated it to herself daily, like a mantra, over and over again.

Tor sent her a card which she had blu-tacked to the wall above her bed. It said:

God only ever has three answers to our prayers:

1) Yes

2) Not right now

3) I have something better in mind.

When she read this she felt empowered. It wasn't a yes for her and Alex, and that wasn't going to happen again in the future, of that she could be sure. So God must have something better in mind for her. Lucy was going to find out what it was; she was going to take control of her life and her circumstances for once and for all.

After two weeks had passed, she had phoned her boss and asked her if she could take two more weeks of annual leave before returning to work. She was thankful that she had only taken five days for Sicily and that she had plenty left. It was a quiet time of year in the office as everyone wound down for the summer, and so her boss didn't mind her taking all her holiday in one fell swoop. She knew it meant she would be manning the fort in July and August as the rest of the troops set off for family holidays overseas.

In the next couple of weeks she intended to come up with a plan for the next phase of her life. She thought about her future and what she wanted. At this point in time she had reconciled herself with the fact that she wasn't going to find someone to share her life with. She longed more than anything for the kind of unconditional love and security that only a family could bring. Her mind kept on returning to the same thing, day after day, hour after hour, minute after minute. It was so clear to her. She wanted a baby. Her whole body ached with the desire to have a child. She had been ready for years, just waiting for the right man to come along so that she could start a family. The realization that was beginning to dawn on her, as clear as day, was that she was no longer willing to wait. She knew that she was going to try and have a baby on her own.

Lucy sat down one evening with her parents and waited for them to help themselves to the shepherd's pie that was fresh from the Aga. As they sat down at the table she broached the subject, unsure of how they might react.

'Mum, Dad, I want to talk to you about something,' she said.

'Okay,' said Ginny. 'Go ahead.'

'I have been doing a lot of thinking recently about my future, and I think I've come to a decision about what I need to do.'

'About returning to work, you mean?' asked Ginny, mid-mouthful.

'No, not work related. I know my job isn't the best in the world but it's not that that's really upsetting me.'

'What is it, darling?' asked Gus, pouring them all glasses of red wine.

'Well I know that I'm still getting over Alex, there's no denying it. But I've been thinking about what has upset me the most about our break-up. The loss of Alex, yes, but also the loss of everything he represented, everything he offered. I realize now that what upset me most about him leaving was the prospect of having a family being ripped from my grasp.'

'I don't understand,' said Ginny, putting down her knife and fork to give her daughter her full attention. 'What can you do about that?'

'Well these days there are options to a single woman of my age,' explained Lucy. 'Lots of people do it.'

'Do what exactly?' asked Ginny, looking somewhat alarmed.

'Have a baby by themselves,' said Lucy, determined to maintain eye contact with both her parents.

'That's the most ludicrous idea you've ever had!' said Ginny.

'Ginny! Just let her explain. Go on, love,' said Gus.

Lucy felt a pang of love for her gentle father, always calm, always supportive, even with something that Lucy knew would be far outside his comfort zone.

'The thing is, Mum, I know it sounds ludicrous, but I cannot imagine a future without any children. What will I do when I am your age? Who would be there for me? Who would I talk to? Life would be so empty and unfulfilling without children. I really can't imagine it and I know that I will do anything to stop that from happening,' explained Lucy.

'I can see that life would be pretty different if we hadn't had you and Ollie,' acknowledged Ginny, 'but being a single mother all alone, are you sure that is better?'

'I have never been more sure about anything in my life,' said Lucy, determined to convince them, and herself, that she was doing the right thing. They spent the rest of the evening talking about it and, though initially extremely suspicious of the whole idea, Ginny began to come around when she realized how deadly serious she was about it. They both acknowledged that she could keep on waiting for the next couple of years to meet someone, but that by then it could be too late for her to conceive. She would be forty in four years' time. It was a risk that she just wasn't willing to take any more.

She was pleased that her brother Ollie, whom she had been Skyping regularly, backed her decision. The free spirit that he was, he told her that the modern family unit was as varied as could be, and that he knew she would be a fantastic parent, which was all a child needed.

She spoke to Claudia and Tor for hours, discussing the pros and cons, the minute details and contemplating thousands of possible scenarios that may happen along the way.

'I don't know, Luce, what's so wrong with not having kids?' asked Claudia. 'I'm not going to!'

'I know you don't want to, Clauds, but you and I are wired so differently,' explained Lucy.

'I think it would be fun if neither of us are lumbered with puking, snotty children. Think of the holidays we can go on! Think of the freedom we will always have,' said Claudia.

'But that's the problem! I want all of that, the puke, the snot, the mess, the chaos! I know it's hard for you to understand but the idea of not having that is awful to me. Don't get me wrong, I understand why you don't want to go down that route, of course I do, but I just *have* to be a mother,' said Lucy. 'I have to have a family.'

'Dan and I can be your family,' said Claudia.

Lucy laughed, 'That's very kind of you but probably not quite the same!'

'If you do decide to go ahead with this, you have to know that it's going to be totally shit at times,' said Claudia, who was renowned for her bluntness. 'You are going to feel lonely, overwhelmed, you might have doubts or regrets. Are you sure you are willing to sign up for that?'

'I know it's not going to be easy, Clauds.'

'I will be there to support you, no question, if you go ahead. But I do think you need to spend more time thinking about it. Have you done any research?'

'I haven't done much but I am definitely going to do as much research as possible before I commit to anything,' said Lucy.

'How about talking to someone who has been through it?' suggested Claudia.

'Yes good idea, I'll see what I can find online.'

Lucy spent the rest of the day googling 'single parents' and reading lots of blogs and posts on various single-parenting forums. There were some interesting articles, websites and support groups available to those who were keen to learn more about it and she realized that she was in no way the only person who had come to the conclusion that they wanted to have a baby by themselves. She registered on a support group as a starting point to finding out more about the whole process, keen to talk to other women who had been in a similar position or who were currently contemplating it. It was called singlemothersbychoice.org, and she read the statement from the founder: 'The word "choice" in our title has two implications: we have made a serious and thoughtful decision to take on the responsibility of raising a child by ourselves, and we have chosen not to bring a child into a relationship that is not a satisfactory one.[1] Lucy felt that this echoed her own thoughts exactly and was excited at the prospect of happiness at long last now that she might finally be able to fulfil her dreams and have her own child. The testimonials she had read made her eyes well up with tears, these women were so happy with their decision, they felt so blessed to have been able to have a child. She thought the whole thing sounded surprisingly empowering.

Lucy knew that it would take time to research everything, to get the money together and to prepare herself fully for the procedure. She thought about whether she might adopt but she decided that she wanted to experience the miracle of being pregnant. She wanted to see her genes in her child, to be connected by that physical bond that adoption couldn't provide. She would use a donor's sperm and she would carry the baby herself, supported by her family and friends. She didn't need a man's help.

[1] https://www.singlemothersbychoice.org/about/philosophy/

Chapter Nineteen

Midway through June, Alex sent Lucy a message telling her that he had moved his stuff out of the house and posted the keys through the letter box on his way out. She dreaded returning to the empty flat, knowing that it would feel eerily quiet without his presence, that it would be so painfully obvious where the gaps were in the cupboards and drawers. Fortunately, Cornwall was so breathtakingly beautiful in the summer months; it truly worked wonders for the soul. It was as though all the rugged wilderness of the coastline, combined with the crashing power of the waves, had a healing effect on her. She would sit on the little stone bench at the top of the hill above the golf course and look down at the estuary, mesmerized by the give and pull of the tide, the waves rolling in constantly, hypnotically.

She continued to find out more about single parenting. The more she found out the more empowered she felt. She started running again, building up her strength. She felt like the faster she ran, the more she could distance herself from Alex, as if she could get rid of him, bit by bit, through her own sweat and tears, exorcizing him from her system. By the end of June she felt ready to return to London, strong enough to deal with work and the empty flat, full of determination to move on, and pleased with her progress so far. She was still overcome by frequent bouts of painful, harrowing sorrow, but they were becoming less frequent as she slowly learnt to live with her new reality.

She gave Gus and Ginny a hug at Bodmin Parkway, thanking them from the bottom of her heart for being there when she needed them most and promising to call if she had any low moments. She watched them drive off in their Land Rover, Tiggy resting both paws on the rear windscreen as if waving goodbye. Gathering her bags, she collected her ticket from the ticket machine and made her way to the platform to wait for her train.

As the train rumbled out of the station and made its way through the sun-drenched fields, she remembered making the same journey with Alex the previous summer. The emotions that she thought she had done such a good job of repressing bubbled to the surface once again. She tried to look ahead and think positively. This was a new phase in her life. She told herself to be strong, that she would be okay by herself, that she didn't need him or anyone else.

Having made her way through Paddington station and the throng of commuters that were heading out of the city, she descended into the underground, rummaging in her bag for her Oyster card, which hadn't been used for quite some time. It felt good to be back in the hustle and bustle of the city. She had relished the peace and quiet of Cornwall during those weeks of rest and recuperation, but there was something incredibly satisfying about the hubbub of city life. She felt like a tiny, insignificant cog in an ever-changing machine, and that anonymity reassured her. She knew that her decisions and her life were of little consequence in the grand scheme of things. It was a thought that gave her a healthy dose of perspective, an antidote to any self-pity that she might have been feeling, and she drew strength from the knowledge that whatever she might be going through, there were always people who were coping with worse.

She emerged from the tube and soaked in the familiar sites of Baron's Court as she made her way home, noticing the small changes that the onset of summer had brought with it, the new roadworks and building developments that had sprung up while she had been away. She decided to go straight home so that she could dump her suitcase before heading to the shops to restock her fridge.

Her resolve began to wobble as she approached Mayfield Road and she braced herself as she opened the front door and climbed the stairs to her flat. She unlocked the green door, noticing that the paint was peeling slightly near the lock and making a mental note to do something about it. As she pushed open the door she was struck by the slightly musty, stale smell of an unoccupied house. It looked a little sad and neglected, and she felt bad for having abandoned her home. Lucy turned on the lights, dumped her bag on the floor and scanned her eyes around the flat. It felt surprisingly normal, as though the absence of Alex and his belongings was barely noticeable. The flat had been the same for so many years before him: she supposed, that it was only natural that it still looked like home without his possessions scattered about. It would be in the storage spaces that she would notice the emptiness more.

She walked into the bedroom, turning on the lights as she went, and opened her cupboard doors. Someone, Alex or more likely Claudia, had thoughtfully spread her clothes evenly across the railing so that a large gap was not evident. There was a lot more space, no boxes and bags, and no set of golf clubs. Lucy's heart wrenched as she remembered the day when she had found the ring, how her emotions had danced the tango as she had opened the little velvet box, how happy she had been. But now there was nothing there. Tearing herself away from the wardrobe, she moved to the chest of drawers. Likewise there were no gaping, empty drawers; her clothes had been neatly folded and redistributed to fill the spaces that Alex's jumpers and boxers had vacated. She went back into the sitting room and looked around.

Claudia had a spare set of keys and had been letting herself in once a week to forward any mail and to water her beloved plants. They had flourished in her absence and the bright red geranium in her window box was in full bloom; a vivid splash of colour that brightened up the sitting room. She knelt on the cushioned window seat and raised the sash window, letting some much-needed fresh air seep into the flat. There was a note from Claudia on the kitchen table:

Welcome home Luce! London has missed you. Can't wait to see you! Look in the fridge for your dinner... can't have you rushing to the shops the moment you get back!

Love you C and D xx

In the fridge she found a chicken casserole, a bag of potatoes for baking, some butter, broccoli, milk and a packet of microwaveable chocolate soufflés. Lucy was so touched by this sweet gesture that she immediately reached for her phone and called Claudia.

'Lucy! Are you home?' said Claudia.

'I just got here, thanks so much for stocking up my fridge. You honestly are the best friend a girl could ask for... mini chocolate soufflés?! You know me so well!' she said.

'Well it has been thirty years, I've had plenty of time!' laughed Claudia. 'How does it feel to be back, not too weird I hope?'

'Do you know what, it's not half as bad as I was expecting,' said Lucy, surprised. 'Thanks so much for rearranging my things so that I wouldn't be faced with too many empty spaces. I think I had made it into something so traumatic in my head that the reality was much easier to deal with! Though ask me again in the morning when I've been sobbing into my pillow all night and I might have a different opinion!' said Lucy wryly.

'Don't you dare, he is not worth it!' exclaimed Claudia.

'It's okay, Clauds. I promise I'm feeling much stronger now.'

'Are you still having bad days?' Claudia asked.

'The odd one, but generally I'm so busy focussing on the future that I am trying hard not to look back into the past, it's a great distraction,' Lucy explained, determined to put a brave face on and to try her best to sound positive.

'The best distraction of all: having a baby!' Claudia squeaked. 'How are you getting on with your research?'

'Not bad actually. It seems that I'll have to have artificial insemination, where they'll use a donor's sperm to impregnate me!'

'Right. So you don't have to have IVF or anything?'

'I don't think so. Not to begin with anyway. I'm going to make an appointment with my GP so I can find out more.'

'Good idea. If you do go ahead with your plan, I'm definitely going to be god-mother, right? You've got to promise me that!'

'I promise. Speaking of which, I had better go and see my godson soon, I can't believe I haven't seen him for so long, what a bad godmother…'

'Tor will understand. You can offer to babysit and get some lessons,' Claudia suggested. 'You're going to need them!'

'I might actually start paying attention to some of the more graphic pregnancy stories too, perhaps it'll put me off!' she joked, knowing full well that there was nothing that could put her off now that she had her heart set on it.

'So long as you don't feel the need to pass them on to me. That is one part of life that I am very happy to remain out of the loop on, thank you very much!' stated Claudia firmly.

'Changing the subject entirely, have you heard from Dan how Alex is doing?' asked Lucy, trying to keep her voice casual but instantly feeling sick at the thought of him having a separate life, separate experiences that she knew nothing about.

'Ummm… not really. He has moved in with his sister for the time being, living in the spare room apparently,' Claudia said.

'Which one?'

'The one that lives in London?'

'Oh, Isabel, well yes that makes sense,' Lucy said. 'Is he dating anyone?' she asked tentatively, hoping beyond hope that the answer would be no.

'I honestly don't know, Luce,' Claudia said. 'But you've got to try not to think about that. What he does now is no longer your concern, as painful as it may be.'

'I know, you're right. But it's not easy. The thought of that still makes me feel physically sick.'

'Will you see him?' Claudia asked. 'Are you going to try and get in touch?'

'No,' said Lucy. 'I've thought about it, but I just can't. It's too hard. I feel like I'm doing fairly well by myself now, and I know that if I see him it will send me hurtling back to square one.'

'I think that's very sensible,' Claudia said.

They proceeded to chat about Claudia's work for a while. She was a PA for a monumental bitch in the world of finance, and Lucy loved nothing more than listening to Claudia's character assassination of her boss and the accompanying stories. She had been particularly bad recently, and Claudia's daily texts reporting on her antics had been a wonderful source of amusement over the course of the last few weeks, proving to be a fantastic distraction from her blue moods.

Sending Dan lots of love and promising to come over the next evening for supper, she eventually hung up the phone. She then texted Tor to see if she could pencil in lunch for the following Saturday with her and her godson, Otto. Tor immediately phoned back to check in on her, to find out how she was feeling being back in the flat, showering her with positive messages about the future and motivational talk as only Tor could, mid breast-feed! Otto suddenly appeared to have had enough of his mother's attentions lying elsewhere, proceeding to scream in protest, forcing Tor to hang up the phone whilst apologizing like crazy for her son's rude manners.

Chuckling to herself and feeling lucky to have such amazing friends, Lucy turned on the oven to the maximum temperature and shoved one of the potatoes into bake. Next she began to unpack her clothes, all carefully washed by her darling mother and smelling of home, before pottering around the flat tidying and cleaning happily, with an episode of *New Girl* playing on the television. She had a glass of crisp, white Sauvignon Blanc, cold from the fridge, as she ate her dinner, perusing the channels to choose a movie. She settled on an old favourite, *The Bridges of Madison County,* and sank back to enjoy it. She tested her emotions to see how she felt, as though dipping her toes into the sea to test the temperature of the water. She realized to her satisfaction that she was okay, and she knew, from that moment on, things would begin to get better.

Chapter Twenty

The next day Lucy got dressed for work in a navy shift with a black belt and some strappy gold sandals. It felt good to be back in her routine. She didn't even mind the early, piercing wake-up call from her alarm clock. She had missed Lettie, Simon, Jack and the rest of her colleagues and was looking forward to catching up on all their news. She was especially looking forward to seeing Jack. She had missed his company. She wondered how he was getting on, whether he was back in the family home or not.

She was relieved that no one approached her to talk about the break-up. There were no insensitive comments and the prying eyes and pitying looks that she had been dreading barely made an appearance. Jack came over to find out how she was and to talk to her about the latest updates on their social enterprise project: a campaign to promote a telecoms brand that was aiming to connect thousands of people in rural Africa. It sounded like they had made great progress with it in her absence.

At midday Lettie and Simon announced that they were taking her out for lunch to the local Leon. They filled her in on all the office news, including the big scandal that arose when the head of Human Resources, Sandra Wysowski, had been caught in the stationery cupboard kissing bald Alan, her underling. Lucy cackled with laughter, trying hard not to regurgitate her lunch at the thought! It felt good to be back.

Lettie and Simon were both dating. Simon was still seeing the man that he had been dating since March, a Spanish guy called Andre who worked in IT. It seemed to be going well and Simon was optimistic, for once, about the future. He was even talking about moving to Spain, which Lucy thought was a bit drastic. Young love, she reminded herself, was very fanciful. Lettie was dating a string of men that she had met on match.com and spent most of lunch regaling them with stories of the dates that she had been on so far, ranging from the bizarre to the outright extraordinary.

'You guys are not going to believe this one!' Lettie said with glee. 'Last week I went on a date with a guy called Mark. He seemed perfectly normal when we were messaging but seriously… he was anything but!'

'Go on!' urged Lucy, taking a slurp of her Diet Coke and leaning closer in anticipation.

'Okay, so we met at this bar in Soho. I spotted him immediately and went over to meet him, he bought me a drink and it all seemed to be going quite well.'

'And?' asked Simon, intrigued.

'Well we sat down at a table in the corner and he took a deep breath and said, "Look, I don't mean to be rude, but you don't really look like your profile." I didn't really know what to think seeing as it's a close-up of my face and it looks just like me, so I asked him to clarify exactly what he meant. He replied that he had hoped that I would be larger than I was, explaining that he wasn't really in to "slim women", apparently he only fancies women that are in the unhealthy/obese category of the BMI scale!'

'No!' exclaimed Simon.

'Maybe he's one of those feeders that you see on TV!' shrieked Lucy. 'What did you do?'

'Well I couldn't leave with a full drink so I apologized for being too slim, secretly congratulating myself on the compliment, and decided to pry into this bizarre fat fetishist a little further. He told me that he was extremely attracted to the sight of rolls of fat. I began to feel a little queasy and started downing my wine in bigger gulps. He proceeded to explain a particular fantasy of his where he would lift up a fat roll...'

'Nooooo!' shrieked Simon and Lucy, wincing at the thought.

'...insert a slab of cheese, wait until it had melted slightly and then eat it!'

'Aaaah!' screamed Lucy. 'No *way*!'

'Eurgh, I'm going to be sick again at the thought!' Lettie shuddered.

Apparently Lettie had almost vomited on the spot and knocked over a table in her haste to get out of the bar. Lucy was encouraged to find herself really laughing, a deep, belly-rippling laugh that she hadn't emitted in a long while.

That afternoon she ploughed through the rest of her emails and made sure that she popped into see her boss, Jill, to thank her for her understanding, for letting her take the time she needed. She bumped into Jack again on the way back to her desk. He seemed to have resumed his old flirtatious manner, giving her a cheeky wink as he passed her, no doubt encouraged that Lucy was now single once more, but she was determined not to encourage him. Ignoring his complicated home life, she was so focussed on her plans for motherhood that she didn't want or need any distraction.

As the weeks rolled by, Lucy settled into the routine of work, running home once or twice a week, catching up with friends, seeing her granny and spending her free evenings researching.

One Saturday in late July, she met with her GP. As she sat in the chair and the doctor asked her what she could do to help, Lucy almost wimped out. She felt embarrassed to say that she was interested in finding out about donor insemination. She was worried that the doctor would judge her somehow, that she would think her naïve or foolish, that she should wait until she met a man like everyone else before having a child. She steeled herself and tentatively broached the subject, her desire to find out exactly what her options were overriding her embarrassment. Her doctor was surprisingly sympathetic. She asked her whether she had thought carefully about proceeding down this path, then recommended various websites that she could go to to get advice and support.

Feeling slightly more positive about the choices that lay ahead and armed with some literature that the doctor had given her, she set off to meet Tor in the park. The sky was a warm, cobalt blue. A light scattering of cloud streaked above the horizon as if a piece of white chalk had been dragged across it. Even the pavement beneath her feet seemed to radiate with the dry heat of the day. Lucy fumbled in her bag for her sunglasses, squinting against the bright light of the sun.

As she walked through Holland Park she inhaled the floral fragrance that permeated the air, noticing with joy that the towering delphiniums and scarlet oriental poppies that blossomed at this time of year were out in full force. She telephoned Tor, who was en route, to find out what she wanted to eat and then went inside the cafe to order, carrying her tray full of sandwiches and crisps out to their usual table in the sunshine.

About five minutes later she saw Tor approaching, pushing her enormous pram, looking slightly dishevelled but grinning happily and waving as she spotted Lucy. Putting the brakes on the pram, she gave Lucy a hug, plonking herself down on the chair and saying, 'Phew, I made it!' with a sigh of relief.

Lucy peered into the pram and admired the sleeping baby.

'I'm telling you, Luce, it's a bloody nightmare trying to get anywhere with one of them!' she moaned, pointing at the pram.

'I can imagine!' said Lucy. 'I'm going to push him around the park later, see if I can steer it. It looks like an awkward contraption to manoeuvre!'

'It is! It's supposed to be top of the range, but surely they can come up with something better than that. I mean, in the first few weeks, I'm not exaggerating when I say that it took me about five minutes to work out how to stop at the pedestrian crossing and press the button to cross without letting the pram slide into the road!' she laughed, rolling her eyes at her own hopelessness.

'I honestly don't know how you do it!' laughed Lucy.

'It's trial and error, that's all,' confided Tor. 'I haven't really got a clue! Anyway, much more importantly, tell me how it all went with the doctor this morning.'

'I was pretty terrified, to be honest,' said Lucy. 'It all feels a lot more real when you find yourself eye to eye with a medical professional.'

'Has it put you off?' asked Tor. 'I remember my first consultation when we started IVF… it sounded frankly horrific: the needles, the injections… et cetera. But in a way I was grateful that I knew what lay ahead; forewarned is forearmed, as they say.'

Lucy had been there for Tor the whole way through, it was too late to spare her the gory details. 'It turns out that IVF is only used if you have had trouble conceiving naturally. Because I haven't tried to get pregnant yet, there is no reason why I shouldn't be able to without any help.'

'Thank goodness for that. So what did they suggest?' asked Tor.

'Something called IUI.'

'Oh yes, I remember that. What does it stand for again?'

Lucy glanced down at her leaflets, riffling through them to find the one she was looking for. She showed it to Tor. 'Intra-Uterine Insemination.'

'I've heard of that,' said Tor. 'We were offered it but I think our chances were better with IVF so we went straight for that.'

'Well apparently it is a pretty straightforward procedure. They wait until you are at your most fertile and then inject you with sperm with some kind of turkey baster!'

'A glorified one-night stand!' laughed Tor.

Lucy raised her eyebrows as she took a bite of her sandwich, contemplating the prospect. 'It would certainly be a lot cheaper!' she agreed.

'And you can choose what they look like.'

'Apparently I can do that anyway at the sperm bank,' said Lucy.

'I've always wondered about sperm banks,' said Tor. 'Do you think they are literally warehouses full of frozen sperm in test tubes?'

'I have no idea!' said Lucy. 'What a disgusting image!'

'Do you have to go along and pick your sperm in person?' asked Tor.

'No, I think it's more digital these days. I can look at the website apparently.'

'Can you get it done on the NHS?' asked Tor.

'Sadly not. I need to find a private clinic that specializes in donor insemination. I'm planning on doing lots of research this week and then I'll make an appointment for a consultation. There's so much to get my head around!' said Lucy.

'Don't rush into anything,' warned Tor. 'Having IVF was the best thing I've ever done, but also the hardest.'

They both looked at Otto, still sleeping peacefully beside them in his pram. Lucy knew in her heart of hearts that however tough the road might be, she was determined to take it.

'I don't want to be too negative, but have you thought about the cost of it all too?' asked Tor. 'It's a bloody expensive process, well, IVF was anyway, hopefully IUI is cheaper?'

'It's definitely cheaper than IVF but it's still going to cost me a lot, especially cos it's so unlikely to work on the first attempt. I managed to save a few thousand pounds from Alex's contributions towards the mortgage repayments while he was living with me, so that will help.'

'At least there was one perk to that arsehole moving in,' said Tor.

'And I've also made some general savings over the last few years, so hopefully that will be enough to cover the costs of the treatments.'

Having finished their lunch, they decided to set off for their customary walk around the park. Lucy pushed the pram while Tor entertained her with stories of her experiences of motherhood so far. There was so much to learn, from the painful boobs from breastfeeding to the constant smattering of sick on all of your clothes, the sleep deprivation, the lack of sex life, the over-reliance on microwave meals and takeaway because you're too knackered to cook. But most importantly, there was the total and utter all-consuming love that you felt for your baby that just obliterated all of the downsides completely. It was so obvious in the besotted way Tor looked at Otto, and Lucy just knew more than ever that she was ready to experience it too. Why should she have to wait for a man to have a baby? There was no time to lose, as far as she was concerned. As soon as she got home she pulled out her laptop and continued with her research.

Lucy wanted to find the right place to have her treatment, somewhere approachable and experienced in treating women in similar situations to her. She found a fertility centre called The London Women's Clinic which had been open for over ten years and which she was reassured to find out was one of the pioneering clinics to start treating single women. The website told her they had helped over two thousand women just like her have babies, a fact which made her feel fractionally less alone, thinking of all those who had been in exactly the same boat as her, making this terrifying decision before her. She joined the Facebook group and spent hours poring over the posts and articles, fascinated to hear from all these women who had chosen to have a baby by themselves. The more Lucy read, the more empowered she felt, and the more excited she became about the prospect of motherhood. She made an appointment for the twenty-third of August where she would be able to talk to a doctor and have a proper consultation.

Chapter Twenty-One

In the meantime, work was fairly relaxed as the big firms wound down over the summer, resting before the onslaught of Christmas campaigns. Lucy found regular entertainment over her lunch breaks with Simon and Lettie as Lettie shared yet more trials and tribulations from the internet dating scene. The more she heard, the more Lucy was put off the idea of ever bothering to date again. Who would go to the trouble of putting themselves through this seemingly humiliating and soul-destroying process? Though, to her credit, Lettie seemed to be taking it all on the chin with a remarkable sense of humour.

'You can't just sit at home moping,' she laughed, as Lucy vowed out loud she would never go on an internet dating site.

Simon agreed, 'It's high time you got back out on the dating scene, Luce.'

'Well there's no hope in hell I am joining match.com!' she said, shaking her head vehemently at the thought.

'What about Tinder?' suggested Lettie. 'It's free and you can see if you've got Facebook friends in common.'

'I suppose that is slightly better,' said Lucy. 'At least then you know you are not going to get a cheese-eating-fat-fetishist!' They all laughed and Lettie visibly paled once again at the thought.

'Exactly!' groaned Lettie.

Simon had already swiped Lucy's phone out of her hand and was busy tapping away on it, ignoring Lucy's cries of 'Oy, give it back!' She admitted defeat, knowing that protesting was futile. Within mere moments, Lucy's Tinder account had been set up. Despite her initial reluctance, when they showed her how it worked Lucy found herself somewhat intrigued. It seemed like a fairly easy method of filtering out the total mingers: swipe right to like and left to pass. Even she could manage that. She promised Lettie and Simon that she would give it a try and she meant it. It would do her no harm to give dating one last attempt. If she was brutally honest with herself she knew that despite having resolved to go it alone, she would never give up hope on a last minute intervention from the fates. The thought that there was a man out there waiting for her could never be eliminated from her mind completely.

Lucy couldn't believe how addictive Tinder proved to be. When she was bored at work she would surreptitiously swipe all sorts of eligible-looking men, determined to get at least one date under her belt. She pinged messages to a few of the guys who she liked the look of, doing some background investigation by texting the mutual friends they had in common to find out if they were normal.

Eventually she set up a date with a guy called Ted. His profile picture revealed him to be a nice-looking ginger-haired man with a rather juvenile-looking quiff, and they had exchanged a series of pleasant messages before agreeing to meet for a drink. Simon and Lettie were extremely chuffed with her and took her out for a pre-date drink to 'warm her up'.

They were to blame for the fact that she found herself turning up a good twenty minutes late at the pre-arranged meeting place, a bar in the city. She crossed her fingers as she entered, hoping that he wouldn't be too deranged. Lucy hadn't got much info out of the random Facebook friend she had got in touch with to do her background check. Apparently he was a vague acquaintance rather than a good friend, but there were no skeletons in the closet as far as her friend knew. She felt the familiar kick of nervous anticipation low in the pit of her stomach and acknowledged that it was quite fun even having the prospect of a new love interest. It had been a while. A pang of sadness flashed through her as she thought of Alex, and everything that a future with him had offered her. But there was no point in dwelling on what might have been. Tearing her thoughts back to the present, she forced a smile as she thought of Lettie, also on her way out to meet a date, if nothing else it would be fun to compare notes with her and swap stories the next day.

She scanned her eyes across the dimly lit bar, hoping to recognize her date from the photo. With a sigh of relief she spotted him sitting at a table in the corner. It had to be said, in the flesh he was nothing much to write home about. *Oh well*, thought Lucy, *looks aren't everything…*

'Ted?' she asked as she approached the table.

'Oh, hi. Lucy is it?' he asked, looking up at her with mild interest as she came to sit down. He didn't stand up to greet her, so she awkwardly stuck out her hand, which he shook somewhat unenthusiastically.

She sat down and placed her bag on the floor, filling the awkward silence that hovered between them with a stream of chatter about her tube journey.

Obviously unimpressed by her thus far, judging from the lack of response, Ted said, 'Can I get you a drink?'

'Oh yes please!' said Lucy, a little over-excitedly.

'What?' asked Ted rather curtly.

'A glass of white wine would be absolutely lovely!' said Lucy.

As she watched him make his way to the bar she wondered why he appeared to be moving at the speed of a snail. Maybe he was not in a rush to get back to her verbal diarrhoea. She mentally reprimanded herself for being incapable of letting awkward silences pass. Why should she always be the one making people feel comfortable? He should be polite enough to put her at ease, not the other way around! She decided that when he came back she would sit back and wait for him to begin a conversation. She wanted to regain a balance of power where she didn't look like a gibbering idiot. This time, she was determined to appear aloof.

After what felt like an age, she spotted Ted weaving his way through the office workers, carrying a bottle of sparkling water and the tiniest glass of wine she had ever seen.

'I got you a small,' he said as he put it down in front of her, before adding, 'We don't know how this is going to go.'

How charming! thought Lucy, grabbing the wine and purposefully knocking at least half of it back in one.

The rest of the date went from bad to worse. They had nothing in common, or at least they never had the opportunity to find out, thanks to Ted's complete lack of communication. Lucy almost wanted to ask him why he had agreed to come on the date if he was clearly so uninterested in getting to know a single thing about her. Despite having resolved to let him take the lead she tried to ask him questions and salvage what was rapidly becoming one of the worst dates of her life, but was met with monosyllabic answers. She found herself wondering what a socially acceptable amount of time to make an exit might be. When she could bear it no longer she looked at her phone, ignoring the excited message from Simon asking her how it was going and checking the time. It was 8.35, precisely forty-five minutes since she had set foot in the building and the longest forty- five minutes of her life. She couldn't stand it a second longer. Wincing as the chair legs scraped across the floor, she stood up to make her excuses and say goodbye, apologizing that she had forgotten she had made plans for dinner with a friend. He didn't even bat an eyelid, in fact he couldn't have looked less bothered.

As she sat on the tube on the way home, she tried to compose a text to Lettie and Simon that suitably portrayed the awfulness of the date. She started with his opening line of 'I got you a small' (he was right about that one!) and ended with her falling asleep on the table. Only a minor exaggeration. What a disaster! She couldn't help but laugh to herself as she thought of his expressionless face as she had left him. Oh to be such a vacant and emotionless soul; she almost felt sorry for him! That was it; she had done what she set out to do. She had proved to herself that meeting someone through a virtual medium was no indicator whatsoever of chemistry, let alone personality, and she knew that she would not be dating anyone else unless she had physically set eyes on them.

That Friday she found herself leaving the office at the same time as Jack. 'What are you up to?' he asked, holding the door open for her as she stepped out onto the busy street.

'Nothing much. You?' she asked.

'Home to an empty house.' He clearly hadn't moved back into the marital home.

'Aren't we cool!' she said. 'Friday night and no plans.'

'Tell me about it,' laughed Jack. 'I don't suppose you fancy a drink?' he asked.

Lucy contemplated this offer for a moment or two. It was that or another evening sitting in front of the TV. She knew the sensible answer would be to say no, to stay well away from him, but the reckless part of her brain replied before she had time to rationalize her response. 'Sure,' she said. 'Why not!'

Jack led the way to a bar around the corner. 'What can I get you?' he asked.

'I'll have a G and T please,' said Lucy, taking a seat on one of the empty bar stools.

'Single or double?' asked the barman as Jack placed his order for two G and Ts.

'Double,' said Jack without hesitation. Lucy made a mental note not to let herself get drunk. They started talking about work but after a short while Jack announced that the topic was banned. 'That's all we ever bloody talk about!'

'Good point. Who wants to think about work when they aren't even in the office?!'

'Or when they are in the office, for that matter,' laughed Jack. 'I'm desperate for a break.'

'Yes, having all that time in Cornwall did wonders for me. What about you? Have you got any holidays to look forward to?'

'I've got the usual trip to Mallorca with the family,' said Jack. 'Though Penny is still deciding whether or not I am allowed to come.' He laughed wryly at this.

'I see,' said Lucy. 'And what do you think the verdict will be?'

'I have absolutely no idea. It's a strange position to be in. I can't bring myself to walk away completely, that's for sure, so if she'll have me I'll definitely go. Penny and the kids are my family. As I can see all too clearly every night that we've been apart, my life doesn't add up to much without them.'

'It's tough,' said Lucy. She felt a wave of affection for him, he was clearly a great father and had been a good husband. It seemed unfair that things weren't working out for them. 'Do you miss her?'

'I do and I don't,' he said. 'In some ways I miss her unbelievably, but if you mean do I miss the humdrum and monotony of our daily lives together... not so much. I think the problem is you get into such routines as a married couple, the same meals, the same drink, the same TV programmes, the same bloody annoying arguments time and time again. It all begins to grate on your nerves after a while.'

'I must say, the one advantage of being single again is having my flat to myself. The remote control especially,' laughed Lucy. 'That's one thing I don't miss! Sharing in general. And compromise, I don't miss compromise either.'

They were now on their second G and Ts and Lucy was beginning to relax into his company. He really was an awesome guy, and the fact that he was ridiculously handsome certainly helped her to enjoy being in his presence. It felt good to be able to talk so openly about Penny, and Alex too.

'So what actually happened with Alex in the end, if you don't mind my asking?'

Jack listened carefully as Lucy told him about the break-up. When she had finished, he announced, 'That is a really shit way to end things. It would have been better if he'd at least had sex with someone else so you could have a reason to hate him.' He ordered another round of drinks. 'To being independent!' he said as he chinked her glass.

'That's a good way of putting it!' laughed Lucy. 'To being nag-free,' she added, clinking his glass once more as she downed half of her drink. They were going down surprisingly easily.

The evening passed in a blur. The more drinks they had, the more flirtatious they both became. Jack hadn't taken long to get up to his old tricks and Lucy found herself both unable and unwilling to resist his charms. *Why the hell should I?* she thought. *Haven't I been through enough crap?* She decided it was her chance to have a bit of fun. She reassured herself that flirting wasn't going to hurt anyone. Anyway, he was still married. Just because he was taking a break from his relationship didn't mean he was available.

'So how is the dating scene? If I'm about to re-enter it I need you to prepare me.'

'Are you about to re-enter it?' Lucy asked.

'I've no idea at this particular moment in time. But say if I were to find myself back on the single scene all of a sudden. It's been bloody ages since I've been on a date… in fact, I'm not sure I've ever really dated anyone apart from Penny.'

She told him about some of Lettie's most hilarious encounters and ended up recounting her recent date with Tinder Ted. Jack was in stitches.

'What a moron. Didn't he realize who he was on a date with? He must be devoid of a personality. And blind.'

'You are too kind!'

'No seriously, you are gorgeous,' said Jack. 'I'm sure I've told you before, but you never believe me.'

'You are not too bad yourself,' admitted Lucy. They were now sitting so close that their knees were touching. Jack had taken off his tie and undone the top few buttons of his shirt, revealing a sexy smattering of grey hair on his chest. It felt good to be flirting with Jack, and even better to be flirted with.

Realizing they hadn't eaten yet they ordered a round of bar snacks and washed them down with a couple of cold beers. Then a couple more.

As they stumbled out onto the street, Lucy fumbled in her bag for her phone with the intention of booking herself an

Uber. Not paying attention to where she was going, she accidentally stumbled on an uneven paving stone and tripped. Jack caught her by the arm just in time as she lurched towards the road. He pulled her away from the curb. She fell against him heavily and found herself clutching his arms. Even through the fog of alcohol she could feel how strong he was. Looking up at him, she suddenly realized how desperately she wanted to kiss him. It felt so good to be in a man's arms once again. Like a rusty engine rumbling into life, she felt something ignite deep inside her. He was looking down at her and she could tell that something in the air between them had subtly shifted. Her heart pounded in anticipation. Was he going to kiss her? She moved closer to him and stood up slightly, her face now inches away from his. She could feel his breath against her skin. She could smell his aftershave. She pressed herself against him and willed him to kiss her. She knew she wouldn't make the first move. She was desperate to feel his touch against her skin, to eradicate the memory of Alex for good. Just as she thought that the moment was about to pass, he pulled her towards him. He had clearly been battling with himself but something had given way. He held the back of her head and he kissed her, softly at first but then urgently, as though he had been waiting to kiss her like that for a very long time. Unable to break themselves apart they kissed on and on.

Eventually, they hailed a cab and went back to her flat, undressing each other as soon as they got in the door. Their clothes lay in a tangled trail to her bedroom. Jack pushed her down on to the bed and forced any lingering thoughts of Alex firmly out of her mind, once and for all.

Afterwards, Lucy drifted in and out of sleep, waking up in the morning with a pounding head, an aching body and an empty space next to her. She felt a strange mixture of elation and guilt. She reached for her phone. Sure enough there was a message from Jack:

Last night was amazing. I'm sorry I didn't have better self-control, I couldn't resist you. Hope you are okay? J xx

Lucy could tell that he wanted to make sure she was all right. He probably felt as if he had taken advantage of her.

My self-control also to blame. And it was great, L xx

Jack replied:

I'm sure I don't need to say this but can we please keep this between ourselves? X

As she read this, Lucy felt slightly sick. She suspected he was regretting mixing business with pleasure. Not to mention the thought of Penny finding out if word got out that they had slept together. Given how up in the air things were between them that would be the last thing he needed. Her eyes filled with tears. She should have known better. It was impossible to have a night like that with someone like Jack and stay emotionally unattached. They had been colleagues for so long, and she had always been so attracted to him. She had thought it would make her feel better but she felt worse. Why was it that all the men she had feelings for didn't quite reciprocate in the way she wanted them to?

Mum's the word!

Replied Lucy, cringing at the false joviality of her text as she wrote it.

With a sigh she got up and made her way to the shower. She wanted to wash the night away. She felt very uncomfortable about Penny. She had vowed that she would never touch Jack, that he was completely out of bounds as long as he was married. She felt ashamed of herself that she had given into temptation, and for what… one night of fun? It had been amazing but that didn't make it all right. He wasn't single, that was a fact, and so what they had done was wrong. She vowed not to tell anyone about it, ever. Not even Claudia. She would never risk it getting out. It wouldn't be fair to Penny or Jack for this to become public knowledge. Most importantly, it wouldn't be fair to his children.

On the twenty-third of August, Lucy went for her initial consultation with The London Women's Clinic. She was impressed by the reception area. With two huge green plants on either side of a black and white, chequered marble floor and a sweeping, wrought-iron stair case ascending from behind the wooden desk, it looked more like the reception area of a smart hotel than a clinic; the only telltale signs were the artistic images on the wall, clever photographs of sperm, eggs and embryos rather than the usual landscapes. As she sat in the waiting room, she was enchanted to see a beautiful little dark-haired girl with the most gorgeous ringlets toddle over to her. She must have been no more than two years old. She was drawn like a magpie to the fake jewels on Lucy's gold sandals and kept trying to pick them up. Her mother came over to try and dissuade the child from bothering her, saying apologetically, 'I'm so sorry, she just loves sparkly things!'

'Don't worry at all, she's adorable!' said Lucy.

'She really is, isn't she?' said the woman, looking lovingly at her child. 'Although I know you're not supposed to say that about your own child! I'm Nicola and this is Maisy,' said the lady, brushing her long dark hair over her shoulder and picking up her daughter. Proffering a slender arm that jangled with bangles, she said, 'Nice to meet you.'

'I'm Lucy,' she said, shaking her hand and watching with amusement as Maisy clambered onto Nicola's lap, pulling at the stretchy fabric of her mother's navy maxi dress.

'Have you been to this clinic before?' asked Lucy. 'It's my first time, so I'm a little nervous!'

'Oh poor you, don't be nervous! Everyone here is so lovely, honestly. I remember feeling the same when I first came here, several years ago now!' Nicola confided. 'Is it your first consultation, then?'

Lucy nodded. Deciding to be brave, she took a deep breath and said, 'I'm thinking of having a baby but I don't have a partner. So I'm contemplating DI.' She knew that she would have to get used to talking about it without feeling ashamed.

Nicola nodded her head and pointed at Maisy. 'That's exactly what I did. Look at me now!' she said, kissing her daughter on the head, who had now decided to curl up and have a rest on her mother's lap. Lucy couldn't believe her eyes, she didn't know why but she hadn't suspected that Maisy could be a donor baby. Chiding herself for her own narrow-mindedness, she realized that she hadn't thought someone as gorgeous as Nicola would have been down this route. *But why on earth not*, she thought to herself, *if I am?*

'That's amazing!' cried Lucy. 'Oh wow, it's so inspiring to see you now, on the other end of the process. To think that I could be you in a couple of years!'

'I'm in for a possible round two now,' whispered Nicola. 'I want her to have a brother or sister. I'm going to try and use the same sperm so that they are genetically full siblings.' Lucy hadn't thought about that possibility yet, but she was impressed that it was feasible to have a real family, sharing the same genes, through DI.

Lucy and Nicola chatted about her experiences during her last round of treatment. It had taken her four attempts, or cycles, of IUI before she had become pregnant. Lucy felt as though she had found a real kindred spirit in Nicola, a high-flying accountant who said she had genuinely never had the time to meet anyone and settle down. She had been thirty-seven when she fell pregnant with DI, and at thirty-nine she knew that she was cutting it fine but had decided to try again. As Lucy was called in for her appointment, Nicola offered to swap phone numbers, saying that she would really love it if they could stay in touch, and that she would be happy to answer any questions Lucy had if she decided to go ahead with it. Lucy gratefully accepted and they saved each other's details in their mobile phones.

She left the waiting room and shook hands with her doctor, a beautiful Asian lady with a kind smile, following her up the staircase and along the corridor into her office.

Lucy was relieved to find the clinic a warm and friendly place where her doctor, a fertility specialist, was able to explain answers to the hundreds of questions that she had amassed over the last couple of months. She was reassured to find out that, in co-operation with the London Sperm Bank, this clinic had the largest donor insemination programme in the UK. She felt in safe hands.

The doctor explained the steps that would follow if she decided to go ahead with the treatment. She would have roughly an eighteen per cent chance of each cycle working. She worked out that she had enough money in her savings to have three rounds of treatment before she would have to start saving up all over again. She prayed that this would be enough.

Lucy waited with bated breath as the doctor did a pelvic ultrasound scan on her. She thought of all of her friends with children and wondered whether they had any idea just how lucky they were that they had got pregnant naturally, that they had met their partners at the right time to start a family. After an agonizing few minutes she was relieved to hear that everything seemed to be in perfect working order. Despite her relief she couldn't help but wish that all of this hadn't been necessary. It seemed like an enormously long road ahead and the chances seemed all too slim. She knew that all she needed to do now was make her final decision and get the ball rolling.

Chapter Twenty-Two

In September the work started rolling in as usual. The Christmas advertising campaigns would take over their lives from now until the end of the year and Lucy was working on several all at once. She felt like she was juggling too many balls in the air and that a momentary slip in concentration would cause them all to come crashing down. Despite the stress that this time of year brought with it she was quite happy to be so busy. Jack and Lucy had made a valiant effort to put their brief encounter behind them. It was never mentioned. For the most part they restricted their conversation to work-related topics, and no attempt was made by either party to arrange another drink. They both knew that the timing, and their circumstances, were wrong. Though she did occasionally blush when she caught him looking at her. God only knew what memories he was conjuring up!

When she wasn't working, often late into the night, she spent hours on the London Sperm Bank website looking at the potential donors. She was able to choose preferences for race, eye colour, hair colour, height, skin tone, nationality, education and occupation. She decided she wanted to choose someone as similar to her as possible. Her new friend Nicola was a wonderful help, they met up for coffee several times, discussing the ins and outs of the process. Lucy found it unbelievably helpful to talk to someone who had been through it already. Nicola was a very down-to-earth person; she took it all in her stride and was always ready with a well thought out answer to any of Lucy's questions or doubts. This helped Lucy come to terms with what lay ahead. Lucy began counting down the days until November when she was going to have her first round of IUI.

Towards the end of the month, Tor had booked Lucy in for a Saturday evening of babysitting. It was the night of her and Will's wedding anniversary and Lucy was excited at the prospect of spending some quality time with her godson. She knew that it would be good experience to have a tiny baby in her care, something that she hadn't had to do much of since the days when she helped Ginny look after Ollie. Right from the start Lucy had adored her baby brother, constantly helping to change his nappy and feed him, covering him in kisses and often picking him up and carrying him around like a doll… much to Ginny's horror! Quietly laughing at her younger self as she reminisced, she rang the doorbell of Will and Tor's smart town house and waited. A couple of minutes later Tor opened the door to let her in, giving her a warm hug and launching into a constant stream of instructions as she clattered around the hallway in her heels, fastening gold studs into her ears. To say she was overexcited at the prospect of having a night out with her husband was an understatement. However, this was also coupled with anxiety at the thought of being separated from Otto for the first time, resulting in Tor at her most chaotic. Trying to calm her friend down, Lucy nodded her agreement at each instruction, reassuring her that she would phone immediately if there was anything wrong.

Just then William came down the stairs, obviously straight out of the shower. He said hi to Lucy as he fastened the cufflinks on his shirt. Tor reached up to straighten his tie; they looked so smart, such a handsome couple, that Lucy stood back for a minute to admire them. Lucy was reminded of when her own parents would go out for the evening and the babysitter would arrive. She had flashbacks of her mum looking incredibly glamorous, smelling of perfume, a slash of bright pink lipstick across her lips as she kissed her good night.

Following Will and Tor into the sitting room, Lucy found Otto sleeping peacefully in his Moses basket. He looked positively angelic in a pale blue babygro, soft, downy hairs covering his head; a miniscule hand curled into a fist by the side of his face.

With one eye on the clock as their reservation time approached, Will and Tor reluctantly tore themselves away from their son and set off for dinner, leaving Lucy in charge. The television flickered in the background with some Saturday evening game show but Lucy was so mesmerized by little Otto that she barely took any notice, staring instead at his delicate little face and his minute features. Her tummy began to rumble so she heated up some of the lasagne that Tor had left out for her, eating it quietly while sitting on the sofa, reluctant to leave Otto by himself in case something awful should happen.

After about an hour and a half of peaceful sleeping, Otto woke up, making little gurgles and squeaks which slowly became moans before developing into a full-blown wail. Lucy followed the instructions to warm up his milk then picked him up. Nestling him in the crook of her arm, she began to feed him from the bottle. This seemed to do the trick and she relaxed as the rhythmic glugging echoed into the room. Having had his fill, she gently removed the bottle and carefully draped a muslin cloth across her shoulder, softly rubbing his back to wind him. As she settled back into the sofa with the tiny bundle in her arms, now sleeping contentedly once more, she prayed that she would be lucky enough to have her own baby soon. She was overcome with the all too familiar emotions of regret that she couldn't have experienced all this with Alex, that she was going to have to go through it all alone. It felt like such bitter bad luck. She wouldn't allow herself to miss out though. The thought of never being able to experience motherhood because she hadn't met her perfect guy at the right time was just too awful to consider. If and when he came along he would have to accept her for who she was, with or without a child. But she wasn't going to waste her last child-bearing years dreaming and hoping in vain for something that may never happen.

The following weekend Nicola had invited Lucy for lunch at her mews cottage in Notting Hill. Intrigued to get a glimpse into life as a single mother, and to have a peek inside Nicola's home, Lucy had eagerly accepted. She knocked on the door and shortly afterwards heard little footsteps padding towards her in response. She could see Maisy's curly hair through the frosted glass as Nicola appeared behind her, reaching to unlock the door and let Lucy in.

As Lucy had expected, Nicola's home was tastefully decorated and amazingly tidy considering the toddler entwining herself round her legs. Nicola kissed Lucy hello and then ushered her through into the kitchen; a huge vase of lilies rested on the granite breakfast bar while a wooden bowl piled high with fruit lay on the table. There were boxes of Maisy's colourful toys lined up along the wall but otherwise the home just looked like any other.

While they were eating their lunch, Lucy took the opportunity to ask Nicola how she had come to the decision to 'go it alone' to have her daughter, wondering if their stories would be similar.

'To be honest,' said Nicola, 'when I was younger I always thought that it would happen naturally, like everyone else, with the man of my dreams. But when I was thirty-six and I found myself single, I suddenly realized that perhaps that wasn't going to happen.'

'Exactly what I've been thinking,' agreed Lucy. 'It's different for guys, they can have children whenever they want. We've got a biological time bomb strapped to us and there's nothing we can do to slow it down!'

'Quite!' exclaimed Nicola. 'So I simply weighed up my options. I don't meet that many men that I actually consider eligible enough to date, I work quite long hours and I had broken up with my last boyfriend two years earlier and still hadn't met a replacement... so I knew that if I wanted a baby I would have to go about it in a rather different way!'

'How did you decide on donor insemination? Did you consider any other alternatives?' asked Lucy.

'I thought about adoption but I really wanted to experience being pregnant and I also wanted to be genetically related to my own child,' said Nicola.

Lucy nodded in agreement.

'The other alternative was co-parenting with a friend but I just couldn't think of anything more complicated than that, plus I'm quite an independent person and I'd rather make decisions affecting me and my family by myself than have to take a third party into consideration,' explained Nicola.

'Do you mind me asking you a personal question?' asked Lucy.

'Go ahead.'

'Have you ever regretted your decision? I mean, have there been times when it has been too hard, or you've felt too alone and wished you had waited to meet someone? I just want to know exactly what I am signing myself up for, so please be as honest as you can,' said Lucy.

'I'm not going to lie… there have been times when I have felt so lonely I just cry myself to sleep, even knowing Maisy is in her room next door. It is not the same as having another half, the love you receive and feel for your child is a completely different ball game. It would be amazing to have someone to support you through it, in particular during pregnancy and the first six months. But if you are asking me whether I would change my mind if I could go back in time, there is absolutely no way I would do it any differently. You are right to be realistic though, it is tough. You will tear your hair out at times.'

'I'm sure,' said Lucy.

'But it *is* worth it,' said Nicola. 'If you are really serious about having a family then you shouldn't let the negatives put you off.'

'Maisy really is a gorgeous little girl,' said Lucy. 'You're very lucky.'

'Fourth time lucky and we'll see how the next cycles work! I know my chances are getting pretty slim, but what will be will be! Won't it, Maisy?' she said, scooping her up and flying her through the air, prompting a fit of giggles from her daughter.

'I expect I'll be talking all about this next week with the counsellor,' said Lucy.

'Oh, have you got your implications counselling?' asked Nicola. 'It's actually really useful, I found. Talking things through makes you feel really sure about it all before you definitely decide to go ahead with it.'

'When have you decided to try again?' asked Lucy.

'I'm going to wait until the New Year,' explained Nicola, 'and then I'll just have to see what happens.'

After lunch they took Maisy down to the local playground and watched her as she played on the swings with some of the other local children. Lucy was grateful for Nicola's honesty; she knew she had some thinking to do that evening.

Lucy settled in for a quiet evening of soul-searching. Negative thoughts kept popping into her mind. Was it fair on the baby not to have a father? Was she being selfish? Would other people judge her, or worse, judge her unborn child as he or she was growing up in a single parent family? She ran through the conversations she had had with Nicola earlier that day, questioning herself over and over, allowing the doubts to well up and trying her best to rationalize and reason with herself. In the end her total and utter longing for a baby always won. It seemed to her that no matter what the downsides were, she could and would accept them for the sake of being a mother. She would do whatever it took.

As she set off to the clinic for her implications counselling session at the beginning of October, Lucy was crippled with nerves, despite Nicola having reassured her that the anxieties she was feeling and questions that she wanted to ask would be nothing unusual for the counsellor.

The lady she saw was incredibly calm and reassuring. She answered all of her questions and was honest about what Lucy might expect to feel and how she would be able to get the support she needed during the difficult times that would undoubtedly accompany the roller coaster of emotions to follow. Lucy found it extremely useful and left the session feeling much more positive. By this stage, there was absolutely no doubt in her mind that she would go ahead with the insemination.

'So?' asked Claudia, when they met up later that evening. 'Have you decided when D-day will be yet? Or should I say DI day?!' Claudia laughed at her own dreadful joke as she glugged red wine into a glass.

'It's going to be next month,' said Lucy decisively. 'All we have to do now is decide on the donor…'

'That's what I'm here for!' interrupted Claudia, peering at the website.

'…and then I have to call the clinic and schedule an appointment,' continued Lucy.

'It has to be when you ovulate, right?' asked Claudia.

'Yup.'

'How will you know?'

'It'll be between days ten and sixteen of my monthly cycle. I've been given ovulation tests that should tell me exactly when I am ovulating.'

'How are you feeling?' asked Claudia.

'Nervous and excited in equal measure!' explained Lucy. 'It's such a big step into the unknown!'

'It sure is! Right then, let's get to work!' said Claudia, rubbing her hands with glee. 'Here's to finding the ideal genetic father of your child!' she said, clinking her glass against Lucy's as they settled in front of the laptop.

They had spent hours choosing the ideal donor, poring over the website with Claudia opening another bottle of wine. As planned, she had chosen the donor that most closely matched her, hoping that the baby would look as similar to her as possible. It had to be said, Claudia had been an absolute godsend, always there for her to talk through any doubts or concerns with. She had also volunteered to accompany her to the clinic for her first round of treatment despite her personal hatred of hospitals. Lucy was glad that she would have some moral support to steady her nerves and reassured Claudia that it was nothing like a hospital.

As she finally went in for her appointment in November she prayed and prayed that it would work, that a miracle would happen and that in nine months' time she would be holding her very own baby. Claudia and Lucy arrived at the clinic and took their seats in the waiting room. As Lucy reached into her handbag to turn her phone off, she saw a reminder from her planner that had popped up onto her screen. It read **13th November: By today you will feel normal.**

'Oh my god, look Clauds!' She showed her the screen.

'I remember you telling me about this,' said Claudia in disbelief.

'How ironic that it should have been *this* day, six months previously, when I set that alert!' said Lucy. She checked herself to see how she felt, reaching deeply into the darkest recesses of her heart, searching for signs of that familiar despair and anguish over Alex. There was barely a trace left.

Chapter Twenty-Three

Lucy would have to wait until two weeks had passed before she could take a pregnancy test to find out whether the insemination had worked. Those two weeks were the longest of her life. She struggled to sleep because her mind was spinning with the enormity of the situation. She felt unbelievably excited at the prospect of what might be, whilst at the same time she couldn't bear the thought that it might not have worked. Knowing the odds, she tried hard to keep her expectations in perspective. Luckily that weekend she had the wonderful distraction of Otto's christening.

She arrived at the church dressed in a smart navy shift dress with discreet jewellery and a pair of kitten heels. In her arms she carried a huge box, carefully wrapped in paper that was printed with little sailing boats. She had bought Otto a bouncy seat that could be suspended from a door frame. As a child Lucy had loved to dance and swing from the beam above the kitchen door in her own bouncy chair, and she hoped her godson would love it too. The other godmother was Tor's best friend from university, Kate. They had met whilst studying Spanish and had spent a year abroad in Seville together during their third year. Lucy had gone out to visit them, taking a break from her History of Art dissertation, and had had a wonderful time eating tapas and experiencing the local nightlife. Her dalliance with a sexy Latino man had almost resulted in her missing her flight back home! Ever since then, Lucy had been firm friends with Kate, and they squealed with delight as they saw each other, both so thrilled to be Otto's godparents, promising to take him under their wing and spoil him rotten. The two godfathers were old friends of Will's, and together the four of them solemnly promised to look after Otto and care for his spiritual development at the requisite points during the service.

Otto behaved like a little saint, not even making a squeak when the vicar doused his head with water from the baptismal font. He had an antique lace christening gown that had been passed down through the family for generations. It was a strange thought trying to imagine Will wearing the same tiny outfit thirty-six years ago!

They posed for photographs outside the church before heading over to Will and Tor's house for tea and christening cake.

Tor discreetly caught Lucy in the kitchen. 'So, how was the first cycle?' she asked in muted tones so that no one could overhear. 'How are you feeling?'

'It was okay I suppose. It's so hard to tell if it has worked… I can't stop thinking about it. I just want to know now!' said Lucy.

'I know, I remember… it's like torture,' empathized Tor.

'Would I have felt anything change in my body yet if I was pregnant? What are the telltale clues?' asked Lucy.

'At this stage it's very unlikely that you would notice anything,' said Tor. 'I know it's really hard but you've got to try and lower your expectations a bit. It is so unlikely to have worked the first time… I don't want to be pessimistic but I remember how crushing dashed hopes can be.'

'You're right,' said Lucy. 'It's just so hard when you want it to work so desperately.'

'Just remember, if this one hasn't worked you need to focus on looking forward, plan the next cycle, never give up hope,' said Tor, giving her friend a reassuring hug.

Lucy remembered this advice as she waited for the result to reveal itself. It was two weeks since her first insemination and she was sitting on the loo, her hands trembling as she clutched onto the little stick that she had just peed on. There was no one else in her flat but her. She had promised to call her friends if there was good news, but she wanted to find out whether it had worked or not by herself. In the days that had passed since her appointment she had scrutinized every twinge that her body had made, trying to detect a change. At night she found herself dreaming of babies, she would even dream about being pregnant, then wake up expecting to feel a bump, reaching down to her tummy only to realize that it had just been a figment of her imagination. It was a strange experience, this waiting process, but it was now time to find out if the insemination had worked. She could have waited one more day to see if her period arrived but she just couldn't bear not knowing for a second longer.

Having waited the requisite three minutes, she looked down at the stick, her trembling hand covering the important part to the left which would reveal her fate. The little diamond window which showed her when the results were ready to read had a thick blue line running through the centre. It was the moment of truth. She slowly uncurled her hand from the small circle that hid the results. A horizontal line across the middle meant not pregnant, while the shape of a cross would mean that she was pregnant. As her eyes focussed on the results, disappointment flooded her body like a tidal wave. A single blue line was all she could see. She was not pregnant. It hadn't worked. Tears sprung into her eyes and she was hit like a sledgehammer by the realization that her dreams had not come true. Lucy had never before been so aware of just how desperately she wanted this baby. She felt crushed with disappointment. It was only when she saw the evidence that it had failed that she really knew how much she wanted it to have worked. She repeated the test three times, each time knowing that she would see the same thin, blue line; the bitter disappointment was so strong she could almost taste it.

She texted Tor, Claudia and Nicola, and rang her mother, who did well to mask her relief. Each woman gave her the same reassuring message; these things take time, that's all. It doesn't mean anything. No one really gets pregnant on their first attempt, after all. Lucy knew that the statistics were not in her favour and that it was extremely unlikely that it should have worked straight away. She knew that she would go ahead and book in for her second cycle the following month, and tried hard to keep thinking positive thoughts as she counted down the days until her next appointment.

As the second treatment day dawned in December, Lucy's nerves jangled as she made her way to the clinic. This time she had decided to go alone, feeling less nervous now that she knew how the procedure worked. She took her seat in the now familiar waiting room, struck as always by how many other women were seeking fertility treatment of some kind. Some were alone, like her, and others were with their husbands or partners. As she waited, a rather red-faced man came rushing back to the reception desk, blushing furiously.

'How can I help you, sir?' asked the receptionist politely.

'Oh, err, gosh… this is rather embarrassing…' stammered the man.

The receptionist waited patiently for him to continue. 'I've just come out of one of your… err… treatment rooms and well, I err… I appear to have left something in there…' he tailed off awkwardly.

'Okay,' said the receptionist. 'Not to worry. If you could just tell me what it is, exactly, that you left behind I will go and have a look for you.'

Lowering his voice to barely more than a whisper, he muttered, 'It's my wedding ring.' By this point the man had gone puce. Lucy surmised that the room was clearly where the sperm samples were collected!

Her eavesdropping was interrupted by the sound of a nurse calling her name and she duly followed her to the treatment room. As she had done the previous time, she climbed onto the couch and the nurse asked her to put her legs into the stirrups. It was a bit like having a smear test, the nurse inserted the speculum and Lucy closed her eyes and prayed as she went through the motions of carrying out the insemination, willing her body to do whatever it took to get pregnant; repeating positive mantras over and over in her mind. She envied all the women who were able to conceive naturally, in the privacy of their own homes, without being prodded and poked in the process.

Having waited a short amount of time following the treatment she set off for home. Her mind was reeling with the momentous events of the day, with each cycle of treatment she felt as if the stakes were increasing, not least due to the expense of each round, yet at the same time she tried to take the pressure off herself, knowing there was nothing she could actually do but wait. It was in the hands of fate. As a reward for her efforts, she decided to treat herself to a chai latte from the coffee shop in Holland Park on the way home. She felt the need to be in familiar surroundings, unready to go home quite yet, and she wanted to walk around the gardens, giving herself space and time to think.

The bus trundled slowly along Bayswater Road as she made her way from Harley Street to Holland Park and Lucy sat on the top deck, looking out of the window as they passed Hyde Park and Notting Hill Gate. She saw the Irish guy from the coffee shop walking along the pavement with his dog, the one who had spilled coffee all over the table. *What was his name again?* she thought to herself. *Rory, that was it.* Seeing him brought back memories of the day she had found Alex's ring. She blinked as the old tide of emotion flooded through her, the aching sense of loss that still surprised her with its force from time to time. She acknowledged the memories and let them go, smiling to herself as she reminded herself to stay in the moment.

She got off the bus and strolled from Holland Park tube through the top part of the gardens towards the cafe, occasionally moving her hand to her belly, as if willing a miracle to occur deep within her. The crisp air nipped at her cheeks as she retreated deeper into her coat. A bright pink cashmere scarf was wrapped around her neck and the matching gloves that Claudia had given her the previous Christmas kept her fingers from turning numb. The thought of Christmas made her think of heading home to Cornwall in a few weeks' time. She was looking forward to it and most especially to seeing her brother, who was once again returning home for his annual visit to colder climes. This time he was coming over from Argentina, having relocated across the globe to follow his beautiful, new South American girlfriend, Sofia. Unfortunately, she wouldn't be coming with him, as she wanted to spend Christmas with her family in Buenos Aires. But still, Lucy was longing to see photographs of the happy couple and to see for herself how smitten Ollie appeared to be. At long last, a woman had managed to capture his interest for longer than a few months. She must be something special!

As Lucy walked through the gardens, she was struck by how barren the trees looked, they seemed naked without their coating of leaves. The four seasons had always been one of Lucy's favourite things about living in England, though as she was getting older the frequency and speed at which they seemed to come and go alarmed her more and more. She had always looked forward to the oncoming change. By the time the summer was over she longed for the warmth of her winter clothes, wrapping up tightly against the cold, the dark evenings spent next to burning log fires, sipping red wine and staying inside as the wind roared and the rain banged against the window panes. By the time winter had got into full swing she began to long for the awakening of spring, the days getting longer, and the air beginning to warm. Then came the summer, with melting ice creams and long limbs lounging on the grass, basking in the sunshine; before autumn came and the perfect cycle began once again. She had always felt there was something immensely reassuring about the passing of the seasons and had felt sorry for those who would never know what it felt like to live under the influence of this ceaseless tide. She hoped that during the next few seasons her own body would go through a changing cycle of its own, that this time next year she would have her own baby, her own new life to celebrate.

Chapter Twenty-Four

When the day came to head home for Christmas, Lucy collected Granny Annie on her way to the train station. She didn't trust her ninety-one-year-old grandma to get herself to the right place at the right time without any help. Annie couldn't figure out how to work the mobile phone they had given her last year for Christmas so was unable to communicate with anyone from the minute she left the house. It therefore made sense for her to stay put and for Lucy to collect her en route.

Having fetched Annie and her suitcase and bundled her into a cab along with her own luggage, they set off for Paddington and the great expanse of countryside that they would soon be speeding across before reaching Bodmin and the little village of Trebetheric, their final destination.

Lucy was grateful for their pre-booked seats on the busy train. It was full of people making their way home for the festive season. Sipping cups of tea from the trolley while sharing a KitKat, Annie and Lucy chatted about life, love and family, catching up on each other's news and reminiscing about years gone by.

The countryside zoomed past the windows; the winter had muted the riotous colour palette that Lucy had seen on her way down to the southwest that summer. Remembering how heartbroken she had been seven months earlier, she felt immensely proud of herself for the long way she had come since. She felt stronger and tougher, as though she had built a little protective wall around her heart. Her grandmother was a source of massive inspiration for Lucy. She had an incredible youthful energy and such a sharp sense of humour, that, despite the occasional muddle where she would forget names or faces, she could keep up with the rest of them without any problem. Lucy hoped that she would be just like her grandmother if she was ever lucky enough to reach that age.

Taking a deep breath, Lucy decided to take the opportunity to talk to her about her decision to go it alone. It occurred to her that now would be the ideal time. There was nothing her grandmother hated more than making a scene in public so she would have to behave herself and control her reaction appropriately, no matter how shocked she might be. The concept would be a hard one for anyone of Annie's generation to get their head around.

Lucy turned to face her grandmother in the seat next to her. 'Granny,' said Lucy, 'I have something I want to tell you.'

'Yes darling,' said Annie, putting her novel down to give her granddaughter her full attention. 'Go on.'

'Well, the thing is… I'm not sure you are going to really understand.'

'What are you talking about, darling? Of course I will understand!' said Annie, amused.

'It's something that would have been unheard of in your day, you see…' said Lucy.

'There are plenty of things that were unheard of in my day, Lucy. I can tell you!'

'Okay, so have you ever heard of a woman having a baby by herself?' asked Lucy.

'Of course I have!' said Annie. 'I am a woman of the world, I know these things happen.'

Lucy relaxed slightly.

'I mean, I'd think you were a fool if it happened to you, but I know these things do happen,' added Annie, inspecting her granddaughter a little more suspiciously. 'Don't tell me, you have been sleeping around?' she asked, suddenly horrified at the prospect.

'No, Granny, of course not!' laughed Lucy, amused at the conclusion her grandmother had jumped to.

'Are you pregnant?' demanded Annie.

'No,' said Lucy, crossing her fingers under the table. She would be finding out whether the cycle had worked while she was in Cornwall.

'So what are you talking about?' asked Annie.

'Well, I have made a tricky decision that I want to share with you. It would mean a lot to me if I had your support,' explained Lucy.

'Right...' said Annie dubiously.

Lucy took a deep breath, 'I have decided to try and have a baby by myself. Not by sleeping with random strangers. Not by sleeping with anyone at all, in fact.'

'Are you going to adopt?' asked Annie, her eyebrows hovering somewhere near her hairline.

'No, not adoption. There is a different way. It is called donor insemination and they do it at a private fertility clinic.'

'Hang on a minute, why would you consider having a baby when you haven't got a boyfriend? Let alone a husband?' asked Annie, as Lucy had suspected that she would.

'Because I am getting too old to wait any longer to meet the man of my dreams. I don't want to waste my last fertile years hoping I will meet someone,' explained Lucy.

'But a child needs two parents,' said Annie, unable to keep the certainty out of her voice.

'Well, yes, I suppose in an ideal world you would want all children to have a mum and a dad. But I know plenty of lovely, happy people who have been brought up by one parent. Say if the father died and the mother didn't remarry, the child would only have one parent, and no one would complain about that,' said Lucy.

'Well yes but that is entirely different darling,' replied Annie. 'You would actively be choosing to bring a child into your life without a father. It wouldn't be right.'

Lucy winced. She wasn't surprised at her beloved granny's reaction but it didn't make it any easier. 'But I will have my family. I will have you and mum and dad, and Ollie. And my friends. We will be enough to look after the baby. And I would love it *so* much. Being a mother is the one thing I want more than anything and I just can't accept that it won't happen. Please try to understand…' Lucy felt her eyes welling up with tears.

'I'm sorry, Lucy, but I really don't agree with it. Perhaps I am too set in my ways, but it just seems selfish to bring a baby into the world just because you want one. If you are meant to have a child then God will give you one. You will meet a man and have a baby the way nature intended. And I am sure that it will happen, you aren't past it yet, darling!'

'I'm not so sure about that,' said Lucy.

Annie raised her eyebrows and chuckled to herself at the utter absurdity of the suggestion. She shook her head and reached for her book.

Lucy blinked away a few tears and picked up her magazine. She understood that the conversation was closed. It would be too much to tell Annie that she had already had not one but two rounds of treatment. She had to hope that if she fell pregnant, Annie would come round to the idea and accept it.

But for now, she would have to leave it at that. Talking about it further would just upset Annie, and that was the last thing Lucy wanted.

After eating some sandwiches from the buffet car, Annie drifted off for an afternoon nap, not another word on the topic was mentioned. Lucy followed suit. She thought there was something incredibly soothing about the rhythmic chugging of the train. Ever since she was little, Lucy had loved dozing in the back of a car, on trains or airplanes, during any long journey, finding the thrum of the engine naturally soporific.

Having slumbered on and off for the rest of the journey, they found themselves arriving at Bodmin Parkway in no time. As always, the reliable Ginny was there waiting for them in her Land Rover. Scatty though she may be, she had never once missed a train's arrival or departure.

They made their way home through the winding lanes in record time. As they parked outside the cottage, Tiggy raced up to the car, barking and wagging her tail in an ecstatic greeting, sniffing their luggage to see if they concealed any doggy treats for her delectation. They opened the door just as Ollie was padding down the stairs into the hall, rubbing his eyes sleepily, his hair perfecting the just-out-of-bed look much sought after by surfers and teenagers alike.

'Granny Annie!' he cried as he came over to the door. 'Don't you look gorgeous! You haven't aged a bit since the last time I saw you!'

'Oh, Ollie, you charming young man. Come here and give your ancient granny a kiss!' she chuckled, pointing to her wrinkled cheek and puckering her bright red lips.

Having kissed his grandma, Ollie turned his attention to Lucy. 'Sis!' he teased, giving her a massive bear hug, 'You don't look too bad either!'

'Thanks Ols,' she said, shoving him in the ribs. 'Have you ever heard of the saying "People in glass houses shouldn't throw stones"?!'

'Oy! This is a carefully styled casual chic look, I'll have you know,' he said playfully, pouting and striking a pose.

'I think you look very handsome,' said Granny Annie, taking him by the arm and leading him into the kitchen.

Just at that moment Gus came in from the garden, wiping his feet on the doormat. He was blue from the cold, having been fixing the fence all morning; Tiggy had managed to find a new escape route.

'Lucy darling, Annie… you've arrived in one piece!' he said, kissing them both.

Lucy looked at her bespectacled, kind old father, covered in mud stains and shivering, and felt a rush of fondness. She went straight over to the Aga to put the kettle on, offering to make him a cup of tea to warm him up.

Ginny helped her fetch the teapot and cups, unveiling her speciality: a freshly baked chocolate cake covered in thick butter icing which she placed in the centre of the pine table, prompting a flurry of applause from Ollie, Annie, Lucy and Gus. They ate the cake, as light and fluffy as air, the icing gooey and sticky on their fingers, and sipped cups of steaming tea. It felt so good to be home again.

Lucy grilled Ollie about Sofia, and wanted to hear all about the job he had found himself in Buenos Aires, working in a wine bar. She thought about planning a trip to go and see him there, after all it was about time she went to visit him again. She had had a wonderful time in Thailand the last time they had met up on their travels. Though it might depend on whether her second cycle of treatment had worked, of course. She only had another few days left to wait until she would find out. She felt nervous butterflies flutter in her gut at the thought and sent up another silent prayer.

After tea, Ollie and Lucy pulled on their winter wetsuits and walked down to the beach with their trusty old bodyboards under their arms.

'So, sis, how's the baby plan working out for you?' asked Ollie.

'It's still in motion,' said Lucy. 'Though my plans are currently shelved until the new year.' She didn't want him to know that she would be doing a test any day now. It was easier to keep it to herself.

'Sensible,' said Ollie. 'Who wants a booze-free Christmas?'

'My sentiments exactly!' laughed Lucy. 'I told Granny on the train.'

'Woah… how did that go down?' asked Ollie, looking at his sister with raised eyebrows.

'Let's just say the conversation is closed. I think it's probably best if we don't talk about it again.'

'She didn't agree with your decision?'

'No. She can't get past the idea that a baby needs a father.'

'I kind of thought that's how she'd react.'

'You can't really blame her, I suppose,' said Lucy.

'No… it's a different world for her these days. Too much change,' mused Ollie.

'I wish I had her support though, I'm sure as hell going to need it.'

'You will. If it happens, she'll come around. She loves you, Luce, we all do. We'll be there for you. You'll see.'

'Thanks Ol. It's good to have you home,' said Lucy, throwing her wetsuited arm around her brother's shoulders as he ruffled her hair.

The clouds parted slightly as they reached the sand. The distant sea looked like pale sheets of beaten silver, shimmering in the beams of light that sliced down through the sky. Seagulls darted around, skimming through the spray as it rose off the white horses that pranced and galloped in the surf. Lucy and Ollie waded in through the foam, shrieking as the ice-cold water turned their feet instantly numb. They were taken straight back to their childhood as they lay on their polystyrene boards, pushing off just as the waves broke behind them and hurtling through the sea, revelling in the full force of nature. Laughing uncontrollably, they zoomed through the surf, full of adrenalin. Their hair was plastered to their faces; salty spray blew into their eyes.

After about forty minutes, teeth chattering and blue from the cold, they dragged their boards back up to the house, arriving at the kitchen door dripping watery puddles everywhere, looking like two drowned rats. It was the ideal start to her Christmas.

Over the next few days Annie and Lucy helped Ginny to prepare the house for Christmas with trips to the local Morrisons, last-minute shopping and putting up lots of decorations around the house. They hung the baubles and fairy lights on the huge Christmas tree that Ollie and Gus had carried in and propped up, somewhat precariously, in a bucket of sand. This year it was their turn to host the annual Christmas Eve party that had been going on for years with a group of local families. Lucy took charge of the menu and the necessary shopping for the canapés. She would make them on Thursday with the rest of the family all taking up posts around the kitchen table with carefully allocated jobs to carry out: chopping, slicing, stuffing and artfully arranging.

Lucy bought a couple of packets of pregnancy tests with her shopping, deciding that she would do her test the next morning, on Christmas Eve, two weeks after her second round of insemination. She had fobbed her parents off in the same way she had done to Ollie by saying that she wasn't going to have her second round until the New Year. She didn't want them to know if the news was not good, believing that any fussing over her would make her feel worse, not to mention put a dampener on Christmas. This time, she was keeping it to herself. Besides, if she did turn out to be pregnant, it would be a wonderful surprise for them all, the perfect Christmas present.

The next morning, creeping out of bed and into her en-suite bathroom, she unwrapped the little Clear Blue box with trembling hands. Her plan this time was to do the test as quickly as possible, not thinking about the consequences, a bit like ripping off a plaster. Without hesitation, she peed on the stick and looked at the clock to check the time, brushing her teeth and washing her face as a distraction. As soon as three minutes passed, she picked up the stick, her heart thudding in her ears. She peered down at the little diamond box, the controller was showing her that the results were in... With baited breath she moved her hand to reveal the little circular window that would tell her her fate. A single line ran through the centre. She was not pregnant. It had failed again. Disappointment coursed through her veins once more. She fell heavily to the floor and gave herself a few minutes to absorb the news. The realization that her hopes were, once again, dashed into smithereens felt like a crushing weight on top of her. The desire to become pregnant had become an obsession. It filled most of her waking minutes. She had never known that you could want something so desperately... something that in moments like this felt so impossible, so completely unachievable. She lay on the cool tiles, focussing on her breathing, in and out, in and out, her eyes smarting with tears, her body heavy with the dead weight of disappointment. She knew that her only option was to keep looking forwards; she would have to move on but it was so hard to put herself through this emotional roller coaster every time.

She knew that there was one person who would understand how she felt more than anyone.

'Hello?' said Nicola as she answered the phone. 'Lucy, are you okay?'

'Hi Nicola, yes I'm fine thanks. Sorry for the early phone call.'

'Don't worry, I've been up for hours thanks to Maisy!'

'I just did the test,' explained Lucy. 'I'm not pregnant.'

'Oh Lucy, I'm so sorry,' said Nicola. 'How are you feeling?'

'Not great,' said Lucy, her voice wobbling.

'It's so hard,' Nicola sympathized. 'You just have to try and stay strong.'

'I know…'

'I remember feeling so depressed every time it didn't work, but you just have to pick yourself up and carry on. Remember it took me four times to fall pregnant with Maisy, but it did happen in the end.'

'I just feel like I've failed,' said Lucy.

'You haven't failed. It's just probability and chance, and nothing anyone can do can change that.'

'You're right,' said Lucy. She told herself that all was not lost; she had known that it would take time. She could and would cope with the disappointment. All she could do was begin to prepare herself for the build-up to round three, there was no way she was giving up now.

Lucy decided to go for a run, the best possible tonic for depressing news. Before setting off she messaged Claudia and Tor, letting them know the news and reassuring them that she was okay, that she was trying to stay positive. They replied with messages of encouragement, telling her to stay strong, and promising to call her later. Her friends really were an invaluable support network, and once again she counted her blessings, so thankful for everything that she did have in her life. As she ran, the pale mist of early morning hovered above the sea. A flight of birds migrating home flew over her head in a perfect V and Lucy marvelled at their uniform formation. Nature really was a miraculous force, so mysterious and yet somehow managing to work symbiotically, everything in delicate balance, in perfect harmony. She pounded the pathways, Kate Bush singing 'Wuthering Heights' in her ears, and let the beauty of the views uplift her spirits and revitalize her. Returning home, she felt renewed with energy and ready for anything.

As she looked through the windows into the cosy warmth of the kitchen, she saw Ollie standing at the sink, downing a pint of orange squash, still wearing his pyjamas. Annie would be eating her breakfast in bed by now, brought to her on a tray by Ginny each morning, and would eventually make her way downstairs by about eleven o'clock. Ginny and Gus were sitting at the breakfast table eating toast and marmalade, reading the morning papers while the television flickered in the background.

'Hi darling,' Ginny said as she opened the door. 'Good run?'

'Lovely thanks, it's cold out but there's a beautiful mist over the sea that's really stunning,' Lucy said.

'Oh great, I'll take Tiggy down there after breakfast!' said Ginny.

Gus asked, 'Do you want a cup of coffee? I'm going to make another one.'

Lucy shook her head saying that she would shower first and then come and eat something. She climbed the creaking stairs to the attic, stripping off her clothes and throwing them into the laundry basket before stepping under the power shower in her bathroom, letting the hot water stream over her and wash away her disappointment, preparing herself for the day ahead.

Later on that day she instructed her family members on their roles for the canapé manufacturing chain she had set up around the kitchen table. They spent a happy couple of hours at work, chatting as they went. By the time they had finished, the pine table was covered in plates and dishes of various shapes and sizes. Each one had an appetizing selection of canapés arranged across its surface: smoked salmon on brown bread covered with curls of lemon zest and black pepper, cherry tomatoes stuffed with blue cheese, prawns on mini pastry puffs, cheese twists, blinis with cream cheese and caviar, and honey and mustard sausages. She surveyed the spread with satisfaction as Gus stocked the fridge with champagne and Ollie lit the fires to warm the house up.

As their guests arrived, the house was warm and cosy, the decorations radiated festive cheer and Christmas carols filled the air. The festive spirit cheered Lucy up enormously. She loved catching up with old family friends at this time of year, it was a lovely tradition that she hoped would last long into the future, with the new generations that were hopefully to come. Granny Annie charmed the socks off everyone in her sweet little dress and matching turquoise jewellery, she was always everybody's favourite guest and she loved regaling the young with stories of her misspent youth. Gus and Ollie made sure that no one's glass was ever empty and Lucy and Ginny handed around the plates of canapés, which everyone said were the best they had had in years.

After everyone had left, the five of them sat down for dinner, their annual Christmas Eve feast of baked ham, Cumberland sauce, cauliflower cheese and jacket potatoes. They played a game of charades; Gus had everyone in stitches as he tried to act out *Pretty Woman*. Afterwards the four of them flopped on the sofa to watch a bit of Michael McIntyre's Christmas special. Granny Annie had already gone to bed, exhausted after such a busy day. Lucy and Ollie stayed up till midnight in honour of the tradition they had started as children, much to Ginny and Gus's annoyance as they had waited for them to finally go to sleep so that Santa Clause could come undetected.

The rest of Christmas passed in a blur of food, champagne, carols, church and frosty walks, before Lucy set off once more for London. She had been touched to receive an envelope from her parents which contained a cheque to put towards her treatment. She realized that this was a sign of them giving her their blessing and was very grateful; every penny counted as the process certainly wasn't cheap. She only had enough money for one more round so this would enable her to continue with a fourth cycle if she needed it. Finding a moment alone with her parents, she had thanked them for their present.

'I hope you know how much it means to me that you are supporting my decision,' said Lucy.

'We know, darling,' said Gus.

'If you're really sure it's what you want…' added Ginny, still not entirely convinced by the whole thing.

'It is. Has Granny told you that I've spoken to her about it?' asked Lucy.

'No!' exclaimed Ginny. 'I had no idea… good heavens!'

'What did she say?' asked Gus.

'I told her on the train. I didn't know whether she would talk to you about it, she's so old-fashioned about these things. I think she has chosen to simply forget I ever mentioned it.'

'So she was against the idea?'

'I'm afraid so.'

'Oh darling, I'm sorry, but I'm not surprised. I must be honest… I still find the idea hard to get my head around, and she is my mother!' said Ginny. 'These things just wouldn't have been acceptable in her day.'

'I know, I know…'said Lucy. 'It's just that her opinion means the world to me, so it's hard for me to know I'm going against her wishes.'

'Darling, it's your life,' said Gus. 'You have to do what feels right for you.'

'You're right, Dad,' said Lucy, giving her parents a big hug and thanking them once again for their support and generosity.

Annie was staying in Cornwall for a few more days to spend New Year's Eve with Gus and Ginny after Lucy left, while Ollie was going to a friend's house party in Gloucestershire. Lucy spent New Year's Eve as planned with Tor, Will and Otto. They had a very pleasant and relaxing evening, and as she had promised herself, she woke up on January the first feeling as fresh as a daisy, full of excitement about the New Year ahead. She began to count down the days from day one of her cycle, ready to telephone the clinic to let them know when she needed to be booked in for round three of her treatment.

In mid-January she went back to the clinic, now a familiar journey for her, and sat once again in the clean, white waiting room, flicking through a magazine and waiting for her name to be called. The fertility specialist came to collect her and led her up the spiral staircase to one of the treatment rooms. She lay on the bed, her legs in the stirrups, and tried to relax, unclenching her muscles and visualizing the fertilization process, willing it to succeed.

Lucy sat in the chair for ten minutes after the insemination was over and done with, praying for the miracle that she so desperately wanted. She then got dressed, flung her handbag over her shoulder, and set off to catch the bus towards home.

She decided to keep to her tradition and stop off at Holland Park for a chai latte and a wonder around the gardens on her way home. She pulled down the sleeves of her green cashmere jumper underneath her trusty duffle coat, a pair of black skinny jeans tucked into leather boots. The air was bright but icy and she wriggled her toes to stop them feeling numb, they already felt blue with cold despite the angora socks that she was wearing. She was feeling the beginnings of a winter cold and knew that catching a chill wouldn't help her chances of conceiving.

As she arrived at the café, she pulled open the door, enjoying the warm air from inside as it made contact with her chilly cheeks. She approached the counter, taking her place in the queue and eyeing up the pastries and cakes behind the glass, wondering whether she should treat herself. Suddenly she felt herself sneeze, she reached into her pocket to try and find a tissue.

The man in front of her in the queue turned his head slightly to say 'Bless you.' As he did so, a flicker of recognition passed over his face, and he said, 'Oh hello! It's Lucy... isn't it?'

Lucy remembered their last meeting as clear as day and was mesmerized for a second by his piercing blue eyes. Realizing she hadn't answered him but had instead been staring at him rather obviously, she quickly stammered, 'Rory... Hi! How are you? And where's your lovely dog?' she asked.

'Well, I'm not sure that he deserves to be called lovely, but he's tied up outside. I won't be letting him inside here again in a hurry, don't you worry!' said Rory with a smile. 'I still feel terrible about him spilling your drink that time. Please, allow me to buy you a coffee today, I'd like to make up for it.'

'You really don't have to do that!' Lucy said, touched by his thoughtfulness.

'I insist!' said Rory. 'What'll it be?'

'A chai latte please. It's very kind of you!'

'A chai latte?! What on earth's that when it's at home?' he asked.

'It's a sort of spiced milk, it's delicious! You should try it!' Lucy laughed.

'Nah, I'll be sticking to my coffee till the day I die,' said Rory, 'I'm a creature of habit, I'm afraid!'

Rory ordered their drinks, looking to Lucy to confirm her choice, and then paid for them. He bought her a little bag of wafers tied with a ribbon in a clear plastic bag as an extra treat. Lucy popped the biscuits into her coat pocket, thanking him for his generosity. They made polite conversation as they collected their drinks in takeaway cups.

As they made their way out of the café, Rory held the door open for Lucy. She stepped out into the cold, noticing Rufus waiting patiently. He was tied up to a metal hook on the wall, and Lucy went over to him to stroke his long, brown nose, running her fingers down the soft hair on his neck.

'Hello Rufus!' she said. He wagged his tail and tried to lick her fingers as she stroked him, nuzzling her with his nose, his almond eyes twinkling mischievously. Carefully holding her drink aloft, she stood up, saying, 'He's such a gorgeous dog!'

Clearly disappointed not to have her attention anymore, Rufus emitted a high-pitched whine, looking pleadingly at his owner.

'All right, all right! We're going for a walk now, Rufus, don't you worry, old boy!'

Rufus began to wag his tail frantically at the mention of the word walk. Rory bent down to let him off his lead and he immediately darted off towards the orangery, relishing his new-found freedom.

'Lucky Rufus! I love walking around Holland Park,' said Lucy. 'I come here most weekends and I never seem to get bored of the gardens. I love watching them change as the seasons come and go.'

'Well, you're welcome to join us,' said Rory. 'I'm a big fan too; the gardens are so well designed. I particularly love the Kyoto garden, it's so calm, though I certainly don't take Rufus in there, he would ruin everyone's peace and quiet!' he laughed.

Lucy and Rory fell into stride with each other, wandering away from the orangery and along the winding path that cut through the Dutch gardens. Lucy sipped the delicious chai as she walked, she could feel it warm her from the inside out.

'The gardens are beautiful,' agreed Lucy, 'but I think I almost prefer the wild parts of the park.' They walked past a water feature trickling peacefully into its pool. 'It's amazing to think that a couple of hundred years ago all of this land was rural. It's hard to imagine now but in the woodlands you can almost catch a glimpse of how it would have looked in the past!'

'I once entered a competition calling on architects to submit plans for a giant tree house for children to play in. It was going to be constructed in the wild woodland here,' said Rory gesturing to his left. 'I don't know what happened to the idea in the end; I think it must have been pulled by the council.'

'Oh, what a shame! That would have been amazing! Are you an architect?' asked Lucy.

'I am indeed. I wanted to follow in the footsteps of my mad great-uncle, Seamus. He built the most incredible tree house for me and my brothers and sister to play in. It was deep within the woods that surround our house in Ireland,' explained Rory. 'Though had I realized architecture would take seven years of training I might have reconsidered my childhood ambition!'

'Seven years, wow! I thought a three-year degree course was long enough!' agreed Lucy sympathetically.

They paused along with another group of onlookers to watch a peacock as it shimmied its magnificent, iridescent feathers. The vibrations made a strange, low thrumming; a mating call. Rory summoned Rufus to his side so as not to pester the bird and he sat obediently at their feet, looking quizzically at the peacock's bizarre ritual.

'Tell me about the tree house,' said Lucy, as they walked away from the crowds amassing around the exotic creature. 'I always longed to have one as a child. It seemed like the coolest thing!'

'Ah, the tree house… now it truly was a work of art, a labour of love some might say. The minute Uncle Seamus finished it, me and my brothers and sister spent every waking minute of our childhood there. My mother must have loved him for the peace and quiet she got!' he said, smiling at the memories.

'I'll bet!' Lucy agreed.

'It was like a castle for us, the sort of thing you might see in a Disney film. He built it across several trees, with platforms, ropes, rooms and real, working lights. But the best thing by far was this high-sided tray that was on a sort of pulley system, it could be raised and lowered from the ground underneath up into the tree house itself. Mum would bring us jugs of fresh lemonade and biscuits and put them on the tray, and we would haul them up for our tea.'

'Oh my goodness that sounds like every child's dream! Is it still there?' asked Lucy, intrigued.

'Yes! Overrun by my nephews and nieces mostly nowadays!' laughed Rory.

'And Uncle Seamus?'

'Oh, he's still around too, at the grand old age of ninety-two; he's still more with it than most! He's quite a character,' said Rory. 'He certainly enjoys a drink or two, and he still fishes and plays golf every week. You're most likely to find him down the local pub, singing some old Irish tunes to entertain the tourists!' he chuckled. 'He loves to be the centre of attention.'

'I've got a grandmother who sounds just like him,' laughed Lucy. 'Granny Annie, rarely to be seen without a glass of wine or a G&T! They would be a match made in heaven!'

'We should introduce them,' agreed Rory, before dashing over to stop Rufus who was getting suspiciously close to a toddler sitting on a rug, munching a soggy Rusk biscuit.

Rory and Lucy carried on walking and chatting for a long while, looping all the way around the park and then back again. They swapped stories about Granny Annie and Uncle Seamus, laughing at their similarities in eccentricity. As they drew near the turning to Rory's house, which he explained was only a few roads away from Holland Park, he stooped down to attach Rufus's lead. As he stood up, he said, 'It's been really great talking to you,' looking directly at her with those piercing blue eyes, and Lucy really believed that he meant it. She felt the same. It was so easy chatting to him, he was mesmerizing company. He was witty and amusing, but not at all over the top; just so laid-back and down-to-earth. What is more they just seemed to get on so well. She realised to her surprise that she hadn't even thought about that morning's treatment the entire time that they had been talking. Lucy found that she was reluctant to leave him, and she hovered for a moment or two longer than was necessary, holding his gaze.

'It has been really great,' she agreed smiling up at him, her blue eyes shining.

Rory cleared his throat, shifting from foot to foot a little awkwardly. 'Look, this might sound a bit strange, but do you fancy walking together again sometime, maybe?' he asked, a sheepish grin on his face, his eyes downturned slightly towards the ground.

'I'd love to!' said Lucy, feeling herself flush at the very thought of him wanting to see her again. Hiding her blushes, she bent down to say goodbye to Rufus, whose tail was wagging at a rate of knots.

'Same time, same place next weekend?' he asked.

'Sure!' she said, and then she took a step towards him to kiss him on the cheek, amazed at her own bravery. His stubble grazed against her skin, sending a thrill of micro shivers down her spine. She caught the scent of his aftershave, such a delicious, musky smell, it drew her towards him and she had to force herself to tear away. They grinned inanely at each other, saying 'Bye!' neither one quite ready to leave the other.

In the end, it was Lucy who turned first and began to walk off towards home. After several metres, she spun around to give Rory a cheery wave and was thrilled to see he was still standing there, so handsome, with Rufus by his side, watching her walk away. He gave her a wave back, and she continued on her way, a smile spreading across her cheeks that lasted all the way home. She had never felt so at ease in a stranger's presence. She felt as though they had known each other for years. There was just something about him that made her feel completely relaxed in his company. She found him completely intriguing.

As soon as she got through the door, Lucy rushed over to the mirror above the mantelpiece, checking her appearance. She was suddenly paranoid that she might have had smudged make-up or a bright red nose from the chilly weather. She told herself off for being so silly; after all, she was supposed to be off men for good, wasn't she? Even so, she was happy to see that she looked all right, her blonde fringe fell prettily over her eyes, her freckles had faded somewhat since they had last seen the sun but there was a healthy, rosy glow to her cheeks and her eyes shone brightly.

She may not look too frozen, but in reality she felt like her internal organs had become blocks of ice. On a cold winter's day there was nothing she liked more than to have a warming bath before settling in for the evening. She turned on the hot tap and soon the room began to fill with clouds of steam as the water ran into the enamel tub. Lucy lit an aromatherapy candle and added a few drops of lavender oil into the water.

She lowered herself into the bath and the intoxicating fragrance washed over her, relaxing her tense muscles. As she lathered soap over her body, she allowed her mind to wander back to Rory and she found herself once again blushing at the very thought of him. She had never met a man with such rugged sex appeal; her imagination ran away with her and she found herself picturing his stubble grazing her chin as he kissed her, her hands running down the lithe muscles on his back. The sensible part of her brain tried to stop her, but she was unable to resist.

Chapter Twenty-Five

Over the rest of the weekend, Lucy's mind swayed like a pendulum between chubby-cheeked babies and distracting daydreams about Rory. Pondering the potentially imminent prospect of motherhood, now a familiar thought at the forefront of her mind, she noticed that she felt slightly different. Deep within her, in her gut, where the usual sense of anxiety normally nestled, an inner sense of calm resided, as though everything was working out just as it should be. She wondered whether this might have something to do with a certain handsome Irish man – the perfect distraction perhaps. Or maybe she had just got used to the process of trying for a baby; that with her third cycle of treatment under her belt she wasn't so nervous anymore. She knew that she would have to wait until the following weekend to do the test and find out whether the latest insemination had worked, so she tried to shut out thoughts of pregnancy and focus on work and the menial tasks that filled her days. At night, however, when she had less control of her subconscious, she would dream endlessly of having her own baby, of holding her own tiny son or daughter in her arms. She woke up experiencing such pangs of longing for her imaginary child that she could hardly bear it. She was so ready for this next stage in her life.

Lucy arrived at work on Monday morning to a noticeably quieter office. Lettie, always the first to arrive at their pod and as reliable as clockwork, was nowhere to be seen. Even by the time Simon rocked up, casually as ever, just as the clock struck nine, Lettie still hadn't made an appearance. As always first thing on a Monday morning, having caught up on the weekend news of her Facebook friends over breakfast, Lucy liked to spend the first half hour of her working week perusing the right-hand column of the *Daily Mail* website. She was in the middle of scrutinizing some particularly fascinating images of Kim Kardashian's derrière, trying to decide for herself whether or not she had had butt implants, when Lettie came scurrying over, clutching three cinnamon lattes wobbling precariously on a Starbucks tray. Having not yet seen her colleagues since she returned from an extended Christmas break at home, Lettie was clearly bursting to tell them her news. Lucy helped herself and Simon to a coffee, and instructed Lettie to sit, take a deep breath, and spill the beans. Simon trained his expert eye on her, giving her his full attention, ready to critique the latest hopeless man she was undoubtedly dating.

Both Lucy and Simon had sat through endless stories of Lettie's first encounters with all sorts of different weird and wonderful men over the years, and they diligently prepared themselves for the usual saga. However, this time, things appeared to be somewhat different.

'So the elongated lie-in has a male explanation, no doubt?' asked Simon.

'How did you guess!' asked Lettie, blushing a deep red that clashed with her hair.

'There's only one reason why you'd look this excited!' laughed Lucy.

'You're right! Oh my goodness, you are so right!' said Lettie.

'Go on then, spill the beans…' said Lucy.

'You can't keep us in suspense,' agreed Simon.

'I suppose it could have something to do with the fact that *I've got a boyfriend!*' blurted Lettie, unable to keep the pride from her voice.

'Whaaat?!!' shrieked Lucy and Simon.

'I know! Can you actually believe it! A real boyfriend!' said Lettie, ecstatic. 'He's called Luke.'

'Ooh, Luke!' said Simon.

'Great name,' said Lucy.

'Who is he? How did you meet?' asked Simon.

'I met him at a Christmas drinks party back home in Worcester. He's an old family friend, when I was younger I used to babysit him and his little sister.'

'No way!' said Lucy.

'I hadn't seen him for years and hardly recognized this handsome stranger when he came over to say hello, but we got chatting and ended up swapping phone numbers, agreeing to meet up in a local pub the next day.'

'And did you remember him when you realized who he was?' asked Lucy.

'Yes, but he was four years younger than me and I wouldn't have even really noticed him back then to be honest. But it turns out that all the years I was his babysitter he had a massive crush on me!'

'How cute!' said Lucy.

'He clearly had a thing for geeky-looking redheads!' laughed Lettie. 'I was *so* not a looker!'

'Don't be so cruel to your young self,' admonished Simon. 'I bet you were gorgeous.'

'Anyway, he's actually turned into an extremely attractive guy, despite his receding hairline.'

'Show us a photo,' said Lucy.

'I've got loads on my phone, I'll show you later…' said Lettie.

'So did you see each other lots after that?' asked Simon.

'We went on that date to the pub, which was amazing, and then we met up quite a few times… we even spent New Year's Eve together, just the two of us.'

'How romantic!' said Lucy.

'Last weekend he took me on a romantic mini-break to a luxury hotel! And we had "the chat"! He said would I mind if we made it exclusive…'

'OMG!' said Simon.

'This is too exciting!' said Lucy, thrilled for her friend. Lettie was, quite clearly, over the moon. She looked like one of those cartoon characters who, struck by cupid, had heart-shaped pupils in their eyes.

Amidst the verbal diarrhoea, Simon and Lucy grilled their friend to check whether Luke had been conducting himself in a gentlemanly fashion, to siphon out any arsehole-type behaviour, but he genuinely seemed irreprehensible. They were thrilled for her and decided to go to the local pizzeria after work for dinner and a couple of glasses of wine to celebrate.

That's it, then, thought Lucy. *First Simon and now Lettie, all coupled up! I really am the last one on the shelf!* Her mind darted towards Rory and she wondered at the possibility that things might develop with him.

Following an unsurprisingly dull few days at work to end the week, she found the weekend soon upon her. Lucy was undecided about whether to meet Rory again in Holland Park. She had promised herself she wouldn't waste her time pursuing men any more but there was just something about him she couldn't stop thinking about. She wasn't entirely sure whether he would even turn up. He had no obligation towards her and they hadn't even swapped numbers to confirm the time or place. Imagine if she showed up and waited there for an hour or so and then had to go home again, cold and disappointed. Not to mention looking foolish and desperate to boot. Yes, perhaps it was more sensible to just stay at home. She decided to Google him to see if she could find out more about him. She remembered his name, Rory McCullan, and was able to find him pretty quickly thanks to his website, Rory McCullan Ltd, which not only had a biography and a photograph but also lots of examples of his work as an architect and links to various articles he had written. It seemed like he did very well for himself. She couldn't help but doubt whether he could truly be interested in her.

She was still in two minds come Saturday morning. She had a bath, relaxing into the scented water and scrutinizing the soft flesh of her belly, trying to work out whether there was a tiny baby growing inside her, or not. She still felt remarkably calm about this round of treatment; she had a real sense of acceptance about her future, she felt sure that everything would happen at exactly the right time and in just the right way. She placed the palm of her hand on the centre of her tummy and sent lots of positive thoughts through it to any baby that might be in the earliest stages of development within. It was a very curious state of mind to be trying for a baby. Lucy found it a strange contrast; she had spent the whole of her twenties obsessively hoping that she wasn't pregnant, that some accident had not happened during a moment of passion that would have everlasting consequences. Each month, when she was due to get her period, she would pray for it to come and only when it did would she relax, grateful in the knowledge that she wouldn't have a baby to contend with in nine months' time. Now, however, not only did she spend all her time hoping and praying that she *was* having a baby, she was even going to extraordinary measures to do so!

In the end, she decided to flip a coin; heads she would go to Holland Park, tails she would stay at home and get on with her weekend admin. Wrapped in her fluffy dressing gown, she went into the sitting room and found her handbag, extracted a coin from her wallet and tossed it in the air. She caught it as it fell and placed it in the palm of her left hand. She took her hand away and saw tails. Tails. She would stay at home. Her heart fell. Within an instant she had flipped the coin back over to heads. Of course she would go. The best-looking man she had practically ever laid eyes on had asked to see her again; she was hardly going to turn it down. She had so enjoyed talking to him the week before, she couldn't wait to spend more time with him. And if he didn't turn up she would have lost nothing, she could just go and buy herself a coffee and all she would be doing was sticking to her usual Saturday routine.

Taking a deep breath, she undid her dressing gown and began to get ready. The cold air outside had left her skin feeling particularly dry so she reached for her moisturiser and rubbed it all over her body, luxuriating in the feeling of silky soft skin. She dried her hair and straightened the ends and her fringe, before going through the ritual of applying her make-up, step by step. At the last minute she decided to shave her legs, just in case.

'What to wear for a walk in the park, whilst still managing to look attractive?' she pondered. She walked over to her big, walk-in wardrobe and flung open the doors, peering inside. Riffling through the coat hangers, she found a pair of black jeans, a stripy long-sleeved T-shirt, and a soft jumper the colour of forget-me-nots. Lucy pulled on her brown suede ankle boots and fixed a pair of gold hoops into her ears, checking her appearance in the long mirror. *Not bad*, she thought, *not bad at all!* She glanced out of the window to check for the possibility of rain. The clouds looked grey and menacing. She pulled on a coat and set off.

At roughly the same time that she had arrived at the cafe last week, Lucy walked nervously up the pathway leading to the Orangery. There was clearly a wedding going on that afternoon. The Orangery was often hired out for events and caterers were coming in and out of their vans carrying trays of food. She sidestepped a young man carrying a topiary, ornamental bush teetering far above his head, and looked up at the cafe feeling sure that she was about to be disappointed. To her amazement, there was Rory, standing rather awkwardly, with Rufus on a lead at his feet; the lead was in one hand with a takeaway cup balancing on top of it, and in the other hand was another cup. As soon as he saw her, his eyes twinkled; the crow's feet that were etched around them deepened as a smile spread across his face. Lucy approached him somewhat shyly, partly due to the cast of River Dance that were currently tap-dancing in her stomach. Shivers ran through her chest and down her spine.

'Lucy!' he cried, obviously very happy to see her.

'Hi Rory,' she greeted him with a kiss on the cheek. 'Nice to see you! Hello Rufus,' she said as she bent down to pat him on the back. He wagged his tail appreciatively.

'I got you a coffee. Well, a chai thingy anyway. Was that right?' he asked.

Touched that he had remembered her drink of choice, she said, 'How kind of you! Yes, a chai latte… you remembered!'

'I tried my best!' he said, smiling. 'I wasn't actually sure whether you'd make it. It was a bit foolish of me not to take your number, really.'

'I was thinking something similar! I'm glad you are here,' she said, taking the lid off her cup and sipping the comfortingly sweet spiced milk. It was a little cold. She wondered how long the poor man had been waiting with it. The thought of him arriving early enough to buy her a drink made her warm to him even more.

'Shall we walk?' asked Rory. 'I think Rufus is desperate to get off this lead.'

'Sure,' said Lucy. 'Let's go!' and they started off down the path, looping away from the Orangery, past the remains of Holland House. 'It's sad to see what's left of it now,' she said as they passed the grand Elizabethan building.

'It must have been quite something in its prime. Though I kind of love the contrast of its use today. An open-air opera at the front and a youth hostel round the back!' said Rory. 'I'm not really sure how well the two go together!'

'I know,' laughed Lucy. 'Probably not at all what the owner had in mind five hundred years ago! Have you ever been to the opera here?' Lucy asked.

'Not for years. I used to go quite often, actually, with my wife,' he said.

'You're married?' asked Lucy in surprise, her heart jumping into her throat.

'I'm a widower,' said Rory, looking at the floor in front of him as he walked.

'Oh my god, I'm so sorry,' Lucy muttered, shaking her head. 'That must have been awful.'

'It was pretty awful,' nodded Rory; a mist of sadness shadowing his features at the memory.

Lucy's heart reached out to him. 'What did she die of, if you don't mind me asking?' she enquired tentatively.

'Not at all, it was a long time ago. It was breast cancer, she battled it for fifteen months, but sadly she lost...' he said. 'Have you been to the opera here?' he asked, changing the subject.

'Actually, yes, I went the summer before last with my granny. They have an OAP scheme where you can enter a ballot to win a pair of free tickets right at the front. Someone told me about it at work and I decided to enter for her, then promptly forgot all about it. I got an email a couple of months later telling me that I'd won! My grandmother was thrilled, she's always one for a bargain. So am I, for that matter!' Lucy added.

'What did you see?' Rory asked.

'*The Barber of Seville*,' said Lucy.

Rory laughed as Lucy told him how Annie had insisted on accompanying the opera singers by reciting the translation displayed high overhead on the subtitle screens at the top of her voice, much to the chagrin of the opera enthusiasts surrounding them in the first few rows. Despite Lucy's best efforts to shush her, she refused to stop until some poor usher was sent over to ask her to be quiet. She then continued sotto voce throughout the remainder of the performance, somewhat hampering Lucy's own enjoyment of the music.

Just as they rounded the path that ran behind the Kyoto gardens, the heavens opened. It was the kind of downpour that is hard to believe is possible. The air was dry, if a little damp, moments before; seconds later huge bulbous raindrops were pelting down from the sky like bullets of glass. Rufus was darting frantically from puddle to puddle as they formed, chasing the rivulets of water that were gushing down the sides of the path. Lucy shrieked and ran to the measly shelter of the nearest oak tree, still clutching her cup. Rory, similarly badly dressed for rain in a thick Guernsey jumper, chased after Rufus before clipping on his lead and shouting to Lucy, 'Follow me!' setting off at a run. Lucy braced herself and then ran after him, through the park, out of the gate and down a few criss-crossed streets before arriving at what was presumably Rory's house. Despite the utter drenching she was currently experiencing she couldn't help but notice the size of the place. It was almost a mansion; architecture was obviously not a bad line of work.

As Rory scrabbled with the lock and flung open the door, he called, 'Come in!' and ushered her through the front door. Slamming the door shut behind him and sending Rufus to his bed to lie down and dry off, Rory and Lucy looked at each other in amusement, both panting and soaked to the bone. She was sure that her face must now resemble a smudged panda, the rain having coursed down her hair was still dripping off her chin and her fringe was plastered to her eyes. Rory looked even more handsome than before; his hair was swept off his face and his eyes were shining with mirth. They took off their shoes and left them on the entrance mat. Her suede boots would never be quite the same again.

Suddenly overcome with a fit of hysteria, they both collapsed in laughter.

'What the bloody hell was that monsoon all about?' Rory hooted, clutching his sides as he tried to catch his breath.

'I have *never* seen a rainstorm quite like that!' giggled Lucy, taking a few steps over to the huge gilded mirror that hung in the entrance hall, trying not to fall over on the slippery tiles. As she walked, she left a watery trail in her wake. She looked in the mirror and cringed; as she had suspected her make-up had smeared in a comic fashion across her cheeks. She looked like she was wearing a sad clown mask. 'Look at my face!' she exclaimed.

'There's a bathroom just across the hall if you want to go and get some tissue?' he suggested.

'Thanks,' said Lucy. 'Not a bad idea.' She went into the bathroom and wiped her cheeks with a wad of tissue. She couldn't believe it! Of all the days for a torrential downpour, did it really have to be today?

It felt a bit odd finding herself inside a stranger's house, though, on second thoughts, at least she could have a look around. She was glad that she had done some snooping online to make sure that he was who he said he was. Remembering what he had told her a short while ago about his poor wife, her mind began to wander. Had he bought this place with her? She couldn't imagine the unfairness of having finally found someone only to lose them to illness; it was something that she had never even considered. Being wrenched from your partner in the prime of life must be one of nature's cruellest fates. She flushed the loo and stepped out into the hall.

Hearing Rory call her name from a room that opened up at the end of the corridor, she followed his voice, ending up in a huge kitchen with a large cast-iron wood-burning stove as its focal point. Rufus was lying on his bed in front of the fire, looking sorry for himself. His large shaggy head rested on his long copper paws. Rory had fetched a couple of towels and was rubbing his hair roughly with one. He handed the other to Lucy, who accepted it gratefully, without being entirely sure how dry it was going to make her.

'I know this is the first time you have been to my house, but, given the circumstances, would you like a shower? I can lend you a T-shirt and a jumper, and if you want, I can put your clothes in the tumble dryer?' Rory offered.

Lucy wasn't sure what to do. She was soaking wet and desperate to get out of her clothes. She thought about calling a taxi to take her straight home and rearranging the whole thing but there was something about him that made her want to stay. She didn't want to risk missing out on getting to know him better. What if they postponed and then a second opportunity never materialized? She debated with herself for a moment or two before deciding that he was worth the risk.

'That sounds like a great idea,' Lucy said, following him back into the hall and up the stairs to the first floor. The staircase kept on going for at least one more flight beyond that, if not two. Lucy marvelled at the incredible house, the carpet was thick beneath her feet. Rory showed her to the bathroom where a phenomenal power shower awaited her. He stood for an awkward moment outside the door while she peeled off the sodden jeans that clung to her legs. Wrapping herself in her towel, she opened the door slightly and proffered the wet bundle apologetically.

Rory took them and said 'Enjoy!' before retreating down the corridor presumably to change his own clothes and find her something to put on.

Not wishing to take too long but reluctant to switch off the wondrously soothing hot jets of water that were propelling forth from the vast shower head, Lucy spent a good few minutes in the shower. She came out and proceeded to do what she could to resurrect her make-up, wiping the smudges from underneath her eyes with a corner of the towel and pinching her cheeks to add a dash of colour. Hoping Rory had found something for her to put on, she opened the door and peeped out into the corridor. Resting on the carpet was a neatly folded T-shirt, a thick, woolly jumper and a pair of tracksuit bottoms. She pulled them on, noting the fresh smell of laundry powder, and turned the waistband down several times to shorten them.

She padded downstairs looking admiringly at the beautiful paintings and drawings that were hanging on the walls. The house was painted a shade of cream with neutral carpets throughout. Soft lighting from lamps and ceiling lights glowed discreetly from every nook and cranny.

Lucy came into the kitchen and saw Rory stirring milk into two steaming cups of tea. The tumble dryer was whirring in the utility room off the kitchen and logs were crackling in the wood burner. Rory had changed into jeans and a dry grey jumper; his wet hair stuck up in spikes, the resulting dishevelled look made him look even more rugged. Lucy felt her stomach lurch at the sight of him. Her ankle boots were sitting in front of the crackling fire, drying out.

'Better?' asked Rory.

'Much better, thanks,' said Lucy. 'I haven't been caught out like that in years! Thanks so much for letting me come and dry off.'

'My pleasure!' said Rory, handing her a cup of tea. 'Second time lucky perhaps? Not quite a chai but tea nonetheless!' he said cheerily. There was a low and comfortable-looking sofa perched in front of the fireplace and Rory gestured for her to sit down. Rufus was still drying out in the flickering heat from the flames; he looked up at them and wagged his tail, then sighed contentedly as he rested his large head back on his paws.

Still chuckling about the ridiculous rainstorm, they chatted over their mugs of tea. Rory asked her all about her job, interested to know how the world of advertising worked. In return he told Lucy about his job as an architect. As she had previously discovered, he worked freelance for his own company, Rory McCullan Ltd, mostly designing commercial buildings for big corporate firms across the UK.

As they sank back into the sofa, gazing at the flickering flames and listening to the logs crackle and spit as they burned, Lucy asked him how long he had been living on Thurloe Crescent.

'I bought the house five years ago from an American couple who were desperate to get rid of the place,' explained Rory.

'Why on earth would anyone be desperate to get rid of this house?' asked Lucy, bewildered. 'It's incredible!'

'They had inherited it from a distant relative and had no interest in owning property in the UK; they wanted the whole thing over and done with as quickly as possible. I was selling my house and looking for somewhere new to develop, and it all just sort of fell into my hands!' said Rory. 'I was in the right place at the right time, I suppose.'

'Did you have to do much to it?' asked Lucy.

'Oh yes, it was completely decrepit. Apparently the actual owners hadn't set foot in it for years... the building was so run-down. As soon as I was granted planning permission I gutted the whole place and redesigned it entirely.'

'Were you the architect?'

'I was indeed!' confirmed Rory.

'Oh my goodness! You are so talented. I mean, this place is just the dream home. I can't imagine living anywhere more incredible, and the location too!' exclaimed Lucy.

'You are too kind!' said Rory, taking a miniature bow and laughing. 'It's really not that hard, when you know how!'

'I'd love to know how to do this. I was completely obsessed with *Changing Rooms* when I was younger and drove my parents crazy redesigning my bedroom. I can't tell you how many different looks my childhood room has had over the years!'

'Did you have any disastrous moments as a novice interior designer?' asked Rory.

'Oh my god too many to even mention,' chuckled Lucy, rolling her eyes at the memory. 'I think my parents really had a fit when I decided to streak my yellow silk curtains with fluorescent pink hair mascara. Turns out that isn't such a good look.'

Rory laughed at the thought, telling her that she needed a tree house to experiment on far from her parents prying eyes, like the McCullan kids.

Looking at the clock and noticing that it was now half past two, Rory asked Lucy if she would like something to eat. Her stomach started to rumble at the very thought of food, and before she knew it he had thrown a whole packet of smoky, streaky bacon into a frying pan and started sizzling the rashers on the hob. Soon the room was full of the mouth-watering smell of bacon; Rufus suddenly perked up and looked pleadingly at Rory, almost begging not to be forgotten. Rory set Lucy the task of cutting wedges of fresh white bread, straight from the bakery that morning. She dropped them into the toaster and opened the fridge to see if she could find butter and tomato ketchup. She was relieved that he had both; a bacon sandwich was just not the same without ketchup. When the bacon was crispy enough, they set about making their sandwiches. Rory cracked open a bottle of chilled Sauvignon Blanc and poured them two enormous glasses, chinking Lucy's glass with his. His bright blue eyes shone and his crow's feet crinkled whenever he smiled at her; Lucy could barely take her eyes off his face.

As she sipped the wine, the soothing, sharp liquid ran down her throat, flooding her senses with that heady relaxation only alcohol could give. They sat at the table and ate their sandwiches, talking about their families and Rory's eclectic collection of brothers and sisters. His mother was called Catriona and his father Padraig, but everyone called them Trina and Paddy. Then he had an older brother called Ronan, an older sister called Trish and a younger brother called Dermot. They were all scattered about Ireland: only Rory had moved to the UK when he had started studying architecture at UCL. He had met his wife, Abigail, at university, and stayed with her in London to be near her family when they got married several years later. He had stayed in London ever since. Lucy asked him if he missed living in Ireland.

'I do miss it, yes. Everyone is so much friendlier and relaxed there. I miss the sense of community, and the lushness of the countryside. It really is the Emerald Isle. I'm not so sure about the rain though...' he winked at Lucy, and they both laughed.

The conversation flowed as though they had known each other all their lives. Lucy felt so drawn to him; it was as if he were emitting some kind of magnetic pull. She wanted to get to know him on every level; he intrigued her as no man had ever done before. There was such a gentle side to him; she could sense a certain vulnerability that she imagined came from knowing such deep and harrowing loss. This was coupled with the most engaging sense of humour and a genuine interest in the world around him; it was an incredibly endearing combination. Rory told her the most wonderful tales about growing up as a young boy in rural Ireland, helping the farmers with the harvest, pinching apples from the neighbour's orchard, getting into all sorts of mischief.

'I once got into terrible trouble for burning down the hay barn next door!' he laughed.

'No way!' said Lucy. 'How did you manage that?'

'It was an accident caused by a contraband match that I'd stolen from my father's desk. I was a total pyromaniac and, unfortunately, a somewhat clumsy ten-year-old!'

'Oh dear,' said Lucy. 'What happened?'

'Unbeknownst to me, Trish was hiding up at the top of the haystacks…'

'No!' shrieked Lucy.

'Yup! Don't worry, as soon as I heard her squeals I clambered up the burning bales, grabbed her and deposited her safely on the ground. However, Trish was more concerned about her new pink gloves which remained where she had been sitting. She insisted I risk my life to rescue them, which I duly did!' he laughed, shaking his head at the thought. His lilting Irish voice added extra charisma to his storytelling, and Lucy found she could picture him very clearly as a scruffy, dark-haired child. She loved the way his boyish charms had stayed with him until this day.

Her tongue loosened by the wine, Lucy told him about her own childhood growing up in Cornwall with Ollie. The scavenger hunts and rounders' matches on the beach, the barbeques in the sand dunes and endless games of forty forty. He asked her so many questions, curious to know every detail about her, as though he were trying to piece together a puzzle to find out what had made her who she was today. He made her feel like she was the most fascinating person on earth; she basked in his attention as if soaking up the sun's rays.

When the bottle of wine was empty, Lucy wondered whether Rory would want her to leave. It was becoming dark outside; the dull shades of dusk were lowering slowly over the city like thick fog. The log fire was so warm and cosy, the company so excellent, that Lucy couldn't bear the thought of making her way home. Obviously having the same thoughts, Rory asked her if she had made plans for the evening or whether she would like to pop out to a local cocktail bar down the road for another drink. Relieved, and unwilling to part from his company quite yet, she said yes, though she suggested that it would depend on whether her clothes had finished drying. Rory went into the utility room to check, and, pausing the tumble dryer to open the door, declared them dry. He took them out, passing them to Lucy who retreated to the bathroom to change.

When she was ready, or at least as ready as she would ever be without her make-up bag to hand, Rory opened the front door, leaving Rufus munching contentedly on a huge bowl of dog biscuits, and they stepped out into the crisp, cool evening. The clouds had dissipated since their outpouring earlier that day, rolling back to reveal a clear sky. A huge moon hovered low above the rooftops, surrounded by a halo of orange light.

'What a beautiful evening!' cried Lucy. 'Look at that moon… it's enormous!'

'Stunning. That's another thing I miss about Ireland,' said Rory. 'The sky at night, you really can't beat it. It looks almost heavy with stars, as though you could just reach up and pluck a handful.'

'It's such a shame we can't see the stars properly in London. Too much light haze and smog,' said Lucy.

'I've always been fascinated by space… the planets and stars and so on,' said Rory as they walked down the street towards the wine bar. 'It's just mind-boggling.'

'I read that there are more stars in the universe than there are grains of sand on earth!' Lucy told him. 'Can you believe that?!'

'I know! And apparently Earth can fit into the Sun one million times!' he said. They both walked for a moment in silence, marvelling at the enormity of the universe above them, humbled by the reminder of their own insignificance.

As they rounded the corner, they came to the bar, Penhaligons. A crowd of smartly dressed people were clustered around the door, smoking and chatting. Rory and Lucy made their way through, squeezing into a space with two free barstools near the wall, which was papered with a decorative print. The bar was decked out in a speakeasy style, with twenties music playing from a crackling gramophone in the corner. Lucy loved the revival of prohibition era bars that had recently sprung up all over London; she perused the typewritten menu, scouring all the tantalizing cocktails on offer. She had asked her doctor whether it was safe to drink in the weeks between fertilization and implantation and she had reassured her that it was fine.

Rory ordered a Campari-based cocktail, the smell of which made Lucy want to retch but that he declared was delicious. Lucy ordered a mojito. As they sipped their drinks, they hypothesized on the personal histories of the people around them… one of Lucy's favourite pastimes, and Rory's, as it turned out. He explained how, in the years following Abigail's death, he had spent an awful lot of time on his own. He had realized that he needed to get used to his own company and would come to restaurants or bars after work, often too tired and emotionally drained to cook, where he would people-watch to pass the time. He had found it very reassuring to muse over the lives of others, taking comfort in the knowledge that he was not alone and enjoying the happiness of those who were lucky enough to be with loved ones.

They finished their cocktails and ordered another round. As they perched on their barstools, their knees touched. Lucy felt acutely aware of how close she was to him, she wanted to reach out and rest her hand on the denim that covered his thighs. The dark grey jumper he was wearing stretched slightly over his broad chest; she could see how muscular his physique was underneath. His arms and shoulders looked so strong that she could imagine him picking her up and throwing her over his shoulder with ease. For an instant a crazy image of him doing just that before marching her back home to ravish her in his bedroom flashed into her mind. She blushed at the thought, thankful that he couldn't see into her overactive imagination.

Realizing she was now hungry, she suggested that they might eat some dinner. They had only had a bacon sandwich for lunch and she was starving. Rory paid for their drinks and they left the little cocktail bar, turning left and walking further down the road past a row of shops and a bank before arriving at a little Italian place.

'This is my local Italian,' said Rory as they neared the restaurant, 'and, in my opinion, it serves the best Italian food in London.' Fantoni's was written in large italic script across the dark green door. Dark wooden tables and chairs were scattered about inside, with bunches of flowers and candles on every surface. The smell of freshly baked pizza wafted from the open pizza oven, where a chef stood shovelling round discs of dough into the mouth of the fire, pulling them out a few minutes later, risen and bubbling. Lucy's mouth watered.

Lorenzo, the owner, greeted Rory warmly, chatting to him with a heavy Italian accent, asking him how he was and what was new in his life. He gave Lucy the once-over, smiling his approval at Rory and congratulating him on his beautiful choice of companion, before ushering them to a little table towards the back. Lucy ordered a Diet Coke, Rory ordered a Peroni and they both pounced hungrily on the basket of warm ciabatta, drizzling olive oil and balsamic vinegar all over it before biting into the chewy dough.

Lorenzo brought the menus over. After several minutes' perusal, they both decided to get pizzas, they just looked too tempting to resist.

'Oh how I *love* Italian food,' said Lucy. 'I could have ordered anything on that menu!'

'I can never decide between pizza and pasta, it's really the food of the gods!' agreed Rory.

'Have you been to Italy and eaten real Italian food?' asked Lucy.

'I've been a couple of times.'

'Whereabouts?'

'Venice and Florence, both beautiful cities. What about you?' asked Rory.

'Well I did a history of art degree; one of my modules was on the Sistine Chapel so I managed to go to Rome to get an up-close and personal look at the place as part of my course! I ended up doing my dissertation on the Baroque period in Italian art, Caravaggio is my favourite artist, so I travelled around Italy one summer, exploring and visiting lots of art galleries and churches,' explained Lucy. 'I've actually visited quite a lot of Italy, and Rome is definitely the best city.'

'I'm ashamed to admit that I have never been to Rome,' confessed Rory.

'Shameful indeed for an architect,' agreed Lucy, teasing him. 'You should go!'

'Maybe you can give me the grand tour?' suggested Rory, smiling at Lucy with a cheeky look in his eyes.

She knew that he was joking, they had only met twice after all, but she was encouraged nonetheless that he would even make such a suggestion. Could it mean that he thought they might see more of each other, that he might like to? She wondered if he was feeling as deeply drawn to her as she was to him. She crossed her fingers and toes and said, 'Yeah, maybe, if you're lucky!' laughing it off with a shrug.

'Anyway, Rome isn't the most beautiful place in Italy; there is somewhere else that wins hands down. Do you know the Amalfi coast?' asked Lucy.

'I've heard of it but I've never actually been, I think Dermot might have been there when he went inter-railing as a young lad. Is it near Naples?'

'It's about an hour and a half from Naples; you can catch the ferry the whole way there, following the coastline. It's such a stunning journey. Anyway, there's a little town called Positano, it's just a cluster of pastel houses scattered on a steep hillside across a cut-away valley. The sea is bright turquoise and crystal-clear, the whole place looks like it has been dreamt up for a fairy tale, it's just the most breathtakingly beautiful place on earth.' Lucy reminisced about her time there as a student, she had taken the train to Naples with another friend from her course and stayed in a little hostel with magnificent views of the town beneath them.

'I'm sold!' said Rory. 'It sounds amazing… I can't imagine how there are people in this day and age who have never left their own country, or worse, their own county! There's such an incredible world out there to explore.'

Lucy nodded in agreement, loving Rory's enthusiasm for just about everything.

Just then their pizzas arrived, piping hot. Strings of melting cheese stretched from slice to slice as they pulled them apart. They devoured them hungrily, chatting happily about all the places they had visited and making a wish list of top destinations still to explore. It was such a happy evening.

Lorenzo brought over huge bowls of gooey tiramisu for pudding accompanied with little shots of limoncello, the sharp sweetness the perfect digestif after the richness of the cream and coffee. Lucy felt so full and so content; her cheeks were glowing with a combination of flirtation, good food and drink. She knew that Rory must be feeling the same way too, they hadn't run out of conversation even for a moment and they seemed to have the same views on all sorts of unexpected subjects.

As the last customers trickled out of the restaurant, Rory asked for the bill and insisted on paying for Lucy's meal. As they walked down the road, Rory took Lucy's hand in his, it felt like a perfect fit and she felt energy coursing through her at the physical contact. Her heart felt like it was skipping every other beat. They didn't speak, they just walked along in silence, their breath like little clouds of mist in the cold air. She thought about stopping to flag down a taxi to take her home, but every atom of her body refused to leave his company, all she wanted to do was talk to him more, look at him more and memorize every gorgeous part of him. She had never felt like this before; she was amazed at the strength of her attraction towards him.

Before she knew it they were back outside his house. Her heart was hammering in her chest like a stampede of wildebeest. He turned to face her, his hand still holding hers, staring with those mesmerizing blue eyes into hers. She opened her mouth, about to thank him for dinner, her breath coming in shallow gulps of air; she couldn't believe the physical reaction her body was having to him. The chemistry was palpable. And then his face was nearing hers, as if in slow motion. His lips brushed against hers, the lightest graze, sending shivers of electricity through her body. She dared not move, willing him to kiss her again, unable to breathe. He stroked a lock of blonde hair behind her ear, smiled tenderly at her, and then kissed her again, still barely brushing her lips with his. He repeated the exquisite torture a few more times, each time pressing his lips a little harder against hers, each kiss lasting a little longer. The heady smell of his musky aftershave was having a dizzying effect on her.

Suddenly, it was as if he could resist the temptation no longer; he put one hand behind her head and the other around her shoulders and kissed her properly, pressing his body firmly against her. She almost fainted with the rush of blood from her head down to her pelvis; it was as though her libido had been jumpstarted with an electric shock from the National Grid. Lucy kissed him back, wrapping her arms around him, running her hands through his thick, brown hair, oblivious to any passers-by. She knew that every rule book ever written would tell her to go home right this second, to end it now before he got what he wanted and completely lost interest, but there was no way she could stop.

Pausing for breath, he held her face in his hands, brushing her cheek with his huge thumb. She felt so tiny and fragile in comparison to him, like a dainty porcelain doll. Looking tenderly into her eyes, he whispered, 'You are the most beautiful, intriguing woman I have met in a long, long time. You have no idea…' he muttered, his eyes shining with emotion.

Lucy felt overwhelmed looking at him, she felt so fond of him already as though they had been in each other's lives for years. Unable to speak, she kissed him again, lightly on the lips, as he had done, despite the huge, beaming smile that was spreading across her lips.

Brushing her blonde fringe away from her eyes, cupping her face in his hand, Rory leant closer to her ear and whispered, 'Do you want to come in?'

Hesitating for a moment, but only for a moment, Lucy nodded her head, knowing exactly what she was agreeing to. Rory unlocked the door. Both he and Lucy were greeted rapturously by Rufus, who, having been alone for several hours, was desperate for company. Poor Rufus's audience was far too distracted by each other to pay much attention to him, so he retreated to his bed with his tail between his legs, back to the still glowing embers of the fire.

Rory took off his jacket and hung it on the peg by the door then took Lucy by the hand and led her upstairs. Her whole body was trembling with desire, her knees felt weak underneath her and she used her free hand to clutch the banister as she climbed the stairs.

In his bedroom, a huge four-poster bed awaited them, clean white sheets beckoned invitingly. The enormous full moon shimmered just outside the window. Lucy stood by the glass looking at the night sky as Rory closed the bedroom door behind them. Suddenly, she felt his warm body press against the length of her back as he wrapped his arms around her, she could feel his breath hot against her neck, his breathing heavy. He kissed her softly on the side of her neck, again and again; spine-tingling tremors ran down her body with each kiss. Unable to bear it a second longer, she turned around to face him. They fell onto the bed, removing their clothes, kissing and exploring each other's bodies, devouring each other hungrily, losing themselves with complete abandon.

Much later, having been unable to resist a repeat performance, they lay entwined in bed, propped up with soft, feathery pillows, Lucy's head resting on Rory's chest. She placed the palm of her hand on his chest, nestling against the dark hairs that covered it, and felt the gentle thump of his heart beating. They talked about their past relationships, about Abigail, and about the string of girls that Rory had dated over the years since she had passed away, how singularly unimpressed he had been with them all. Not one of them had managed to capture his interest even remotely as much as Lucy had done. He told her that she was the first person he had met who he had been properly attracted to, who he had really, really liked, in all the years since his wife had died. Lucy smiled to herself, thanking God and her lucky stars that she had met this wonderful, kind man. In return, she told him about all her single years, and then about Alex, and the disastrous end that their relationship had had.

'I can't bear the thought of you going through all that,' said Rory. 'It must have been awful.' *Hardly awful in comparison with what happened to you*, thought Lucy. 'But I'm secretly glad of course,' Rory added, 'because otherwise you wouldn't be lying here next to me right now, and for that I am eternally grateful.'

'Very true!' said Lucy, smiling and reaching up to kiss him.

'Any other skeletons in the closet?' he asked, clearly sensing her hesitation.

She paused, wondering whether she should tell him about Jack. 'Well… I promised I'd never tell anyone this. But in the spirit of sharing all of our deepest secrets… I did something last year which I've been feeling pretty awful about.' She paused. 'I had sex with someone at work, a guy called Jack.' Taking a deep breath, she continued, 'He was married.'

The hand that had been gently stroking her back stopped. She turned her head to face him. He was looking at her quizzically, unimpressed, waiting for further explanation.

'I know it was wrong, I feel terrible. We were really drunk; he had just separated from his wife... One thing led to another and... I wasn't thinking...'

'Well,' said Rory. 'I'm glad that you added that bit about him having separated from his wife. I guess you could call me traditional, or blame my Catholic upbringing, but I'm of the old-fashioned belief that marriage vows mean something. I really can't understand why people cheat. You have to try and put yourself in the wife's shoes. How would it feel if it happened to you?'

'I know. That's why I feel so awful. I hope I never have to find out.'

'Me too,' said Rory.

'Do you think I'm a terrible person now?' asked Lucy, worried that she had blown it.

'I think he is the one most at fault, and no... we all make mistakes. But I would hope, sincerely, that you wouldn't be the cheating type. That that experience has put you off.'

'I promise. It's the last thing I would ever do.'

'Okay then,' he said. He held her in his embrace, stroking her hair and kissing her head. In his arms she felt totally secure, as safe as she had ever felt. She imagined herself staying there forever and could think of nothing she would want more. Eventually, they drifted off to sleep, still lying in each other's arms, the moon watching wistfully on, bathing them in a silver pool of light.

Chapter Twenty-Six

Sunday dawned bright and cheerful; Lucy was awoken by the chirruping birds tweeting from their high viewpoint on the leafy tree outside Rory's bedroom window. Taking a moment to gather her thoughts and get her bearings, she turned over to find herself face to face with him, breathtakingly gorgeous in sleep, his stubble darker and thicker, his dark eyelashes curling from eyelids still heavy with dreams. She smiled contentedly to herself, stretching out her aching limbs, the post-coital glow still radiated from every cell in her body. Tucking herself near him, he rolled his arm over her, pulling her closer to him in his sleep, spooning the back of her body. She couldn't put her finger on it but she knew something was different this time, that Rory was somehow different from any other man she had met. Blissfully happy, Lucy allowed herself to close her eyes, drifting back into a deep sleep.

She awoke a while later and turned over to find an empty bed. She rubbed her eyes sleepily and yawned, stretching once more like a starfish across the bed.

Lucy looked blearily around the room, spotting a cosy-looking tartan dressing gown hanging on the back of the door and wrapping herself in it. She went to the bathroom and borrowed Rory's toothbrush to brush her teeth. Then she padded down the corridor, the lush carpet soft underneath her feet, and tiptoed down the stairs, listening for any noises from around the house. It was eerily quiet. She made her way to the kitchen, calling out 'Rory?' but there was no reply. Rufus was nowhere to be seen either. All of a sudden she heard the front door slam shut and the light patter of Rufus's claws clattering against the tiles.

Rory called out 'Lucy?' in his deep voice.

She replied, 'In here!' from the kitchen.

He burst into the room with Rufus lapping around his ankles, bringing a blast of fresh air in with him. His cheeks were rosy from the chill outside and his eyes sparkled. The crow's feet seemed deeper than ever as he beamed at her; in his hand he held two takeaway cups and a paper bag full to the brim with pastries.

'Morning!' he sang, coming over to Lucy and kissing her warmly on the lips, causing her stomach to lurch. His kiss lingered for a second or two, then he kissed her again. 'You look gorgeous! My dressing gown really suits you!' he smiled.

'Why thank you, kind sir!' Lucy replied, doing a little twirl and striking a pose. 'I have rather a limited selection of clothing to choose from!'

'We'll have to get you home to get a change of clothes at some point,' said Rory, putting the coffees and the paper bag onto the kitchen table. 'But I'm not sure I'm going to be able to let you out of my sight,' he muttered, looking at her with a mischievous glint in his eyes as he wrapped her in a bear hug and kissed her again. 'I got you a cappuccino, I'm afraid there were no chai lattes at the local cafe, but they do serve excellent coffee.'

'I love coffee in the morning, that's perfect. Thank you so much. Is that breakfast you've got there?' asked Lucy, feeling hungry after their late night activities.

'Rufus needed to go out so I took him for a run around the park, hence the tracksuit,' he said gesturing to his grey joggers, 'we stopped off to buy croissants on the way back. They're still warm!'

'Yum!' said Lucy. 'My favourite.' Her tummy was rumbling at the thought.

He popped back to the front door to collect the paper, which had been delivered, and they sat at the kitchen table, sipping their coffee, eating their croissants with generous lashings of black cherry jam, and reading the *Sunday Times*. Lucy was more interested in the magazine supplements than anything else, but Rory filled her in on the headlines. Rufus snuffled around underneath the table, hoovering up any crumbs or flakes of pastry that made their way down to him. Lucy couldn't believe how at ease she felt in Rory's presence. It was as if she had known him all her life, she couldn't understand how it was possible to feel so comfortable with a virtual stranger but she did.

When breakfast was over, Lucy said, 'Do you mind if I have a shower?'

'I think that is a fantastic idea,' said Rory, leaning closer to her and kissing her on the lips. 'Do you mind if I join you?' he asked, resulting in another hour or two back in bed.

Lucy had never felt so completely and utterly satisfied by a man; he was amazing… such stamina! Her lips stung from being kissed so much and her muscles ached even more. Her phone was buzzing manically with voicemails from Claudia, her mum, and Tor. All of them rightly assumed that she would be available on a Sunday morning for their weekly catch-ups. Only Claudia was suspicious, wanting to know exactly what reason Lucy had for not answering her phone.

Having finally wrenched themselves apart and out of bed, Lucy insisted that it was about time she went home to get a change of clothes. It was already way past midday and the sun was still shining, Rory clipped the lead on Rufus and they set off towards Baron's Court. They held hands as they squinted in the bright sunshine, their spirits sky-high, laughing and stopping for the odd kiss as they went, not a care in the world.

Lucy had sent a cryptic text to Claudia and Tor, saying something about being otherwise engaged and promising to fill them in as soon as possible. This had resulted in another barrage of texts from Claudia, the detective, determined not to be left out of any potential gossip. Tor had merely sent back a cheery:

Sounds interesting! No rush...Enjoy!xx.

Lucy had also sent her mother a message saying she was busy and promising to call in the week.

As they rounded the corner towards Baron's Court, Lucy pointed out all her favourite local spots to Rory. The whole of London looked infinitely more attractive and charming in the bright light of a sunny day, and Lucy found herself feeling incredibly fond of where she lived. They turned onto Mayfield Road and sauntered up the street, two lovebirds beaming from ear to ear. Rufus sniffed happily at tree stumps and lamp posts as he went.

At number 13, Lucy announced that they had arrived at their destination, unlocking the front door and picking up some post that had arrived yesterday from the communal letter box as she went in. She led Rufus and Rory up the three flights of steps to her flat, letting them in and saying, 'Welcome to my humble abode!' As Rory took a step inside and looked around, Lucy felt proud of her little flat; it was at its best with the beams of light streaming through the big bay window by the window seat, illuminating everything with a warm glow.

'I love it!' declared Rory. 'It's so cute! Such a homely feel to it…' he said, as he wondered around the sitting room, looking at the higgledy-piggledy books stacked on the shelves. 'You've done a great job. All the distressed furniture is such a great look.'

'Thanks! I distressed it myself,' said Lucy.

Rory raised an eyebrow in admiration before asking, 'Where shall I put Rufus?'

'Good question!' said Lucy, 'I hadn't really thought of that. Is he okay in the corner on the rug for now?'

'He's grand anywhere,' said Rory. 'Aren't you, boy? So long as it's okay with you.' Rufus wagged his tail obligingly and settled, as directed, on the stripy rug in the corner of the room, under a free-standing lamp.

Lucy offered Rory a drink, pouring him a glass of elderflower cordial from the fridge, before popping into her bedroom to change her clothes, leaving Rory skimming through a magazine from the pile on the coffee table.

Alone in her bedroom, Lucy pondered what to change into. She wasn't sure if they would be spending the night with each other, but she certainly hoped they would; she didn't want to spend a second without him if at all possible. She changed her underwear, choosing her best matching set, a pretty shade of coral silk, and pulled on a stretchy jumper dress in black and white stripes, and a pair of black tights. She applied some make-up for the first time since yesterday morning, only a little so as not to be too much of a contrast to her nude appearance of the last twenty-four hours, and subtly straightened her fringe. Spritzing herself with her Chanel no.5, she flung open the bedroom door and went back into the sitting room, eliciting a long, drawn-out wolf whistle from Rory followed by an approving 'Woof' from Rufus, which made them both chuckle.

'She looks nice, doesn't she, Rufus? You daft old boy!' Rory said, laughing at his dog, who was sitting with his head cocked to one side, looking quizzically at them both. 'What do you want to do now?' asked Rory, as Lucy sat on his lap at the kitchen table and gave him a kiss.

'Do you fancy watching a movie?' suggested Lucy.

'Great idea,' agreed Rory.

Lucy reached for the remote control and they scanned through the movies on the planner, then the box office, finally settling on some new thriller that they had both missed at the cinema. They spent a relaxing afternoon on the sofa, cuddled up to one another, gripped by the twists and turns of the plot

After the film had finished they took Rufus out for a walk on the green nearby then popped into Sainsbury's to buy ingredients for a roast dinner, leaving Rufus whining on the lead. Lucy put a small, corn-fed chicken into her basket, some roasting potatoes, onions for bread sauce, vegetables and milk. With their stomachs starting to rumble at the prospect of a traditional Sunday roast, they returned to the flat. Rory had picked up an enormous cardboard box from outside the shop, and he ripped off the edges to make a low, makeshift basket for Rufus in his little corner. Lucy found an old, ripped sleeping bag that Ollie had left behind the Christmas before last and donated it to Rufus's new bed. Having wolfed down the dog food that Rory had bought him from Sainsbury's, he settled happily with a sigh of contentment into his cosy basket.

Lucy put her iPod in the dock, filling the room with the spellbinding, deep voice of Nina Simone. Rory and Lucy worked in the kitchen in perfect harmony to prepare their meal, chatting all the while, teasing each other about how to improve on their culinary techniques, competing over whose mother had taught whom best. Once again she marvelled at how completely at ease she felt in his company. She hadn't found the tiniest thing about him annoying or off-putting, it was as if he were too good to be true.

Lucy rubbed butter into the prickled skin of the chicken, chopping a lemon in half and inserting it deep into the cavity, then she turned the oven on to heat up. Rory set about peeling and chopping the potatoes ready for roasting, while Lucy placed a baking tray of fat in the oven to heat up in preparation. With the potatoes parboiling, they put the chicken in the oven and carefully spooned the potatoes into the steaming hot fat, spitting and hissing as each fluffy potato hit the pan. Lucy made the bread sauce, setting Rory the task of chopping the onions, and they got the vegetables ready to cook later.

Standing back to take a look at Lucy, Rory said, 'Oh dear, I'm afraid you've been a little bit clumsy,' his hands on his hips. 'What a messy pup!' he said, getting a wet cloth from the sink to attempt to wipe her face.

'Oy, you can't talk!' screeched Lucy as she dodged the incoming cloth. 'You've got a piece of potato peel in your hair, you muppet!' she said as she extracted it, dangling it in front of him as proof.

'Who are you calling a muppet?' asked Rory, chasing after Lucy with the cloth. Shrieking, she ran around the kitchen table, Rory in close pursuit. He pinned her down by the window seat, tickling her until she begged for mercy, and wiping the flour from her face. Barely able to breathe from laughter, they lay collapsed on top of each other, gasping for breath.

'What are we going to do while we wait for the roast to cook?' asked Lucy, batting her eyelashes innocently.

'Mmm, I can't think,' muttered Rory, as he pinned her down with the full length of his body. 'Actually, I've got an idea,' he said, his voice deeper and lower all of a sudden as he kissed her, grinding his hips against hers, before picking her up as though she was as light as a feather and carrying her into the bedroom.

Wrapped once more in a dressing gown, Lucy padded out of her bedroom an hour or so later to baste the chicken and turn the potatoes, by now a crisp, golden brown. Having worked up an impressive appetite once again, she set about blitzing some bread crumbs in the blender for the bread sauce. Stirring in milk, onions and seasoning with salt and pepper, she flicked on the kettle, smiling to herself as she heard Rory's rich baritone singing from the shower. Rufus came over to sniff around her feet as she cooked. It was so nice having a dog around, she chatted away to him merrily as she laid the table, setting two place mats and a candle in the centre. She opened a bottle of red wine and poured herself and Rory a glass, it was a Spanish Rioja, and as Lucy sipped it, she savoured the rich, fruity taste.

She poured boiling water over the cauliflower florets, fetching some peas from the freezer and putting them in a small pan. As she stirred the bread sauce, Rory came out of the bedroom, wearing a T-shirt and her kikoi draped around his legs. He wrapped his arms around her and she leant back into him, enjoying having someone to cook with and chat to once again in her flat.

Rory insisted that his speciality was making gravy so he took over the final stages of the roast, setting the chicken to rest on the carving board, sprinkling plain flour and some of the red wine into the juices from the meat, and adding some of the water from the vegetables. He left Lucy to stir it while he set about carving the chicken, shaving thin slices of breast meat as juicy and succulent as could be. With the roast finally ready, and Rufus satisfied with a couple of scraps from the carving board, they piled their plates high and sat at the table, eating their hard-earned meal and listing their favourite foods, the best meals they had ever eaten, and the most exotic.

'I'll win this one, hands down!' announced Rory.

'What was it?' asked Lucy,

'Lambs testicle!' he said proudly.

'Eurgh,' said Lucy. 'That is disgusting... why? Where?'

'It was a dare while I was travelling in Africa after finishing school. It was pretty horrendous, I'm not going to lie. What about you? Can you trump that?'

'Cow stomach.'

'That does sound pretty rank.'

'But I'm ashamed to admit I couldn't eat it. It was like a sheet of the thickest rubber imaginable, and worse, you could see the spiky villi all over it...' Lucy went green at the thought.

'I definitely win then!' laughed Rory. 'I'm no wimp!' Lucy gave him a playful shove.

After their meal, pleasantly full and with wine glasses topped up, they settled on the sofa to watch some Sunday night television.

Later, as they got into bed, Rory having taken Rufus out for a last run around the green, she felt as deep a sense of contentment as she had ever felt. She knew, without the slightest trace of doubt, that she was in exactly the right place at the right time, and, most importantly, that she was with exactly the right person.

Chapter Twenty-Seven

'You dirty stop-out!' shrieked Claudia. Her reaction to Lucy's dramatic update on her love life was so extreme that Lucy had to hold the telephone well away from her ear. It was Monday lunchtime and she had called Claudia the second her break had started to fill her in. After another late night with Rory she had struggled through the morning replaying memories of their weekend together to keep her going.

'I know! Can you actually believe it?' laughed Lucy. 'He's literally the most gorgeous man I've ever met in my life, so sexy, so awesome. I can't wait for you to meet him!'

'He sounds divine!' said Claudia. 'When is he going to get my seal of approval?' she asked.

'I'll see if we can get a pub session together next weekend maybe,' suggested Lucy. 'It would be nice for him to meet you guys.'

'Good plan,' agreed Claudia. 'It sounds like he absolutely knocks the socks of Alex. Irish *and* an architect… the dream!'

'When I'm with him, I honestly can't even remember who Alex is, he doesn't even compare! It's so weird, Clauds, I can't describe it… I know we've only known each other for a short time but I feel like I've known him all my life,' explained Lucy. 'I've never felt like this about anyone before.'

'You know that's exactly how I felt when I met Dan?' said Claudia. 'It was the strangest thing, if I were to believe in something as horrendously naff as the notion of soulmates then that's kind of what it felt like. As if you knew each other inside out right from the beginning.'

'Exactly! It's as if we just "get" each other,' expanded Lucy. 'We love all the same things, we laugh at the same jokes, we even have practically the same dog for Christ's sake! Size excluded obviously!'

'Oh, Luce, I'm *so* happy for you! Fingers crossed that you have finally met your Mr Right! Although, on second thoughts…'Claudia tailed off somewhat awkwardly.

'Yes?' asked Lucy.

'Well, when are you going to find out the results of your last treatment? What if it worked?' asked Claudia, raising the question that had been hovering like a rain cloud over Lucy's head all day.

'To be honest, I can't even think about that right now,' said Lucy, rubbing her forehead.

'But you kind of have to, right?' encouraged Claudia. 'I mean, just imagine…'

'I can't even begin to imagine what I would do if I found out I was pregnant right now, the timing would be utterly insane. I'm sure I'm not pregnant, anyway. I can't feel anything different within me, surely I would know?'

'You still better check, Luce,' said Claudia, the voice of reason. 'It's better to know, even if things have changed for you somewhat.'

'I know. But it's still too early to test yet.'

'Did you use protection?' asked Claudia.

'Yes…' said Lucy, holding her breath and wondering whether to come out with the truth of the matter. 'Although on one occasion the condom split… but it was only for a second before he noticed and then we immediately dealt with it, so I'm sure it's fine.'

'What do you mean you're sure it's fine? What you are saying is that you had unprotected sex?' asked Claudia in exasperation. 'Did you get the morning after pill?'

'No,' said Lucy. 'I'm sure the timing of my cycle was in my favour. I was supposed to be at my most fertile the weekend before this thankfully. And I have had two rounds of IUI which didn't result in pregnancy so this is hardly likely to have done so…'

'But you wouldn't want to fall pregnant with a virtual stranger's child!' said Claudia.

'Look, I'm sure nothing happened… anyway, it was an accident,' said Lucy, as if that made it better.

'Okay Luce, I'm not trying to be a pain in your arse here but I am after all the expert at avoiding impregnation, that's all.'

'I know, I know! God, life all seems way too complicated all of a sudden,' groaned Lucy.

'What is meant to be will be,' Claudia reassured her.

'Anyway I've been wittering on about Rory and myself for the last twenty minutes, how's Dan? How's work? Is the mega bitch still being bitchy?' asked Lucy. Having changed to her favourite subject, Claudia nattered on happily for the rest of Lucy's lunch break.

She had decided to eat her sandwich sitting on a bench in a nearby park, making the most of yet another sunny day. As she walked back to the office, her mind shifted back to Rory. He had left early that morning to take Rufus home and get ready for work. He was going to spend the day working partly in his office, and partly at Thurloe Crescent, where all of his architectural equipment was set up in one of the downstairs rooms overlooking the garden. Rory was at a work event that evening and though she would happily have seen him she was looking forward to having the evening to herself. She had made plans to see Rory on Tuesday. She missed him already and could hardly believe that she was falling for him so quickly; she hadn't thought it was possible.

Lettie and Simon were fascinated by her account of what had happened that weekend. They gave each other knowing looks as she described Rory, hoping along with her that her turn might have finally come. She quickly hushed them, knowing that that kind of talk got her nowhere whilst secretly hoping they might be right. Even the usual Monday morning hello from Jack had failed to have its usual stomach churning effect on her.

In the afternoon, Tor had emailed her trying to get a date in the diary for lunch that weekend, so Lucy had also given her a call and filled her in on the new developments in her life.

Tor had been an absolute rock during Lucy's donor treatments so far. Having been through a similar, if more gruelling, process herself she was more interested in knowing how Lucy was feeling following the third cycle than anything else. Lucy explained the dilemma about Rory and the split condom. Tor reassured her that it was incredibly unlikely that she could be pregnant from those few moments but warned her that these things did happen occasionally nonetheless. It only took one sperm to fertilize an egg, after all, and it was possible to release more than one egg in a cycle. In fact, it turned out that one of Tor's sister's friends had got pregnant through exactly the same slip-up. This did not make Lucy feel much better. She thought long and hard about how she would feel if it were true. She realized that to her a baby would be a blessing no matter who the sperm came from, and she was sure that the chance was so slim she needn't worry about it too much.

Tor offered to be there when she did the pregnancy test, knowing the time would be coming up soon. Lucy thanked her but knew she would rather do the test alone. Tor was very sensitive to the situation and knew there was no need to push the matter. Instead, she patiently answered all of Lucy's questions about what she should expect to feel if she was pregnant. All of the symptoms that Tor described had no resonance with what Lucy's body currently felt like so she prepared herself to accept the fact that she would remain childless for a while longer. This time it was with mixed feelings that she contemplated the prospect. Perhaps now that she had met Rory it wasn't the best time for her to be trying to fall pregnant after all. Maybe she should concentrate on seeing what happened with him over the next few months before pursuing her quest for motherhood further. It was funny how life could throw curveballs at you. Just one chance encounter and her entire world had turned upside down! Suddenly she no longer knew what to think, what to hope for, or what to do. She decided to put her next treatment cycle on hold for a while, until the earth stopped shifting beneath her feet and she felt settled once more.

Rory had been texting her throughout the day and Lucy's heart had leapt every time she saw his name flash up on her screen. When she finished work she decided to run home. She needed some time to straighten out her thoughts and running was the perfect way to do so. It was already dark when she left the office and the lights of the city flickered all around her, the noises of London's traffic accompanied the rhythm of the music pumping in her ears as she ran. She slowed her pace as she neared her flat, walking the last few blocks and feeling her heart rate return to normal, her forehead damp with sweat, her backpack resting heavily on her back.

The flat seemed very empty without Rory and Rufus there. Bizarrely she seemed to feel their absence even more acutely than the empty feeling the flat had had when Alex had moved out. After a refreshing shower she popped to the shops to buy some dinner before curling up on the window seat to phone Nicola.

'Lucy! How are you?' her friend asked warmly as she answered the telephone.

'Not too bad, thanks! How are you?' replied Lucy.

'Not bad at all! Maisy is keeping me busy as ever.'

'I'll bet!'

'Work is manic, but I'm sticking to my guns and leaving early so that I can spend time with her in the evenings.'

'Well done you, stay strong. Don't let them bully you into working late; they need to honour the terms they agreed to when you came back.' Her bosses had been giving her a hard time recently, trying to pressurise her into working into the evening with the rest of the team.

'Don't worry, I'm not going to let them take advantage. They know Maisy is my priority and they are just going to have to like it or lump it,' said Nicola firmly. 'How are you feeling, anyway, since the last cycle? You must be nearly ready to do a test, right?'

'I feel fine...' Lucy pondered whether to share her predicament with Nicola, and realized that she would really like her opinion, so she talked through her thoughts on whether to quit IUI to pursue a relationship with Rory. . Nicola listened carefully before offering her opinion.

'Look, Lucy, life has a wonderful way of keeping us on our toes. I know the timing is not exactly ideal, but look at it this way. You want a baby and you want to meet an amazing guy. In the last few weeks you could have achieved both of those goals, admittedly it might not be in the traditional way, but the world is changing. Whatever happens now is in the hands of God. You just have to accept it! There is a Chinese saying that when the sky falls down, you should pretend it's a blanket, it's a bit like blessings coming in disguise. Only good things can come from all this. You'll see! Try not to worry.'

Lucy thanked her for her kind words and realized she felt much better. Trying to control life was impossible, Nicola was right; she just had to roll with it.

'Have you thought more about your own situation?' asked Lucy. Nicola was trying to decide when she was going to start her treatments to try for a brother or sister for Maisy.

'Yes, I have actually. I'm going to start trying in the summer, when things should have calmed down a bit at work,' explained Nicola.

'Okay. Well remember what I said about being there to look after Maisy when you do. I doubt you want her toddling around the treatment room after all!' chuckled Lucy.

'Thanks Lucy. You are a star, I might well take you up on that,' said Nicola.

As they ended their conversation, Lucy set about making some dinner, watched a bit of television and then got ready for bed and an early night. Just as she was settling in under her duvet, her phone started to ring. It was Rory; he was just taking Rufus out for a final walk and was ringing to find out how her day had been. They chatted for twenty minutes or so, making plans to meet at The Troubadour near Earls Court for dinner the next day. Lucy fell asleep with a grin on her face, dreaming of Rory.

On Tuesday, Lucy just couldn't stop smiling at the thought of seeing him again that evening. She found herself humming cheerful tunes at her desk; work suddenly seemed much less of a chore. She was actually enjoying herself for once working on a new campaign that she had just been assigned. She felt as though she was viewing the world through rose-tinted glasses and she loved it.

After work, she dashed for the tube and found herself arriving at The Troubadour a little earlier than expected. The tables of the little bistro were covered in chequered table cloths and the walls were plastered in retro French memorabilia. Her internal butterflies had reached dizzying new heights. Every time the door opened she would lift her eyes in nervous anticipation, expecting Rory to walk through the door. When she realized it was someone else, the disappointment would overwhelm her and she would return to her careful studying of the menu. When he did finally walk in, her heart melted at the sight of his sparkly blue eyes and his broad smile, which widened as he saw her.

Rory came over and kissed her on the lips. The delicious smell of him made her want to run out of the restaurant with him that second, straight home, forgetting about dinner altogether. As he sat down opposite her, tucking his long legs underneath the little, wooden table, she contented herself with drinking in every gorgeous detail of him instead. He began to fill her in on his new project, a commission for a new art gallery in Edinburgh that was to be constructed purely out of metal and glass. As he talked about his ideas, Lucy marvelled at his talent and creativity. She could never dream something up from thin air like that; it was such an incredible skill. The more she found out about Rory the more flawless he seemed to be. She couldn't believe her luck.

For dinner they ate coq au vin with creamy mashed potato and drank glasses of red wine, listening to the band that was playing live in the corner. They talked about their most embarrassing memories, their first kiss, when they lost their virginity and with whom. The more they discovered about each other, the closer they became. They had an endless appetite for talking; no sooner had one topic of conversation finished had they started the next. A thousand questions brewed in Lucy's mind; there was so much she wanted to find out about him. She thought of all those dinners with Alex when he would retreat inwards and barely talk to her. She hadn't thought anything of it at the time but she realized now that she had had nothing like this level of interest in getting to know what really made him tick, what made him who he was. Lucy was beginning to see what her granny had meant all along about Alex not being quite right for her. She wondered how long she should wait until she introduced Rory to her family. She couldn't wait for them to meet him.

The next evening, Lucy and Rory went to the cinema together to watch an Indie flick that Rory had read about in *Time Out*. They sat in the comforting darkness of the movie theatre, sinking back into soft chairs, a huge barrel of popcorn perched between them. As they munched their popcorn and slurped their drinks, they became lost in the virtual world projected on the screen before them, resurfacing a few hours later back into reality, discussing the ins and outs of the plot as they walked hand in hand back to Thurloe Crescent once again. They received another rapturous greeting from Rufus, his tail wagging as he begged to be taken out. Obliging, they walked around the block with him and then settled him into his bed in the kitchen before heading upstairs to bed.

As Rory wrapped her in his arms under the white sheets, every cell in Lucy's body tingled with the warmth of his embrace.

On Thursday morning she got a taxi back to her flat at the crack of dawn, tearing herself away from Rory who was having a mini lie-in, not needing to be in the office until later on. She showered and dressed before heading straight into work. Lucy envied Rory who was no doubt still tucked up in bed as she joined the mindless traffic of commuters heading into the city. But for once, she felt so relaxed that she didn't even mind when her head ended up being rammed too close to a sweaty armpit, choosing instead to retreat inwards into her mind, imagining herself back in the snug king-size bed at Thurloe Crescent.

Rory was at a work event on Thursday evening so Lucy went to see Granny Annie for dinner. They had steak and chips in the studio, followed by apples and ice cream, one of Annie's many specialities. Lucy told her grandmother all about Rory.

'It has to be said, darling, he sounds like just about the most wonderful thing since sliced bread!'

'He is an absolute dream,' said Lucy. 'I can hardly believe my luck.'

'Darling, will you bring him over for dinner next week?' asked Annie.

Normally Lucy would have thought long and hard about introducing someone new to her grandmother, but not this time. 'Absolutely. I'm sure he would love to come!' said Lucy.

'And, darling, now that you have such an eligible man, I do hope that you are putting your crazy ideas about having a baby by yourself to rest?' asked Annie. Lucy had been waiting for this. She had suspected that Annie was particularly thrilled about Rory's arrival on the scene for this exact reason.

'You never know, granny. Perhaps I won't need to be a single mother after all!' said Lucy.

'I must say I'm jolly glad to hear it!' said Annie. 'I couldn't have been more shocked when you told me you were planning on doing it alone. Daft idea... quite extraordinary!'

'Yes, granny, you made that quite clear,' said Lucy, hoping beyond hope that she would never have to face explaining the truth to her grandmother if events did not work out in her favour. She realised just how different her circumstances were this time around as the day she would be able to take a pregnancy test approached once again. She suddenly found herself unsure as to whether she would prefer to be pregnant or not.

Ginny had made her nightly telephone call to her mother between courses, so Lucy had also finally filled her in about Rory too, playing the romance down as much as possible, determined not to raise her mother's hopes. Ginny sounded terribly excited nonetheless. And like Granny Annie, asked Lucy whether she was still going to pursue the 'donor route', as Ginny referred to it, now that she had met a nice young man. Ginny and Gus didn't realize that she had received another round of treatment earlier in the month, and Lucy hadn't enlightened them. She merely told her mother that all plans were on hold for a while, to which she could hear her mother's audible sigh of relief.

Kissing her grandmother goodbye after dinner, she headed towards home, flagging down a black cab as she went. She called Rory and passed on Annie's dinner invitation. He was delighted to accept, having heard so much about the infamous Annie. They planned to have a night in at Rory's house the next day before going to the pub on Saturday, as promised, with Claudia and Dan. Lucy couldn't wait to see the look on Claudia's face when she saw him. She knew that they would get on incredibly well.

Chapter Twenty-Eight

Having spent the whole of Friday night and Saturday cocooned in the love shack that Rory's house had become, wrapped up in the all-consuming mutual adoration that was peculiar to lovers still dazzled by new romance, it was with reluctance that they geared up for their night out in the real world. They had barely left the house. Lucy had decided to see whether her period came the next day rather than going out to buy a pregnancy test. She was always extremely regular, so she knew that if she was late she could then take a test to confirm whether she was pregnant. The outcome didn't feel quite as critical now. She still wanted to be a mother, of course, but now that she had Rory she realised she was prepared to wait a while.

Lucy was very excited at the prospect of Claudia and Dan meeting Rory. Her best friend's approval was of paramount importance to her. She knew that as soon as other people got to know him and see for themselves what an incredible man he was, the more real it would become for her. She might be able to stop pinching herself at her astounding good luck in finding him.

Rory continued to amaze her on a daily basis. Physically, he was such a strong and striking man, yet he was so kind and vulnerable underneath. He had endless time for her. He had told her that this was the first time he had really let someone in, let someone get to know the real him, since Abigail died, and she was so glad that he had chosen her to be the one to do so. When he gave her his attention she felt as though he was thinking of nothing else apart from what she was saying, as though there was nowhere in the world he would rather be, no one else in the world he would rather be with. She had heard him on the phone talking to his various family members, giving the same tenderness and affection whether he was talking to Trina and Paddy, his brothers or sister, or any one of his numerous nephews and nieces. Occasionally he would just double up with laugher, a booming deep laugh that would reverberate around the room, echoing warmth through the house, and Lucy would find herself laughing along with him, having no idea what about. It was contagious.

They had developed a jokey banter between them, lightly teasing each other and steadily building up the foundations of a deep friendship, which felt as secure and unshakeable as her relationships with Claudia and Tor.

On Saturday lunchtime, Lucy called Claudia to confirm their plans to meet up that evening.

'Luce?' said Claudia, answering the phone at the first ring.

'Hi Clauds,' said Lucy. 'Are you excited?'

'OMG I can't wait!' shrieked Claudia. 'I feel like I'm going on a first date… I'm nervous!'

'Steady on, Clauds, he *is* taken you know!' laughed Lucy. 'As are you, need I remind you?'

'I know, I know! Dan thinks I'm completely crackers. He just sounds so great and I'm so happy for you. It's too exciting!'

'So where do you want to meet?' asked Lucy.

'Mmmm, not sure. Where's convenient?' asked Claudia.

'I reckon Putney is about halfway.'

'How about the Rose and Chalice?'

'Brilliant, I love that pub,' agreed Lucy.

'Cool, see you later then,' said Claudia, getting ready to hang up the phone.

'Wait… *wait!*' said Lucy, lowering her voice so that Rory couldn't hear her. 'Remember, Clauds, not a word about *anything.* I mean it.' She hated the fact that she wasn't being completely open with Rory, especially when he had been so honest with her about Abigail, but she didn't want to scare him away when there was no indication at this stage that she was even pregnant.

'Yes, yes, I know. I mustn't mention a thing,' said Claudia, having already been lectured several times about the impossibility of Rory finding out a single detail of donor insemination gate.

'See you later,' said Lucy.

'Byeee! Can't wait!' added Claudia, blowing kisses down the phone.

That evening Rory and Lucy both had showers before getting ready to head out, Rory going first and Lucy, for once, managing to resist his persuasive offers to join him, knowing that would make them very late indeed. Later, as she emerged with pink cheeks in a cloud of billowing steam from the en suite into the bedroom, she was greeted by the sight of Rory, his white towel wrapped around his hips, doing a Michael Jackson impersonation to 'Thriller' which was playing on the radio. Not wishing to be outdone, she joined him, moonwalking across the floor, her hair in a turban like the Queen of Sheba, prompting an energetic dance off that ended up with both Rory and Lucy collapsed on the bed, trying to catch their breath through hysterical laughter.

'I definitely beat you,' said Rory, bending over her and kissing her on the neck.

'You did *not!*' shrieked Lucy. 'My moves are *much* better than yours!'

'Oh, *really*... well we'll have to see about that!' chuckled Rory, showing her exactly what moves he was talking about.

Shoving him off her, Lucy screeched, 'Rory! You are incorrigible! Not now... we're going to be so late!'

'But you're so irresistible, it's not my fault!' complained Rory, a wicked glint in his eye, trying to tug her towel down.

Wriggling out of his grasp and bolting to her overnight bag that was lying in the corner of the room, she promised him that he could have his wicked way with her later if he got a move on now. She pulled on a set of matching underwear and a royal blue patterned dress, spraying herself with perfume and running a comb through her hair. No straighteners would mean she would have to embrace her natural wavy hair, but she felt confident enough to go au naturel with Rory, having crossed that bridge early on thanks to the rainstorm. She couldn't believe it was only last Saturday when they had got together, it seemed like months ago!

Rory pulled on his trusty jeans, some loafers and a pale blue shirt that brought out the striking colour of his eyes, then tousled his fingers through his hair, declaring himself good to go. Lucy's stomach flipped at the sight of him, she couldn't wait to see Claudia's jaw hit the floor.

Having finished off her make-up while Rory took Rufus out for a quick walk around the block, they were ready to leave. They hailed a taxi and set off for the pub.

The Rose and Chalice had such a rustic, cosy atmosphere, complete with burning fires and comfortable looking sofas, that it felt like an authentic country pub. Lucy began scanning the faces scattered about the place, looking for one she recognized, but she needn't have bothered... Claudia's shriek would have been audible across the river! Following the ear-piercing decibels, they spotted Claudia and Dan sitting at a table near the fireplace at the back of the pub, already halfway through their first drink.

They made their way through the crowded pub to their table, being careful not to nudge any drinks over as they did so. Lucy clocked Claudia's gobsmacked expression at the sight of Rory, which, with a well-timed elbow in the ribs from Dan, she hastily rearranged into a normal smile. Both Claudia and Dan stood up to kiss Lucy and greet Rory, welcoming them and exchanging the usual platitudes of 'Nice to meet you' et cetera. Lucy was so proud to be here with such an incredible catch, she could feel the envious eyes of all the other women on her back, and felt a wave of smugness rise within her. She had been very impressed with the confident way in which Rory had introduced himself, firmly shaking both Claudia and Dan's hand, saying their names whilst looking them directly in the eye. He asked Lucy what she would like to drink and offered to buy another round for Claudia and Dan, before turning to weave his way back through to the bar.

Immediately, Claudia burst out with, 'Oh my god, he is just divine! You lucky cow!' to which Dan retorted, 'Easy, Clauds or I'll start to get jealous!'

Lucy beamed. 'I told you he was good-looking!' she said as she helped herself to a handful of salt and vinegar crisps from the packet that was lying open on the table. She was really craving salty food at the moment, and thought she might get some chips with her meal to hit the spot. 'I'm starving... in fact I think I'll go and get some menus and help Rory carry your drinks. You're eating right?' she asked.

'Definitely,' replied Dan, peering over her shoulder to scan the specials that were chalked up on the blackboard.

Lucy joined Rory at the bar and grabbed a couple of menus from the stand, tucking them under her arm then waiting for the barman to pull their pints.

'They seem like a lovely couple!' said Rory. 'And this pub is a great find. The food looks amazing… check out that burger over there,' he said, pointing over at a table to their left where a tower of pulled pork was spilling over a brioche bun.

'Oh yum! I might have to get one of those,' agreed Lucy, taking the two glasses of wine and following Rory back over to Claudia and Dan.

'Here we go!' announced Rory. 'Yours was the Guinness right?' he joked with Dan, before proffering a lager. 'Only having a laugh, we Irish aren't all as obsessed with the black stuff as you might think, you know!'

They settled into a happy chat about Ireland. Dan had been on a recent work trip to Dublin which had included an enlightening tour around the Guinness factory. Claudia asked Rory all about his family, clearly doing her best to get as much information out of him as possible, eager to size him up. She shrieked with disbelief when she heard that he had seven nephews and nieces; three from his sister and four from his older brother.

'Wow! I think having one nephew is more than enough responsibility for me!' said Claudia, referring to Sebastian, now, incredibly, over one year old already.

'I don't think anyone would disagree with you, Clauds!' laughed Lucy. 'You're not exactly what I would describe as a natural with kids after all…'

Rory asked Claudia and Dan what they did for a living, showing interest in hearing about their respective careers, asking plenty of questions.

As their food arrived, they passed out cutlery and condiments, marvelling at the mouth-watering pies and burgers. During dinner the conversation moved on to Rory and his architecture and Lucy began to tell them about his amazing house in Holland Park. Claudia was fascinated to hear about the development of the house from its less than desirable beginnings: her father had run a business renovating properties for years. As the conversation flowed, Lucy sat back and admired Rory, his endearing self-deprecation, the way the vowels rolled lazily off his tongue and those frequent bouts of deep laughter. She loved listening to all his anecdotes about life and could tell that both Claudia and Dan were held captive by him too.

The two couples ordered a round of highly calorific desserts followed by coffees. By this time the alcohol had loosened their tongues and, as was so often the case, lowered the tone of the conversation. It was always at this stage of the night that Claudia was at her most hilarious, with Dan her witty sidekick, and she had all of their attention gripped as she described a recent sex-tape scandal at work that would have had even the most liberal of people blushing to the very roots of their hair!

As the pub began to close, they spilled out onto the pavement along with the other punters, kissing each other goodbye and promising to organize another date for the diary soon.

Claudia hugged Lucy tight and whispered in her ear, 'This is it, I think it really is *it!*'

Lucy beamed at her friend. If anything tonight had confirmed what she was beginning to suspect, that this really was different, that Rory really could be the one she had been waiting for.

Chapter Twenty-Nine

On Sunday morning Lucy was rudely awakened by Rufus's sandpapery tongue licking her toes as they stuck out of the end of the duvet. He had somehow made his way up into the bedroom. Groaning, she whipped her feet back into the warmth and safety of her bedcovers and tried to shoo Rufus back downstairs to his bed. Hearing a wry chuckle, she opened one eye and peered out into the light of a new day. Rory was standing by the open door, his tall frame leaning against the wall, an eyebrow raised and a smile spreading across his cheeks.

'Up you get sleepyhead!' he sang.

'Nooo…' whined Lucy, burying herself deeper into hibernation and asking in a muffled voice from beneath the duvet, 'what are you doing up at this hour on a Sunday morning anyway, you crazy man?'

'We're going on an adventure!' said Rory. Rufus was wagging his tail so loudly in appreciation of this early morning activity that Lucy could feel it whipping against the valance beneath her.

'Really? Now?!' asked Lucy, still firmly ensconced in bed. 'Can't we have a lie-in first?' she pleaded.

Suddenly the duvet had been sliced off the bed and Rory was poking her. 'Up, up, up!' he chanted, aiming for the ticklish side of her tummy. That did the trick, along with the cold blast of fresh air that was nipping at her skin; Lucy was out of bed like a shot.

'Okay, okay... where are we going?' she asked, flicking her fringe out of her eyes, feeling abnormally exhausted considering she hadn't drunk more than a couple of glasses of wine the night before.

'It's a surprise. Somewhere cool, that's all you need to know!' announced Rory. 'Jump in the shower and get dressed, I'll take Rufus out and see you back here ready to go at nine?!'

'Okay boss,' Lucy said, giving him a weary salute. Despite her protestation, she loved him for his spontaneity and sense of fun; you never knew what he was going to do next, that was for sure.

As always the hot pelts of water that sluiced over her body reinvigorated her. The fresh mint shower gel that she rubbed all over her skin made each cell tingle in preparation for the day ahead. She dried her hair vigorously with a towel before running a comb through it, detangling it as best she could and then brushing her teeth. Prepared for anything, she pulled on a pair of jeans, a red cashmere jumper and a pair of worn-out, old ankle boots. She did her make-up and gave her hair a final rub, trying to squeeze the water droplets out so that she didn't catch a cold... there was no such thing as a hair dryer to be found at Thurloe Crescent, it occurred to her that she might have to rectify that soon.

Still yawning, she went downstairs and made herself a coffee while she waited for Rory and Rufus to return from their walk. Despite the light drizzle that had lasted for most of the day yesterday, Sunday had dawned bright and crisp, a perfect start to February, full of promise of the coming season.

Lucy pondered where Rory might be taking her as she caught up on the news on the BBC. She checked her phone for messages, having received some lovely texts from Claudia last night singing Rory's praises, and noticed that she rarely felt the need to log onto her favourite social media sites any longer, her go-to iPhone apps of Facebook and Instagram hadn't been accessed for quite some time. Not to mention Tinder, she cringed at the thought of her awful date with that guy Ted. Perhaps she had finally got bored of snooping on other people's affairs, or maybe it was because her life was now so full and happy in itself that she no longer had any need for it. Her lifelong obsession with comparing herself to others appeared to have come to an end, a wonderful side effect of getting older, she mused.

Just then the front door banged shut, rousing her from her thoughts. Rory called her name to see whether she was still upstairs. Answering back, she tipped out her coffee and put her cup into the dishwasher before traipsing up the corridor to meet him in the hall. They were taking Rufus with them, it seemed, and travelling to their mysterious destination by car. Lucy clambered into the front of Rory's Audi A3, Rufus lying down across the back seats as Rory revved the engine, pulling his sunglasses down over his eyes as he did so.

They drove through the streets of London, blissfully empty in the early hours of Sunday morning, and listened to the strains of Steve Wright's Sunday Love Songs. Rory accompanied each song, with Lucy doing her best to join in. They laughed at her unbelievably bad knowledge of song lyrics. Rory stopped frequently to ask her what she thought the words were to some of the most famous songs, correcting her moments later with something blindingly obvious and completely different. He told her that he preferred her versions, they were much more amusing.

They continued driving east for about forty minutes before Rory pulled over and parked on an empty street in the middle of Tower Hamlets. With Rufus on the lead, they walked down

Baxendale Street, the sun still shining proudly in a clear stretch of blue sky. As they neared the end of the road, Lucy began to hear what sounded like the hustle and bustle of a market up ahead. They turned into Columbia Road where they were instantly hit by a wall of riotous colour, an assault on the senses. The chatter of market shoppers mingled with the sing-song calls of East Londoners selling their wares. Lucy could not believe it: as far as the eye could see the street was lined with thousands upon thousands of flowers of all sizes, colour and description. Huge sunflowers as big as footballs unfurled their sunshine yellow leaves, their necks twisting towards the light from thick green stems. Stalls with every herb known to mankind filled the air with their aromatic aroma: purple sage, sweet basil, lemon thyme and coriander to name but a few. Calla lilies and amaryllis, shamrocks and chrysanthemums nestled next to towering ten foot banana trees. The barrow boys' rhythmic chanting of 'Everything a fiver!' punctuated the chatter of shoppers at regular intervals.

As Lucy feasted her eyes on her surroundings she turned to Rory and kissed him, 'I *love* this place!' she grinned. 'It's my idea of heaven!'

Rory smiled at her, his arm around her shoulders, saying, 'I had a sneaking suspicion you might say that! Now let's walk all the way around the market, and you better choose the ones you like best, cos I'm going to *fill* your house with flowers when we get home!'

Lucy clapped her hands in anticipation, giving him another kiss and declaring him to be officially the best boyfriend in the entire world.

Upon hearing the word boyfriend, Rory spun her around to face him, raising an eyebrow and saying, 'So I'm your boyfriend, am I?!'

Lucy blushed as she realised that she may have jumped the gun a little. 'Do you want to be?' she asked somewhat hesitantly.

'Are you kidding? I would like nothing more!' he said, bending down to kiss her. He spun her around in delight. Rufus was bemused at all the kerfuffle but wagged his tail happily.

Soon, Lucy and Rory's arms were both full with huge bunches of flowers, bursting from their sheaths of brown paper and tied with long strands of hessian. They stopped at the edge of the market and stacked their bundles of flowers high up against the wall, ordering coffees from a little cafe and perching on stools that wobbled precariously on the pavement. They sipped their drinks and people-watched, absorbing the wondrous scene before them and marvelling at the variety and infinite beauty of nature, so very evident here.

Lucy thanked Rory again for bringing her and made him promise that they would come here all the time now that she had discovered it. They watched the crowds of shoppers passing by, Rufus sitting happily at their feet. A young family caught her eye, the toddler holding his mother and father's hands as they swung him in the air, ruddy cheeks glowing as he laughed in delight. Lucy found herself caught unawares by an overwhelming pang of longing for a baby. She wondered whether Rory had similar thoughts. Meeting him had changed everything for her, but it hadn't lessened her desire to become a mother. If anything, it had almost made it stronger, as she felt so secure and settled in her new relationship. She suddenly realised that her period hadn't arrived. It was due today but she had forgotten all about it in the madness of the morning. The thought that it might be late terrified and excited in her in equal measure. She promised herself that she would take a pregnancy test at work the very next morning if it hadn't come by then, though she was sure that it would have. Her body was no doubt slightly out of sync with all the excitement of these last couple of weeks with Rory. She didn't want to do it when she was with him, anyway.

After a while, they walked back through the throngs of people towards the car, the Victorian buildings of Columbia Road a striking backdrop to the endless market stalls. They piled the bouquets into the boot, momentarily cutting off their supply of sunshine for the journey home.

Having made it back across London to Mayfield Road, they burst into the flat balancing bags, flowers and Rufus, while somehow managing to keep hold of Lucy's keys. The sun was streaming in through the windows. Rufus went over to his now familiar makeshift bed and settled down for a rest after the excitement of the car journey. Lucy and Rory cut the ends off the stems of each gigantic bunch of flowers and arranged them into all sorts of containers and vases, filling every nook and cranny of the flat. It looked as though a florist had exploded. Lucy had never seen her flat look so beautiful! Within minutes, the room was filled with the sweet perfume of the flowers' scent. As they stood back to admire their handiwork, Lucy's mobile rang.

'Hello?' she said as she pressed the green button on her handset.

'Hi darling, it's Tor! How are you? What are you up to?' she asked.

'Oh we've just been to the most amazing place in the whole world, Columbia Road Flower Market. Have you ever been?'

'Oooh… I've heard about it but no, never been. Is it wonderful?'

'It's breathtaking! My house looks like the Eden Project, I've got so many flowers here, you have to come over and see it!'

'I'm having tea with mum in Hammersmith this afternoon, why don't I pop over on the way? I feel like it's been a while since I've seen you and you can see your godson too!'

'Great idea! Come over whenever you want. We'll just be having some lunch.'

'We?! Does that mean I'm going to get to meet the mysterious Rory then?' asked Tor, clearly delighted at the prospect.

'If you're lucky!' chuckled Lucy, winking at Rory who could overhear their entire conversation.

'Well now just try and stop me!' cried Tor. 'I'll be there within the hour; it takes me an age to get out of the house with all the baby crap.'

'Okay Tor, see you when I see you,' said Lucy.

After that they nipped out to the local deli and bought some salads for lunch and a loaf of sourdough bread from the bakery. Lucy heated up some chicken mulligatawny and they dunked their crusty slices of bread into the creamy soup. They had picked up the Sunday papers and read them while they ate, Rory starting with the real news and Lucy with the supplements before swapping over... Lucy was now determined to keep up with Rory's impressive knowledge of current affairs.

She hadn't been feeling quite herself that morning so she declined Rory's offer of coffee opting instead for a pint of Berocca to try and give her immune system a boost. The liquids seemed to rush straight through her and suddenly she found herself desperate for the loo.

To her surprise and disappointment Lucy found that her period had started. Her eyes filled with tears. Her head started to spin with a mixture of emotions at the realization that once again she was not pregnant. She hadn't been thinking about it nearly as much as she had done in the two weeks that followed each previous cycle. She had spent more time and energy convincing herself that what would be would be, but now that the reality hit her she felt absolutely devastated. The by-now familiar and all-encompassing disappointment of yet another failed round of treatment washed over her like a tide of despair, rising up through her body and spilling out in her tears. It was bitter and almost tangible in its strength. She forced herself to try and be positive: this clearly hadn't been the plan for her. And anyway now she had Rory, maybe she was meant to have a baby with Rory instead, following the traditional route of falling in love, marriage and starting a family. She dreaded to think how she would have broached the subject with Rory had she been pregnant and felt the tiniest flicker of relief that now she would never have to.

She splashed water on her face and took a deep breath. There was nothing to be done but to resign her future to the fates. Life really was full of surprises, she thought. You could plan all you liked but it did no good. She remembered an old poster that she used to have blu-tacked to her bedroom wall saying, 'Life was what happened when you were busy making other plans!' It was true, she thought as she looked at her reflection in the mirror, wiping the tears away. She knew now was not the time to sort through the puzzling and conflicting feelings that were currently zooming through her head like a snowstorm. She pushed them to one side and promised herself she would process it all properly the next time she was by herself. Rory, and Tor's imminent arrival, were far too much of a distraction for any serious soul-searching to take place at this precise moment.

About an hour after Tor's phone call, as predicted, the doorbell rang. Lucy buzzed Tor in and she stomped up the stairs heaving Otto in his little car seat under one arm. Lucy felt her eyes smart furiously at the sight of baby Otto, the bittersweet realization that she was not pregnant swung dramatically towards disappointment at the sight of her godson. Pulling herself together, Lucy offered to help. Tor insisted on lugging it all the way up, saying it was the only exercise she got, eventually arriving at the top of the steps with slightly red cheeks, huffing and puffing. Brushing her blonde curls out of her eyes and kissing her friend hello, she walked into the flat to find Rory waiting to greet her.

'You must be Tor,' he said warmly, giving her a kiss on both cheeks as she said, 'Nice to meet you, Rory!'

'And you, little man, must be the famous Otto that your godmother has told me so much about! I can see why, he's darn cute!' said Rory as he tousled the baby's slightly ginger hair.

Otto gurgled in response, a spit bubble forming on his rose-bud lips, before a beaming smile spread across his chubby cheeks.

'He loves you!' said Tor. 'He doesn't smile for just anyone, you know.'

'He's grand!' said Rory. He seemed genuinely interested in little Otto.

'Can I hold him?' asked Lucy, feeling very hormonal all of a sudden.

'Be my guest!' replied Tor as she unclipped the strap around Otto's chest, releasing him from the car seat. Lucy picked him up and held him out in front of her, kissing his soft little cheeks and cooing over his beautiful blue eyes. 'I can't believe how much he has grown!' she said to Tor.

'Tell me about it!' Tor rolled her eyes and collapsed onto the sofa.

'Would you like a cup of tea?' asked Rory.

'I'm absolutely gasping for one, thank you. I haven't had a second to make one for myself all day.'

'Where's Will?' asked Lucy.

'Oh he's away on business so I'm coping with Otto all by myself, lucky me! The flowers are stunning by the way. You're right, Luce, it is like the Eden Project in here!'

'I know, I'm a lucky girl!' grinned Lucy, reminding herself to count her considerable blessings.

'I'll say!' agreed Tor with a wink, mouthing, 'In more ways than one!' while Rory busied himself in the kitchen.

Rory came over to join them with a tray of biscuits and three cups of steaming tea.

Tor thanked him as she took a sip, relaxing back into the cushions and heaving a deep sigh of relief. 'It's so nice not to have to be in charge!' she said, yawning. 'You just keep hold of him for me! Don't mind me if I nod off... I'm so sleep-deprived!'

'We'll look after him, don't worry. I absolutely adore children, and so, it would seem, does Lucy. You should let us babysit for you!' suggested Rory. 'Give yourself a break.'

'Definitely!' said Lucy. 'I love looking after him, anytime, just give us a call.'

'Thanks guys, I really appreciate it,' said Tor gratefully.

Lucy knew that Tor was absolutely dying to quiz her to find out whether she had done her pregnancy test yet, but thankfully she was too discreet to try and ask her anything so personal in front of Rory, particularly given the dilemma Lucy had recently explained over the phone. She decided she would text her the news that she was not pregnant later. If she told her that she had got her period, she might well up and burst into tears. She felt extremely hormonal, the usual PMT undoubtedly kicking in.

Rory took Otto from Lucy and bounced him on his knees, provoking another bout of rapturous giggles from the baby who was as smitten with Rory as his godmother, and mother, appeared to be. Tor praised him on his natural ease with babies, saying it was quite unusual in her experience for men that didn't have any children of their own. Rory explained that he had seven nephews and nieces and was therefore an experienced uncle.

'It's easy!' said Rory. 'You just bounce them around, chuck them up in the air, or fly them like superman. In my experience, one of the above normally gets a baby to stop crying sooner rather than later.'

Watching him with Otto, Lucy felt another pang of sadness stab through her.

'He's the baby whisperer!' laughed Tor as Otto began to close his eyes.

The three of them dunked their biscuits in their piping hot cups of tea and chatted for an hour or so before Tor announced that she had better go if she was going to make it to her mother's and back ready for bedtime. Gathering all her stuff together, she put Otto back into his car seat and clipped his little safety belt together. Unfortunately, Rufus, who had been sleeping docilely in his bed the whole time that Tor and Otto had been in the room, chose that exact moment to bound out of his bed straight over to the baby. Whisking Otto up and out of Rufus's reach, Rory offered to carry him down to the car for Tor, and so the three of them made their way outside, with

Lucy clutching on awkwardly to Rufus's collar in case he took his liberty too seriously and ran away.

As they waved Tor off with Otto safely ensconced in the back seat and Rufus straining to chase after the car, Rory turned to Lucy and said, 'Your friends are so lovely! I think it's about time you met some of mine.' He looked at her with a mischievous grin, adding, 'Though I wouldn't want you to be put off now, would I?'

Lucy shoved him and said, 'Why would I be put off? Are they going to reveal all sorts of dark and mysterious secrets about you that I haven't found out yet?' She laughed as she kicked the front door shut behind her with her boot. Rufus rocketed forward like an uncoiled spring as she released her grip and bounded up the stairs with the agility and speed of a greyhound.

'Well, you'll have to wait and see! I'll text Ben now and see if I can organize something for the weekend,' said Rory, pulling his phone out of his jeans pocket.

Lucy knew all about Ben. He had been Rory's best man when he married Abigail. Rory had talked to her about the wedding a couple of times, and as always whenever she thought of Abigail Lucy felt moved to the point of tears. She couldn't bear what he had been through. She felt nothing but sadness on their behalf, laced with a touch of gratitude that, though she wouldn't have wished it on anyone, least of all Rory, she was able to be with him now. Ben was a friend of theirs from University College London, now a successful doctor married to an Australian physiotherapist called Chrissie, and with three children to boot. Lucy had heard lots about him and the rest of their university gang and couldn't wait to meet them. She suggested that they hosted a dinner party at Thurloe Crescent, which Rory thought was a fantastic idea. He tapped at the screen and sent Ben a message, trying to ignore Rufus who was running about like a headless chicken, clearly full of far too much energy having spent the afternoon cooped up inside.

While he was texting Ben, Lucy swallowed her disappointment and sent a message to Tor, Claudia and Nicola explaining that she had got her period. She tried to put a positive spin on the news, asking them not to worry, saying that it was probably for the best now that she had found Rory. She knew she was trying to convince herself more than her friends. They all pinged messages back agreeing that it was for the best, hoping that she was okay and asking her to call when she was next free.

By this stage Rufus was about to explode with pent-up energy, so they decided to take him out for a late afternoon walk. Nipping into the bedroom, Lucy changed into her trainers and pulled on a warm gilet to protect herself against the evening chill. If she was coming down with something that was the last thing she needed.

They strolled around the block and into the local park, letting Rufus off the lead and watching him bound like a cheetah across the expanse of green grass, revelling in the space around him. Lucy and Rory walked hand in hand through the park, admiring the changing colours of twilight, that warm glow that bathed everything around them in a blanket of hazy light as though someone was twisting a giant dimmer switch up above them.

As they walked, Lucy asked Rory to tell him about how he had met Abigail. Rory obliged and began to describe their first encounter, two fresh-faced, rosy-cheeked freshers, innocent and nervous in equal measure as their friendship, forged over pints of lager in the union bar, slowly developed into something more. Rory, fresh off the plane from Ireland, was infatuated by this freckly, green-eyed redhead and her English accent. Abigail was equally blown away by Rory. They had lived together in their second year with Ben and a couple of other medics, including their close friend Ed, before moving in on their own during their final year at UCL, getting married soon after graduation.

'Have you ever considered getting married, Luce?' asked Rory.

'I've always wanted to get married,' replied Lucy. 'And I always assumed that I would…'

'Did you ever come close?'

'I suppose Alex was the closest I ever got to seriously considering it,' said Lucy. 'But that didn't end so well. All in all, I guess the right man has just never come along.'

When she said that, Rory looked at her long and hard and said, 'Do you still believe that?' He held her hand softly as he spoke and she felt as though the rest of the world surrounding them just melted away, that they were locked in a bubble of their own creation.

'I'm not sure,' she replied, barely able to process the hidden meaning behind his question, a flutter of excitement flickering through her like flames licking at burning coal. In response, he kissed her. It was such a tender, soft kiss that she felt her insides dissolve.

Lucy felt a calm sense of reassurance settle over her like a blanket. With Rory by her side, she felt utterly protected, as though she could survive anything, that no matter what happened, she would be okay.

Chapter Thirty

The following day Lucy had a much-needed evening in to sort through some admin at home. Rory had some work to finish and so he was spending the evening at Thurloe Crescent. Though Lucy would prefer to be with him she was looking forward to having some time to sort through some of the domestic chores she had been neglecting of late.

At seven thirty the doorbell rang. She skipped over to the intercom with a smile on her face, assuming that Rory had been unable to resist and had decided to come over and surprise her. 'Hello?' she said as she held down the intercom. It was so crackly she could barely hear anything other than a garbled male voice rustling down the line. She held down the buzzer and left the door ajar, rushing back to the hob to lower the heat on the soup she was making for her dinner.

There was a knock at the door, which was odd, seeing as she had left it ajar. Suddenly on alert that it may not be Rory, she rushed back to the door, ready to defend herself from an unwanted visitor and kicking herself for not getting the intercom repaired.

As she pulled open the door, the person she saw standing there was the last person in the world she had been expecting. Her heart skipped a beat and her stomach lurched at the unexpected sight of him. She couldn't have been more shocked to see him standing there. 'Alex!' she said. 'What are you doing here?'

'Hi Lucy, I'm sorry to turn up unannounced. Can I come in?'

'Err…' She wasn't sure. 'I suppose so.'

He took a step forward and came into the sitting room.

She felt unbelievably awkward in his presence. 'What do you want?' she stammered. She couldn't think of a single reason why he would turn up out of the blue like this. Her head was spinning slightly as she took in his once so familiar features, now strangely unfamiliar. She had only seen him on Facebook since they had broken up. It was as if she was seeing him in a dream or a memory, not in real life.

'I just wanted to talk to you,' he said, somewhat nervously. 'Can we sit down?'

'Sure,' she said, intrigued to find out what he had to say for himself.

He sat on the sofa and she sat down on the chair next to it.

'I didn't know if you'd answer the phone if I called, it's been so long…' he tailed off.

'It has,' she agreed.

'I drove past and saw that your light was on so I knew you must be in, I guess I just took a chance and rung the bell, hoping you'd agree to see me.'

'The intercom is broken, I actually thought you were someone else…' said Lucy unapologetically.

'Oh. Are you expecting someone?'

'Not especially.'

'Right.' They sat in awkward silence for a few minutes before Alex plucked up the courage to speak. 'I guess I just wanted to apologize for everything I did to you. I have felt so guilty. You were nothing but amazing to me and I treated you badly, I know that now… I was moody, work-obsessed… I'm surprised you didn't kick me out yourself.'

Lucy was amazed at this apology. She still couldn't get used to him sitting on her sofa, being in her flat. It was hard to believe that he used to live there. 'I see. Well thanks... I guess?' she said.

'The thing is, Lucy, I've been doing a lot of thinking recently. I was wondering, hoping, if maybe...we could give things another go?' He looked up at her with his brown eyes full of hope, yet nervous at the same time.

Lucy couldn't believe what she was hearing. The words that she had so desperately longed to hear for all those months, which would once have been music to her ears, now just seemed ridiculous. 'Another go?!' she repeated, incredulous.

'The thing is... I think I just freaked out. I really loved you but I don't think I was ready to commit. I think I just ran away because I was too afraid. I thought I could love someone more, but I know now that I was wrong. There is no one out there better for me than you. I don't think I'll ever find someone as good for me and I just hope that I'm not too late... that you might consider giving me another chance?'

Lucy felt a little bit sorry for him sitting there, wearing his heart on his sleeve, but his words just left her cold inside. And at the same time slightly offended. She didn't believe what he was saying, not for one second. She knew that he was probably feeling sorry for himself and a bit lonely, and he obviously thought she was an easy bet, that he could click his fingers and come crawling back with his tail between his legs. Well she wasn't that woman anymore. Even if she hadn't met Rory, who was so incomparably amazing, so completely out of Alex's league in every way, she wouldn't have bought his sob story. She was not going to accept anything like this as good enough for her. She wanted to be with someone who couldn't live without her, not someone who would settle for her because they hadn't met someone better.

'Alex, I'm sorry but it's far too little too late. I've moved on. And, to be perfectly honest, I don't think we were ever right for each other in the first place. I see that now. I was so in love with you at the time, I couldn't see our relationship clearly, but with distance I know it was far from perfect. It just wasn't good enough, I need so much more than that. I *deserve* so much more than that.'

'I know you do... that's why I want you to give me another chance. I'll change. I'll be better this time, I promise. I've missed you so much.'

'I'm sorry but no. I'm seeing someone else, anyway, as it happens. And he's amazing. I wish you the best of luck, I really do, but now I'd like you to leave.' Lucy stood up and walked over to the door. She had nothing else to say to him. She just wanted him to get out of her flat as quickly as possible.

He nodded his head. 'I see,' said Alex sadly. He stood up and walked over to the door. 'You're probably right. I'm sure there are many guys out there who are much better than me...'

She didn't want to encourage his self-pity so she just stood there, holding the door open.

'Goodbye Alex,' she said firmly.

'Goodbye Lucy.' He looked at her sadly, hesitating as to whether to kiss her or not. He obviously thought better of it and walked through the door, taking one last look around her flat as he left.

She shut the door quickly behind him, her heart pounding. She couldn't believe what had just happened. Walking back to the sofa where Alex had just been sitting, she sat down heavily. She went over the conversation once again, marvelling at his audacity to turn up unannounced like that and casually ask for her back, as though nothing had ever happened, as if none of this time had passed. The cheek of it! Seeing him again confirmed what she had suspected, Rory already meant more to her than Alex had ever done. She never felt on her guard with him, she was so relaxed in his company. He didn't have any character traits that she disliked. His personality was so unselfish, so genuine and he was such a positive guy. Alex had been the opposite and she thanked her lucky stars that she could now see him and their relationship for exactly what they were.

She picked up the phone and called Claudia. 'You'll never guess who's just been around...' Lucy said.

'Who?' asked Claudia.

'Alex!'

'Alex? No way! Why? What did he want?' she asked, clearly shocked.

'He asked me to give him another chance,' said Lucy, still unable to believe it.

'What? That's ridiculous. As if you would take him back after everything he did to you!'

'I know!'

'Did you tell him to get lost?' asked Claudia.

'Of course I did! Even if I didn't have Rory I would have... the audacity of the guy!'

'What did he say exactly?'

'That he's realized I was as good as he'd get, basically, and would I be happy to try again on those oh-so-flattering terms.'

'Idiot!' said Claudia. 'Dan said that he's been feeling pretty down recently, but he had no idea that he was going to turn up on your doorstep! If he had given me an inkling that he suspected that, I would have told you, obviously...'

'I know you would have, Clauds. It's just so odd to think how much I once prayed that he would do exactly that. Now everything is so different, *I'm* so different...'

'And you've got Rory… much more importantly!'

'Yes thank god for that too…'

'Did you tell Alex about him?'

'I said I was seeing someone.'

'Well at least that should shut him up. Hopefully he got the message.'

'Exactly.'

'Are you going to tell Rory?'

'I'm not sure,' said Lucy.

In the end she did tell him when he phoned her later on in the evening, just as she had tucked herself up in bed. She played the whole episode down and reassured him that she hadn't even considered saying yes for a millisecond, that she was completely over him and that she was really only interested in one man, and one man only.

'I'm glad to hear it,' said Rory. 'I couldn't bear to lose you now that I have finally found you. It sounds lame, but I honestly didn't know if I'd ever meet someone I could trust, someone I liked, after losing Abi…'

'I know. And I promise you, I'm not going anywhere,' she said. 'You're stuck with me now, for as long as you want me!'

'You'd better get very used to me then!' he laughed. They talked for a while longer before hanging up the phone.

Lucy dozed sleepily, dreaming of Rory morphing into Alex and back again as she allowed her mind to drift off into a deep sleep.

Chapter Thirty-One

On Wednesday evening, Rory had been invited to dinner at Lucy's grandmother's house in Chelsea. Lucy had been looking forward to it all week, glad that she had something positive to focus on after the disappointment of realising yet again that she wasn't pregnant. Annie had been calling her daily to confirm that the meal was still going ahead, to discuss the menu and to make sure that she had written down the right time to expect them in her diary. Lucy promised her grandmother that they would both be there by 7.30 p.m. and that they were very much looking forward to it. She was sure that Rory and Annie would get on like a house on fire.

She met Rory at the tube and they walked to Annie's little studio together. Lucy was carrying a big bunch of lilies and Rory had bought a bottle of champagne, a sure-fire way to win over her grandmother. They walked down the narrow streets lined with mews cottages, peeping through the windows as they passed by to spy on the residents as they settled in for the evening, shedding the stresses of the day.

'Have you heard anything more from Alex?' Rory asked, trying to maintain a casual interest in the subject but clearly desperate for reassurance that she wasn't about to run back to her ex.

'Not a word,' said Lucy.

'That's good,' said Rory.

'As I said, he could do nothing to persuade me. I've got you now! And who could want anything else?' she laughed as he bent across and kissed her.

The melodic chime of the doorbell announced their arrival at number 34. Lucy could see her granny pottering around in the kitchen through the window as she rang the bell. Annie was wearing her most sophisticated dress and a set of diamanté jewellery, her trademark red lipstick was painted brightly on her lips; she looked like a glamorous yet tiny Mrs Pepperpot.

Opening the door with a waft of Dior perfume, she embraced Lucy and then set her beady eyes on Rory, sizing him up as potential grandson-in-law material within seconds, an enamoured smile beaming across her face, radiating her approval.

'Champagne? Why you shouldn't have, you naughty boy!' said Annie playfully as Rory proffered his bottle. 'And flowers... I keep telling you not to spend your money on me, you terrible children!'

'We like spoiling you!' said Lucy. 'And anyway you're the one spoiling us tonight, by cooking us a delicious dinner.'

'Well, I wouldn't say anything until you taste it. It could be ghastly!' warned Annie. 'Let's open this, shall we?'

Rory did the honours and cracked open the bottle of champagne. Lucy collected three champagne flutes from the corner cupboard and poured them each a glass, tilting the bottle as she did so to prevent the bubbles from overflowing onto the Persian rug beneath them. Rory proposed a toast, and as they chinked glasses, he complimented Annie on her home, resulting in a fairly detailed 'tour' of the property, surprising given the size of the place; you could glance an eye over it in a matter of seconds. In response to her captive audience, Annie seemed to develop verbal diarrhoea, regaling Rory and Lucy with endless stories from the long and rich tapestry of her life. Somehow, mid chatter, she managed to assemble their dinner, with a little help from Lucy.

They dined on prawn cocktail with baby gem lettuce, followed by chicken with grape and celery sauce and new potatoes. It was clear that Rory was as smitten by Annie as she was by him. Enjoying the new-found friendship that was blossoming before her eyes, Lucy watched Rory as he threw his head back and laughed time and time again at one or another of Annie's scandalous stories or peculiar mannerisms and sayings. Her grandmother's conversation was peppered with 'Annie-isms' as Ollie and Lucy liked to call them; she often slipped in and out of an American accent at random intervals and was truly the most entertaining company.

After a cup of Annie's best filter coffee accompanied by bittersweet Bendick's mint chocolates, Lucy and Rory finally stood up to leave, mystified at how quickly the evening had flown by as they suddenly realized that it was eleven o'clock. Annie was clearly besotted with Rory, she announced that she had adopted him already. They kissed her goodbye, making the usual promises to call and come and see her soon, then set off for Thurloe Crescent, both of them filled with admiration at how much energy a ninety-one-year-old could have. She made them both look positively lame in comparison. The sparkle and mischief in her eyes, the sheer sense of fun she had, was inspiring, and Rory announced that she would indeed make the perfect match for Great Uncle Seamus, as Lucy had suggested.

Lucy spent the next couple of evenings planning the dinner party that she and Rory were hosting on Saturday night. They had invited Ben and Christina originally, but since then the numbers had grown somewhat with the addition of two more couples: John and Anna, and Daniela and Ed. Anna and Ed were both members of Rory's old gang that had formed so many years ago back at university; Daniela and John were their other halves, all firm friends now and extremely close to Rory. Lucy knew that she would be under close scrutiny from all parties; she felt under pressure to make sure the menu was up to scratch and that the evening went off with a bang. Lucy also wanted the opportunity to see Rory in his natural habitat surrounded by his oldest mates. It always provided a fascinating insight into a person, meeting their friends. Lucy believed that you never really knew someone one hundred per cent until you had also met their friends and family, for a person's character could only really be revealed in the context of those who know them best. She couldn't wait... Lucy was happy with her decision to shelve any plans for future rounds of IUI for the time being. She had a feeling that she may not need to continue down that route now that she had Rory.

After careful consultation with Tor and Claudia, as well as advice from Ginny, the best cook of all time, she came up with her perfect menu. For the first course she was going to serve little cheese soufflés on a bed of watercress, followed by beef Wellington (her personal favourite) with potato dauphinoise, spinach and tender stem broccoli. The dessert was in Rory's hands and he insisted that he was going to make something; Lucy was suspicious as to his capabilities but appreciated the gesture nonetheless.

On Saturday morning they went for a long run around Hyde Park, Rufus racing ahead of them. After a few miles circuiting around the outer edge of the park, they stopped to catch their breath and walked back to the Serpentine Lake. They sat at the open air cafe watching the tourists feed the swans and ducks. A huge wealth of birdlife had settled in the area thanks to the regular feedings and the cafe by the lake was an ornithologist's utopia. Rory was in charge of restraining Rufus who was interested in the variety of birds for entirely different reasons. Lucy went inside to order a couple of lattes and bought some huge oatmeal and raisin cookies that were begging to be eaten in a glass jar by the till; they were soft and chewy and the perfect accompaniment to the rich coffee.

As they sipped their drinks and admired the view of the lake Lucy asked Rory to give her the low-down on the couples that were coming over that evening. She knew quite a lot about Ben and Christina but wanted to be armed with some information about the others before she met them.

'Okay, well in a nutshell… Ed is an incredibly successful investment banker; he often travels to New York and all over the world and is disturbingly good at his job. He works quite long hours but so does Daniela so they don't seem to mind too much. They have an amazing nanny.'

'Wow!' said Lucy. 'What does Daniela do?' she asked.

'Daniela is a human rights lawyer. She did languages with Abi at university and is trilingual, seriously intelligent and also doing something to really help the world. So not at all sickening!' laughed Rory.

'Oh my god I'm so intimidated!' cringed Lucy. 'What am I going to say? I spend my days selling new flavours of toothpaste, it doesn't really come close!'

'Luckily they are very self-deprecating and a totally chilled-out couple, you would never guess in a million years how high-powered they are, which is what makes them so awesome in my view…' said Rory.

'Such an attractive quality,' agreed Lucy.

'Anna and John met when they used to work in a hospital; they are both GPs now.'

'Fellow medics with Ben and Christina… Okay I get the picture. I shall try and spend the rest of the day thinking of something even remotely interesting I can say about advertising should the conversation of careers arise! Or maybe I'll just plan a good diversion tactic to keep up my sleeve!' she laughed.

'Stop worrying! They're going to love you,' said Rory, giving her a kiss. 'Of course they will!'

At that moment, the lead slack in Rory's hand, Rufus caught him unawares in a well-timed dash for the lake, plunging in head first and leaping through the water. A flock of birds of all shapes and sizes flapped their wings and headed for a mass exodus, fleeing for their lives at the sight of this hairy, copper monster. A startled Rory jumped to his feet and ran after him, shouting his name and wading into the water, mortified at his disobedient dog's complete lack of response. Eventually, with Rory lowering his voice to its most ominous pitch and growling 'Rufus', the Irish setter finally stopped and turned his head to face up to his owner. With a little bark and a wag of his tail he reluctantly reversed his way out of the lake. Rory grabbed hold of the lead; he was soaking wet up to his knees. Noticing the interested crowd of onlookers, he raised both his hands in a shrug with a resigned and bashful grin on his face. The tourists burst into an impromptu round of applause at this handsome hero with his renegade dog and the whirr of cameras clicking announced a flurry of photographs being snapped. Lucy joined them, having enjoyed the whole spectacle more than most, taking out her iPhone to snap the bedraggled pair, before bending down to tell Rufus off for being so naughty. Rufus looked extremely pleased with himself, encouraged by the crowd that he had attracted to undoubtedly repeat the stunt again at his next opportunity.

That afternoon, Rory drove Lucy to the nearest supermarket and they filled their trolleys with all the items on the shopping list. By the time they had finished, they had a boot full of goodies and Lucy's excitement levels had begun to rise at the prospect of what would no doubt be an incredible party.

They unpacked the shopping bags in the kitchen and filled the drinks fridge with white wine and bubbles. They set the huge, mahogany table in the dining room with eight places. The walls were lined with coral wall paper, giving the room a warm and cosy feel. While Rory assembled the most enormous trifle Lucy had ever seen, layer upon layer of colourful calories, Lucy set about preparing the mixture for the cheese soufflés. When she was happy with its creamy consistency she poured it into eight individual ramekins and set them to rest in the fridge until she was ready to cook them later on. With a quick phone call to Ginny to run through the recipe for beef Wellington, she began to prepare the meat. Rory wanted to learn how to cook it so was getting a step-by-step tutorial from Lucy as she went. He was so impressed with her cooking; he proved the theory that good food was the way to a man's heart.

'You know you really are the ideal woman,' he announced admiringly, watching Lucy wrap the pastry carefully around the cylinder of beef as she rolled it up snugly in its pastry blanket.

An hour or so later, both Lucy and Rory were showered and dressed. They lit candles in the kitchen where they would have pre-dinner drinks and also in the dining room. The fire was flickering in the wood burner at the end of the room, the only kitchen in London with a fire, as far as Lucy knew, and bowls of crisps and dips were scattered across various surfaces. Rory had cranked up his old record player. The needle ran smoothly around the ridged orbits of the disc, filling the room with crackling, atmospheric blues.

Ben and Christina were the first to arrive.

'Lucy how lovely to meet you!' said Christina.

'It's lovely to meet you too,' said Lucy, kissing Christina and then Ben, who were both clearly thrilled at the opportunity to have a night without their children.

'Can I offer you my cocktail of the night?' asked Rory.

'And what might that be?' laughed Ben.

'It's gin and tonic with elderflower liqueur… as yet to be named,' said Rory. They both wasted no time in accepting.

The other two couples arrived simultaneously a few minutes later and soon they were all chatting happily in the kitchen, sipping their refreshing drinks with remarkable enthusiasm. As their cocktail glasses slowly emptied, Ben and Rory reminisced about their days working in a cocktail bar as students.

'I didn't know you were barmen,' said Lucy.

'We were indeed,' said Rory proudly.

'They were both savvy enough to realize that their chosen trade would not only give them extra, much-needed, beer money but also teach them a trick or two to last them into later life. Am I right, lads?' laughed Ed.

'It was definitely a sure-fire way to meet lots of women,' said Anna.

It seemed that Ben, a blond Leonardo di Caprio look-a-like in his youth, valiantly took on the challenge single-handedly, doing his utmost to plough his way through both men's allocation of ladies with serious dedication.

Amused by the recollection of their *Cocktail* days, John challenged Ben and Rory to see if they could still remember any of the tricks they used to practise from their days of flair bartending. Both men accepted the contest with relish, surprisingly competent given their years out of practice as they flipped and spun the bottles on their arms.

'Come on boys… you have to show Lucy your old party trick,' said Anna to rapturous cheers from the rest of the gang. Their party trick double act seemed to involve passing the bottle between the two of them with a risky catch in the air, three hundred and sixty degree turns and a bit of juggling. Rising to the occasion, they gave it their best shot, but unsurprisingly the bottle slipped from their grasp mid-air and went crashing to the floor, covering the tiles in Tia Maria. The whole party collapsed in laughter, with Rufus doing his best to lap up the spillage.

'Oy Rufus, no!' shouted Rory, shooing him away. A drunk dog would be just what they needed to add to the chaos the evening would undoubtedly bring.

A short while later they sat down for dinner, everyone well-lubricated and bright-eyed after their cocktails. The soufflés were crisp and golden brown on the surface but perfectly mousse-like in the middle. The watercress with balsamic glaze was the ideal combination of bitter and sweet to go with it.

'This is absolutely delicious,' said Daniela.

'May I propose a toast?' said John. 'To the chefs!' he said, raising his glass.

'Hear hear,' cried the others, clinking their glasses.

'To the chefs!'

'And to Rory… for his *amazing* taste in women!' said Ben, winking at Lucy as he did so, prompting another flurry of cheers and chinking glass around the table as Lucy tried not to blush.

The beef was resting and the potato dauphinoise was bubbling happily away in the oven so Lucy stayed at the table and settled back into the conversation. 'So Ben, tell me more about your lothario days,' said Lucy.

'I blooming wish I still had that pulling power!' laughed Ben.

'I don't know what went wrong,' chuckled Christina, 'You were so promising when I married you!'

'I think it's called middle-aged spread…' said Ben, patting his slight paunch and reaching for the wine.

'Better keep working on it,' agreed Ed. 'This kind of peak physical condition doesn't come easily you know!'

Glancing at her watch five minutes later, Lucy excused herself and popped back into the kitchen to steam the spinach and broccoli while Rory began to carve the meat. She could tell he was thrilled to have the house filled with his friends, good conversation and a delicious meal. It was great to see him so happy. Not that he ever really seemed to get down. Unlike Alex. She raised her eyebrows and shook her head once again in disbelief at him turning up out of the blue like that earlier in the week. She marvelled at how far she had come since their break-up and smiled to herself when she thought how much better Rory was for her in every respect.

Together, they plated up the food. The beef was perfectly cooked, rosy red in the middle and oozing juices, the pastry flaky and golden on the outside. Lucy's stomach rumbled at the sight of it, the creamy, garlicky potatoes smelt amazing. She carried two plates at a time into the dining room, another rapturous round of applause erupted from Rory's friends as she set the plates down in front of them. As Rory came and poured a bottle of his finest claret into their bell-shaped red wine glasses, Lucy insisted everyone start to eat before their food began to cool. It was thankfully as mouth-watering a meal as Lucy had ever cooked, Ginny would have been proud of her, and she enjoyed every mouthful, relaxing into the sparkling conversation that flowed around and across the table now her catering duties were over.

The group of old friends had a wonderfully amicable ease with each other. The girls had formed a sort of triple entente against the boys, resulting in a comedic battle of the sexes which Lucy thought was hilarious. They would reprimand the men whilst the men wound them up purposefully, all resulting in some highly entertaining conversation.

Having given themselves enough time to digest their first two courses, Rory asked whether everyone was ready for pudding. He received a resounding cheer and went to fetch his pièce de resistance, the trifle. He dolloped huge portions into bowls, which were passed out along the table. Tasting a big spoonful of the gooey pudding, Lucy was impressed. It was a superb trifle; she had forgotten how much she loved it.

By the time Lucy had finished eating, her tummy was straining against the waist of her jeans; she was full to bursting. The conversation had moved onto the charming and not-so-charming antics of the accumulated couples' children. Between them they had six children aged between one and nine years old. Rory was godparent to two of them and clearly loved hearing what they had been up to recently. It seemed that children really did say the funniest things. Much to their embarrassment with the neighbours, John and Anna's eldest had screeched from the top floor out into the garden last week that her brother Freddie had punched her in the vagina. They couldn't understand where she had even heard of that word and assumed that it was from the older children at school; they could only hope that she didn't really understand what she was talking about. Along the same vein, Daniela and Ed's eldest, nine-year-old Joe, had been humming along to the *Harry Potter* theme tune when he had suddenly sung the word 'erection' quietly to himself. Not wishing to embarrass their son, Daniela and Ed had barely been able to disguise their giggles.

By one o'clock in the morning, everyone was more than ready for bed. The parents amongst them were conscious of their babysitters who would be annoyed if they didn't come home at a relatively decent hour. Taxis were summoned and everyone kissed and hugged goodbye, declaring themselves thrilled to have met Lucy and over the moon for Rory at his wonderful girlfriend. Lucy was sure that the flattery was partly down to the booze but was secretly delighted that they all seemed to rate her so highly. Rory looked proudly at her as she said goodbye to all his friends, an expression of adoration plastered across his face. It had been a truly fantastic party.

They cleared up happily, loading the rest of the dirty dishes into the machine and washing the dishes that were too large to fit in under the tap. Lucy went up to get ready for bed while Rory took Rufus out for a quick walk around the block. She was half asleep by the time he joined her and she snuggled into his arms, kissing him and resting her head on his muscular chest as she drifted off to sleep.

'Luce?' asked Rory in the darkness.

'Mmmm,' said Lucy drowsily.

'Do you want kids some day?'

'Yes... I do,' said Lucy, her heartbeat quickening. She immediately felt guilty that she still hadn't told him about the IUI yet she felt excited that he was bringing the topic of conversation up in the first place. 'Do you?' she asked.

'I want a few,' said Rory, stifling a yawn as his breathing deepened. 'Quite a few...'

Within minutes he was asleep, leaving Lucy to contemplate what he may have meant by asking her that question. Did he think they might have children together? Did that mean he might have been okay with it if she had turned out to be pregnant last week? In the silence of the room, with the rhythmic breathing of Rory's breath in the background, she considered what his reaction might have been. She dared to imagine what he might have done if he had found out the baby wasn't his.

Chapter Thirty-Two

The following weekend Ginny and Gus were making a rare train journey up to the big smoke for Ginny's birthday. They were planning on taking Annie out to the theatre and had invited Lucy and Rory to join them. Lucy wondered whether their biennial trip to London had arrived a little earlier than usual, suspecting that it was probably connected with enormous curiosity on both their parts to meet the by-now famous Rory. Especially since Annie had not stopped raving about him during Ginny's nightly telephone calls ever since their dinner in the studio the previous week.

Rory couldn't wait to meet Lucy's parents and was excited about their evening together. He wasn't a massive fan of musical theatre but was more than happy to make an exception to spend the evening with her family. Gus was treating them all to dinner afterwards at a French restaurant in the West-End. They were going to see Ginny's best-loved musical, Lloyd Webber's *The Phantom of the Opera*, and Lucy spent the whole week looking forward to it.

Rory's friends had all written charming thank you letters after the dinner party, singing Lucy's praises and thanking them both for such a fun and spoiling evening, promising to invite them back for a return meal soon.

During the week, Rory and Lucy spent most of their evenings together in the familiar routines they had established as a couple. On Thursday they stood side by side brushing their teeth before bed. As Rory put his toothbrush back in the holder, he asked her whether she was around in the first week of March.

'I should think so,' said Lucy. 'How come?'

'Would you like to meet my folks?' asked Rory. 'I really want you to.'

'Are you kidding?' asked Lucy. 'I would *love* to!'

'I think it's unfair that I am going to have met Annie, Ginny and Gus by the end of the week and none of my family have had the chance to meet you. They're all dying to lay eyes on the famous Lucy Johnston! What would you say to a weekend jaunt in Ireland!' suggested Rory.

Lucy couldn't think of anything she would rather do. She was thrilled with the way things were going between them; it felt like every piece of the puzzle was falling into place. Meeting each other's families would be the icing on the cake.

That Friday evening they celebrated Valentine's Day, until recently Lucy's worst day of the year. Not anymore. Rory cooked Lucy a romantic, candlelit meal and they exchanged cards with heartfelt notes written inside. Lucy felt closer to him than ever and loved him for spoiling her so much; he made her feel like the luckiest woman alive.

Saturday was a drizzly, damp day; a day for winter warmers, leather boots and duffle coats.

'I don't want to go outside in this,' Lucy sulked, looking out of the window.

Rory mimicked his mother Trina scolding, 'There's no such thing as bad weather, only unsuitable clothes,' as he zipped up his oversized waterproof jacket and pulled on his beloved Caterpillar boots.

Having travelled underground into central London, Lucy and Rory emerged from the tube and bowed their heads as if in prayer as the misty rain sprayed their faces. Rory unleashed the catch on his enormous umbrella, which sprang into a full arc above their heads, protecting them from the elements as they trundled through the throngs of Saturday night drinkers that flocked to Soho each weekend. Gus was waiting for them, his hands thrust deep into the pockets of his coat, seemingly lost in his thoughts as he stood at the entrance to the theatre like an off-duty security guard. Spotting his daughter as she approached, he roused himself from his thoughts and stepped down from his vantage point to greet them.

Having kissed Lucy, Gus turned towards Rory held out his hand and gave him a firm handshake, saying, 'Rory, lovely to meet you' as he did so.

'It's very good to meet you too, Gus,' said Rory. 'I see London's pulling out all the stops for your visit!' he joked, gesturing at the water that was gushing along the gutter.

'Yes, I know! We don't seem to have the best of luck with our wonderful capital, it would appear. I would hazard a guess that eighty percent of our trips up to London have been exactly like this, while there's nothing but blazing sunshine back home in Cornwall!' said Gus as he showed their tickets to the doorman. 'Sod's law I suppose!'

'Poor dad,' consoled Lucy. 'How was the train journey?' she asked.

'Oh, fine, fine thanks, darling. It only takes four hours you know, it's so much faster than driving!' marvelled Gus.

'That's what I've been telling you for years! It's so much more comfortable too,' said Lucy. 'I can't bear the thought of driving down there now; sitting in traffic on the motorway for double the amount of time it should take!'

They climbed a flight of stairs, admiring the framed pictures of actors and actresses that lined the walls, before arriving in the opulently decorated bar. The seats were covered in red crushed velvet and gold light fittings mimicking chandeliers hung from the ceiling. Annie and Ginny were waiting at one of the tables with a bottle of prosecco and five champagne flutes full to the brim. They both stood up as they entered the room, two matching grins mirrored each other on both of their faces, so similar despite one being slightly more wrinkled than the other.

'Darlings!' cried Annie as she held out her arms to embrace her granddaughter and her 'beloved', as she called Rory. 'So lovely to see you both!' she said, kissing them both on each cheek.

'Annie, I see you're looking gorgeous as ever!' replied Rory. 'And you must be Ginny,' said Rory, turning to face Lucy's mother with his most charming smile as he, in turn, kissed her on the cheek.

'I certainly am. It's lovely to meet you at long last,' simpered Ginny. 'I've heard so much about you from both Lucy and my mother... I feel like I know you already!'

'I hear many happy returns of the day are in order?' asked Rory.

'Yes, happy birthday Mum,' said Lucy. 'Let's have a toast.'

They clinked glasses and drank to Ginny's good health, making small talk about the weather, the journey from Cornwall, Tiggy and Rufus, and how much they were all looking forward to the show.

At the five minute warning, Lucy and Ginny nipped to the loo to spend a penny. Embarrassingly Ginny shouted, 'SUCH a gorgeous man!' at the top of her voice the minute they turned their backs on the others, firmly within Rory's earshot; subtlety was certainly not her forte! They dried their hands in the blade hand dryer that suctioned the water from your skin in seconds as though you were shoving your hands inside a Hoover, a novelty for Ginny who declared that it was very space age. Lucy was fairly sure that these inventions had reached the south-west coast but they apparently had not come to Ginny's attention as of yet. She loved to associate anything remotely modern with the city and often said 'city folk' were far too 'technological' for their own good.

As the two minute bell rang, they made their way into the Grand Circle to sit down. Lucy loved the murmuring chatter of the theatre, the atmosphere was always tense with anticipation as everyone took their seats, nothing to do for the next three hours except to sit back, relax and be entertained. As the curtains rose, the familiar strains of Lloyd Webber's music rose from the orchestra and swelled up to the rafters of Her Majesty's Theatre. Lucy was swept away.

After the performance they headed for a nearby brasserie where Rory successfully managed to win over both Gus and Ginny with his charming repartee and courteous manners.

'After you,' said Rory, holding the door open as they made their way inside. Having been shown to their table he then helped Annie into her chair, pulling it out and supporting her elbow as she lowered herself down.

'What charming manners you have, Rory!' said Ginny. 'You must have been brought up very well! I do love a bit of old-fashioned chivalry.'

'There's not much of that around these days!' agreed Annie, patting Rory's hand in thanks as she settled into her chair.

'Speaking of bringing up children well, I must compliment you in return! I can't think of a lovelier person than our Lucy here,' he said, dropping a kiss on her head and ruffling her hair as he sat down.

'That's got nothing to do with them, I can assure you!' laughed Lucy. 'When you meet Ollie you'll soon realize that!'

'Oy!' said Ginny in mock offence. 'It is entirely down to us, thank you.'

'Of course, Mum... I'm only joking!' said Lucy. 'Now what's everyone having?' she asked as she opened her menu. 'Starters or just mains?'

'I'm starving,' said Gus. 'Let's have starters and mains, the whole shebang! After all we are celebrating!'

Later, having consumed what felt like enough French food to feed a small army, Lucy realized it might be time to make a move when she noticed Annie start to go slightly cross-eyed.

'Right, Mum, I think we'd best be off,' said Lucy, nodding in her grandmother's direction.

'Darling! But we're having so much fun!' slurred Annie, more than a little tipsy after sinking most of a bottle of white.

'A little too much fun perhaps!' laughed Lucy.

'Impossible!' declared Rory.

'Will you drop Mum at the studio on your way?' asked Ginny.

'Of course,' said Lucy. 'Where are you staying again? Do you want us to drop you off en route too?'

'I'm treating your mother to a night at that fancy hotel down the road,' said Gus.

'Ooh la la!' trilled Annie.

'It's walking distance, so don't worry about us,' said Ginny.

Rory and Lucy set off in a taxi, taking Annie with them to drop her off on the way home. They left Gus and Ginny to have a nightcap in peace to continue the birthday celebrations. Annie was singing the phantom's theme tune all the way home, making them (and the taxi driver) chuckle as she warbled her way to the top notes, the wine she had consumed at dinner helping her soprano voice reach new heights. It was raining again, so Rory escorted Annie inside her studio, holding his huge umbrella over her head, leaving Lucy to wait in the warmth and comfort of the taxi. Rory unlocked the front door for Annie, returning to the taxi only when he was sure that she was safely inside and settling herself in to her bedtime routine. He was so kind and patient with Annie and both of her parents, Lucy just couldn't ask for anything more. He was a true gentleman. She was counting down the days until their trip to Dublin, where she would finally get to meet the rest of the McCullan clan.

Irritatingly, Lucy began feeling a little out of sorts towards the end of the following week. She had packed her running kit on Friday morning, determined to run home before another weekend cosily settling in front of Rory's fireplace, but had felt so tired and under the weather that she couldn't face it.

Rory and Lucy had a quiet weekend at home, taking it easy to ensure a rapid recovery for Lucy. They had started watching the hit TV show *Breaking Bad* on Ollie's recommendation after a recent Skype call to Buenos Aires. The show was bizarrely compulsive viewing considering the fact that it was all about crystal meth drug dealers. Lucy and Rory became rapidly addicted, devouring each episode with a fearsome appetite, allowing themselves only intermittent breaks to cook and take Rufus out to the park.

Lucy's lurgy continued throughout the next week. There were plenty of bugs going around the office, Lettie and Simon had both been suffering, so Lucy popped into Boots on her lunch break and bought a tube of Berocca, determined to nip any lurking germs in the bud.

On Saturday, they planned their trip to Ireland the following weekend.

'I've booked us flights leaving from Gatwick on Friday straight after work,' said Rory looking up from his laptop. 'The neighbours have agreed to look after Rufus for the weekend.'

'I'm so excited!' said Lucy. 'I've never even been to Ireland.'

'You know this is our first proper holiday together?' asked Rory as he got up to join her on the sofa where she was reading one of his old Ireland guidebooks.

'I know, that's partly why I can't wait. But I'm just *so* excited about meeting your family!'

'They can't wait,' said Rory, throwing his arm around her to pull her closer to him and kissing her on the forehead. 'I kind of wish we were going for longer, we're not going to have nearly enough time to do everything I would like.'

'That's okay… all the more reason for me to come again!' said Lucy with a wink.

Rory talked her through all of his favourite places, narrowing down a shortlist of highlights for Lucy to see on her first trip to his home. He was so excited about showing her around, and although he knew there was no way she would be able to see everything that he wanted her to, he reassured her that there would be plenty more opportunities in the years to come, so not to worry. Whenever he made reference to them still being together way into the future, Lucy felt a warm glow spread throughout her insides. She couldn't think of anyone she would rather be with in a week, a month, a year's time, or even longer, for that matter!

On Sunday Lucy went to meet Tor and Claudia for lunch. She explained that she had been feeling rough all week and told the girls to stay away from her in case she had germs.

'What symptoms have you had?' asked Tor, looking quizzically at Lucy.

'Nausea and a cold mainly, and I've felt really tired. Half of my office have got it.'

'You know the nausea and tiredness could both be pregnancy-related, right?' said Tor.

'I've had my period!' said Lucy. 'There's no way I could be pregnant… is there?'

'It's funny you should say that. I've just heard from a colleague that she's twelve weeks pregnant,' said Claudia. 'She got two full periods before she realized, she had absolutely no idea. So I guess it can happen.'

'Oh my god!' said Lucy. 'I'd heard of people having very light ones and being pregnant but mine was totally normal.'

'I'd say it was unlikely,' said Tor.

'But I've been drinking this past two weeks,' said Lucy, suddenly feeling guilty at the thought of how the drinks she had consumed might have affected a developing baby if the impossible were true, that she had been unknowingly pregnant all this time. Her heart started to race slightly faster as she processed this possibility. She didn't know why she hadn't thought about looking it up before, she had just assumed getting her period meant that she wasn't pregnant, as it always had before. She felt a hot flush creep up the back of her neck. A confusing mixture of fear and excitement coursed through her.

'Don't worry, my colleague had been drinking the usual amount too and her GP said the baby would have been so small at that stage it would hardly have affected it. Maybe stop drinking now though until you do a test… just to be safe.'

'Would it be safe for me to fly if it turned out I was pregnant?' she asked.

'It's fine at this stage,' said Tor. 'If I were you I'd take a test and find out.'

'Okay, I will...' Lucy tailed off. Her head spun. 'If I am pregnant, what the hell will Rory say?' Her eyes welled up with tears at the thought of his reaction. How could she tell him? It would ruin everything.

'It might be okay,' said Tor. 'But you'll have to be honest with Rory. He deserves that much.'

'I agree,' said Claudia. 'He's a good guy, Luce. He might surprise you...'

Lucy was pretty sure she wasn't pregnant, but having heard the story of Claudia's work colleague there was no way she could be certain until she saw the proof, in black and white, in front of her eyes. There was no denying it, if she was indeed pregnant, there was also a slim but equally likely chance that the baby could be Rory's, thanks to the split condom. But the thought of confessing her predicament to him was just horrifying, she felt ashamed that he might think her desperate and stupid for having pursued the route of artificial conception in the first place. Her hands trembled at the very thought.

On her way home Lucy popped into Boots. Spotting the aisle that housed the pregnancy tests, she made her way over to it. Despite her worry, the part of her that was so desperate for a baby began to feel a flutter of excitement. She went over to the rows and rows of little rectangular boxes. She stood there gormlessly for five minutes, staring at the selection. Eventually a shop assistant came over to ask her if she needed help. This kicked her into action and she grabbed a couple of packets, uttering a garbled 'no thanks' as she rushed over to the self-checkout to make her purchases. She shoved the tests deep into the bottom of her handbag telling herself that she would do one very soon, just so she could have peace of mind.

Each morning that week she contemplated taking one of the packets from the stash in her washbag and doing a test but somehow she just couldn't bring herself to go through with it. She told herself it would be better to do it when Rory was not around, just in case. She knew that she was being a spineless wimp but she was in such a quandary. What if she was pregnant? What would she do? This internal battle went on every morning until she decided to give up, let herself off the hook, and deal with it the next day. On Friday she even got as far as unwrapping the little white stick from its packaging, her heart pounding in her chest with nerves, before slamming it back in the box. She reasoned that it would be less than ideal to meet his family for the first time with such a big secret hanging over her head so she decided to give herself until Monday. That was the deadline, under no circumstances was she allowed to put it off any longer. To make doubly sure that she would not fail, she decided to call Tor, who had been contacting her daily to find out whether she had done it yet.

'I promise you I will take the test on Monday,' said Lucy.

'Why wait until Monday, Luce?' Tor asked. 'Are you still feeling rough?'

'I have to wait until the weekend is over until I feel strong enough to find out, once and for all. And yes, I am still feeling rough…'

Tor wasn't too happy about the delay. She told Lucy that if she hadn't had a phone call by Monday afternoon with the results she would be marching over to her flat and forcing her to do it right then and there. Lucy promised fervently, telling her she would phone Claudia too so that they could both hold her accountable to her promise.

Lucy was still feeling nauseous as she made her way to the train station later that afternoon, pulling her little wheelie suitcase behind her. As she was squeezing herself through a particularly congested tract of the Victoria line, a horrible man barged past her and shouted, 'Get out of my way, you stupid woman!' Lucy felt her bottom lip wobble at his acidic remark and tried to pull herself together before her eyes welled up with tears in response. She was all over the place! Thanking her lucky stars that it was the weekend and praying that she would feel better by the time she arrived in Dublin, she caught the train out to Gatwick Airport. As she watched the peaceful countryside roll by through the window her phone rang.

'Hey!' said Rory. 'How are you getting on?'

'I'm on the train,' said Lucy. 'You?'

'I'm already here. My client meeting finished early,' explained Rory. 'I'll meet you at security, shall I?'

'Great, have you got the boarding passes?' asked Lucy.

'I sure do!' he said. They were both taking carry-on luggage only, so thankfully they wouldn't have to join the horrendously long queues that there would no doubt be at the check-in desks.

As they went through security, Lucy could tell Rory was delighted that she was there with him. He had explained a couple of nights previously that she was the first girl since Abigail that had meant enough to him to even consider bringing back to Ireland to meet his family. This did nothing to abate her guilt about the secret she was concealing from him. She knew how important this weekend was to him and was annoyed that she didn't feel one hundred percent well. Conflicting emotions welled within her. She knew perfectly well that it could be explained as morning sickness despite the fact she hadn't actually been sick, more tired and run-down, and she knew that she only had two more days until she would find out and be forced to face facts.

As they took their seats on the busy flight, Lucy blew up her little air pillow and decided to try and sleep. Rory was already engrossed in the new Dan Brown, so she didn't have to make conversation, for which she was grateful. As she dozed off, visions of babies, pregnancy tests and the horrified look on Rory's face if he found out she was pregnant filled her mind. She tried to push these to one side, focusing instead on imagining his family, what they would be like, what they looked like, piecing together all the snippets of conversation she had overheard, all the stories Rory had told her and the photographs she had seen of them all.

Just an hour later the captain announced over the tannoy that they would soon be landing in Dublin. It was such a short and easy flight, nipping across the Irish Sea. The twinkling lights of Dublin sparkled in the twilight as they touched down, the plane bouncing off the tarmac before juddering to a grinding halt. They were going to pick up a hire car from Avis and then it would just be a short drive to the little village of Renwood in the Wicklow Mountains, where Rory had grown up and where Trina and Paddy still lived.

Unfortunately, the dim light of dusk did not display the countryside at its best as Lucy and Rory wound their way through Wicklow. She tried to make the landscape out as best she could, but she knew that she would have to wait until tomorrow to really see it in all its glory. Her excitement at having arrived and being so close to Rory's childhood home and family had certainly acted as a good tonic to her sense of fatigue, she was suddenly buzzing with excitement. Doing his best as a night-time tour guide, Rory told her when they were passing the snow-capped Sugar Loaf peak that she would be able to see from the bedroom window. Lucy loved even the very sound of the names as they rolled off Rory's tongue. His

Irish accent seemed to have trebled in strength automatically upon touching down on home soil.

After an hour or so, they drove through the tiny village of Renwood, turning up a long curving road that climbed uphill and soon became nothing more than a dirt track. A hand-painted sign in the shape of an arrow read 'Renwood Farm' amidst the peeling white paint. They followed the direction of the arrow for a while longer, the track winding around a sharp bend to the left. Suddenly the rambling farmhouse appeared before their eyes, a mishmash of stone buildings with cheery, warm light flooding out of each criss-crossed window.

Lucy gasped in delight, 'It's so cute!' she said, 'I love it already!'

Rory laughed, a huge grin on his face at the sight of his home, clearly very happy to have made it.

Trina opened the front door, obviously having been listening out for the car. She cried, 'Rory, my dear boy, you're home!' rushing over to fold him into her ample bosom, enveloping him in a homely hug. 'Lucy dear, thank you so much for coming to visit us, how was your journey, darling? Terrible bore planes, aren't they? Are you hungry? Tired? Come in, dear, come in!' She rattled out sentences at the speed of light in her sing-song voice whilst simultaneously kissing her hello, giving her a hug, taking her bag from her hands and ushering them both into the house. Quite impressive, Lucy thought, seeing immediately where Rory got his warmth of character from, and his lovely gift of being able to put any newcomer at ease within seconds of being in his presence.

Trina had soft grey hair that had been set with rollers and bounced in gentle curls around her cheeks. This was coupled with a broad grin and a welcoming face, all smiles and dimples.

Lucy and Rory came into the warmth of the house; a little wood-burning range was doing a valiant job at blasting heat out into the hall. Several dogs of various shapes and sizes rushed around their feet, welcoming them with little sniffs and yaps and plenty of wagging tails.

Rory's father, Paddy, a rosy-cheeked, roundish man with a waistcoat and a pipe, came to greet them. 'Lucy, my dear, it's a pleasure to meet you,' he said as he kissed her on each cheek. 'It really is,' he repeated, smiling at her with great affection before turning to greet his son.

Rory's older sister Trish, her husband Andrew, and their younger brother Dermot came out of the sitting room to join the welcome party.

'The whole McCullan clan!' said Rory. 'Aren't we spoilt!'

'Well yes, except for Ronan, but he doesn't count,' said Dermot, giving his brother a bear hug.

'What's he doing again, the cheeky blighter?' asked Rory.

'Poor old thing's at some big family do with the in-laws,' explained Trina. 'We barely see him these days.'

'Unlike some people who we can't seem to get rid of no matter how hard we try,' laughed Paddy, gesturing towards Dermot with his pipe.

'I thought you lived in Dublin?' Lucy asked him.

'I do!'

'He just comes home pretty darn frequently for a bit of home cooking and Trina's free launderette service!' said Paddy.

As they made their way through to the sitting room, Lucy chatted to Trish. 'You live in Dublin too, don't you?'

'Yes just south of Dublin, though sadly we rarely get the chance to make the most of it these days,' said Trish. 'We don't get out much now we've got the three little ones.'

'You should get Dermot to babysit!'

'Hah, fat chance!' laughed Trish. 'Though all three of my brothers are excellent uncles, so I shouldn't complain!'

'Are they asleep? I'm dying to meet them,' said Lucy.

'Mercifully they are, though they will no doubt be hammering on your door in the morning at some ungodly hour, begging Rory to take them on one of his famous adventure treasure hunts. They've been banging on about it all day! I can only apologize in advance for my unruly offspring… especially the twins!'

Rory, having overheard their conversation, decided that it was a great idea. They would set up a trail in the woodland surrounding the house; it would be a good way to show it to her. The children could then follow the trail to the treasure later on.

As she watched the McCullans, Lucy decided that Dermot was a very handsome younger version of Rory, with slightly paler brown hair that was even more dishevelled. He looked like an Indie pop star and Lucy could imagine young girls swooning at his green eyes. Trish was more like Trina in appearance. With Rory's hazel eyes and her mother's dimples, she was a very attractive lady. They had clearly had a boozy Friday night dinner as they were all cradling glasses of red wine and tumblers of whisky. Drinks were quickly fetched for the new arrivals and the rest of the evening was spent catching up on all the family gossip, and the more important task of getting to know Lucy. She felt one hundred per cent relaxed in the McCullans' presence, they were incredibly genuine, down-to-earth people and, as she had expected, made her feel like she was part of the family within minutes.

When the grandfather clock in the hall chimed midnight, their conversation finally paused and motions were made to start drifting up to bed. Trina and Paddy went up first, closely followed by a yawning Trish and Andrew, no doubt conscious of the fact that their children's natural alarm clock would be waking them at the crack of dawn, and promising to try to delay the terrible twins' exit into the rest of the house for as long as possible. Dermot, Lucy and Rory finished off their drinks as the last flickers of flame crackled and hissed before finally dying out, leaving a bed of embers glowing in the great open hearth beside them. Rory picked up the gilt fire guard and moved it in front of the fireplace before they heaved themselves out of their comfortable chairs to retire for the night.

As they climbed the creaking wooden staircase, Rory hauling both of their bags up with him, they whispered goodnight to Dermot, trying not to make any noise that might wake the little ones. They crept down to the room at the end of the corridor and dumped their belongings on the floor, collapsing in an exhausted heap on the hand-sewn patchwork quilt that Rory's grandmother had once made him.

As Lucy's eyes adjusted to the dim light, she gazed around Rory's bedroom, imagining him as a small child, this view of the world being the one most familiar to him, and she felt a real pang of love for that little boy and the man that he had become. She suddenly had an overwhelming need to tell him that she loved him, though now was hardly the right time. If she was about to find out she was pregnant he might then feel pressured into staying with her, or worse he might leave her and then where would she be…how would she cope knowing that he loved her but that she had ruined everything? She had known for quite some time that she loved him with every single cell in her body and she simply couldn't imagine her life going forward without him in it. She wondered if he felt the same way… she fervently hoped that he did. She had often felt sure that he was about to tell her, but so far neither of them had bitten the bullet. She knew that she would wait until he told her that he loved her first, it was such a big deal to utter those three little words out loud. There had been too much heartache in her life and for once she wanted to be sure that he wasn't saying anything because he felt he ought to, or worse, as Alex had told her when they broke up, because he felt under too much pressure from her, her family or her friends due to their age.

Her gaze settled on a row of little trophies. They were lined up on a wooden shelf by the windows, which were draped with red and white chequered curtains. 'What are these?' asked Lucy, sitting up and pointing at what was clearly his prize collection.

'They're sports trophies from school,' explained Rory. 'I used to be quite the sportsman when I was younger, don't you know. PE was definitely my favourite subject!'

'Sweet! A young athlete,' said Lucy, wandering around the room to look at his old photographs, books and the pictures that hung slightly lopsided along the walls. There was a little framed pencil drawing of the farm, signed 'Rory, age 10', hanging by the bed. 'Did you do that?' she asked, laughing. As Rory nodded, she said, 'Wow, you were so talented even back then!'

'You're too kind,' he said, taking off his jumper and T-shirt in one fell swoop, revealing his muscular torso and dark, hairy chest. 'So, what do you think?' he asked.

'I think I want to rip off the rest of your clothes!' said Lucy, running her fingers down his chest and breathing in his musky aftershave, as always a stream of electricity darting through her from head to toe.

Rory laughed, 'That is *not* what I meant!' taking both her hands in his as he faced her and kissed her lightly on the lips. 'What do you think of the place, of my family?' he asked, sincerely waiting for her opinion.

'I adore them; they are just the loveliest people I could ever hope to meet. And I love the farmhouse, I just wish it was morning already so we could go and explore! I am dying to see it all in the light of day.'

'Well that's just as well,' said Rory, 'because if I get my way you'll be coming here an awful lot more as time goes on, not to mention spending a lot more time with my family!'

'That's good,' said Lucy, as she kissed him, and they lay back on the bed and tried hard not to make any sounds that might give away their late night activities to the rest of the household.

Chapter Thirty-Three

As expected, Lucy and Rory were rudely awakened by the pummelling of tiny fists against the wooden door. There was no lock, but at least the twins had knocked before bursting in with the strength and enthusiasm that only two nine-year-olds could muster. Despite the early hour, the identical blond boys came barrelling into the room at what felt like a hundred miles an hour, with decibel levels through the roof as they shrieked, 'Uncle Rory!!' and jumped on to the bed, paying little attention to the newcomer in the room.

Muttering under his breath, 'Don't worry, I'll get rid of them!' to Lucy who was still half asleep, he shouted, 'Right, you little rascals!' and got out of bed. He scooped up both of the offending children, one under each arm, and carried them out of the bedroom so that Lucy could have a little longer in bed. She could hear the boys shrieking in delight as they were taken downstairs and out of earshot by their beloved uncle.

Having given herself time to wake up properly, Lucy tiptoed down the corridor and washed herself in the ancient enamel bathtub, brushing her teeth and drinking some water. She was still feeling tired and a little disorientated, something she hoped was down to waking up somewhere new and nothing more. She was beginning to feel terrified that she might be pregnant. Excited too, in a way, for the desire for a baby had not left her, but terrified about what such a revelation would do to Rory, to their relationship. It was all so perfect, she was so happy and she just couldn't bear the thought of putting it all in jeopardy. She knew that she couldn't go back in time, but if she had only known Rory was about to come into her life she doubted she would have gone through with the treatment. She would much rather have the chance to create a family with him, with the man she loved.

Back in the bedroom, Lucy opened the little curtains and gasped as she took in the view. The rolling hills, all different shades of green, were spectacular, some covered in woodland and some stretching up and out towards the sky. In the background she could see the famous Great Sugar Loaf. A smattering of snow coated the top like white icing on a sticky bun. She could see at once why Ireland was called the Emerald Isle and in particular why Wicklow was known as the 'Garden of Ireland'. It was breathtaking.

Suddenly feeling as excited as she had done as a small child on Christmas Eve, she longed to get outside and explore. She pulled on a pair of jeans, some boots and a coral jumper, applied some make-up, and then went downstairs to find Rory. He was in the kitchen with Trina, Trish, the twins Connor and Darragh, and Trish's younger daughter, Rosie, who was five. They were all sitting at the table happily munching on bowls of cereal of various sizes, reminding Lucy of the bears in the story of Goldilocks with their bowls of porridge.

The children peered shyly at Lucy through their blonde fringes, pausing mid mouthful with spoons in the air to size up this newcomer into their midst.

Trina said, 'Good morning, love!' giving Lucy a hug before turning to her grandchildren. 'Kids, I would like you to meet Lucy, Uncle Rory's lovely girlfriend!' she said.

They spluttered 'Hi!' and 'Morning!' in response, the boys giggling into their cereal at the word 'girlfriend', before returning to the much more important task of eating breakfast. Rosie continued to fix Lucy with her dark brown eyes, smiling coyly whenever she caught Lucy returning her gaze.

Rory set about making Lucy a cup of coffee while Trina enquired whether she had slept well and if she was feeling okay. She wasn't feeling particularly hungry, but thought it would be rude to turn down breakfast, so she agreed to a piece of toast and sat down with the others at the large, scrubbed pine table, the wood etched with markings from over a century of happy family meals.

After breakfast, Rory announced that he and Lucy had work to do. 'We'll be gone for an hour or so,' he said.

The twins started to bounce on their seats in excitement.

'Are you going to make us a treasure hunt, Uncle Rory?' asked Connor.

'Pleeeeeeease!' begged Darragh.

'PLEEEAASE!' they all pleaded as Rory and Lucy pulled on coats and boots and made their way to the door.

Refusing to reveal the motive behind their early morning excursion, he said, 'You'll have to wait and see,' ruffling the three curly mops of hair and laughing at their expectant, pleading faces.

He led Lucy out of the back door and they stalked across the lush green grass down the hill away from the house. The sun glistened on the coating of frost that clung to each blade, creating an optical illusion of stalks of crystal shattering underneath their wellington boots. Behind the house the mountains stood majestically like ancient leaders calmly surveying their realm. At the bottom of the hill dense woodland spread out before them, an enchanted forest full of whispering trees and secret hiding places.

'These are the famous woods,' said Lucy, clapping her hands in glee. 'Are we going to see the treehouse?' she asked.

'We certainly are,' said Rory. 'And on the way, we'll set out our clues.'

'What'll the treasure be?' asked Lucy.

Rory reached into his Barbour pocket and pulled out a bag of sweets that he had picked up duty-free. 'Trish'll kill me for the sugar high!' he chuckled mischievously as he dangled the cellophane bag stuffed with jewel-coloured wrappers in the air.

'Oh dear! As if those boys need any more energy than they already have!' laughed Lucy. 'Right, you had better show me how to make the trail; I've never made a treasure hunt before!'

For the next hour or so they trudged through the woodland, stamping on bracken and flattening out the pathway as they went. They used little twigs to create arrows at various intervals along the way, showing the route. Whenever the path became unclear they made a cross on the floor, instructing the explorers to turn back. It was great fun. Rory was fuelled by memories of his childhood, mucking about in the woods with his siblings, and he recounted them to Lucy as they worked. At the end of the trail, Lucy finally laid eyes on the huge, ramshackle tree house that Uncle Seamus had built.

'There it is!' Rory said.

'Oh, WOW!' said Lucy. 'It's so much more incredible than I expected.'

It really was quite a feat. The rooms were constructed around the thickest, sturdiest boughs of three towering oak trees. A complex system of ropes and pulleys threaded through the woodwork. A recently replaced rope ladder dangled from the left-hand side.

'Wait there,' said Rory. 'I'm just going to check it out to make sure it's all safe then you can come up.' Rory grabbed hold of the ladder and held it steady before scrambling up it with surprising ease. A patch of sunlight streamed through an opening in the trees where a tree stump stood like a welcoming seat.

Feeling ludicrously exhausted after the morning's exertions, Lucy sat down and basked in the sunshine while she waited.

A few minutes later, having completed some basic checks on the tree house, Rory helped Lucy up the ladder, holding it for her as she pulled herself up. She gasped in delight as she reached the top, imagining how exciting it must have been for them all as small children to have this amazing den. Rory showed her around and they peered out from the windows, the perfect position to spy on the world below. He proceeded to show her all the best secret hiding spaces, and how to operate the pulley to haul up the tray for snacks. Lastly, Rory led her over to his favourite spot, a wall full from top to bottom of carvings, etched by tiny hands with rusty penknife blades, their names and the names of their friends, complete with dates and coded messages in spiky, childish writing.

'How sweet!' Lucy cried, running her fingers over the uneven surface of the wood. Suddenly, she spotted a new addition to the etchings, clearly freshly carved in the top right-hand corner a short while before, while Lucy had been waiting on the tree stump. The letters R and L were encased in a wonky heart, the date etched beneath it. Lucy looked up at Rory who was watching her reaction. 'You did one for us!' she cried. 'I can't believe it!'

'It's meant to tell you something,' he said. 'I wouldn't put just anyone's name in this sacred space, y'know!' he muttered, pulling her towards him and wrapping her in his warm embrace. He kissed her, and said, 'I love you, Luce.'

Overwhelmed with emotion, tears sprung into her eyes as she kissed him back, happiness radiating from every cell in her body. 'I love you too, Rory,' she whispered, hugging him back. She had no idea how long they stood there, kissing and holding each other through their smiles, a bubble of happiness isolating them from the rest of the world.

Later, having hidden the bag of sweets in a suitably secret alcove in the tree house, Lucy and Rory walked hand in hand back to the farmhouse, unable to wipe the broad grins from their faces, like a pair of lovesick teenagers.

By the time they got back to the house, Connor, Darragh and Rosie were about to explode with excitement. They barrelled into the garden at breakneck speed, sprinting down the grass to start looking for clues, Rosie trying her best to keep up with her brothers. The adults all joined them as they walked through the woods, following the trail that Lucy and Rory had carefully laid out for them. The treasure was discovered by the boys in record time, and kindly shared with Rosie who was teetering from her father's shoulders, having grown tired of the search. With the bounty safely stowed in the children's coat pockets, the whole party trudged back to the warmth of the cosy farmhouse, ready to devour a hearty lunch of fish pie and peas that Trina had prepared that morning.

In the afternoon, Rory took Lucy on a tour of the local area in their hire car. On the way home they stopped off at his local pub. Lucy was delighted to discover a group of musicians playing Irish jigs on their fiddles in the corner. The rest of the customers all seemed to know the tunes and were singing along. There was a lot of feet stamping, impromptu shouts and trills, and even a sweet little girl who was ushered into the middle of the pub to dance. Lucy was very impressed with the speed at which her legs moved, flicking upwards and side to side as though she were a puppet with strings being pulled this way and that. All the while her back was straight, with her arms held firmly by her side, a lovely smile fixed on her sweet little face. Lucy was feeling rather nauseous. She ordered a Diet Coke, hoping the bubbles would help settle her stomach, while Rory had the obligatory pint of Guinness.

That evening the whole McCullan family sat down to dinner together, a tasty roast that everyone had helped to prepare that afternoon while Lucy and Rory had been out exploring. It was a very happy meal, full of laughter and chatter. Lucy had to strain her ears at times to stay abreast of the conversation, they all certainly had the gift of the gab and she had to concentrate to keep up with their rapid-fire talking. Rory's accent was now stronger than ever and she loved seeing him so relaxed in his home surroundings.

On Sunday morning, after a deep and undisturbed sleep thanks to the depths of the countryside and without London's sirens and building works to awaken them, Lucy and Rory made their way down for a late breakfast. Paddy was in charge of cooking breakfast on Sunday mornings.

'The full Irish, my love?' he asked Lucy.

'How kind!' she said as he presented them with a plate of bacon and eggs with sides of mushrooms, tomatoes and fried bread. Lucy's stomach turned slightly at the sight of it, but she was determined not to be rude, and gratefully accepted the plate before sitting down at the table, breathing deeply to rid herself of the wave of nausea that was washing up the back of her throat. She felt so sick at the thought of having to eat the eggs that she felt absurdly close to tears.

Rory noticed her expression and the greenish tinge to her complexion, and whispered, 'You okay?' with a concerned look on his face.

'I'm just feeling a little bit sick,' said Lucy, trying to put a smile on her face.

'You haven't been right for some time, have you?' said Rory, looking worried. 'Perhaps you should see a doctor when you get back home?' he suggested. 'These things don't usually last so long.'

'Perhaps you're right,' agreed Lucy, crossing her fingers tightly behind her back as she did so, unable to even contemplate where this conversation could end up. Forcing herself to be brave, she loaded her fork with a mouthful of eggs, took a bite, and realized too late her mistake. There was no way she was going to be able to keep that down. Overwhelmed with the sure knowledge that she was about to be sick, she pushed her chair back from the table as fast as she possibly could and ran to the nearest bathroom, reaching the loo just in time.

After she had been sick she felt slightly better, but the feeling just wouldn't go away. She knew that she could put it off no longer, her heart began to sink as she realized that the feeling of being under the weather that she had been unable to shake off for the last few weeks may well be easily explained. The bittersweet realization hit her: she must be pregnant.

Rory was waiting outside the door. Checking whether it was okay to come in, he nudged the door open and came and sat next to her on the floor, rubbing her back. 'You poor thing,' he said. 'What can I do to make you feel better? I can't bear seeing you like this.'

She suddenly realised that she couldn't put it off a moment longer. She had to know once and for all. 'Rory,' said Lucy, taking a deep breath, 'would you mind driving me to the pharmacy?' she asked. 'I think I had better do a test.'

A shadow of confusion flickered over Rory's face, swiftly followed by understanding. 'Oh, you think you could be pregnant?' he asked, unable to stop the beginnings of a smile from twitching at the corners of his mouth.

Lucy shook her head, 'I don't know.'

Rory gave her a hug and said, 'Well, that wouldn't be a bad thing, y'know. I mean, I haven't really thought about it, but definitely someday I'd love nothing more.' Seeing her worried expression, he said, 'It'd be okay, Lucy, really it would.'

She loved him even more for his reaction, but the truth was, it would not be okay if the baby was not his. She felt as though she was on the precipice of a cliff about to step off the edge. As soon as she crossed that point she knew there would be no going back. She just couldn't put it off any longer.

The rest of the family were heading out for a long walk up the Sugarloaf. They were very understanding and sympathetic when they heard that Lucy wasn't feeling well and agreed that it would be best if they just stayed at home so she could rest. As soon as they had gone, Rory nipped out to the local pharmacy to buy Lucy a test. The wait for him to return was one of the longest of Lucy's life. She felt as though her perfect future was in the palm of her hand but that it had suddenly started to crumble, sliding through her grasp like grains of sand disappearing into the wind.

A short while later Rory came back, clutching a paper bag. He seemed in an indescribably happy mood, the prospect of impending fatherhood did not seem to worry him in the slightest; in fact, Lucy realized, his eyes were full of hope. He was hoping the result might be positive. If only he knew what that could mean, that the baby could just as easily not be his. How could fate be so cruel?

Smiling thanks to Rory for buying her the test, she went into the bathroom, clutching the little box. She knew the routine; she had done it many times before, remembering the crushing disappointment each time a single blue line appeared. As she peed on the stick, she caught a flicker of hope, of excitement, that the baby she had longed for, had worked so hard for, might finally have arrived. But this was overshadowed with utter dread for the implications of what that would mean. If she was pregnant, the baby would either be Rory's or an unknown donor. If it was Rory's then she could allow herself to believe that he could forgive her, that he would stay by her side and everything would be okay. It might be a bit soon in their relationship but she was confident they would be strong enough to make it work. But if it turned out the baby wasn't his….she couldn't bear thinking about it. She couldn't believe the timing. He had just told her that he loved her and now she was potentially about to destroy everything. She had to be honest with him.

Rory knocked on the door, and said, 'Luce, let's wait for the results together, okay?' He saw tears wetting her cheeks and wiped them away with kisses. 'Hey, don't cry, I know that this is scary but we'll get through it together. I love you, Lucy,' he said, wrapping his arms around her.

'I love you too,' whispered Lucy, knowing that those words had never been more truly spoken.

They sat on the sofa, the stick in front of them, waiting. Nothing happened. They stared at the little square window where the results would show. The seconds ticked by. Eventually two thin blue lines began to emerge. Instantly, Lucy knew that this time was different. She felt time slow down as her mind spun with a million different emotions. A tidal wave of joy rushed over her: pure, undiluted joy at the knowledge that she was finally, *finally* pregnant. She was also flooded with a feeling of relief that she had been able to conceive when she knew only too well how many women could not, but mostly she was filled with terror at the thought of having to tell Rory that this baby may not be his. All these emotions came at once, a wall of feeling that she was slammed into with full force.

Meanwhile Rory had been giving a running commentary of 'There are two lines, are there two lines? What does that mean? That means you're pregnant, right? Oh my god, let me check the packet. Yes, it says two lines pregnant. Oh my god. Oh my GOD... you're PREGNANT!!!' This last bit he shouted so loudly, a grin exploding from ear to ear as he grabbed Lucy and kissed her all over her face, saying over and over again, 'Oh my god, I can't believe it, I just can't believe it.'

Lucy quietly said, 'Rory,' trying to get his attention. She repeated it several times but to no avail, eventually she rose her voice and shouted, 'Rory, *stop!*'

He looked at her in confusion. 'What is it?' he muttered quietly, seeing something in her eyes that filled his face with instant doubt.

'I've got something I need to tell you,' she whispered, her eyes filling with tears.

'No!' said Rory. 'I don't want to hear it.'

'You have to,' said Lucy, shaking her head. She took his hands in hers and whispered, 'I'm so sorry.'

'You've cheated on me, haven't you,' whispered Rory, tears suddenly glistening in his eyes too, his voice unsteady.

'No, I swear. I would never, *ever* do that to you. I love you. I love you so, so much,' she said softly, her eyes drinking in the man of her dreams as he sat before her, the man she adored more than life itself, that she couldn't bear to live without. 'I don't know how to tell you this. I've wanted to, so many times, but I couldn't find the words. I didn't think you'd understand.'

'Try me,' said Rory, his voice sounding tight and firm.

She could feel him trying to distance himself from her, trying to regain some ground as he felt the world shift beneath him. He had already experienced so much loss, so much heartache, she couldn't bear the thought of hurting him.

'Before I met you, I had given up on men. When Alex left me, I thought that was it, that I had had my chance at love, at having a traditional family with a husband and a child. It hit me very hard. I was so lost. I decided to take control of my life once and for all. The thing that I knew I wanted more than anything else in the world was a baby. I knew that at thirty-six I didn't have long left to try. I thought long and hard about it, I really did, and I decided that I wanted to have a baby, no matter what. I didn't have a partner but that didn't mean it was impossible. I did lots of research and I found an amazing clinic. They helped me to go through a process called intra-uterine insemination. It meant that I would try to conceive using a donor's sperm. The first and second rounds of IUI failed.' Taking a deep breath, she continued, 'After my third round of treatment I went to Holland Park to go for a walk and clear my head. That's when I met you in the queue to buy coffee…'

As Lucy spoke, understanding dawned on Rory's face, the creases around his eyes and on his forehead grew deeper, a look of exhaustion, maybe anger, passed over his face. He lowered his head into his hands and rubbed his forehead. 'But, that time, when the condom split… I thought, I assumed, it was my baby,' he muttered.

'That was only a week later. It could be yours. I have no way of knowing,' she whispered, as tears slowly rolled down her cheek. 'I'm so sorry,' she said. 'I'm so, so sorry. I didn't know how to tell you. I didn't know what to do, and then I got my period and I thought I definitely wasn't pregnant so it would all be okay. But now...' she shook her head, sadly.

'How could you not have told me?' he asked, his eyes full of hurt. 'How could you? I don't understand...' he trailed off. 'If there's one thing I thought we had it was honesty, no secrets...'

'Please forgive me,' she whispered. 'It'll be okay, I promise, we'll figure it out. Please forgive me. You have to forgive me,' she begged, her shoulders racking with sobs.

He just looked at her, a long and sorrowful look, and shrugged his shoulders. 'I don't know, Luce. I don't know if I can. This whole situation it's just... I don't even know what to think. I've waited so long to meet you. You're the first person I've really cared about in such a long time and now this? You could be pregnant with another man's child? What am I supposed to do with that?'

She tried to put her arms around him, desperate for reassurance that everything would be okay, but he shrugged her off. His eyes were full of tears. She could see how disappointed he was. He muttered something about needing space then he got up from the sofa, walked over to the back door, grabbed his coat and went outside.

She watched him as he walked head down towards the woods at the bottom of the hill. She felt her heart wrench in pain and collapsed to her knees on the floor, unable to stop the tears from falling. She prayed that he would come back to her, that he would find it within himself to somehow understand, to somehow forgive her for not telling him the truth, but she had a sickening feeling, deep within her core, that it was too much for him. She couldn't even let herself think it, but somewhere in the depths of her soul she knew that she had crossed a line that would be impossible for him to forgive, after everything he had been through, after all the loss he had known. If the baby wasn't his, how could she expect him to stay with her and bring up another man's child?

When Rory returned to the house quarter of an hour later, he was very quiet. He had clammed tightly shut like a sealed shell and Lucy was unable to draw anything out of him.

'Rory, please talk to me,' said Lucy.

'I'm sorry, Lucy, but I just don't want to talk about it anymore; I need time and space to think. This has been a lot for me to take in.'

When his family got back he did a valiant job of covering up what had happened while they were all out walking. He explained that Lucy had come down with the flu. The family were all too happy to send them off on their flight back to London later that afternoon, unwilling to catch any germs that could be avoided. They waved at Lucy, not getting too close for fear of infection, and she smiled gratefully at their warm, kind faces as they said goodbye. She watched them from the front seat of the car as Rory loaded their bags in the back, and felt her eyes fill once more with tears at the prospect of never seeing them again. Everything had been so perfect, too perfect perhaps.

Rory got in the car after saying a falsely cheery goodbye and revved the engine, putting his foot on the accelerator and swinging out of the drive. Lucy asked him if he was ready to talk. He shook his head. The look of hurt and confusion in his eyes broke her heart.

As they drove through the rolling hills, Lucy looked sadly out of the window and contemplated her new fate. Feelings of bitterness welled inside her at the thought of how unfair life was, at how awful the timing seemed to be. Just when she had her perfect future in the palm of her hand it was wrenched away and thrown into chaos. She couldn't bear the irony of it all. In any other circumstance the sight of those two blue lines would have been the cause of the most immense joy, but now it was all unbearably bittersweet. Lucy was grasped once again in the disturbing clutches of the unknown, and the familiar feelings of doubt that she had tried so hard to get rid of settled over her, wrapping around her like a cloak.

The journey home was spent in silence. Lucy began to feel angry with Rory's refusal to engage with her. This was the man who had sworn blind earlier that day that he would be there for her, no matter what. That he loved her. And now he could barely look at her, let alone talk to her about how he was feeling. She wished she could get inside his head and know even a tiny bit of what he was thinking. Did he hate her? What if the baby was his, what then?

She closed her eyes and wished herself anywhere but here, in this awful situation. The awkward silence continued as they made their way into the arrivals hall back in London.

He turned to face her and her heart melted at the sight of him, there were shadows under his eyes and his brow was twisted and creased with the weight of his thoughts. As they stood in the middle of the big, open space, he took a deep breath and said, 'I think I'd better get home,' his voice cracking slightly.

Tears sprung into her eyes once more. 'Rory, don't do this. We need to talk about it. Please… if we don't, then we'll never get through this…' she begged.

He just looked at her, there were tears in his eyes once again.

'What's going to happen?' she asked softly, hardly daring to even utter the words.

'I don't know,' he said, looking at her with sorrow and regret. 'I just don't know,' he repeated, shaking his head. Then he turned his back on her and strode off towards the train station, leaving her standing there with her little suitcase, bereft and miserable.

She had a sudden urge to scream his name and run after him, but she stood as though paralysed to the spot. She didn't know what she could say to change his mind.

A few minutes later she followed in his footsteps, numbly making her way back home, her mind working overtime to process the day's events. When she got back to her flat, she telephoned the clinic and told them that her recent pregnancy test had shown a positive result. The nurse said, 'Oh what fantastic news! Congratulations! I hope you don't mind me asking but why hadn't you taken the test earlier?'

'I had a completely normal period,' Lucy explained. 'I just assumed that it hadn't worked… it wasn't until I started feeling unwell that I thought I'd better take a test just in case…' she trailed off.

The nurse said, 'That is unusual but it's not the first time I have heard it happen. You must be delighted. We'll have you in tomorrow to see the sonographer for your early pregnancy scan.'

As Lucy put down the phone, she walked over to the long mirror and lifted up her top. She prodded her tummy, looking for any signs of change.

Lucy spent the evening in quiet contemplation, trying to accept the path she had chosen to take without regret. Every time a thought along the lines of *Why did I do this?* popped into her head, she let it go. She reminded herself that there was absolutely no way she would do anything to harm this life that she had created. It had been her decision to have the treatment, she could never have guessed in a million years that someone like Rory was going to come along, out of the blue, and sweep her off her feet. Despite the unbearable sadness she felt when she thought about him, and the raw pain of the distance between them that grew with every second that passed, a quiet smile spread through her body at the knowledge that the baby she had dreamed of, the baby she had longed for, was growing safely inside her. A sense of peace settled on the part of her heart that had been desperate for a child. She was going to have a baby, and as long as she had that she would be fine, heartbroken maybe, but she wouldn't be alone, she would have her own family. All she could do was give Rory space and time to process the bombshell she had dropped on him, and pray for him to come back to her. As she rested her hands lightly on her tummy, she told her baby that she loved it, that she would never, ever regret it.

Chapter Thirty-Four

The next morning, Lucy called in sick to work; seeing as she had spent the past couple of hours with her head over the loo, she didn't even have to lie. It would appear her morning sickness had finally kicked in.

A few hours later, her nausea having mercifully beaten a temporary retreat, she caught the bus to the London Women's Clinic. This time, it was with a very different feeling that she made her way through to the waiting room. A sad smile played on her lips as she looked at all the nervous couples and single women who sat around her, desperately hoping and praying for a miracle to happen to them, a miracle just like the one that had happened to her.

The sonographer came to collect her, calling out, 'Lucy Johnston?' and looking expectantly around the room. Lucy stood up and shook her hand; she followed her to one of the little private rooms upstairs. All at once she felt incredibly nervous, what if the test had been wrong? But she knew deep inside that there had been no mistake, she was certain of it now.

As she lay on the bed and the cold gel was applied to her flat stomach, she prayed for a healthy heartbeat. Her body was full of mixed emotions, nerves and excitement in equal measure. She had to pinch herself to believe that she was about to catch her first glimpse of her own baby. As the sonographer chatted merrily away to her, she felt herself relax. Before long the image was projected on to the screen in front of her. The nurse smiled happily as she pointed out the tiny embryo in the black cavity of her womb. It looked like a little gummy bear. Lucy couldn't believe her eyes. There was her baby, right in front of her! Her heart swelled with pride and love for this little smidgen of life. She could see the heartbeat flickering on the screen and tears rolled freely down Lucy's cheeks as she repeated over and over again, 'I can't believe it! I just can't believe it!' The relief she felt that she was finally, undeniably pregnant was immense.

When the scan was over, Lucy went to see the nurse who talked through the next steps with her. Everything seemed to be in order and there was nothing for Lucy to worry about, so from this point onwards she would be placed back into the care of the NHS, and the pregnancy would be treated as any natural conception would have been. The next scan would be in four weeks' time. Lucy prayed that Rory would be back by her side by then. She resisted the temptation to call or text him, desperate to talk to him but aware that the best thing she could do right now was give him space. She was given a little photograph of the scan to keep and she stared at it all the way home, her heart swollen to bursting point with love for this miniscule little baby.

That afternoon was spent making telephone calls. One by one she telephoned Tor, Claudia and Nicola. She told them the whole truth, leaving nothing out. They were ecstatic to hear of her pregnancy and sad but unsurprised to hear of Rory's reaction. They all comforted her with reassurances that he would come around, especially because of the possibility that the baby could be his.

'He'll come back, Luce, I know he will,' said Tor. 'If not, if you have to go it alone, then you know I'm here for you… one hundred per cent,' Tor added. 'We all are.'

Lucy knew that this was true; she thanked her lucky stars once more for her incredible friends.

Ginny and Gus's reaction was slightly different, as expected. She had to come clean about the round of treatment she had hidden from them in January. 'Do you know what, darling, I really hate to say it but I almost feel sorry for him, I really do,' said Ginny. 'I blame myself for letting you go down the donor route in the first place.'

'Don't be silly, Mum, there was nothing you could have done to change my mind. Who would have thought someone like Rory would come along?' said Lucy.

'But if only we hadn't given you that money at Christmas…' Despite their feelings of regret, they were incredibly supportive of Lucy.

Gus, more matter-of-fact than his wife, said, 'Look, it's happened now, love, so there is no point having regrets. We'll do whatever we can to help you going forward, with or without Rory.'

They were both desperate to be grandparents, and even though the circumstances were not perfect, Lucy could tell that they were both excited at the prospect of a new member of the family arriving in seven months' time.

That evening, she Skyped her brother and explained all the latest developments. Nothing fazed Ollie, and he congratulated her on the happy news, excited that he would be an uncle, telling her in his karmic way not to worry, that everything happened for a reason and what would be would be.

Before hanging up the phone to each of her friends and family members, she made them promise not to tell another soul until the twelve-week scan was safely out of the way. It was only then that she would begin to tell everyone that she was pregnant, for until twelve weeks had passed anything could happen. They promised to keep it to themselves, especially Ginny with regards to Lucy's grandmother. Annie wouldn't understand the situation at all. If she ended up on her own, she would just have to come up with a way of explaining things to Annie, but she would cross that bridge if and when she came to it.

Claudia came over that evening and they talked about Rory and what to do next. 'I've got faith in him,' she said. 'Anyone who had seen you together could see how much he loved you. I'm sure he'll decide that he can't live without you.'

Lucy hoped she was right with all her heart. The thought of not seeing Rory again, of not holding him in her arms, of not hearing him laugh, was too awful to consider. She knew that it was a possibility that Rory wouldn't come back, but she just couldn't face the thought of going through the next seven months of pregnancy alone, without him by her side. Her eyes filled with tears at the thought. She refused to believe it could happen. They were meant to be together, of that she was completely sure. No one else had ever come close to him. Their relationship had felt different right from the start, so natural and uncomplicated.

'Have you thought about maybe doing a paternity test? Can't you do them before the baby is born these days?' asked Claudia.

'I've thought about it, but it seems there are always so many complications with these things. I think I'd rather wait until the baby is born.'

Perhaps if he knew the baby was his, Rory would come around, and they could slowly build the foundations of a relationship once more and finally become a family.

'I think you should wait until tomorrow to contact him,' said Claudia. 'After two days of silence and time to think, he might feel ready to talk.'

Lucy agreed that this was probably the best approach. She kissed Claudia goodbye and got ready for bed, suddenly exhausted after the roller coaster of emotions that she had been on for the last two days. An early night was exactly what she needed.

Lucy found work the next day a brand new experience. She kept on thinking about her secret, she felt unbelievably distracted from the task in hand, and had to stop herself from blurting out to everyone that she was pregnant. She decided not to mention anything about Rory to Lettie and Simon, telling them the truth about the weekend up until Sunday, then describing how ill she felt when she got home and how she had spent yesterday tucked up in bed. With no reason to doubt her, Lettie and Simon believed her story and continued to treat her perfectly normally, for which she was grateful. They did not notice the obsessive refreshing of her email inbox, or the constant furtive glances at the display window of her mobile phone, desperately hoping for Rory to contact her, to tell her everything was going to be okay. But nothing came.

That afternoon she had a meeting with Sharon and Jack to review their social enterprise telecoms project. At the end of the meeting after Sharon had left, Jack called out her name as she was leaving, 'Lucy, can you just hang on for a sec?' he asked.

'Sure,' she said. It was the first time they had found themselves alone in a room together since they had spent the night with each other. It occurred to her that there was absolutely no interest left as far as Jack was concerned. Her feelings for him had well and truly disappeared. 'Did we forget something?' she asked.

'No, no… it's nothing to do with that.' He looked past her to make sure the corridor was clear and lowered his voice. 'I just wanted to let you know that Penny has asked me to move back in. We are going to give things another go,' he said.

'That's wonderful news!' Lucy was genuinely pleased for him. 'I'm really happy for you. I hope it all works out for you both.'

'Thanks Lucy. I appreciate it. And thank you… for your discretion…' He looked slightly embarrassed as she nodded to show him that she understood what he was saying.

She stood awkwardly and smiled at him, mumbling, 'Of course…' She didn't know what to say next. She hesitated by the door, not knowing whether to leave or stay and talk. Jack started shuffling his papers so she took the opportunity to say, 'I'd better go… I've got a conference call in a couple of minutes…' He nodded and she closed the door behind her and walked back to her desk. That conversation had made her feel surprisingly uncomfortable. She was glad for Jack and Penny though, and for their children. Maybe all was not lost for her and Rory. It was clearly possible to survive difficult times in a relationship if you were prepared to work at it. She just hoped that this wasn't going to prove too much to ask of him.

That evening she spent ages composing a text, unsure of what to say to him. In the end, she settled on:

I hope you have had time to think, are you ready to talk? Please call me. I love you so much. I hope you are okay. L xxx

Lucy sat by her phone for the rest of the evening, willing a message to appear on the screen or the ringtone to chime out its cheery tune. At times she would walk away, thinking of Ginny saying 'a watched pot never boils,' her ears straining to hear the ping of a new text, before hurrying back over to it just in case she had missed something. Still nothing came.

She could picture Rory sitting by his fire, a glass of whisky in his hand and Rufus at his feet. She couldn't bear to think of the inner turmoil she had plunged him into. She knew he would be torn up inside, that he wouldn't want to hurt her but that he didn't know what to do, how to react. If he came back to her, he would face the possibility of raising a child that was not his. The thought of him sitting there by himself made her cry; she ached for his arms to be around her, for his eyes to crinkle as he smiled at her, stroked her cheek and told her that he loved her, that nothing else mattered.

That week, the silence continued. She tried calling him several times; she even went to his house one evening and rang on the doorbell, sitting on the steps for half an hour, just waiting. She became enraged at him, shouting through the letter box, pummelling the door with her fists, begging him to shout at her, scream at her, tell her to go to hell... anything but this silent treatment. She couldn't bear it. She telephoned her father in tears and asked him what she should do. Gus advised her, 'Go home, my love. You're going to have to leave him alone. If Rory is going to come back, he will come back of his own accord, you can't force him. It's going to take time for him to think through his options. If it is meant to be, then sooner or later he will realize that he can't imagine his life without you, despite the circumstances.'

Realizing the wisdom in her father's words, Lucy decided to stop contacting Rory. As hard as it might be, she couldn't make him come back. He knew how much she loved him, but if he felt coerced or pressured it would make him less likely to return to her. If he did come back, he needed to know that it had been his decision, and his alone.

Two painful, horrendous weeks of utter heartbreak had passed since Ireland. Lucy had never known pain like it. When Alex had left her she thought she had felt the depths of despair, but that was nothing compared to this. Rory was her whole world, and she loved him, she really loved him. She was painfully aware that *she* had chosen this path; it was her fault and hers alone that Rory was no longer with her. After Alex had left she would reassure herself with the thought that there was nothing she could have done differently, he just hadn't loved her enough. She had taken comfort in that. Besides, she had always disliked the darker, more negative side of his personality. She had known deep down that she could have found someone better. But there was no one who could ever come close to Rory. He truly was her perfect man. There was no denying that Lucy was responsible for the situation she currently found herself in, and that hurt her almost more than she could bear. She refused to blame her baby. She already loved her unborn child with all her heart and felt fiercely protective over it, but the harrowing, heart-wrenching sorrow she felt without Rory was all-consuming. Eventually, she began to feel numb; she had no more tears left to cry.

Before she knew it, the first week of April had arrived and Lucy was due for her twelve week scan. She had prayed and prayed that she would not have to go through this alone, but as the morning of her appointment dawned, there was still no Rory by her side. She turned down offers from Nicola, Tor, Claudia and Ginny to be there. She needed to face facts; she would be doing this alone. Rory had not even sent her a single message since they had last seen each other at the airport. Lucy had started to give up hope. But wasn't this what she'd asked for? She was going to be a single mother and she needed to reconcile herself with that fact.

Taking a deep breath to steady her nerves, she took her seat in the waiting room, surrounded it seemed by nothing but happy couples. She really did feel alone. It was a different environment from the clinic, and as she surveyed the smiling faces, noticing the tender glances and solidarity between the husbands and their wives as they waited for their turn, she felt deep pangs of longing for Rory wash over her.

'Lucy Johnston?' called the sonographer.

Once again she lay in the chair as the sonographer spread gel onto her tummy.

'There we go, my lovely, here's your baby!' she said as the picture flashed up onto the screen.

'Oh my god, I can't believe how much it has grown!' Lucy said. She could make out a real baby now, the instantly recognizable dome of the head with a tiny body curled up beneath it. The baby's heartbeat thudded loudly into the room. Lucy felt euphoric happiness course through her body as she realized that she was past the most risky part of her pregnancy.

The sonographer reassured her that all was well and once again Lucy was given an image of the baby to take away with her. She wrapped her fingers around the picture in her pocket all the way home, swiftly getting out her telephone and sharing the happy news with her family and friends.

Without thinking, she found herself heading towards Holland Park. Having wound her way through the path that led to the centre of the park, she sat down at the table in the cafe where she had first met Rory. She took out her phone once again, her heartbeat thudding in her ears, and sent a photograph of the scan to him, with a message attached.

Just thought you should know, in case the baby is yours, I have had the twelve week scan, here he/she is. I love you. I miss you. I will always love you. L x

The empty feeling in her heart, that she had felt constantly since he left, ached deeper than ever. She wished things could have worked out differently. Thoughts beginning with 'If only…' constantly drifted in and out of her mind. She felt almost crazy with the emotions that were running through her; the depths of despair at losing Rory coupled with the radiant joy of being pregnant. She felt like a madwoman teetering on the edge of hysteria.

Suddenly overwhelmed with missing him, she got up from the table and walked briskly away. That place had too many painful memories, she needed to distance herself. She walked home and ran herself a bath, sinking slowly into the jasmine-scented water. She felt sure that her belly was beginning to look a little swollen now. Looking down at her mini bump, she told her baby how much she loved it, how she couldn't wait to meet it. She would force herself to look forwards and not back.

Chapter Thirty-Five

The next week, it was her thirty-seventh birthday. Lucy woke with a start in the middle of the night with tears streaming down her face. She had been having the same recurring dream since Ireland. She and Rory were blissfully happy together, laughing and dancing, kissing and whispering sweet nothings into each other's ears, then suddenly he faded, growing fainter and fainter until she realized that he had gone, that he wasn't coming back. Each time, the hurt became raw again like an open wound and she would find herself crying into her pillow, unable to cope with the abyss of pain she felt at losing him.

Slowly coming to her senses she realized that it was her birthday and smiled ironically to herself through her tears; what a way to start the day!

She closed her eyes and went back to sleep, forcing herself to dream instead of her baby and the new life of motherhood she was embarking on.

Her alarm beeped rudely and unrepentantly at 6.45 a.m., rousing her from a restless sleep. Her phone was already buzzing with messages from friends near and far, her icons blinking from Facebook, WhatsApp and all sorts of disparate social media sites, sending her birthday wishes. Lucy had always loved her birthday, but as she scanned her messages she was only looking for one name, Rory McCullan, and his was nowhere to be seen.

Slowly waking herself up, she got dressed for work whilst listening to Chris Evans on Radio 2, his upbeat chatter was definitely the most cheerful way to start any day, and today she needed it more than ever. How strange, she thought to herself, that this was the last day she would celebrate a birthday by herself. Next year, she would have her baby with her.

She had decided to start telling people about the baby tomorrow; she just wanted to get her birthday over and done with first before the attention fell to her pregnancy and answering all sorts of awkward questions about Rory that would no doubt follow.

To celebrate her birthday Lettie and Simon had brought in little cakes and a bottle of champagne. Lucy accepted a glass and pretended to sip it.

She kept her phone on vibrate all day. Her heart would leap into her mouth with false hope every time it buzzed as she raced to read the birthday greetings, hoping beyond hope that it would be from the only person that she really wanted to hear from. As the day went on she realized that the last flame of hope that had been flickering inside her was spluttering out. She had been clinging to the idea that Rory would contact her today, that he would be unable to resist the thought of her spending her birthday alone. But she realized now that he was gone. He hadn't been able to reconcile himself with the prospect of her having a child that wasn't his. She was heartbroken, but if she truly searched her soul she couldn't blame him. Would she have been able to bring up a stranger's child as if it were her own? She couldn't be sure.

After work she met up with the girls, Tor, Claudia and Nicola, for supper. They went to a trendy new tapas bar in Borough Market. The others drank lots of red wine and chatted about baby names, trying to steer the topic of conversation away from Rory and men in general, keeping things light-hearted and fun. Lucy grilled Nicola and Tor with a million questions about pregnancy and childbirth, while

Claudia played her comedic role to perfection, rolling her eyes in bewilderment and pretending to pass out in disgust! Lucy was genuinely intrigued to find out exactly what was going to happen to her in the next six months. She wanted to be as fully prepared as possible for what was to come.

After the meal, Nicola gave Lucy a beautiful gold bangle with a turquoise stone for her birthday present.

'It's stunning!' said Lucy as she slid the cool metal over her wrist. 'Thank you so much Nic.'

'It's my pleasure,' said Nicola, thrilled with Lucy's reaction.

'And from us, an envelope!' said Claudia as Tor pushed a card across the table.

'A Mothercare voucher!' laughed Lucy. 'What a good idea!'

'It's to put towards baby stuff,' said Claudia, stating the obvious.

'But only when you have raided all my bits and pieces that I no longer need for Otto,' added Tor. Tor was keen to give her as much baby paraphernalia as possible now that Otto was growing older and no longer needed it; she was desperate to declutter her house a little.

Later, as the time came for them to make their way home, Lucy said, 'Thank you so much, for everything… for your presents and for tonight. But mostly, thank you so much for being there for me, no matter what. It means the world to me and I couldn't do this without you.' She found herself getting a little tearful when she said goodbye as they put her in a taxi, with shouts of 'Happy Birthday' and 'We love you!' fading into the distance as she set off towards Baron's Court.

Lucy sat back heavily in her seat and reached into her bag to check her phone for one last time in the dim light of the taxi. Still nothing. Her heart sank to the bottom of her shoes. A shuddering sigh escaped her lips. With her hand on her tummy, she said to her baby, 'This is it now. It's just you and me.' She sat like that for the rest of the journey, staring out of the window as the lights of London flickered like oil lamps from the inky black silhouettes of the buildings they passed by. Finally, the taxi driver turned into Mayfield Road and pulled up opposite number thirteen. A big van was parked outside her house and she wondered vaguely who it belonged to as she paid the taxi driver and thanked him for taking her home.

Wearily, she clambered out of the taxi and crossed the road, reaching into her handbag to find her house keys. As she weaved her way through the gap between the van and the car next to it, she suddenly became aware of a person sitting on the steps leading up to her flat.

He lifted his head as she approached, 'Lucy?' he asked softly.

Lucy took a sharp intake of breath; she could not believe her eyes. There, sitting right in front of her, bedraggled and exhausted, was Rory. Her heart stopped beating; she was frozen to the spot as though the Medusa had turned her into solid stone. She dared not move, dared not breathe, in case she somehow shattered the illusion and he disappeared, as he had done so many times in her dreams. Finally finding the strength to speak, she whispered, 'Rory... you're here.' A single tear escaped from her eye and rolled down her cheek.

'Happy birthday,' he said, standing up and coming over to her, wrapping his arms around her and holding her as though he would never let her go. She felt as though she had finally come home, this was where she belonged; she knew it with every fibre of her being. She breathed in the musky, peppery smell of him and squeezed as tightly as she could. 'I've missed you so much,' he said, his voice choked with emotion.

'Me too,' she sobbed into his shoulder. 'I thought you weren't coming,' she whispered. She was desperate to know why he was here. She didn't dare believe that all her wishes had come true, that he was back for good, that he had somehow found it in his heart to forgive her.

Gently, he pulled away from her and looked down at her with those beautiful blue eyes, 'I'm so sorry, Luce. I've been in turmoil these last few weeks, I didn't know what to do, what to say, so I just didn't say or do anything at all. It was so cowardly of me. You didn't deserve it. I've been in Edinburgh working this past week or I would have come sooner, but I had to see you.' Seeing that she was crying, he said, 'Don't cry, please don't cry. I'm here now. It's okay, it's okay,' wiping away the tears that were falling down her cheeks. Then he took her face in his hands and he kissed her. The moment she had been dreaming of and praying for had finally arrived; relief flooded through every part of her body as she kissed him back. She hoped fervently that this meant he had indeed forgiven her, that he could see a way forward for them.

'You're freezing,' she said, noticing that his face and hands were stone cold beneath her touch.

Rory rubbed his hands together to warm them up. 'I've been sitting here all evening, waiting for you to get home. I didn't know what time you'd be back, and I didn't want to call you. I needed to speak to you face to face, to explain.'

'Let's get you inside,' Lucy said, fumbling once again for her keys and opening the front door. They walked up the stairs, hand in hand. She unlocked the door to her flat, switching on the light and putting her bag down on the floor. Her heart was pounding.

They crossed over to the sofa and sat down. Rory took both of her hands in his. Taking a deep breath, he said, 'Lucy, before

I start I just have to tell you how much I love you. The thought of living without you these past few weeks has been like torture. I thought about it, I really did. You see I just didn't know what to do; the whole thing came as such a shock, the pregnancy, the donor stuff. I felt like I'd been knocked sideways. It was awful. I love you so much but I had to think carefully, I had to decide whether I could stand by you if the baby isn't mine. I hated myself for not contacting you. When I heard you outside my house all I wanted to do was race to the door and open it, to tell you it would be okay, but I just sat there, unable to move. I knew that I couldn't come here until I had figured everything out. I needed to tell you that yes, I'd stay or no, I couldn't, once and for all. Anything else wouldn't have been fair.'

Lucy listened and nodded, saying 'It's okay. I understand,' as he spoke, holding his hands tightly in hers, her eyes brimming with tears. Her heart sank as she realised that he had come to explain himself, to justify his decision to leave her. It was all too much for him. He couldn't accept what she had done.

'When you sent me that photo of the scan, everything changed. I looked at that baby and I saw you. I felt such a strong pang of love for that little thing, that I knew, instantly, that I could love it, even if it turns out not to be mine, because it is you.' Tears streamed down Lucy's cheeks as she realised she was hearing the words she had so desperately hoped she would hear. 'It is yours. And I love you, Lucy, so much that it hurts. I can't bear the thought of life without you. I don't want to live another second without you. I am in. I am here. If you'll have me, I am yours. Forever. I have already lost love once before, and I am not... I *will* not, lose you. Please forgive me.' He looked at her nervously, waiting for her response, and she could see how much he meant every word that he had said, every beautiful, miraculous word.

'Of course I will, Rory. I love you more than anything,' she whispered, tears once again falling freely, this time of happiness, and they held each other and kissed through their smiles and laughter.

Then Rory placed his hands on either side of her waist, he planted several kisses on her tummy and gently stroked it, saying, 'Hello little baby, I can't wait to meet you. I promise I'm going to take good care of you and your mummy.' He sat back up and kissed Lucy again and at that moment she knew that they would make it, the three of them, their very own little family.

Chapter Thirty-Six

The following weekend Lucy moved into Thurloe Crescent. Rory was certainly determined to make up for his recent absence. She was sure that their time apart had forced them both to re-evaluate their relationship. They were both completely and utterly besotted with each other. It was as if they were in the first throws of young love once again. They spent all their time together. Rory took great care of her, empathizing with the miseries of morning sickness and the overwhelming tiredness she was experiencing. They created space for Lucy's paintings and furniture in the house and soon she felt completely at home. She had always loved Rory's house but now that it was full of her belongings it had started to feel like her home too. Simon had given Lucy a little flipchart which she had positioned on Rory's bedside table. It was supposed to chart the progress of your baby's growth throughout the course of the pregnancy, however instead of the usual fruit-sized comparisons, it was a 'dad-friendly' version. The baby had already passed through 'day-old stubble', 'chocolate drop' and 'cufflink' to become the size of a 'golf ball'.

As her bump passed through 'baseball', 'BlackBerry' and 'loo roll', Lucy decided it was high time she stopped her usual running regime. Instead they took gentle walks around the park with Rufus tearing off at his usual pace, terrorizing the wildlife. Rory tried his best to make life as easy as possible for her. He took on full responsibility for the housework and cooking and generally declared himself at her disposal for whatever she needed, be it foot rubs or endless cups of herbal tea. Rory was so excited about the prospect of fatherhood that he read almost every parenting book going. He made sure that Lucy was taking care of herself, sleeping and eating well and giving the baby everything it could possibly need.

Every night he would crawl under the covers and wriggle down the bed. He would say goodnight to the baby using whatever term of endearment the calendar happened to define the baby's size that week. 'Night night little Benjy,' was a particular favourite for week eighteen, a tub of Ben and Jerrie's ice cream. Or, a few weeks later, 'Sleep well Whoopee. Don't you wriggle too much and keep your mummy awake now.' One night a tiny little fist pummelled the taut skin of her stomach as he was doing so. 'Lucy! Uke gave me a high five!' he squealed in disbelief at the little imprint that he had seen appear for a split second before disappearing just as quickly. The baby was apparently the size of a ukulele now, a thought that somewhat disturbed Lucy.

'I certainly felt that one!' laughed Lucy, reaching around to the spot where the baby had kicked her.

'What does it feel like?' asked Rory. He had been intrigued by every stage of her pregnancy, his fascination increasing all the more as her bump continued to swell.

'Honestly? It feels like an alien is wriggling around inside me,' said Lucy.

'That doesn't sound very pleasant!' said Rory.

'It's not unpleasant exactly, more uncomfortable. But you do get used to it!'

Lucy had loved being pregnant and had never lost the feeling of wonder and gratitude, of awe, at what was happening to her. She knew some women weren't lucky enough to experience it and that it truly was a miracle: a blessing and not a right.

They had decided to wait until the baby was born to find out the sex. For Rory it had been love at first sight; he had been utterly enamoured with the baby at the twenty-week scan. The sight of its tiny curving forehead with its little button nose, its fist curling up towards its face, coupled with the miraculous sound of the heartbeat echoing through the room had moved them both to tears.

'Not long now little one,' he said, planting a kiss on her belly. 'Not long now! You sleep tight.' He crawled back up to the top of the bed as Lucy rolled over; resting her bump on the crescent shape pillow Rory had bought her for extra support. He stroked her hair and kissed her gently.

'I love you Luce,' he said as her eyes began to close.

'I love you too,' she said. She truly meant it. He was absolutely everything to her. She had never felt such peace and contentment, and such hope and excitement for the future.

The next day she was going to meet Claudia for lunch in order to celebrate the first day of her maternity leave. It was a month until her due date; she had decided to give herself plenty of time between finishing up at work and the baby's arrival. She had some last-minute baby-related shopping to do, in particular a tube of nipple cream that Tor swore was a lifesaver. Oh how her life had changed!

Chapter Thirty-Seven

Rory's phone vibrated in his pocket as he walked out of the meeting. 'Clauds?' he said, surprised to see her name flash up on his iPhone.

'Rory! I'm so glad you answered!' she said, her voice sounding strangely high-pitched.

'To what do I owe this pleasure?'

'Without wishing to alarm you, I'm in a taxi with Lucy and we're on the way to the hospital. Her waters broke while we were out shopping and she appears to be having contractions!'

'Oh my god! Is she there? Can you put her on?' His heart rate had skyrocketed at this announcement. 'Luce? Are you all right?'

'Hi Rory,' she said. 'I'm okay, don't worry but I'm afraid the baby might be coming rather early.'

'Have you spoken to the midwife?'

'Yes I've just called the hospital. They think I am in labour. It should be okay, the baby should be fine. Will you come as soon as you can?'

'I'll jump in a cab right now. See you there, oh and keep your phone on you,' he said as he hung up the phone. He flagged the very next black cab he saw and instructed the driver to head straight to the hospital. Unfortunately, just as the driver rounded the corner, they entered an enormous tailback. There had clearly been an accident up ahead. After several minutes they were still sitting stationary as the lights ahead turned from green to orange and back to red without a single car moving. Rory began to tap the keys on his phone to try and find a travel alert. It seemed that the whole area was totally gridlocked. He scanned the map on his screen but there were no tubes or trains nearby. He tried to figure out his best bet. Should he stay in the car or get out and run? He felt sick with nervous anticipation as he willed the traffic to clear. It was an infuriatingly slow process. His knuckles were white as he drummed his fingers on the seat next to him. He wanted to shout in frustration. Finally, after what seemed like hours, the traffic began to get moving. Slowly but surely, they crawled past the accident. Two cars had collided with each other at a set of lights. Unsurprisingly as soon as they passed the incident the roads began to clear. Rory asked the driver to step on it as he picked up his phone to call Claudia and give her an update as to his whereabouts.

When he finally arrived at the hospital, Rory raced through the corridors, asking the first nurse he saw where he could find the labour ward. He held his phone up to his ear as he ran, listening to Claudia telling Lucy to breathe as she groaned in pain. Things seemed to be moving ridiculously quickly with Lucy's labour. 'Tell her I'm almost there!' he shouted into the receiver, pressing the button for the lift frantically, willing it to arrive quickly and for the baby to stay put for a few moments longer.

Arriving on floor five, he hurtled down the labour ward, getting directions from Claudia as he ran. He pushed open the door to room 137 and saw Lucy lying on the bed. A midwife was by her side; things were clearly progressing fast. 'Lucy!' he called as he ran over to her bed. 'I'm here! It's okay, it's okay.'

Claudia let go of Lucy's hand gratefully and stepped back from the bed as Rory bent down to kiss her forehead. It was clammy with sweat and her cheeks were flushed.

'Rory!' Lucy paused mid-pant. 'I'm so glad you're here. I was so worried you might miss it.'

'Me too!' said Claudia. 'You put the frighteners on us, I can tell you. I'm not quite sure how much of a birthing partner I am cut out to be! And this looks like it's going to be the world's shortest labour!'

'You've been wonderful, Clauds…' Lucy tailed off and gripped onto Rory's hand.

He thought his bones might break from the strength of her grip as another contraction swept through her. It was awful to see her in so much pain. She was using the breathing technique they had been taught in their antenatal classes. Short, sharp bursts of breath.

'Good, you're doing your breathing,' he said, joining in for moral support with the rhythmic breaths. After a minute or so the contraction stopped and Lucy's body relaxed once more.

Turning to face Claudia, Rory said, 'Clauds, how can I thank you? You've been amazing taking care of her so well. You are a true legend.' He was eternally grateful to her for stepping into the breach. He knew it must have been difficult for her with her fear of hospitals.

'I'm just so glad you're here now, before the gory action really starts!' laughed Claudia.

'Thanks Clauds,' said Lucy. 'I really mean it; you truly are the best friend a girl could ask for!'

'Right, I think my work here is done! I shall leave you soon-to-be-parents to it and see you when you are a little family!' she said. She gathered her belongings and bent to kiss Lucy on the cheek. 'See you when you are out my little future godbaby,' she said, leaning down to kiss the bump.

'Yes,' said Lucy, addressing her bump, 'the sooner the better please!' With that, another huge groan reverberated around the room as she was swept up in yet another wave of pain. Lucy's body tensed and her cheeks reddened as she gritted her teeth and waited for the contraction to pass.

'Luce, I'm so sorry it took me so long, the bloody traffic was awful…' he said, taking hold of her hand and pushing her fringe away from her eyes.

'Don't worry. I'm just glad you are here now!' she said as she caught her breath. 'I don't think it's going to be too long now.'

Rory thanked his lucky stars that he had made it in time.

'Keep breathing,' he said as one contraction turned into another, and another. She was breathing in the gas and air as though her life depended on it.

Soon the minutes and seconds of labour began to blur into one long, continuous frenzy of breathing, gritted teeth, stamping feet, sighing and groaning. He was vaguely aware of people coming in and out of the room, of the midwife talking to Lucy and giving her instructions. All he could focus on was Lucy. It broke his heart to see her in so much pain. If he could have traded places with her he would have done so in a heartbeat.

Finally, after one monumental last push from Lucy, the baby arrived. As Lucy collapsed in an exhausted heap back onto the pillows, tears of happiness streaming down her face, Rory inspected the baby at close quarters. 'It's a girl!' he cried. He lowered his head to Lucy's to kiss her, his eyes wet with tears. He was shaking his head in disbelief at the miracle he had just witnessed. It was hard to believe that a new life had arrived in the world. In the room where seconds earlier there had been only three of them, now there were four.

A few seconds later the midwife placed their tiny newborn baby on Lucy's chest. Despite having arrived four weeks earlier than planned, she was perfect. Words could not describe the flood of unconditional love that coursed through Rory like a tidal wave. He could barely believe his eyes, this perfect little bundle of tangled limbs and dark hair was his baby, their baby. He knew with absolute certainty that no matter how this baby had been created she was unquestionably his daughter. For a second he was brought to tears at the thought of how close he had been to throwing it all away. How could he have been so stupid? As he touched her miniscule fist with the tip of his index finger, she curled her fingers around his. Lucy looked at him. His heart was swollen with love for her and their new baby daughter. He couldn't stop smiling. He felt like the luckiest man in the world. He bent over and gently kissed her. 'I love you so much.' he said.

'What shall we call her?' Lucy whispered, unable to take her eyes off the baby's face. They were both utterly mesmerized by her charming, tiny features.

'You know what?' he said. 'I think she looks just like an Annie.'

Lucy smiled, staring down at the baby's perfect little face, still red and wrinkled in protest at her abrupt arrival in this cold and mysterious outside world. 'Annie,' she said. 'It's perfect!'

The midwife examined Lucy once again, lifting the blanket that was covering her modesty. Rory saw a flicker of alarm glance across her face. She tried her best to conceal her concern, quickly rearranging her features into a professional smile, but Rory hadn't missed the initial look of worry at whatever it was she had seen.

'I don't want to worry you, my love, but I'm going to have to call for the doctor,' the midwife said. 'There's still quite a bit of bleeding down here.' She pressed a button on the side of the bed.

Rory's heart skipped a beat. This was clearly not what should be happening after a natural delivery. He smiled reassuringly at Lucy who was looking at him anxiously over Annie's tiny head. She looked so tired, after everything she had just been through to safely deliver her baby this was the last thing she needed to hear.

A few moments later a doctor appeared. He was accompanied by a nurse. They seemed to enter the room in a hurry, giving both Lucy and Rory a smile and introducing themselves before huddling around Lucy's notes several paces away from the bed, talking to the midwife. After a muted discussion which Rory was unable to overhear despite straining his ears, they came over, explaining to Lucy that they were going to examine her to see what the problem was. Quickly, they began to attach various monitors to her, picking up her heart rate and inserting an IV into her arm. Rory could see the worried look on the kindly midwife's face once again. Whatever was happening was clearly a cause for concern. He felt a wave of panic rise up in his chest, a tightening sensation that quickened his breath. The doctor wasn't pausing to make chitchat. He examined Lucy and checked the monitors, frowning as he spoke to his fellow medics using jargon that neither Rory nor Lucy understood.

'Is there something wrong?' Rory asked, determined to gain at least some control of the situation, to find out what was actually happening. He put his hand on Lucy's to reassure her as she clutched little Annie close to her chest.

'You are bleeding quite heavily,' the doctor explained to Lucy. 'I'm afraid you're still losing rather a lot of blood.'

'Is that normal?' asked Lucy.

Rory suddenly noticed that she was looking very pale. The shock and emotion of Annie's arrival had been so enormous that he hadn't stopped to think about how Lucy might be doing. Why was she losing so much blood? Something must have happened during the birth. His heart began to pound and he felt a wave of panic rush up his throat.

'Not quite this much, no.' said the doctor. 'I'm afraid we're going to have to get you into surgery as quickly as possible. We need to find out what's going on so that we can stop the bleeding.' The doctor was using a calm and steady tone to explain the situation to them but Rory had had enough experience of doctors to recognize when they were trying their best not to reveal too much. The mere mention of surgery had sent his heart rate rocketing skyward. He was filled with dread at the thought of something happening to Lucy.

The midwife took the baby from Lucy's arms as the medical team, now joined by a second doctor, bustled around her. Lucy sobbed that she didn't want to leave her baby, but the midwife had already whisked her away, giving her no choice. Rory took a couple of stunned steps backwards as they moved Lucy onto a gurney. His heart was beating loudly in his ears; he felt anxiety prickle up and down his spine. His head began to ache. He wished he could slow everything down and just get his head around what was happening but he knew that there was a reason for the urgency. She needed help quickly.

'You'll be all right,' said Rory as he moved closer to her, bending down to kiss her. His eyes were brimming with tears. She looked afraid and frighteningly pale, so small and vulnerable lying there. So helpless.

'But... Annie,' she whispered, her eyes filling with tears once more.

'I'll stay with Annie, don't worry,' Rory said. 'I love you… You're going to be fine, just as soon as they fix you up. It's okay Luce, don't worry.'

It was all happening so incredibly fast. Too fast. Before he knew it they were wheeling her out of the room. He wanted to shout at them to stop, but he stood there, helpless to do anything but watch. 'She'll be alright, won't she?' he repeated to the doctor as he steered the gurney into the corridor. Rory felt his head spin. He could tell just how concerned the doctor was from the look in his eyes. The doctor nodded curtly at him and vanished out of the door.

'There, there love,' said the midwife as Annie began to cry gently. 'It's okay, daddy's here.' The midwife gave Annie to Rory. His eyes brimmed with tears as he cradled the tiny bundle in his arms for the first time. He could hardly believe how light she was. How fragile. His heart expanded yet again with an overwhelming surge of love. Lucy should be here with them. This wasn't right. His heart wrenched at the thought of her scared and alone.

'Where have they taken her?' he asked, dumbfounded by what had just happened. The room seemed desperately empty all of a sudden.

'They've taken her up to surgery, dear,' she said. 'She's in the very best possible hands, don't you worry.' She gave him a kind smile and patted his hand, squeezing his arm gently.

Rory sat down on the chair in the corner of the room as the midwife stripped the blood-stained sheets from the bed, still warm from where Lucy had been lying just moments before. He had heard of complications from childbirth, of course, but never in his wildest dreams had he imagined that something like this would happen to her. He prayed that she would be all right, that it was just a routine procedure, easily fixed.

The midwife chatted happily away to Rory about her grandchildren as she bustled about the room, no doubt trying to distract him from what was currently happening to Lucy. Rory could barely take in what she was saying. His ears were ringing. He felt so helpless, there was nothing he could do to protect Lucy now, she was in the hands of the surgeons. There was nothing he could do but wait. It felt so wrong, so unnatural that she wasn't there with them. His heart felt twisted with angst and his nerves jangled with fear.

He sat in the same spot, waiting for Lucy, for what felt like hours. Every time someone came in to check on Annie, his heart leapt into his mouth. He was longing for news. Whenever he asked for an update, all anyone said was, 'She's still in surgery.' The panic rose steadily inside him as he realized quite how long she had been gone. Annie was sleeping in her tiny cot next to him. Rory kept his eyes fixed on the door, repeating silent prayers over and over again in his head. He had never felt so utterly helpless, so completely desperate.

Eventually the door opened once again. It was the doctor who had come to see Lucy earlier. He walked quietly into the room. Rory felt his heart skip a beat. He felt as though everything was happening in slow motion. As if he couldn't engage with the situation properly. He braced himself for what was to come.

Epilogue

The wind whisked their cheeks as they stood in a huddle on the beach. Annie, zipped into her waterproof romper suit, was picking up fistfuls of sand and dropping them delightedly into her lap. Her chubby cheeks, already red from teething, were flushed from the brisk breeze and her bright blue eyes sparkled. Rufus and Tiggy were racing around chasing the waves and each other, barking at the spray, clearly in their element.

'I can't believe a whole year has gone by already,' said Lucy, crouching down to pull a crocheted blue hat over her daughter's fine brown hair.

'I know!' said Rory. 'It's unbelievable how the time has flown. Just think… a year ago we were in the hospital. You were probably just coming out of surgery…'

'I was so completely out of it, I can barely remember.' Lucy thought back to those first few days with Annie as she had begun her long road to recovery. 'It feels like such a blur.'

Rory shuddered at the memory. 'Didn't that give us a fright?' he said as he scooped Annie up into his arms and swirled her around. She gurgled in delight at her favourite flying trick.

They walked down to the seashore, pulling their coats closer around them. It was a bitterly cold day. The water gleamed silver under the afternoon sun. Rory whistled loudly and Rufus and Tiggy came bounding through the waves, splashing icy cold water as they went, exhilarated from their run along the beach.

'We better get you home for tea!' Lucy said to Annie. 'Granny's made you a very special birthday cake!'

Gus and Ginny absolutely doted on their granddaughter, spoiling her rotten at any given opportunity. They had been unbelievably excited to find out that they would soon become grandparents for a second time, this time to a little boy. Ollie and Sofia had recently come over from Buenos Aires for a few weeks, taking advantage of Sofia still being able to fly. They were currently holed up by the fire with Gus, Ginny and Granny Annie, taking refuge from the cold while Lucy and Rory took the dogs for a walk. They were all so besotted with the newest addition to the family. It would be the McCullan's turn next…they were flying to Ireland in a couple of days' time to continue Annie's birthday celebrations there.

'Are you ready?' asked Rory. 'Shall we head back up?'

'Let's go,' she replied. She leant across and kissed him. 'Happy birthday darling girl!' she said as she kissed Annie on the cheek. Annie smiled at her and Lucy's heart swelled with emotion. She had never known she was capable of such overwhelming love. The love she felt for Annie was limitless; it amazed her on a daily basis. Becoming parents had strengthened her relationship with Rory in a way she had not anticipated. They were so closely bonded after everything they had been through, so completely united in their love for each other and for their daughter. It had brought them closer together and she knew now that she wouldn't be able to survive a single day without her family by her side. She reached for Rory's hand and they made their way back across the golden sand, the three of them together, her own little family, looking forward to a warming cup of tea and a slice of Ginny's famous chocolate cake.

We hope you enjoyed this book!

Georgie Capron's next book is coming in summer 2017

More addictive fiction from Aria:

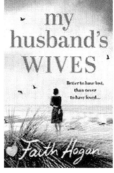
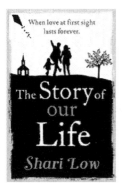

Find out more
http://headofzeus.com/books/isbn/9781784979560

Find out more
http://headofzeus.com/books/isbn/9781784977153

Find out
http://headofzeus.com/books/isbn/9781784978242

Acknowledgements

I would like to thank various people for making this book possible. First and foremost, my sister Emma, an amazing editor who managed to find time to guide me through the formative stages of writing my first novel despite her own formidable workload. Her patience, wisdom and expertise played a crucial part in helping me take the idea that started as a tiny seedling in my imagination and getting it out into the world. I would also like to thank my twin sister Sophie and my mother Polly for reading endless first drafts and giving me invaluable feedback along the way.

As part of my research I would like to thank my friends Carice Irwin-Clark and Sophie Walton for their help and insights into parenthood. I would also like to thank The London Women's Clinic for taking the time to answer my numerous questions about donor insemination.

I owe a huge thank you to Bea Corlett, my agent, who played an enormous part in building the plot and adding depth to the story with her initial edits.

I have been very lucky to work with Caroline Ridding and Sarah Ritherdon at Aria. Their support and encouragement has been invaluable. Sarah's editing is sensitive, meticulous and incredibly skilful and makes the whole process as enjoyable as possible. I would also like to thank Jade Craddock for her detailed and enormously thorough copy editing. The rest of the team at Aria, Nia Beynon, Yasemin Turan and Geo Willis have all helped in bringing my dream of publishing my debut novel into reality, for which I am eternally grateful.

Lastly I would like to thank my family for all their loving support over the years. They always made me feel like achieving anything I put my mind to was possible, and it turned out, they were right. And finally to my husband, Tom, thanks for putting up with me... you are definitely my very own Rory McCullan, and I am very lucky to have you.

About Georgie Capron

GEORGIE CAPRON lives in South West London with her husband. She works as a primary school teacher, and writes during the holidays. She studied Italian and History of Art at the University of Edinburgh, and loves travelling, yoga and all sorts of arts and crafts. Just the Two of Us is her first novel.

Find me on Twitter
https://twitter.com/GeorgieCapron

Become an Aria Addict

Aria is the new digital-first fiction imprint from Head of Zeus.

It's Aria's ambition to discover and publish tomorrow's superstars, targeting fiction addicts and readers keen to discover new and exciting authors.

Aria will publish a variety of genres under the commercial fiction umbrella such as women's fiction, crime, thrillers, historical fiction, saga and erotica.

So, whether you're a budding writer looking for a publisher or an avid reader looking for something to escape with – Aria will have something for you.

Get in touch: aria@headofzeus.com

Become an Aria Addict
http://www.ariafiction.com

Find us on Twitter
https://twitter.com/Aria_Fiction

Find us on Facebook
http://www.facebook.com/ariafiction

Find us on BookGrail
http://www.bookgrail.com/store/aria/

Addictive Fiction

Aria
Clerkenwell House
45-47 Clerkenwell Green
London EC1R 0HT

www.ariafiction.com

Printed in Poland
by Amazon Fulfillment
Poland Sp. z o.o., Wrocław